THE HOUSE AT THE TOP OF THE HILL

Kathlyn S. Starbuck is the author of *Time in Mind* and *India's Story*. She lives in San Diego with her husband, fantasy writer Raymond E. Feist, and their two children, and assorted horses and cats.

GW00454964

By the same author

TIME IN MIND
INDIA'S STORY

Voyager

KATHLYN S. STARBUCK

The House at the Top of the Hill

HarperCollins*Publishers*

Voyager
An Imprint of HarperCollins*Publishers*
77–85 Fulham Palace Road,
Hammersmith, London W6 8JB

The *Voyager* World Wide Web site address is
http://www.harpercollins.co.uk/voyager

A Paperback Original 1997
1 3 5 7 9 8 6 4 2

Copyright © Kathlyn S. Starbuck 1997

The Author asserts the moral right to
be identified as the author of this work

A catalogue record for this book
is available from the British Library

ISBN 0 00 648276 7

Set in Postscript Sabon by
Rowland Phototypesetting Ltd,
Bury St Edmunds, Suffolk

Printed and bound in Great Britain by
Caledonian International
Book Manufacturing Ltd, Glasgow

This novel is entirely a work of fiction. The names,
characters and incidents portrayed in it are the work of the
author's imagination. Any resemblance to actual persons,
living or dead, events or localities is entirely coincidental.

ACKNOWLEDGEMENTS

Thank you so much to the following people for their critiques on the rough draft: Diane Clark, Carol Ding, Diana Domingo, Michele Gillaspie, Kristina Kebow, Deborah Smith, and Glenn Smith.

Most especially, thank you Ray. With your love and support, I feel like I can do anything!

Chapter One

'Balance is the key to the power you wield. If this balance is tipped in any way, the results will be catastrophic.'

The Magic Book, Chapter One

He came to her in the middle of the night; another vivid dream in a long series that had begun when she returned home. His hand closed over her mouth. His head was close to hers and she could smell his breath, hear his breathing in her ears, feel his hair against her cheek.

It was familiar and strange at the same time. The hand over her mouth was much larger and stronger than that of her childhood memories. The smell of him was different, too, slightly musky instead of just soap and water and toothpaste.

She breathed deeply, trying to place the components that were familiar. His hair tickled her cheek and she reached up to touch it. The curls were still as soft as they had been when he was a boy. He wore his hair longer now and it was tied back so that she couldn't run her fingers through it. She settled for brushing it away from her cheek and stroking it instead. He had hated her touching it when he was a boy, but he didn't pull away from her now. His hand relaxed over her mouth.

'Jeremy?' she whispered.

His hand moved to her cheek. 'You remember?'

'I remember,' she turned toward him on her pillow. 'Have you always been here?'

He laughed softly. The sound washed over her, stirring more memories. 'Where would I go?'

'You were gone from my mind for a long time,' she said. 'Now that I'm home here you are in my dream as large as life, but grown up, not a little boy.'

'So you had forgotten,' he said, slightly accusing.

'I didn't mean to,' she said, getting defensive. 'But I was gone such a long time and we were only kids.'

'But we aren't kids anymore,' he said. He moved his hand from her cheek to her jaw in a gently stroking motion.

'No, we aren't,' she breathed. She pulled him to her, seeking his mouth with hers, and kissed him deeply, feeling things that would have disturbed her had this not been a dream. 'And maybe I'd forgotten but I remember now,' she said at last. 'In the morning I'll have to find you to tell you so.'

'What?' asked Jeremy in a somewhat louder voice. 'I'm right here. You just did.'

'Not really,' she sighed.

'Really,' he laughed. He pinched her cheek.

'*Ow!*' she gasped. Her hands flew to her face. 'Why did you do that?'

'You are not asleep,' Jeremy said, laughing harder now. 'You thought this was a dream?'

Lyssa froze but her mind was racing. This wasn't a dream, and she had kissed him, and now he was laughing at her.

'So, you've been wanting to do that for a long time?' Jeremy asked, still laughing. 'I thought you said you'd forgotten me!'

Lyssa drew a deep breath, trying to calm down. 'What I dream about is none of your business,' she said coldly. 'What are you doing in here anyway? This is my bedroom and you're not welcome in it!' She sat up and reached past him to turn on the light. Then she sat back and stared at him, still gently pressing her cheek with one hand.

His hair was still blue-black and longish, the soft curls tied back with strips of colored leather. His eyes were as black as his hair, but his skin was oddly fair and Lyssa remembered how easily he burned if they were out in the sun too long in summer. She had moved away when she was just eight years old and hadn't seen Jeremy or the House since. Now they were both twenty and both in the House again. She could still see the young boy when she looked at him but he had become a very handsome man.

'I'm sorry,' he said.

'No, you're not,' she shot back. Her cheek was still throbbing. 'You always did like picking on me. They told me I was making it up to try and get you in trouble. I hated that!'

'So that's why you kissed me?' he asked, laughing again.

'Get out of my room, leave me alone!'

'I had to prove you weren't asleep.' He was still laughing.

'By causing me pain?' Lyssa stared at him. 'You were a sadistic little bastard. Why did I think we were friends?'

Jeremy shrugged. 'You don't remember everything.'

It was a statement. She thought about it for a long time, watching him as he sat on the edge of the bed.

He in turn studied her. 'You'll remember,' he said, getting to his feet. He looked down at her, unsmiling.

Feeling small and vulnerable for the first time, Lyssa nodded.

Jeremy walked to her closet and opened the door. Turning back he looked at her again before stepping into the closet and shutting the door.

Then she remembered the warrens. The closet led straight to them from Aunt Burchie's part of the House. He wouldn't be coming back tonight.

She turned off the light and settled back into her pillows, quietly resolving to get a lock installed on her closet door. She would have to investigate the warrens around her closet to see if she could keep him from getting that close again. It was one thing if she decided to go looking for him, but it was quite another to be vulnerable to his nocturnal prowling. Maybe she could just borrow an armoire from another room and take all her stuff out of the closet. With

3

the door locked, she wouldn't have to worry about his opening it. But what kind of lock would be best?

Her thoughts started to tangle as Lyssa fell asleep. She dreamed every memory of her childhood that night. Years of information packed into the hours of unconsciousness so that when she woke early in the morning, Lyssa was exhausted and completely unable to go back to sleep.

The clock on the nightstand said six. The sky outside the window was grey both with dawn and clouds: she had forgotten how dreary the weather could be here. She sat up and rubbed her eyes with the backs of her knuckles. The grit made them burn but she continued to rub until she felt she'd gotten out most of the sleep. Opening her eyes, Lyssa blinked at her reflection in the dressing table mirror opposite the bed.

She looked a hundred years old. Her thick chestnut hair was matted and snarled from her restless night and lines of tension were etched on her face. Crease-marks on her cheek from the pillowcase added to her disheveled appearance and the whites of her blue eyes were pink. Her lips were cracked and dry and her tongue felt thick and furry.

'Good morning to you, too,' she told her reflection in a rather sticky voice. A shower wouldn't solve all her problems, but it would definitely make her feel better, so Lyssa pushed back the covers and stepped out of bed onto one of the fussy little rugs she had loved as a little girl.

It was sweet of Aunt Burchie to put her in her old room. It was exactly as she had left it twelve years before, but her tastes had changed a bit since then. Maybe she'd prowl the House for another room and then lock this closet.

Yes. That would be best. Aunt Burchie would never check the room. She'd never know about the lock. The maid would never question it. Perfect. Lyssa could come and go, and Jeremy would be limited to the warrens, unless there were other ways into the rest of the House of which she was unaware.

4

Lyssa sighed.

Shower. Then worry.

The bathroom was very pink and smelled of cheap bubble bath. Lyssa smiled, remembering the hours spent soaking in the small, shallow tub. It was the perfect size for a child of six or eight to flatten out in, head crooked up just enough so the nose and eyes were out of the water; hot water trickling into the already hot bath, head full of dreams and plans while fingers and toes pruned.

Definitely a new room. There must be a dozen standing empty, any one of which would be fine. In the meantime, the tiny stall shower here would do. She returned to the room to get her toiletries.

'Will there be anything else, Miss?'

'No, thank you,' Lyssa smiled at the older woman. Millie had seemed so old when Lyssa was little but looking at her now she couldn't be more than sixty. Her signs of aging seemed peripheral; laugh-lines at the corners of her grey eyes, coarsely-veined hands, noticeable grey in the blonde hair she wore so neatly twisted at the back.

How had Lyssa forgotten so much?

'This all feels so familiar,' she said, as Millie stood by the buffet. 'Like I've come home and discovered I haven't been away as long as I thought.' She sat in silence for a long time.

Millie continued to stand near the buffet.

'Does the cook still make all that food every day?' Lyssa suddenly focused on the table beside Millie.

'She likes it that way,' said Millie noncommittally.

'What do you do with all the leftovers?' Lyssa was incredulous. There was a lot of food on the table and Lyssa knew that besides the staff – and they consisted of only the cook, the housekeeper and the non-resident gardener/chauffeur – she and her aunt were the only people in the House. Well, the *house* part of the House. And the gardener/chauffeur didn't even live there. She was a local kid who was putting herself through college one course at a time.

'There are those who need,' said Millie. 'Old Burchie has never forgotten that.'

Lyssa looked up sharply, but Millie's face was expressionless.

Lyssa decided to change the subject. 'What time does Aunt Burchie get up?'

'She doesn't sleep much anymore,' said Millie in the same bland tone. 'She only gets out of bed to attend to her toilette. Any time you want to talk to her she'll probably be ready.'

'Oh,' said Lyssa and then, 'I'm going to find a different room to stay in.'

'The blue room's shower isn't working right. Any other room should do you just fine.'

Lyssa spent the morning exploring the rooms of the old House. Memories of a childhood spent there welled up from deep inside as she wandered aimlessly, finding furniture, pictures and knick-knacks she had completely forgotten.

Time hadn't touched this place and Lyssa felt she might just stop aging if she stayed here for any number of years.

Lyssa shook her head and looked around. She had been wandering through the rooms and not paying attention to where she might choose to sleep while she was here. And how long would that be? She had been surprised when she'd received a phone call from Aunt Burchie – she hadn't seen or heard from the old woman since she'd left as a child – and had no idea how long her aunt expected her to stay.

The room in which she now stood was typical of this part of the House. The ceilings were so high that it gave the rooms a boxy feeling, like a doll's house with the roof off and long walls stretching upward. The wallpaper borders at table and ceiling levels matched the pattern of the carpet. The paint in between was a paler shade of the predominant color of the furniture – everything was ruffles and lace, china and crystal and frightfully correct. Lyssa still didn't like it very much.

There were some parts of the House that were incredible, some that Lyssa loved and others that terrified her. But the part she was living in at the moment was at least safe. She decided, finally, to choose a room near her old one, so she would have reason to be near the entrance to the warrens.

And as she wandered back to her childhood room to pack up her belongings Lyssa wondered idly if Millie knew anything about the Others.

'Come in,' called Aunt Burchie in a surprisingly strong voice.

Lyssa pushed the door open and stepped into the room. 'A hospital bed?' she blurted before she could stop herself.

Aunt Burchie laughed and her blue eyes sparkled with mischief. 'I fought it long and hard, dear, believe me. Come in and sit down.'

Lyssa sat in an overstuffed chair beside the bed and smiled at her aunt. She must be near a hundred, she thought to herself.

'Ninety-seven,' said Aunt Burchie, with a wry smile. 'And I look like death warmed over, but my mind is still here and my body is actually working pretty well. I'm just stiff, is all. And slow. They think I'm dying,' she snorted. 'I may just decide to after a while, but not yet. I'm glad you came back, child.'

Lyssa smiled. 'You knew I would.'

Aunt Burchie shook her head, stirring wisps of white cotton wool-like hair. 'I *hoped* you would.'

'Why?'

'There are things we need to discuss,' said Aunt Burchie. 'Things about my will and the distribution of my possessions.'

'Aren't these things you should be talking about with my father?' asked Lyssa.

Aunt Burchie shook her head slightly. 'He grew up here, but never really *lived* here,' she said.

Lyssa froze. She sat very still for a long moment before nodding her head forward. 'He doesn't know—'

Aunt Burchie shook her head again. 'And you must never tell him.'

Lyssa sat up very straight. 'Never,' she echoed. 'But what about the rest of the family? Surely someone else is more qualified to handle this kind of thing?'

Aunt Burchie shook her head. 'You're the one to do it, and now is the time to get it done,' she said firmly.

'But settling the estate will take some time, won't it? Isn't there a lot of paperwork involved?' Lyssa asked, feeling a little overwhelmed by the scope of the request.

'For a place like this, and our peculiar family trusts, yes. Quite a bit. I expect it could take months. Are you settled in?'

Lyssa laughed. 'Yeah, I've found another room, though.'

'I know,' Aunt Burchie smiled. 'I didn't think you'd stay there, but I thought you'd get a kick out of seeing your old digs again.' She paused and then changing the subject asked, 'When are you going into town? I'm surprised you came to see me first. You always did love to shop.'

'Well, that hasn't changed,' Lyssa grinned. 'I thought I'd see if you needed anything.'

'Just promise me you'll never bring another packet of that bubble bath into my house!' laughed Aunt Burchie. 'You used to beg advances on your allowance to spend on that stink!'

Lyssa chuckled.

'And I used to give them to you!'

'Your tolerance and generosity are acknowledged. I solemnly promise I will never buy that particular brand of bubble bath again. I've moved up to the really expensive kind, so if I could have an advance on my allowance?' She laughed and stood up. 'Do you need anything?'

'No dear,' said Aunt Burchie, turning her cheek for

Lyssa's kiss. 'You run along and have fun. Come see me whenever you want. I think Millie told you I don't sleep much these days?'

Lyssa nodded.

'Nosy old beast,' Aunt Burchie said fondly. 'Anyway, I'll be here, and we have plenty of time for what we have to cover, so go spend some money.'

She squeezed Lyssa's hand and Lyssa came away with money folded into her palm. She smiled at her aunt and went to do just that.

The town didn't appear to have changed one bit, at first glance. Lyssa felt vaguely jarred then, when the changes began to be apparent. The buildings were the same, but some of the shops were different. Some of the buildings were different, but the shops inside were the same ones that had inhabited the old buildings. Nothing was quite right, even though it was very much the same.

Lyssa found a bench in the park that was the town commons and sat facing the church. It was the only thing that was completely the same. The church was actually older than the village. The popular belief was that the abandoned building had been discovered by the founders of the village, who took it as an omen to settle and build. They rebuilt the church from the foundation up to be exactly as it had been, before building the rest of the town around it in specific fashion. There was nothing haphazard about the village.

Haphazard was the House at the top of the hill.

Lyssa sighed and stirred on the bench.

'A thousand years is a long time,' said a voice beside her.

Lyssa jumped, suddenly aware of Jeremy, sitting on the bench, also staring at the church. 'No one knows for certain how old it is,' she said.

'I figure that's as good a guess as any,' said Jeremy with a smile. 'It's old, in any case.'

9

Well, there was no arguing with that. 'What are you doing here?' she asked tiredly.

'I thought maybe you'd have some questions.'

'Why are you still here?'

Jeremy laughed shortly. 'Where else would I go?'

Lyssa didn't answer and a few moments passed before she spoke again. 'The town hasn't really changed all that much,' she said, looking around her, 'but it feels like coming home from school and finding your old bedroom is now the study.'

'My room will never change,' said Jeremy.

She studied Jeremy closely but his features had hardened into an emotionless mask. She frowned, trying to see past his guard but was exhausted after the night's dreamings and shortly gave it up. 'The Others?'

He nodded. 'You'll see them in time. But it was up to me to come for you.'

Lyssa smiled a small, bitter smile. 'Always. Why am I here? Aunt Burchie says it's to do with the House, but I get the feeling you're tied up in this, too.'

Jeremy shrugged. 'I'm just a fly on the wall.'

'You were never so innocent,' Lyssa laughed a short bark, but something triggered in the back of her mind. When she tried to focus in on the thought, it vanished. For a moment, she'd gotten it – made a leap of understanding that skipped the pieces of the puzzle she didn't have and sparked a connection she knew would take her time to rediscover. With a small cry of frustration she rose from the bench, as if trying to reach for the thought.

Jeremy stood close beside her, his hand on her elbow, holding her firmly. 'It will be like that. As I said, if you have any questions, ask me.'

Lyssa sighed. 'That's the problem. Too many questions. I don't want to be doing this.'

'You have to play by the rules, or you can't join the Game,' he said.

Lyssa's eyes widened. It was the chant from their childhood. She could hear their voices as children singing it: *Play by the rules, or you can't join the Game.* She knew that. But what *was* the Game? And why was it so important that she remember? She thought she had dreamed all the memories of her childhood, so why weren't *these* there? 'Do I have to start over, or can I pick up where I left off?' she asked, as her mind raced in circles searching for clues.

Jeremy laughed outright and his mask vanished. 'Can you even remember the Game? Or do you know exactly where you were?'

Lyssa sighed, rubbing her temple to hide her frustration. His tone and expression were straight out of their childhood. He had always loved knowing what she hadn't yet figured out. He enjoyed making her feel stupid. 'Obviously I haven't remembered any of this for almost twelve years. No, I don't remember the Game. I'm only just beginning to remember about the House.' She frowned and thought for a moment. 'I remember things that happened outside the House,' she began slowly, trying to put words to feelings. 'Those memories are just like small bits of a movie floating around in your brain that you can set in motion if you think about them.' She shook her head, trying to clear the dreams from her mind, and refocused on Jeremy. 'But I don't remember much about what happened inside. I have impressions about things; assumptions, really,' she mused. 'And some images like still photographs taken with only the full moon for light. And I remember fear.' Her brain finally shuddered to a halt, exhausted, and Lyssa collapsed onto the bench.

Jeremy sat back down and put his arm around her shoulder. 'You can't go back to sleep in the House just now. Sleep here and you won't dream.'

'Like a vagrant on a park bench?' Lyssa asked. She didn't have the energy to argue. She put her head down on his shoulder and fell into a deep and silent sleep.

* * *

She woke a long time later in darkness. She could hear quiet breathing nearby, but could see nothing. After a futile time of searching for any pinpoint of light, she gave up and fell back to sleep.

She ran across the long balcony overlooking the dark hall. There were no lights on and only the gibbous moon to illuminate her flight.

Glancing back again she could see a shadowy figure on the balcony above her. The door was too obvious. She yanked it open and let it bang against the wall before darting under the stairs she had just come down.

Then she heard the footsteps on the stairs above. Unexpected, she started violently. The sound was right beside her ear, as if the person following her was right next to her under the stairs. Then she realized what had happened, and hoped she hadn't made a noise that would betray her location. By now she was holding her breath.

The shadowy figure finally walked through the door at the foot of the stairs.

She waited until the footsteps faded before going to another door and stepping through it. The long corridor beyond led to stairs that went back up, so she mounted them and began to climb.

Her sense of panic hit full force as she stepped into the room at the top. Looking wildly about, she could see no one. Nothing that would indicate danger. Still, she was driven by the panic inside her. She plunged across the room and through the only other door.

She slammed the door and ran as fast as she had ever run before, passing doors that she probably should have taken. But stopping was more than she could manage right now. Her only goal was to put as much distance between her and her pursuer as possible.

Lyssa sat up with a start and discovered it was morning. She was in her room. The one she had chosen after deciding there were too many nightmares in her childhood room. Had he known? Or had he put her on the doorstep, rung the bell and run away? Or did he bring her to Aunt Burchie and ask what to do with her? The thought shivered her spine and she glanced quickly around the room. She was alone. Still, she showered and dressed quickly.

Lyssa stood before the closet in her childhood room. Her hand was on the knob, but she ran down the check-list in her mind one last time before entering the warrens: knife, flashlight with fresh batteries, snack. She smiled and patted the pocket containing that last item. The provisions of childhood. When she ran into Jeremy, he would ask what she'd brought to share.

With a deep breath for resolution, Lyssa turned the knob and pulled the door open. Before she could think about it, she stepped through and pushed on the back panel. It swung open and she stepped through into the corridor behind the closet. She switched on the flashlight as the panel shut itself and found herself enclosed once again in the dream-world of the House.

She finally remembered to exhale and took another deep breath before starting off down the hall. The floorboards creaked more than she remembered, but the carpeting muffled them well enough that they wouldn't be heard on the other side of the wall in the Family-occupied portion of the House. The corridor wasn't as long as she remembered, and she reached the door at the end sooner than she was really ready.

Lyssa stood and looked at the door for a long time, running through her mental check-list again and again, stalling. This is silly, she told herself, giving her head a little shake. Open the door and get it over with.

Still she stood in the hall, facing the door, but not touching the knob. You have to do it sometime, she mouthed silently, reaching out with her right hand. The knob felt oddly warm as she twisted it. The door fell open and Lyssa

13

stepped away, shining the flashlight beam down the stairway.

The stair went down in a straight line for about fifty steps and the beam could barely penetrate the darkness at the bottom. Shadows twitched and jumped. Did the door below just close? Or were the shadows playing tricks on her vision? There must be people watching her progress. The Others must be watching. Jeremy wouldn't bother to hide.

Fear prickled on her neck as Lyssa pulled the door shut behind her and started down the steps. It felt like she was deliberately stepping into a dream. Each stair took her further into a world that had nothing to do with reality. Letting go had never been so hard. She glanced back over her shoulder, but there was utter blackness above her. She resisted the temptation to shine the light into that blackness. Another one of the rules. *You can only move forward. A backward move will land you arbitrarily elsewhere in the House.* That was part of the magic.

But purpose? Goal? Lyssa had no idea. She knew those things varied, but she couldn't remember a single one. Only that once the threshold of the upstairs door was crossed, the Game was in play and the object was to finish.

Lyssa had crossed the threshold, and now she was playing, whether she could remember the Game or not. She patted the leather pouch which held her knife. Not much against magic, but it had always been enough when she was a child, so she hoped for the best and reached the bottom step. She opened the door with a confidence she didn't feel and stepped out into the foyer. The panel snapped shut behind her, leaving her in the middle of a two-story entry. She had known it would be there, but it hadn't seemed real until now.

In front of her was a huge glass atrium, etched and frosted in elaborate design, with a large brass-knobbed door in the middle. It had been the House's front door before the hill overgrew it. The floor she stood on was marble. A beautiful pale jade, shot through with fine veins of black ore. It was clean and polished, as were the teak banisters and paneling of the two magnificent staircases that swept up the circular walls to the first floor. An exquisite chandelier of crystal and brass hung from the high ceiling, and mirrors lined the walls that climbed the stairs.

A rail at the top of the stairs created a balcony. Lyssa knew that on the other side of the rail was a huge room with many doors. She switched off the flashlight and put it in her pouch as she climbed the marble stairs and stood at the top to gape some more.

This room was and had always been here and its components remained constant, although the beautiful brocade furniture had often changed position. The floor up here was marble also, but was deep black and polished to a high gloss. The huge, overstuffed couches of cream-colored silk brocade stood about the room in conversation areas. Tables, of the same teak as the banisters and paneling, separated some areas and joined others, making a maze.

Teak doors stood at intervals around the room, and colorful artwork hung on the cream-colored walls between. Lyssa glanced at the brass knobs as her eyes swept the room. She studied the furniture directly in front of her and finally located the entrance to the maze. Feeling a little better about being here now, Lyssa stepped without hesitation into the opening.

The room seemed to shift around her. Lyssa closed her eyes and stood still for a moment, getting her bearings and waiting for the maze to decide where it was sending her. When she opened her eyes, things had settled down and she could see the way to proceed.

Sometimes the maze was easy, sometimes tricky, but she always got stuck in dead-ends. The backtracking rule didn't apply in the mazes. Backtracking is part of working a maze you can't see from above. It was one of the few of the arbitrary and numerous rules of the Game that seemed fair.

When Lyssa finally reached the end of the maze, she was almost back to where she had started, at the door directly to the left at the top of the stairs. Well, that's part of the Game, she sighed as she opened the door and stepped through.

She fell in blackness for a time before slowing and landing softly on an old feather bedstead. Dust billowed up and she sneezed frequently until it cleared. When she was finally able to look around and size up her position, she could hardly believe her eyes.

Slowly, Lyssa crawled out of the filthy bed and stood with her mouth hanging open, staring around the large room. This must be the *original* House! She looked up at the ceiling, through which she must have fallen, but she could find no trace of a trap-door. Lyssa retrieved her flashlight and shined it at the ceiling, but there was still no sign of her entryway. Finally, she climbed back onto the bed and stood balanced against the wall, craning her neck to search, but there was no door to be found. That meant there had to be another way out of here.

Lyssa climbed down off the bed and turned a slow circle, surveying the room. Dust covered everything, fine and layered until it appeared fuzzy white on the table tops and the backs of chairs. The colors of the braided rag rugs on the floor were indistinguishable, and cobwebs festooned the rafters like ratty decorations someone had forgotten to take down after the party was over.

The hair on her arms stood up in goose bumps. She had found the Room. She hadn't even remembered it until this moment, and now here she was. It didn't look anything like the House of Legend should look. It was small and filthy, like a settler's cottage.

Lyssa sneezed again, creating whirling eddies in the dust motes still polluting the air from her fall onto the bed. She wouldn't be able to breathe until she cleaned this place up. She could satisfy her curiosity and look for a way out at the same time. She spun again slowly, daunted by the scope of the task, trying to get her bearings.

The bed stood along the back wall of the large, rectangular-shaped room, with the headboard against the short left wall. A plethora of dusty quilts and blankets covered the deep feather ticking and two huge feather pillows leaned against the dusty wooden headboard. A large leather steamer-trunk stood at the foot of the bed and just beyond that, a wooden clothes cupboard. A small wooden table stood beside the bed.

In front of the bed, four rocking chairs were arranged around a long, low table. There was a thick, crude glass window in the wall, but it was covered with dirt, and no light penetrated. There was a door next to the window and another window on the other side of that. A dining table with four ladder-back chairs stood beneath it. Behind them was the kitchen; a stove, a counter, cupboards, and a sink with a pump.

Two half-walls formed a small alcove between the bedroom and kitchen, dividing rooms without actually blocking off the rectangle. A floor-loom and spinning wheel occupied this space, along with stacks of baskets containing raw wool, carded and dyed wool, spun yarns and threads.

Then Lyssa noticed that the lantern on the dining table had been cleaned and lit. She had been expected.

Well, of course, she told herself as she tried to shake the prickly feeling on her neck and arms. The House had sent her here. But why was the Room so dusty? She couldn't recall ever finding a room in the House before that wasn't immaculate. Everything was scrubbed, dusted and polished as though the Family still lived there. If the rest of the House was so clean, why was this room so dirty? If she had been truly expected, wouldn't it have been cleaned in anticipation, and not just lit?

Finally, Lyssa shook herself into action. Standing there wondering about it wasn't changing the situation. She made one more circuit of the Room trying to find a starting place, and found herself back at the bed she had landed on when she fell through the ceiling. It was as good a place as any, so she dragged all the covers off the bed and pulled the frame away from the wall. Cobwebs made it difficult to see in the corner.

Without much hope, Lyssa went to the sink and primed the pump. Water would certainly make the job easier, but there were enough rags to at least remove the top layer of grime, but she hoped she could do better.

The pump shuddered and spat out a foul brown liquid. Encouraged, Lyssa continued pumping and more dirty water spurted into the sink, but gradually the water ran steady and clear. With a sigh of relief, she got to work. In a cupboard she found lye soap, a bucket and a huge pile of dusty rags, so first she washed the rags, and then set about washing the room from ceiling to walls to floor. As she she cleaned, she touched everything, learning the shapes and textures, placement and layout, she became more connected to the Room and its contents until the magic became palpable and Lyssa finally became aware of it.

Pushing a stray lock of damp chestnut hair out of her eyes, Lyssa looked right through the clothes cupboard and saw the door hidden behind it. Startled, she glanced up at the spot over the bed. She could see the trap-door clearly! She looked around. This place was riddled with secret entrances and exits. The magic pulsing through her allowed her to see them all through whatever was hiding them from ordinary eyes.

And she knew that no one had set foot in the Room in centuries. It had been saving itself for her. Now she had finished cleaning it, she had forged the connections that allowed her to really see it.

It still didn't look like much; more like a pioneer's cabin than anything else. The grandeur of the rest of the House now seemed pretentious to Lyssa. She sighed happily. Here she was at home. She would stay in the room she had chosen in Aunt Burchie's part of the House only as long as it was necessary to be polite, she decided. She would eventually bring most of her things here.

The length of her fall had seemed considerable and she wondered how long it would take her to climb back up to the levels she needed to be in before she could even hope to find her way home. Lyssa opened the doors of the clothes cupboard and stood open-mouthed.

She stepped into her room and took off the leather pouch. She slung it over the chair in the corner and went into the bathroom. Now that the Room was clean, she should be, too.

'So you set off into the warrens today?' asked Aunt Burchie.

Lyssa nodded. 'Everything looked exactly as I remembered it from childhood. A little smaller, perhaps, but just as polished and beautiful as when the Family was living there.'

Aunt Burchie smiled. 'The House takes care of itself.'

'But apparently not in terms of probate court,' said Lyssa with a laugh. 'How specific have you made your will?'

Aunt Burchie sobered. 'As specific as I could, dearie. You know your father. It's his boyhood home, and he feels he should be entitled to it. But I just couldn't do that.'

Lyssa nodded. 'I can't believe he never discovered the warrens.'

'Well, he never was much of a curious child. I never could warm to him for that. I was so relieved you turned out the way you did. It was nice to have someone around that I could talk to about the vagaries of this place.' Aunt Burchie patted Lyssa's hand. 'I guess I'm just being a selfish old woman, but I wanted company. I wanted your company. Millie's a good sort, but she's not Family. She's not you.'

'And you had just the means of luring me here? Telling me you need me to go over details of your estate?' Lyssa snatched her hand out of Aunt Burchie's clasp in mock outrage. Actually, she was glad of the excuse to free herself. 'Letting everyone think you're going to die?'

Aunt Burchie laughed and Lyssa laughed with her, but the magic, which had opened her eyes in the Room at the bottom of the hill, was thrumming insistently as Aunt Burchie spoke and it shook Lyssa's confidence.

'As I said, I may take it into my head to die, but not for a while yet, I think,' said Aunt Burchie. 'I'm just prolonging your father's anticipation.'

Lyssa laughed outright. 'You're torturing him and loving every minute!'

No one in the Family actually disliked Lyssa's father, but he had always been rather grubby about money, and got more than a little rude about it sometimes, especially since he had none of his own, and was constantly asking for advances on his allowance. Each Family member received the same monthly stipend from the estate, but if they wanted more they had to work for it. Most of the other Family members held steady jobs and used the trust money for extras.

But Jordan Anders didn't feel he ought to have to work. He took the estate to court to argue that the cost of living had risen drastically since the trust had been established, and that the equations used to determine the amount of the allowance were hopelessly antiquated. They should all, therefore, be entitled to an increase accordingly. He fought, then pleaded with other Family members, saying he was doing it for them as much as for himself, but they all told him to grow up and get a job, and leave them alone. Not one of them stood with him to argue the case, and eventually the judge told Jordan the same thing his family had: go get a job.

He decided to get married instead, and had a child, entitling him to a greater amount from the estate. He mismanaged this as well, and shortly after Lyssa was born, her mother left and Lyssa went to live with Aunt Burchie. Jordan continued to get the larger sum of money, and he wasn't bothered by the things he'd had to do to get it, so he was satisfied.

Lyssa grew up in the House, discovered the warrens and became entangled in the magic of the place; the ritual and adventure. She saw the Family in small bits when members would come to visit. The Family wasn't very large, and it wasn't very close, but eventually, every one came home again, for a little while. When they visited, Lyssa would hide in corners and watch, because they were all grownups, and they all seemed a little annoyed by children. When she was introduced, they would look through or over her instead of at her, so she knew that she would be tolerated only if they didn't have to see, or hear her. She managed that in order to discover what she could about her Family. Aunt Burchie never really told Lyssa anything except about recent Family history, including Lyssa, her greedy father and her no-good mother. There hadn't been much to tell about Lyssa yet, since she was so young, but there were baby-things that Aunt Burchie happened upon in her wanderings through the House.

Mostly it had been up to a nanny to raise Lyssa, and the nanny didn't talk to her much, being the sort who had come to her station by a loss of income, not a love of the profession. Thinking about it now Lyssa couldn't even remember the woman's name. She sighed. 'So if my father doesn't get the House, who does?' She tried to think of the relatives she'd seen over the years.

'You, dearie,' Aunt Burchie laughed. 'Who did you think?'

Lyssa startled. 'Me?' she squeaked. 'No!'

Aunt Burchie laughed again. 'It's not up to you.'

'Then change your will,' Lyssa pleaded. 'Don't make me do this.'

'It's not up to me, either!' Aunt Burchie protested, beginning to be pained by laughter. She really wasn't very healthy. She took a moment to regain her composure. 'The House decides, and it's chosen you.'

'Yeah, right,' said Lyssa. 'Come on, please? You know how my father can be.'

'Your father can't do a thing against the trust, and neither can you,' said Aunt Burchie rather severely. 'He's just a spoiled child looking for other people to blame for his misery. You tell him so in just that tone of voice, and it will back him right down. We're letting him have more money than he's legally entitled to just because it keeps him quieter longer, but we keep hoping against hope that he'll grow up and learn to take some responsibility for himself.'

'That's all well and good to say,' said Lyssa slowly, 'but he's gotten this far from being greedy and selfish, and I don't see him changing any time in the near future. I mean, he's fifty. If he hasn't willingly changed by now, it probably won't happen.'

'Which is exactly why he was never allowed to discover the warrens,' said Aunt Burchie with a rather smug smile on her face.

'Why?' asked Lyssa.

'Because he hasn't changed, and with what's down there, well –'

Lyssa thought about it for a moment. The rooms had been left exactly as they had been when the Family lived there. All the furnishings, decorations, everything as it had been. For a moment, her mind boggled at the amount of money those antiques would fetch.

'It's part of the trust your father would never be able to uphold,' said Aunt Burchie gently. 'The House must be maintained exactly as it is. More may be added on, but plans must be approved by a majority of living relatives and arrangements for construction made through a certain Bell family in the village.'

'When was the last time the House was added on to?' asked Lyssa curiously.

'I've lived in these rooms all my life,' said Aunt Burchie with a smile. 'My mother designed them and my father had them built right after they were married. I was born a short while later.'

'So these rooms are almost a hundred years old?' asked Lyssa. She looked at the electrical outlets and thought about the plumbing.

'It's been renovated over the years,' said Aunt Burchie, 'But otherwise, it's pretty much the same as Mother designed it.'

'And the Bell family built it?'

Aunt Burchie nodded.

'Why them?'

'Because it's in the trust,' smiled Aunt Burchie. 'Why don't you run along and give an old lady a rest.'

Lyssa stood obediently and kissed Aunt Burchie on the cheek. 'I might go into town. Do you want anything?'

Aunt Burchie shook her head. 'Thank you, darling, no. Run along.'

Lyssa walked through the village, across the park and into a pretty neighborhood. Tall, leafy trees lined the winding streets and the houses sat back on their manicured lawns overlooking flower gardens, ponds, tiny orchards and fountains. The homes were not large, but they were neatly kept and freshly painted, maintaining an appearance of modest affluence.

There didn't seem to be a pattern to the meandering of the streets, but Lyssa knew there was one, and she knew what it was. She walked past one particular house without stopping, and continued on a route through the neighborhood that would take her back past the house again in the other direction.

Shortly, Jeremy joined her. Lyssa smiled to herself. 'I haven't seen *you* in a while,' she said. She glanced over at him, then shut her eyes.

He really was handsome, she thought regretfully, seeing him behind her closed eyelids. His intense, black eyes were large and widely spaced above broad, high cheekbones. His nose was a trifle long, but it was balanced by his wide, full-lipped mouth and strong chin. He was tall and long-legged, with broad shoulders and slim hips. With a sigh, she put herself next to him in her mind. By comparison, Lyssa was a little brown sparrow with bright eyes; engaging, but not remarkable. Jeremy's ebony and marble contrasts were remarkable.

Pretty is as pretty does, she could hear a voice smarming in the back of her mind. She touched her cheek.

'I've been looking for you in the warrens,' he said. 'You haven't been in town and I haven't seen you in the House. I thought maybe you weren't speaking to me again.'

'Nothing so silly,' said Lyssa. 'I went into the warrens about a week ago but I never ran into you. I have a question.'

Jeremy nodded. He stopped and looked at her.

Lyssa stopped also and studied him for a moment. 'How long have you lived in the House?'

'Since I was an infant. My mother came here with me as a baby.'

'How long do the Others live in the House?' Lyssa pressed.

Jeremy shrugged. 'Usually a couple of years.'

'Usually?' she asked. 'Why do they come here?'

Jeremy shook his head.

'Where do they go?' Lyssa waited. Jeremy stood still and said nothing. 'Do you know where they go?' she repeated.

'I don't know,' Jeremy said finally.

Lyssa thought for a long time. He really didn't know. 'Why are you here still? Why aren't you like the Others?'

He said softly, 'I'm here for you.'

Lyssa felt the breath sucked out of her. 'What – I mean, how – why?'

Jeremy shrugged. 'Mother never did understand. She was taking me into the bathroom to change my diaper and she walked through the same door she always had, only instead of going into her own bathroom, she wound up in one of these.' He gestured in the direction of the House. 'She tried and tried, but she never could get back to our home. My father has no idea what happened to us. We just vanished from his life and he evidently couldn't follow us here. The door, or whatever, closed behind us.' Jeremy stood staring into space for a time. 'I don't remember anything, of course. I grew up in the House, with my mother, and that's just how it was. But my mother never got over it. She died grieving for my father and the life we lost.'

'Why have you never left?' Lyssa asked again.

Jeremy's mouth twisted in a bitter smile. 'You think I've never tried? The House won't let me. I get just so far down the road out of town and I'm returned to one of the rooms. I find myself back in the warrens whether I want to be or not! The House won't let me go. It's kept me here for you.'

The implications were more than Lyssa wanted to think about. She shut her eyes, but she couldn't shut out the images of Jeremy's grieving mother. Lyssa had known Magrite, but she had never known this about her. How had Magrite been so gracious with Lyssa all those years, being a surrogate mother to a motherless girl, knowing she was Family? Lyssa shuddered. 'I'm sorry,' she whispered.

'Done is done,' said Jeremy shortly. 'The question is what can we do now?'

Lyssa waited.

'Well?' she prompted.

Jeremy resumed walking slowly and Lyssa fell in step beside him. 'Well?' she asked again. 'What can we do now?'

'I don't know,' said Jeremy thoughtfully. 'But I think the rules are about to change. There's a new magic, I mean a different magic – an *old* magic – in the House. We all felt it. That's why I've been looking for you. Now that I've found you, I know a little more about what's going on but that's still not much.'

'I haven't told you anything,' said Lyssa defensively. 'I don't know anything.'

Jeremy shook his head. 'You didn't have to. You're the source of the old magic.'

Lyssa held up her hands, denying it. 'I've felt the magic, but I'm *not* the source.'

'It's so strong your aunt can't have missed it. That could be trouble,' Jeremy continued as if he hadn't heard her. 'Your magic is wild and strong, but she is entrenched in the House. She knows every nook and nail of the warrens.'

'Not every one,' said Lyssa. Now that Jeremy had named her as the source of the magic, Lyssa knew what had happened.

'You mean –?' Jeremy stopped again and stared intently into Lyssa's eyes.

She nodded slowly.

'The legend?' he demanded.

'I've been so muddled since I got back here I completely forgot about it until just now. I was in the Room,' she started to explain.

'You *found* the Room?' Jeremy asked excitedly.

'I found the Room,' said Lyssa with renewed wonder.

The Others shared a hope and referred to it as the Legend. Somewhere in the House, back at the beginning, was the Room. Apart from the House, but very much a part of it, the Room held secrets that would give the Finder knowledge about why the Others had been brought to the House, and what happened to them when they disappeared. This would, of course, pit Finder against Family, but it was something the Others were infinitely willing to do.

'Wait a minute!' Lyssa exclaimed. 'I can't be Finder *and* Family. The Legend says the two must be pitted against each other.'

Jeremy thought for a moment about this. 'Maybe Finder *has* to be Family. The Others are powerless, brought here against their will and held until they are to fulfill their purpose, whatever that is.'

Lyssa shuddered, thinking of the table in the dining room, laden with food 'for those who need'. She wondered how long this had been happening. Centuries, she guessed, and shuddered again. No wonder Jeremy disliked her.

'The way you say entrenched,' Lyssa began, suddenly remembering something Jeremy had said. She frowned. 'You make it sound like a battle is taking place.'

Jeremy gaped at Lyssa. 'There's been a battle waging in that place forever! You can't have been totally unaware. Didn't your aunt ever say anything?'

'No!' said Lyssa hotly. 'I was eight years old when I left the House and the Family would never fight in front of children. Only Aunt Burchie talked about the House. Mostly about her girlhood playing the Game. She said she was too old to play anymore, but that I could play and then tell her all about it.'

'And you did,' said Jeremy.

'I did,' said Lyssa. 'If the rules are changing, it doesn't matter what I told her twelve years ago.' She looked at him and raised her eyebrows. 'She doesn't know I found the Room.'

'Wanna bet?' asked Jeremy bluntly. He laughed. 'She, better than anyone in the House, would feel the magic waking. She knows, better than you and I, what that means.' Jeremy suddenly stopped and grabbed Lyssa by the shoulders. He pulled her closer to him and looked down into her startled blue eyes. 'Be careful with her,' he said fiercely. He gripped her shoulders more tightly and she winced. 'Promise me!'

'Okay,' Lyssa whispered. 'I promise.'

Jeremy let her go suddenly and stepped back. 'I'll walk you to the square,' he said in a normal voice.

Lyssa nodded and fell into step beside him, thinking about what he'd said. The entire Family at war? Over the House? That had to be it. If the trust was unbreakable, and no one but her father cared anyway, then it had to be the House. But no other Family member lived there for any length of time. Only Aunt Burchie endured. Entrenched? Jeremy hadn't meant it in terms of battle. The imagery had been more spidery, webby.

She still hadn't come to any conclusions when they reached the park.

'I'll leave you here,' said Jeremy, breaking into Lyssa's musing. 'I have errands to run.'

Lyssa nodded. 'See you in the warrens,' she said.

That night after supper, Lyssa decided to go back to the Room and do some more exploring. She wondered about the Legend. If Aunt Burchie knew, and Lyssa couldn't ask her about it, then Lyssa had better undertake her own education as quickly as possible. The idea frightened her, but she didn't think she should involve Jeremy at this point. She needed to have a better understanding of the situation before she could begin to know how he might help.

Force of habit made Lyssa grab her leather pouch. She checked its contents and found she needed a snack, so she ran to the kitchen, made some sandwiches and wrapped several of Millie's huge peanut-butter cookies in a napkin. She thrust these into the pouch with the knife and flashlight, and headed back to her room.

The connection between bedroom and Room was still there. Lyssa stepped into her closet and came out of the wooden clothes cupboard in the Room.

Lyssa had cleaned the Room when she had been here last, but she hadn't cleaned inside the clothes cupboard or the steamer-trunk. Now she looked at the shelves, full of dusty garments, and decided she'd better finish the job. Maybe there would be some clues here, or in the chest at the foot of the bed.

She noticed a lock through the hasp on the trunk, but it was hanging open, so she pulled it out and lifted the lid. More laundry.

Lyssa sighed. Well, she might as well get to it, she thought, and went back to the cupboard for an armload of clothing. She took this to the kitchen and dumped it into the sink. This was going to take all night, but she wouldn't have been able to sleep anyway. Once Jeremy had put the idea of old magic into her mind, Lyssa had thought of nothing else. She had to find out what was going on before it happened and she was left in the dust still wondering what had hit her. With another sigh, Lyssa primed the pump and began whooshing water into the sink. The harsh lye soap was all she had to use, so her hands were red and raw by the time she had dumped the last armload of clothing into the sink.

The chairs and tables, curtain rods, loom and spinning wheel were festooned with garments of all shapes, sizes and colors, since she had no clothes line on which to hang them to dry. Lyssa looked at them, and at the pile in the sink. None of them seemed to form a wardrobe. It was a random collection as though each had been donated to the poor-bag by a different person.

Lyssa frowned. That didn't make sense. When she had gone through the closets in other rooms in the House, they were filled with costumes appropriate to the time that part of the House was inhabited by the Family. She had spent countless hours as a child, trying on the old clothing and clumping around in big shoes in front of the mirror, pretending to be the beautiful young ladies who had worn the ruffles and bows, the lace and silk, hats and high heels.

Jeremy was openly scornful of this practice, but Lyssa didn't care. The closets of the House had always attracted her. She was always glad when he stomped off to find adventure, leaving her to dress up and dreams.

But this closet, this chest, contained the oddest assortment of clothing she had seen anywhere, and none of it was particularly attractive. The first item she picked off the pile was a skirt of fine cloth with a gaudy floral pattern which was large enough for Lyssa and several of her friends to picnic on. There was an old pair of brown, men's trousers, out at the knees; a badly stained baby's shirt; a ratty red velvet bathrobe; several pairs of underwear in all sizes, sexes and styles; a girl's frilly pink blouse; two blue cardigans with buttonholes, but no buttons; a boy's union suit; six women's petticoats, too small for Lyssa, and badly stained and patched; a man's greatcoat; three socks without mates; and an apron.

Lyssa stared at the clothing. Why did it differ so from the other closets in the House? Had anyone actually lived here? She noticed something bulging in the bathrobe pocket, and fished it out. She held up a long silk cord. It made a large loop and was tied in intricate knots around a stone that looked like carved jade or marble, and finally ended in a tassel hanging down below the stone. It was a beautiful necklace, so Lyssa put it around her neck, tucking it inside her shirt. She continued looking at the clothes.

Finally, she shook her head. Maybe it meant nothing. Maybe she was so spooked by her odd homecoming that she was reading meaning into trivia. With a sigh, she filled a bucket with water, picked up the pot of lye soap and some rags, and went to clean the cupboard and trunk.

There was a false bottom in the trunk; and a hidden drawer in the cupboard. Lyssa rocked back on her heels and hugged her knees. She looked around the Room. She had dusted without examining any of the other furniture for secret hiding places. She looked at the items she had discovered in the secret compartments. There were several pieces of jewelry, some lengths of cloth and a lot of books.

Lyssa picked up one of the books and leafed through it, but it was in a language she had never encountered. She glanced over the other titles, but they were all in the same strange alphabet. She frowned. Self-education was all well and good, but how do you learn a language from a book with no translation? She didn't have time for that kind of code-breaking, and she had no translation key.

She combed the Room and furniture for any additional secret hiding places, hoping a search would turn up something to provide a clue, but found none. She wondered briefly if there were other clues somewhere else in the House, but then she thought of all the different rooms she had been in while playing the Game, and sighed. Even if there were clues elsewhere in the House, she had no reasonable expectation of finding them. The House was just too huge. The task would be tantamount to finding a specific shell in the ocean. There were just too many places to hide things; places about which even Aunt Burchie could have no knowledge, despite what Jeremy said.

Lyssa turned her attention to the jewelry, but it seemed straightforward enough. There were four large brooches set with precious stones, a pearl necklace and a tiny golden ring that just barely fit over the tip of her baby finger. None of it was magic, though. Old, rare, priceless, but they weren't even charms. Lyssa bundled them into the toe of one of the socks and placed the jewelry back in the bottom of the trunk.

The cloth was next for inspection, and as she opened the first length, Lyssa noticed her fingertips begin to tingle. The fabric seemed simple enough, a pale pink dimity, but by the time the yardage was laid out flat on the floor, Lyssa's arms were tingling up to the elbows and she was losing the feeling in her hands.

She jumped back away from it shaking her hands, trying to restore circulation. She banged them against her thighs and wiggled her fingers. She twirled around with her arms out, as if centrifugal force would work. Finally, Lyssa just waited until the magic could dissipate. Her body absorbed most of it, and she could feel the tingling work its way up her arms, into her shoulders, neck and head, then down her torso to her legs and feet. Some of the magic went out into the Room, and Lyssa could see it being absorbed by the room itself.

Lyssa sat, fascinated and terrified, not knowing what to do. She had to fold up the cloth again, but she was certain she shouldn't touch it, or any of the other lengths. She would have to put those back in the chest and try to find another means of identifying what they were and how they were to be used. She pulled two socks over her hands and

31

refolded the pink dimity as quickly as she could, making sure to fold it exactly as it had been.

By the time she had finished, Lyssa could feel the magic bleeding through the socks, so she used a couple of the ragged petticoats like pot-holders and got the fabrics put away in the trunk. She then put the false bottom back in place and turned to study the books.

Close inspection of every slim volume turned up no further clues about the language. Lyssa had no idea what it was, or how to translate it. The books could be of no use to her until she could read them. She put one of the smaller volumes into her leather pouch. Maybe the library would have some information she could use.

Lyssa stacked the rest of the books in the trunk and clicked the drawer back into place. It would take the clothing some time to dry, and there didn't seem to be any more she could get out of the Room for now. She slung her pouch over her head and settled it on her hip, and went out into the warrens. She wasn't ready to go back to her bedroom just yet.

Chapter Two

'The Game serves two purposes: It creates the spell for
transition, and it links the player to the House.'
The Book of Rules, Chapter Three

Lyssa didn't even bother to turn around to see the corridor
disappearing behind her. She had never been in this part
of the House before. There were probably many places in
the House she'd never seen. There was a dull nag of urgency
was growing in the back of her mind, but she shook it off
and went to the next door, then the next, and the next.
She no longer tried to skip any, and plodded from one to
another.

The corridor was long and dim. There were doors at
frequent intervals on both sides and Lyssa was obliged to
open each door in order to progress fown the corridor. She
didn't know what she was looking for. So far, there had
been only grey nothingness behind each door, but she had
to stop and look before she could walk any further down
the corridor. Every time she tried to walk past a door, she
was stopped by something she couldn't see or touch.
She would be kept immobile until she made a move in the
direction of the door she was supposed to open. Once she
had seen that it, too, opened onto nothing, she would be
allowed to proceed to the next door.

The hallway had grown longer since she first entered. It
had to have. There couldn't have been this many doors when
she started. Surely she'd have been discouraged just by looking at that many, but now they seemed to stretch to infinity,
and all of them opened onto the same dull grey emptiness,
and she was going to send the rest of her life opening doors.

Lyssa opened the next door and was relieved to find herself on the balcony of a brightly-lit ballroom. The endless, dark hallway disappeared and Lyssa was standing among the tables that had been set here for the older guests who no longer wanted to be a part of the games on the floor, but still wanted to attend the festivities and watch. Lyssa remembered Aunt Burchie telling her it was often referred to, rather impudently, as the grandparents' gallery, and it circled half the dance floor looking down on the orchestra dais. Below it was the bar, a long, highly polished wooden arc, exactly the same dimensions as the balcony above. Stairs on either end swept up to the balcony, making it easier for servers to take drinks and hors d'oeuvres to the guests above.

The ceiling rose to a much-frescoed dome three stories above the inlaid marble dance floor. Cherubs and gargoyles vied for attention in a twisted dance around the huge crystal chandelier which hung from the center of the dome to a point above the balcony where the light was bright, but not intrusive, and on the dance floor it was intimate, but not dim. Wall sconces and ornately-framed mirrors decorated the walls at floor level, making the edges of the room brighter for those not dancing. More tables and chairs were arranged in two semicircles from the orchestra dais to just past the bar on either side of the circular room. A wide aisle between the two semi-circles led from the bar to the dance floor in front of the orchestra, onto which everything looked.

The room was empty, but in her mind, Lyssa could see people dancing, sitting at the tables laughing and talking, standing at the bar drinking and flirting, as clearly as if a movie were running behind her eyes, projecting out into the empty room. She glanced around her and now she could see the guests she stood among. An older woman, with her iron-grey hair arranged high on her head, motioned imperiously for Lyssa to get out of the way, and Lyssa glanced around guiltily. She was blocking several views. She smiled apologetically and went to the stairs, since there seemed no exit from here. She would have to find one down below.

'Would you care to dance?' asked a ghostly young man, as Lyssa reached the bottom step.

She glanced toward the image playing in her periphery and started at the realness of the vision. She could still see through him, but it looked like he was really there. His costume was magnificent, tailored white silk trousers, coat and vest, white stockings and frilled shirt. Everything was fitted to display and enhance his excellent physique.

Lyssa reached for his hand and he smiled dazzlingly. Together they swept out to the dance floor and the orchestra struck up a tune she didn't recognize. Among the imaginary dancers, Lyssa abandoned herself to the waltz and her beautiful partner. She closed her eyes and danced, feeling the music surge in her blood, and her partner's arms strong around her back.

The music changed, becoming faster and more insistent. The young man's arms became tighter and tighter as they spun around the dance floor. Lyssa opened her eyes and found the room going past in a flash and began fighting against her partner's grip.

He was going to crush her. She struggled harder, clawing with her fingernails, but he wasn't really there, so she couldn't hurt him. He was still an image in her mind, but his grip on her was very real. The magic was at work. She would have to meet it on its own terms.

Closing her eyes again, Lyssa reached into herself desperately searching for the old magic. The music grew louder and louder still, until she couldn't hear individual notes anymore; it was just noise making her ears hurt. It also made it very difficult to concentrate.

She used the magic to swell herself in her partner's arms, but was unable to break his grip. Frantically, she tried to slip through them, but each movement made his hold on her stronger.

Chinese finger puzzle! she thought. She went limp in his arms and made herself as heavy and motionless as she could. Her feet dragged on the floor and as her grasp on him relaxed, he was unable to keep going.

The young man vanished, and so did all the other imaginary guests. Lyssa found herself lying alone in the middle of the empty dance floor feeling bruised, dizzy and nauseated. The light in the room was dimming. Groggily, she pushed herself up onto her hands and knees and began crawling across the cold, hard marble floor toward the tables at the side of the room. Beyond them, she knew, were the doors. She'd better find the exit before her flashlight was the only means she had of locating one.

This is ridiculous, she thought fuzzily to herself. I should just go home.

She had taken only brief leaves of absence from school and work. Her mortgage would be drawn automatically from savings, and her Family stipend would cover it, but she wanted to sleep in her own bed. She didn't want to play the Game anymore, and hadn't realized just how much she disliked it until now. Crawling on her hands and knees was humiliating. At home, this would never happen. She wanted the familiarity and predictability of her classes, her job and her friends.

As she moved, Lyssa could feel herself returning to normal, and shortly, she was able to pull herself upright using a chair. Taking stock of the room, Lyssa moved first to one door, then the next, searching for the way out.

The House was big on doors leading nowhere, Lyssa thought darkly as she yanked open yet another. This one opened onto a child's room.

'Hello,' said the little girl on the bed. She was sitting cross-legged, holding a doll on her lap and combing its hair.

'Hello,' said Lyssa cautiously. 'May I come in for a moment?'

The little girl nodded solemnly, her black curls bouncing

against her shoulders, the large bow on top of her head flopping with the movement.

'That's a pretty doll,' said Lyssa, wondering *what now?* This was no imaginary child. She couldn't be one of the Others; they were older.

The little girl nodded, tears pooling in her dark sapphire eyes, her chin quivering. 'I found her here,' she whispered. 'She keeps me company.'

'You're all alone?' asked Lyssa. 'How long have you been here?' She tried to keep her growing outrage from her voice so she wouldn't frighten the child any further.

The little girl shrugged. 'A very long time,' she gulped miserably. 'I'm hungry.'

With a small, anguished cry, Lyssa reached the child in one stride and swept her up in a hug. 'No one has found you? You didn't go looking for the Others?'

The little girl was sobbing now, clinging to Lyssa, the doll cast aside. 'I'm so afraid!' she cried. 'I went to go get my own dolly to show my daddy, but I went into this room instead, and Daddy isn't outside the door like he's supposed to be and I w-want my mommy!' she wailed.

Lyssa hugged the little girl, rocking her back and forth on the bed, murmuring nothings her soft hair until the child had cried herself out and fallen into exhausted sleep. Even then, Lyssa continued to rock, holding the tiny victim, her mind racing in too many directions, trying to grasp meaning in this cruelty.

The Others were older. Very seldom were they younger than their twenties. They tended to be strong and healthy, and they had all enjoyed happy family lives until they walked through a door, and found themselves in the House instead of where they expected to be. They lived in the House, unable to go any further than the edge of town, for no more than a couple of years before disappearing again. It was hoped they returned home, but no one really believed that.

Lyssa studied the girl. She couldn't be any more than

four. She felt a stab of guilt. The House had obviously known the child was here and had led Lyssa to her. No one else in the House was aware of the little girl's presence. The House had been hiding her for Lyssa to find. What if she'd put off playing the Game for a few more days? Would she have found a corpse, instead? She shuddered.

Aside from the bed on which they sat, there were two night-stands, a huge clothes cupboard and a desk and chair. The floor was deeply carpeted and the walls hung with matching wallpaper. If she didn't know better, Lyssa would have thought this room was in the portion of the House belonging to Aunt Burchie. But this room didn't exist in that part of the House. Lyssa had been all through that. Those rooms never changed. They weren't part of the warrens yet. When the next portion of the House was built, the current living quarters would become part of the warrens.

But all that was beside the point. What was Lyssa going to do with a child? She couldn't take her to Aunt Burchie's. She couldn't leave her in the Room and she couldn't leave her here. This was the place she was trapped, this was a prison which had taken her from her father and mother. And Lyssa was a member of the Family who had done this to her.

It always came back to that. The difference between Family and Other. Two groups who inhabited the House simultaneously, but lived apart from each other. Lyssa wasn't sure she knew all that much about either group, in spite of belonging to one and spending her childhood with the other.

Was it reasonable for Lyssa to ask the Others to care for the child? She was so much younger and less able to care for herself – Lyssa bit her lip and studied the child again. Her dark lashes curled against her pale cheeks, making her look even younger and more vulnerable than she had when awake. Lyssa felt the sob rising in her, but couldn't stop it. It tore from her throat like cloth ripping.

There had to be a way to make this stop. It was bad enough to take adults. Stealing babies was criminal.

Lyssa felt a kernel of resolve hardening in her chest. A lump of sorrow and guilt at being the cause of such unhappiness. It slowed her tears, making them part of the resolve to change things. Blinking back the last ones, Lyssa steeled herself as if for a blow. She didn't know what it was she needed to fix. She just knew something wasn't right. She would have to find a way to take care of the child herself. Leaving her with the Others didn't feel right. Lyssa had no idea how she would take care of her, but leaving her in the House wasn't an option.

Unable to continue until the little girl awoke, Lyssa sat for a long while, turning things over and over in her mind. She wanted very much to talk to Jeremy, but she had no way of finding him. If you started the Game in pairs, the House might let you stay together for some or all of the Game, but never were other players allowed to join a game in progress.

Lyssa froze. *Never were other players allowed to join a game in progress.* She looked again at the tiny girl in her arms. The rules were changing. Jeremy had said so. Now she had proof, she thought, growing angrier still. Her grip on the child tightened and her body began to shake. Playing games with the life of a child was unconscionable.

The child stirred in her arms, protesting the confining embrace. Lyssa held her breath, trying to relax. Dark blue eyes blinked open and stared back at her. 'I'm still hungry,' she whispered.

Forcing a smile, Lyssa said, 'I think I can remedy that.' She unslung her leather pouch and pulled out a large paper packet containing the snack she always packed.

'Oh-h, that smells good,' the child said, inhaling deeply as Lyssa opened the packet.

'What's your name?' Lyssa asked, handing the little girl a biscuit that had been split, buttered and stuffed with meat and cheese.

'Molly,' she answered around a huge mouthful.

'My name is Lyssa. Eat slowly,' she admonished. 'You don't want to make yourself sick.'

Molly nodded solemnly, chewing with difficulty. It was clear she wanted to say something, but her mouth was too full even to try talking through it. Lyssa worked on her own sandwich while waiting for Molly to regain control.

'My mommy always says that. Can you help me find her? And my daddy too?' She looked up at Lyssa with hopeful expectation.

Lyssa thought hard about what she could say. At last, hoping it would be enough, she said, 'I'll do what I can.' It felt sadly inadequate especially since Lyssa didn't honestly think there was anything she could do. She gave Molly a hug. 'I'll sure be better company than a doll.'

Molly smiled tentatively and reached for another sandwich and a cookie. When the picnic was finished and the last crumbs had been wadded up in the paper and thrown out, she sighed.

'Better?' asked Lyssa.

Molly nodded. 'I feel dizzy,' she said.

Lyssa chuckled. 'You ate a lot. All the blood has gone to your stomach. We'll wait a minute for your head to settle before we leave.'

'Where are we going?' asked Molly. 'Are you taking me home?'

'I'm not sure where we're going,' said Lyssa slowly. She hated to tell the girl the truth, but she couldn't lie to her, either. 'I don't know where your home is. It's going to be very difficult to take you there, but I'm going to try. It make take a long time. Can you be patient?'

Molly nodded solemnly, but it was clear she had no idea what patience was. 'I'll try,' she said. 'I'm glad you found me.'

'Oh, sweetheart,' Lyssa hugged Molly again. 'Me, too. Do you think you're ready to leave?'

'I guess,' said Molly timidly. The room was strange, but

it had been home since she had gotten lost. With a small sigh, she climbed off the bed and reached for Lyssa's hand. 'Can I bring the dolly?'

'Sure,' said Lyssa. 'Would you like me to carry her for you? She's pretty big.'

Molly nodded solemnly.

Lyssa picked up the doll and looked around the room one last time before opening the door opposite the one she had come in. It opened onto another hallway. 'Gee, what a surprise,' she murmured, leading the little girl out of the room and shutting the door. They walked together down the hall to the only other door. Behind it was a stairway going up into darkness.

'Where are we going?' asked Molly again as they began the climb. She held tightly to Lyssa's hand and tried to peer ahead into the gloom.

'We're playing a game,' Lyssa answered truthfully enough. 'This House is magic and it likes to play games with the people who live in it.'

'Other people live here?' asked Molly, Her breath was becoming shorter, and still they climbed.

Lyssa was beginning to hate the Bell family and their quirky architecture by the time they reached the top stair. The light came up suddenly and a panel swung shut behind them. They were in a huge dining room.

A carved wooden table thirty feet long and ten feet wide dominated the room. There were straight-backed wooden armchairs, ten on each long side, and three at head and foot of the table. Each place was set with enough silver, crystal and china for seven courses. The sideboards along the far wall were laden with food and servants stood at attention beside them.

All but two of the chairs were occupied; young men and women who sat silent with stony expressions, staring at the new arrivals.

Lyssa stood, holding Molly's hand, and stared back, unabashed. They were all her age, and wore clothing made shabby by repeated washing. She guessed they kept what they had worn when they first came to the House, since it was probably the only thing tying them to their past. The sullen expressions were a defense. They were frightened, lonely and hopeful that Lyssa would have the answers they had been unable to find on their own.

With a sigh, Lyssa looked away from their penetrating eyes and toward the foot of the table where Jeremy sat, flanked by the two empty chairs. It was obvious they were for Lyssa and Molly, so she walked around to them, and seated Molly on Jeremy's left. Then she took the remaining seat and waited.

Looking around the table again, Lyssa didn't recognize any of the faces. She hadn't really expected to, since the Others stayed so short a time, but it hadn't registered what that meant until she sat facing the jury these strangers seemed to resemble.

'You have found the Room,' said the young man directly opposite Jeremy at the far end of the table.

She nodded.

'And the knowledge?' he pressed.

Lyssa shrugged. She said slowly, 'I don't know much about it yet.'

'Tell us what you found,' he demanded.

Lyssa shook her head slowly. 'That's not how this works,' she said.

'You are the Finder,' he insisted. 'That makes you one of us.'

'No,' said Lyssa firmly. 'I am Family, I am your adversary. I am Finder, I am neutral.'

A murmur of consternation rippled around the table and the Others leaned toward each other to consult.

Jeremy leaned toward Lyssa and whispered into her ear 'You can't do this. They need something from you. They need to know that they have some charge of their lives now. They can't face hearing that someone else is now in control and still making the decisions for them.'

Lyssa shrugged. 'They *are* helpless. I just don't know what I can do for them, or even myself, yet. Now I've got Molly to take care of and I don't know why. All I have are problems and no solutions. I still have to face Aunt Burchie about her will and estate, and here I am playing this damned Game –' She gestured at the table and, in doing so, glanced up. The Others were staring at them.

The young man at the head of the table stood up. 'This is *not* a game!' he snapped. 'We don't care about your problems. We care very much about solving ours, and we won't permit you to stand in our way. We insist you show us what you found.'

'No,' said Lyssa. 'I didn't mean to imply *this* –' she indicated the table with a sweep of her hand, 'was a game. I meant what the House is doing to me.'

The young man's face darkened a shade or two, but he gestured to the servants, who immediately began circulating with dishes, filling cups and bowls, setting out baskets of bread. The entire group sat silently, watching the young man, who continued to stand, watching Lyssa. She sat unmoving and equally silent.

'If you will not show us willingly, we will have to force you to,' the man threatened, unable to keep quiet any longer.

'You will find yourself unable to act, in the same way you have found yourself unable to leave,' Lyssa said, standing as well. 'You are pawns, not players. I'm sorry about that. It's none of my doing, but that's how it is. I may find the means to stop all this, but that doesn't mean I'm going to be able to solve your problems. Molly?' she turned and looked at the little girl.

Molly looked up from her plate. She had found a pocket of hunger inside her but the anger in the room frightened her so she was afraid to pick up her fork.

'We are going now,' said Lyssa, holding out her hand.

Molly slid out of her chair and went to stand beside

43

Lyssa, hand in hand, ready to leave. 'Thank you for dinner,' she said regretfully to the strangers.

They nodded and smiled, a few said, 'You're welcome,' but none looked happy.

'Jeremy will keep you informed,' said Lyssa. 'You will not meet with me like this again.' She took a side door and wondered where they would come out this time.

'Why were they so angry?' asked Molly rather plaintively as the door shut behind them.

Lyssa looked around for the next step of the Game. They had come out into a largish sitting room. There were two couches, one on either side of where they stood, and chairs in small groups around them. 'I'm sorry, sweetheart,' said Lyssa, absently shifting the large doll on her hip. She had been in this room before. She looked around long and hard, trying to figure out what was different this time, but she couldn't pinpoint it. What was she doing here? She squeezed Molly's hand and pulled her across the room. The pictures were different. There had been portraits on the walls. Now there were nature scenes. Lyssa walked from one to the next, studying them all, but she found nothing out of the ordinary. They hid no safes, escapes or other unusual things.

'What are we doing?' asked Molly as they made their third circuit of the room.

'I don't know,' said Lyssa. 'Looking for something.'

'What?'

'I don't know,' Lyssa said again. 'I'm not even sure I'd know it if I found it.' She sighed and looked down at the little girl. Molly looked frightened and confused. Lyssa crouched down in front of her and took her face in both hands. 'I don't have much to tell you,' she apologized. 'But I will take care of you, and we will try to find a way to get you home again, and that's what I'm doing now: searching for a way to send you home.'

'Is there a way?' The little girl's voice sounded oddly grown up and it took Lyssa aback.

She took a deep breath and held it while she thought. 'I don't know,' she finally exhaled. 'But if there is, we'll find it. Okay?' she smiled encouragingly.

'Can I help you look?' For the first time, Molly looked eager.

'Yeah,' said Lyssa. 'But I don't think we're going to find anything more here. I thought I was missing a clue, but I guess not. Why don't you pick a door and we'll see where it leads us.'

Molly ran to the closest door and pulled it open. There was a deep, black yawning pit just behind it, and Lyssa yanked Molly back from the doorway just in time to keep her from tumbling in. They were both screaming by the time Molly was safely seated in a chair.

'Maybe I'd better tell you a little about the House first,' Lyssa said when she had calmed down enough to speak.

'Someone is following us,' Molly said in a stage whisper. She gripped Lyssa's hand tighter and glanced fearfully over her shoulder. She walked faster, trying to drag Lyssa forward down the hall.

Lyssa slowed her down and laughed a little. 'That's just the House trying to hurry us,' she said, recognizing the same feeling of dread in the pit of her stomach. There was somewhere they were supposed to go, *now*. She used to respond at a run, but she had been a child then, Molly's age or a little older. Now the imperiousness of it bothered her. It made her want to dig in her heels and take her own time.

'Please,' begged Molly, pulling hard on Lyssa's hand. 'Come on!'

'No,' said Lyssa. 'I play at my own pace now.' She reached into herself and found the core of resolve. She held it briefly in her mind to focus herself and she willed the feeling that was bothering them both to go away. She concentrated on this thought harder than she had ever done before, and gradually, she felt the panic recede. 'Is that better?' she gasped. She didn't dare let up, but she had to know if Molly was being helped as well.

'A little,' she whimpered. 'What are you doing?'

'I'm trying to make this feeling go away,' Lyssa panted. 'Shh!'

Molly squeezed her eyes shut and stood next to Lyssa, trying to help, but not knowing how.

Finally, the feeling of urgency disappeared, but Lyssa was spent with the effort, and wondering if it had been worth it. She got to her feet and held out her hand to Molly. 'I'm sorry if I frightened you,' she said. 'It just made me mad that the House was using the same tactics on me that it did when I was a child. We both need to relearn each other. It was a pretty stupid fight, but I think I got my point across. The rules are changing, and I have to deal with that. That's why I have hope we can get you back to your parents.' She looked at Molly long and hard. 'Do you understand that?'

Molly nodded. 'I know about magic.'

Lyssa nodded approvingly. 'Children do,' she said with a smile. 'So, now that you know that you have to be careful, why don't we find another door. There's always another door.'

Molly was much more circumspect in her next approach, but she still shivered a little when another dark and empty place was revealed. 'Why is it like this?' she asked as she slammed the door shut and went on to the next.

Lyssa shrugged. 'It just is,' she said. 'That's how its always been, as far as I know. The people who built the House have a strange sense of humor, and the Family allows them to exercise it. We just play the Game.'

The next door was the right one and the pair stepped through it into a darkly-paneled game room. Only the light over the pool table was on, but Lyssa could see Jeremy sitting in the easy chair in the far corner.

This seemed an odd room compared to the rest of the house. The furnishings were old and threadbare, and the carpeting was cheap and worn. The pool table was bottom of the line, and all the other games set up around the room showed signs of hard use. The dart board was cork instead of hair, and was missing chunks; the chess pieces were chipped plastic on a piece of cardboard covered with paper. The overall effect was depressing. Lyssa couldn't imagine anyone having fun in that room.

'That was quite a show you put on,' Jeremy said.

Molly started and Lyssa realized she hadn't known he was there. Lyssa squeezed Molly's hand reassuringly. 'That's not what I intended to do,' she said. 'I was rather on the spot.'

Jeremy stood up and came over to where they were, still in the doorway. 'You made them pretty angry.'

Lyssa twisted her lip.

'You could have thrown them a bone,' said Jeremy with feeling.

'It wouldn't have done any good,' said Lyssa. 'I had a really stupid fight with the House,' she said, changing the subject.

Jeremy grinned. 'How's that?' he asked, drawing her and Molly into the room and shutting the door behind them.

They couldn't go back anyway, so Lyssa came away willingly enough. Molly looked as wilted as Lyssa felt. She stroked Molly's glossy black hair.

Molly's lower lip trembled, but she said nothing.

'Molly, this is Jeremy,' said Lyssa.

Jeremy nodded acknowledgement and Molly smiled shyly, but neither one said anything to the other.

'Tell me about the House,' Jeremy said, turning back to Lyssa. 'We can search for a while together.'

'Search for what?' Lyssa asked sharply.

'The Room, silly,' Jeremy laughed. 'I know you've found it, but the Game was always to search for the Room. We just aren't bothered by the detail of finding it anymore. Now tell me about your fight!' He started pulling open doors looking for an exit.

'I just objected to being hurried along,' she said, trying to sound nonchalant.

'You withstood the anxiety?' Jeremy sounded impressed.

'I overrode it,' she said. 'I stopped it from affecting Molly and me.'

Jeremy raised his eyebrows. 'But it cost you.'

'Yeah,' she said wryly.

'Why was it a stupid fight?' he wanted to know.

Lyssa laughed. 'Because I'm beat! I'm still going to go where the House wants me to go, and it's still going to take me time to do it. It's going to take more time because I stopped to make it clear I wasn't going to be hurried ever again. And the House, being somewhat vindictive, is probably going to drag it out even further just to prove to me that it doesn't matter what I want anyway.'

Jeremy opened the right door and stood back with a flourish. 'You're right. It was a stupid fight. But, it also gave you a chance to test the old magic a bit. What did you think?'

Lyssa led Molly through the door. They passed briefly through a small bathroom and out the other door into a series of rooms and closets joined by short hallways.

'I think I've still got a lot of learning to do,' said Lyssa with feeling.

They threaded their way through the maze of bathrooms and bedrooms, admiring furniture and artwork, but always trying to find the path through the myriad dead-ends.

The rooms they walked through were huge, with high ceilings and wide doorways, but no windows. There was no way of knowing which direction they were going and Lyssa began to wonder if they were going in circles. Everything looked oddly the same. There were different color schemes in the various rooms, baths and halls, but they all had the same basic shape and appointments, and there were certainly more rooms than colors, so on many occasions it felt as if they were entering a room they had only just left.

Molly walked with her head down, holding onto Lyssa's hand tightly.

Poor thing, Lyssa thought. She's in shock.

Anger welled up in her again, and she gave the tiny hand a gentle squeeze. The core of resolve grew again, just a little, as Lyssa turned the next corner into a short hallway. Jeremy was the only other baby she knew to have been brought here, but at least he had had his mother until her death a few years ago. Molly didn't even have that. Lyssa hefted the large doll again and Jeremy held out his hands.

'I'll carry her for a while,' he said gruffly.

Gratefully, Lyssa handed over the surprisingly heavy doll, and stroked Molly's head. 'Would you like to peek into some of the closets?' Lyssa asked her. 'There are some beautiful clothes and it's fun to try them on.'

Molly shook her head. 'No thank you,' she whispered, without looking up.

Lyssa looked at Jeremy and found him looking at Molly with empathy. 'You've got to help me,' she told him. 'For her sake and your mother's, too, this can't continue.'

Jeremy nodded. 'I was brought here for you,' he said again, rubbing it in.

'What do you mean by that?' Lyssa demanded.

Jeremy shrugged. 'I've never known more than that. I can't even remember who told me or when. It just seems like I've always known that I was brought here for you.'

'Did I ever know the purpose of the Game?' Lyssa asked suddenly. 'I don't remember knowing and the search for the Room never entered my mind when we were playing all those years ago, and that's not the answer I get when I ask.'

'Not what you get when you ask?' Jeremy repeated irritably. 'Ask who, what?'

'I mean, when I ask myself why I'm playing the Game the answer is different,' replied Lyssa trying to explain.

'What answer do you get?' asked Jeremy impatiently.

'It's more like I'm taking an extended and bizarre tour of the House,' she said slowly, thinking about it. 'Like I'm supposed to see every bit of it eventually, but I don't know why.'

Jeremy frowned. 'You know that the Others don't play the Game?'

Lyssa started. 'What?'

'No. They never have. They think what you and I are doing is very strange indeed. You don't remember the conversations around the dinner table when we were children. They always made us tell them about our adventures, but the Others always stay in those rooms back there, and don't go out into the rest of the House.'

'I'll be damned,' said Lyssa with dawning realization. She stopped in mid-stride and leaned against the wall. Molly came to a stop as well, looking up curiously for the first time in quite a while. It took Jeremy a stride to realize he was alone, and he too stopped.

'Yes?' he asked expectantly, shifting the doll from one arm to the other.

'The rules are changing, but they're also finally being revealed. You taught me about the legends the Others tell while I was learning the layout of the House.' Lyssa sighed. 'I learned the legends. But I don't think I could ever learn the House. The magic distorts things too much. I remember bits and pieces, but they have no connection. The start of the Game was always very clear, but after the room with the brocade maze and all those doors, the continuity breaks up completely.' Lyssa frowned and shook her head. 'I don't get it.'

Jeremy spread his free hand to indicate he didn't understand any better than she did. 'Maybe you can find a way to question your aunt without her knowing what you're getting at,' he suggested. 'You said you had some estate stuff to talk with her about.'

Lyssa grimaced and cocked her head to the left slightly. 'I can try.' She pushed off from the wall and continued searching for the way out of the maze. It bothered her a lot to find herself thinking of Aunt Burchie as an adversary.

The three of them plodded through the maze, lost in their own thoughts and moving on automatic pilot until they turned a corner and found themselves on a long, narrow balcony that stretched into the darkness on either side of them. There was darkness above and below.

'Left or right?' Lyssa asked.

'Flip a coin,' suggested Jeremy with a short laugh.

'Left,' whispered Molly.

'Left it is, then,' said Jeremy, shifting the doll to his other arm.

Lyssa was only marginally grateful that there were no doors along the wall they walked beside. She wondered what was off the balcony in the darkness. There had been no light-switch plates on the wall where they had come in, so they were walking in the increasing dimness as the light from the doorway faded. She reached into herself, looking for the slowly wakening old magic, but found nothing there to create light with. She sighed and held Molly's hand more firmly.

'You've spent time in the town,' Lyssa said suddenly to Jeremy. 'Do you know of a Bell family? Architects and builders?'

Jeremy thought for a moment before shaking his head. 'Never heard of them,' he said. 'That doesn't mean anything, though. The town is pretty big. There's close to ten thousand people living here now and I've never had need of an architect before.'

'I didn't realize,' she said, more to herself than to him. 'We're out in the middle of nowhere. How have people heard to move here? There's just not much here.'

'Think about it,' said Jeremy a little impatiently. 'It's a scary world out there. This is a small town with virtually no crime. It's still safe to walk outside alone at night here, no matter what neighborhood you're in. We're really not that far away from things anymore since the highway went in. I'm told it's a comfortable drive,' he finished with a bitter twist in his tone.

Lyssa flinched. 'I wonder if they're still in town, or if they've moved to a more profitable city. I wonder if there are blueprints to this place.'

'Blueprints?' Jeremy laughed. 'Can you imagine what those would look like?'

'It might not give me the specifics, but a general plan?' Lyssa mused. 'It might help.'

'Is there no way to string the pieces together in your head?'

Lyssa shook her head, but in the darkness, no one saw. 'No,' she said when she realized this. 'And now that I can start the Game from either the Room, or Aunt Burchie's, I have even less idea how this is all hung together. A couple of times I've found myself in a room I've been in before, but I have no recollection of how I got there the first time, and no idea how to duplicate the route I used to get there next.'

'I don't remember the magic distorting things so much when we were kids,' Jeremy said.

Lyssa thought about that. They were walking with their hands out in front of them now, hoping they would run into a wall or door instead of a downward flight of stairs, or a hole in the floor.

'I remember the mazes being augmented magically, but you're right, I don't remember hallways becoming unending, or so many empty doorways.' Her foot struck something and she fell forward onto a flight of stairs going up. 'Oh, thank goodness!' she exclaimed as she stood back up. 'Molly, are you okay?' she asked, feeling in the darkness for the little girl.

'Yes,' came the unruffled reply. 'You let go when you fell.'

'Well, I guess we climb,' Jeremy said.

'Do you want me to take the doll again for a while?' Lyssa offered.

'You've got Molly,' he said. 'I'm okay with the arrangement.'

'Then let's climb,' said Lyssa. She was beginning to wonder where they were going, and when the Game would end. Molly needed to rest, and Lyssa still needed to figure out where she would be safest. There seemed to be no easy decisions.

The flight was quite short, and there was a door at the top of the stair. On the other side of the door was a table, laden with food, and the three rushed toward it without a second thought. They grabbed plates and set to eating greedily.

As she neared the end of her second plate, Lyssa began to wonder how Millie had gotten all this down here. Maybe they weren't as far from Aunt Burchie's part of the House as she thought they were. They had been walking forever and could actually be quite near. She looked around the room for a dumbwaiter, or some other means of conveying large numbers platters from one room to another. There were strange pictures on the walls, of bull fighters and waterwheel mills. The walls were painted hunter green and the moldings were all trimmed with gilt. There were several sideboards against the walls, but none had wheels.

With a sigh of contentment, Lyssa pushed her plate and her stray thoughts away. She sat back in her chair. 'I may live.'

Jeremy chuckled in agreement. 'How are you doing, Molly?' he reached out and ruffled her dark, silky curls.

'I'm fine,' she said shyly.

She looked much better now that she'd eaten. Lyssa hoped that all the walking with her head down had been time spent working through her shock. 'I feel like we should move on but I'm so stuffed all I want to do is loosen my belt, lean back in my chair and take a nap.'

Jeremy nodded. 'I think you're right. We should be going.' He stood up and lifted the large doll into his arms. 'Maybe the walking will wake us up a bit.'

There were four doorways in the room. The one through

which they had come was the only one with a door, and it was shut. The other doorways gave free egress into the other rooms clearly visible beyond.

One was a beautiful salon decorated in white and silver, and looked as though it was never touched. It was forbidding and sterile in its splendor. Another was more of a living room, with couches and chairs arranged in conversation areas around beautiful, low, glass-topped tables. It was done in royal blues, gold and cream, and also looked unlived-in. The third room drew all three into it. It looked like every stereotype of a brothel Jeremy and Lyssa could think of: red velvet upholstery on gilded wooden furniture, metallic gold wallpaper with overlapping grillwork patterns in matte white and flocked black velvet. Black velvet draped every doorway. There were vases of peacock feathers on the tables and paintings on black velvet of large-eyed women in brightly colored dresses on the walls. The carpet was sculpted and patterned with roses and leaves. The overall effect made them all a little dizzy, but they couldn't help standing in the middle of the room, spinning in circles trying to look at everything at once. It was grotesque in a fascinating sort of way, and they couldn't stop staring.

'It's like a train wreck!' Lyssa marveled. 'You don't want to look, but you can't help yourself.'

Jeremy shook his head in appreciation. 'It's pretty incredible,' he agreed.

'It's beautiful,' breathed Molly, slewing here and there, wide-eyed.

Lyssa and Jeremy gaped at her a moment, then burst out laughing.

Molly looked up, hurt. 'It is,' she pouted defensively.

'Beauty is in the eye of the beholder,' said Jeremy, with one dark eyebrow quirked.

'This is true,' Lyssa conceded. She smiled at Molly. 'Sweetheart, I'm sorry I laughed. I didn't mean to make fun of you.'

Jeremy nodded. 'Me, too,' he said. 'I didn't mean to make you feel bad.'

'Okay,' said Molly happily. She immediately returned to admiring the room.

'I guess we go on from here,' Lyssa said. 'Pick a door.'

'I guess straight ahead is as good a direction as any,' Jeremy suggested, pointing to the room beyond.

This section of the House seemed to consist of large, square rooms with a large, open doorway in each wall, leading to rooms adjoining every other room. Every room was beautifully decorated with a different theme and color scheme, but it was clear that none of them were to be used.

'This must be a huge square,' mused Lyssa as they walked, 'with walls dividing it into smaller squares, but no hallways, bathrooms, bedrooms and I haven't seen a kitchen through any of the doorways I've looked through. Who in the world would build their section of the house with only living rooms? Or why did the magic change it to be like this?'

Jeremy shrugged. 'I've never understood the purpose of any of this but I've been here before.'

Lyssa looked at him carefully. 'Not with me, though.'

He shook his head. 'I played the Game one day after you left,' he said briefly.

'Did you do that often?' she asked sharply.

'I was hoping to find the Room,' he said, his color deepening a little.

'When did you stop playing?' Lyssa pressed.

'That was it,' he admitted grudgingly.

'Look!' Molly cried, grabbing Lyssa's hand and dragging her forward.

They had reached the center of the square. The room was all crystal and mirrors, ablaze and shimmering with the light of thousands of candles. Larger than the rest, they could see through the doors into the rooms beyond. They were more of the same type they had been passing through. This room, however, was special. There were people here, dancing, talking and laughing in complete silence. A couple, beautifully dressed in brilliantly-colored silks, swirled by but instead of brushing up against Molly, the woman's skirts went right through her legs as if they weren't really there.

Molly gasped and leaped backwards, clinging to Lyssa's hand. 'W-what was that?' she quavered.

Lyssa looked quizzically at Jeremy.

'Probably just more magic,' he said. 'They obviously aren't here, so I guess we push on through to the other side and get to wherever it is we're going.'

'Aren't they here for a reason?' Lyssa asked, unwilling to let it go.

Jeremy sighed. 'What reason would that be?'

'I don't know,' Lyssa shrugged. 'But there seems to be a reason for everything here, even if we don't immediately know what it is.'

Jeremy laughed. 'How do you figure? I haven't noticed a reason for much of anything around here.'

'I don't know,' Lyssa said again, this time defensively. 'I just thought –'

'Please don't fight,' Molly begged, stepping between them and looking up plaintively. 'It's just a pretty party, that's all, we can go; it's alright.'

Lyssa looked down at the little girl, feeling guilty. 'You're right, we'll find our way out of here and try to figure things out when we get back.' Lyssa shot a look at Jeremy.

He glared back, but they set out across the room toward the far door and the other side of the maze.

'I'm tired,' said Molly plaintively. 'I'm hungry.'

Lyssa squeezed her hand. 'Would you like me to carry you for a while?' They had been walking for a long time, and Lyssa was tired also. But she was determined to take care of her small charge. Molly held up her arms and Lyssa swung her up to settle the girl on her hip. Molly snuggled her head into Lyssa's neck and sighed.

Lyssa sighed too. They were still in the odd maze of living rooms and there was no end in sight. She didn't have any better idea about what she was going to do with the little girl she was carrying. The problem had been turning around and around in her mind, and the only thing she knew for sure was that she couldn't keep Molly hidden in Aunt Burchie's portion of the House, and had to keep the old woman from finding out about her at all. Lyssa couldn't figure out how Aunt Burchie hadn't yet found out except, somehow, the House didn't want her to know any more than Lyssa did.

None of it made sense. Lyssa sighed again and glanced at Jeremy. He trudged beside them, still carrying the doll. It was pretty funny seeing the dark, brooding young man he had become, gently holding the large, frilly doll with long, blonde curls and a big, floppy hat. But looking at him, Lyssa didn't feel like laughing. By now, she really wanted to cry. But that wouldn't produce any solutions, and, right now, she needed some.

Eventually, this Game would end, and she would have to go to Aunt Burchie and tell her most of what had happened during the time she had been wandering. Burchie knew about Jeremy and would know about the confrontation with the Others, but she wouldn't have any idea about Molly. How would Lyssa keep the little girl's presence from her?

Lyssa was growing more and more uneasy about her relationship with her aunt. The idea of keeping secrets from her felt like a betrayal. The idea of telling her everything felt very dangerous. Lyssa never had any idea what Aunt Burchie was thinking and she was beginning to understand that she herself had always been an open book.

Maybe that would change with the magic Lyssa had tapped into, but she couldn't take the chance of being found out, and having the evidence in her bedroom.

'Maybe I could help,' Jeremy said softly.

Lyssa was jolted by the sound of his voice and Molly

stirred on her shoulder. Lyssa stroked her silky, black hair and murmured something soothing against her head. 'You?' she asked, somewhat incredulous.

'Well, I don't think you'll like it much, but I know a place where Molly'd be safe,' he offered.

Lyssa was silent for a long moment before she realized what he was talking about. He was right. She didn't like it much. She didn't like it at all, but it might work and, if it did, Molly would be safer there than anywhere else Lyssa could imagine. 'Do you think she would?'

'If I asked, she probably would,' he said. 'She loves kids.'

Lyssa could feel her arms tense and willed herself to relax, not wanting to communicate her unhappiness to Molly, who was sleeping undisturbed in her arms. It would keep the little girl close, but away from the House and Aunt Burchie. It made Lyssa uncomfortable, but that was her problem, not Molly's.

'Will you ask her, please?' Lyssa finally made herself ask. The words tasted bitter in her mouth. She hated to have to do it, but she couldn't see any other way.

Jeremy nodded. 'If we ever get out of here,' he chuckled softly. 'Suppose the House is playing with time, now, too?'

Lyssa shrugged. 'Probably. That or we've been missing for days.'

'It's kind of what it feels like,' he agreed. 'I don't remember the Game ever taking more than half a day when we were kids. Maybe the House thinks we have more stamina these days.'

'With a little girl in tow? I don't think so, but I don't know anything for sure anymore. The House knows about her and brought me to her,' Lyssa said in a voice that sounded uncomfortably whiny in her ears. 'Sorry,' she shuddered. 'I guess I'm tired, too!'

Jeremy laughed softly, trying not to awaken Molly. 'Well, that makes three of us, but what can we do?'

'Lie down on a couch and take a nap?' Lyssa suggested, half-joking.

Then they saw it.

Out of the corner of their eyes, something was different and they both swung toward it at once.

'Wow!' said Jeremy with a low whistle.

Lyssa stood with her mouth open.

It was a jungle. Vast and green and seemingly endless. 'I guess the gardener hasn't been here in a while.' The far wall of the room they faced had a much larger door opening than the other rooms and the growth had taken over, vines clinging to the walls and growing out into the room, spreading toward the corners, making it seem as if the wall was missing entirely. The good news was there were fruit trees.

'I guess we dine before we nap,' said Jeremy. 'Shall I bring you something while you put Molly on a couch? If she wakes up, she can eat, too. If not, we'll save her something for when she does.'

Lyssa laughed. 'If there's anything left!' She moved to the couch closest to the lush green tangle and settled the sleeping child against the pillows.

Jeremy set her doll beside her and smiled down at the pretty picture they made together. 'Someday,' he whispered.

Lyssa wondered what he meant but couldn't bring herself to ask.

'Do you have your knife?' Jeremy asked.

Lyssa handed it over.

The fruit was delicious, abundant and perfectly ripe. Of course, Lyssa thought to herself as she bit into the mango Jeremy had just finished peeling. Juice dripped down her chin and she moaned in exaggerated pleasure. 'What do you suppose mangoes are doing in the House?' she asked through her mouthful.

Jeremy grinned wickedly. 'More of the Others,' he said before biting into a slice of mango. 'They all got turned into plants and brought to this room.'

'So all of you are from tropical climates?' asked Lyssa with feigned innocence. 'And now we're eating the off-spring?'

'Oh!' Jeremy laughed. 'What a revolting thought!'

'You started it,' Lyssa accused, but she laughed also. It felt good to be able to joke about something they couldn't really even talk about. 'So,' she said, changing the subject. 'Do we go in?' She nodded at the jungle.

Jeremy stared at the tangle of vines and leaves for a long time while he finished his mango and peeled another. At last he shook his head. 'Not this time, I think. There's too much in there and we're already pretty tired. I think we need to find our way out of here and see about finding Molly a place to stay. We need to come back here by ourselves when we have the time and resources to explore this place properly.'

Lyssa nodded. She picked another mango and held her hand out for the knife. 'How big do you think it is?'

Jeremy studied it again for a time. 'I don't think it really exists in the House. I think this is one of those strange portals the builders are so fond of. If the Others can come from different places than the here and now, why can't this jungle exist outside the here and now? I'm not even sure if we go in there, we'll ever come out again.'

'I think we will,' said Lyssa positively. 'This House has plans for us. It won't let us get completely lost. Not so that we never come back, anyway. It just wants us in the dark for a while longer.'

'What for?' asked Jeremy .

He had a bemused look on his face, but Lyssa decided the question was rhetorical. She finished peeling her second mango. 'What other fruits are there?' she asked.

They ate while Molly slept, then prepared an assortment of the delicious fruits for her in case she awoke before they did, and lay down on other couches nearby so she would see them and not worry. They were asleep almost instantly, but neither of them slept well.

The dream was shared, and both were aware of the other in the same nightmarish situation. They were in the jungle and they were lost. The machetes they had brought with them to help get through the fantastic growth had quickly dulled, and were shortly useless. They had not thought to bring along anything to sharpen the blades, and the knives seemed to be getting unreasonably heavy. They agreed to abandon them, but then found they couldn't let go of the handles. They continued to drag the increasingly cumbersome burdens as they struggled through the dense greenery.

The humidity was increasing. They could scarcely breathe and their sense of urgency was growing by the moment. Adrenaline surged in their veins and they knew it was the House hurrying them, but even Lyssa couldn't stand against it this time. They had to move single file, but it was so difficult they could scarcely make any headway.

They stumbled into a clearing so abruptly they fell sprawling on the dirt. Lyssa had the wind knocked out of her as Jeremy landed on top of her. To her surprise, her breath blew the dirt away, exposing floorboards. The illusion had been so complete she had forgotten they were inside, and not lost somewhere near the equator in an exotic rainforest.

Then she saw the feet.

There were two pairs. One pair abnormally large, one pair unusually small. She gasped and tried to sit up, but Jeremy was still unmoving on top of her. 'Get off!' she hissed, trying to be discreet.

'I can't move,' he whispered back.

'Why not?' Lyssa was angry now.

'There's a knife at my throat.'

Lyssa couldn't argue with that. Her heart was pounding. She wondered if they were going to die.

'Both of you, get to your feet slowly,' said a rusty, rather high-pitched voice. 'No quick moves or I will have to cut you.' This elicited a reedy giggle; not the same voice.

Lyssa felt Jeremy's weight lift and she rolled over to free her hands and make them clearly visible. Somehow, she had managed to let go of the machete in the fall and it was nowhere to be seen. She got to her feet and looked at their captors.

The large feet belonged to a strange man with equally large hands and a huge, pale, bald head with tiny, delicate features. He wore a dark robe and a strange jeweled ring on his right ring finger. Beside him stood a tiny, red-haired boy with a troll-like face. He wore nothing at all.

'Who are you?' Lyssa quavered at the old man. He held a knife with a wickedly curved blade. A glance at Jeremy told her he, too, was unarmed. The machetes had been too dull to do any real damage but she'd have felt better if she were holding something.

'I'm the Keeper. This is my companion. You will come to me soon. We will talk then. Now, you must go. It isn't safe to be here even in dreams.' His voice cracked from disuse.

'You aren't going to kill us?' asked Jeremy in surprise.

The old man laughed bitterly. 'The spider will kill you.'

He disappeared then, and his companion with him, but their laughter rang in the air for a long time after they had gone.

Chapter Three

'Their magic is different from yours. They control only
a tiny portion of the whole and that is related to building and transportation. They provide you with the
means to weave your spells and you provide them with
the energy they need to build.'

The Symbiosis of Builder and Family, Prologue

Marnie said yes, and Molly had a new home.

For a while, at least, Lyssa kept telling herself. What she
hated most was that Marnie was really nice. She and Molly
took to each other immediately, and Lyssa would have
liked to hate her for that, but she couldn't. To top it off,
Marnie was everything Lyssa felt she wasn't. Marnie was
tall and slender and beautiful, with black hair the same
depth and texture as Molly's. She was obviously very intel-
ligent and had a good sense of humor, laughing delightedly
at the silly things Molly said because the little girl wanted
to hear the slithery, infectious music.

She was nice. Really sweet and it made Lyssa want to
throw up, but she found herself drawn to Marnie just like
Molly. She wanted to do and say things to please this
incredible woman and she wanted to be disgusted by that
impulse, but she couldn't. She finally left the house with
Jeremy, feeling like a complete traitor to herself.

'Molly will be really happy there,' she found herself saying as they left the neighborhood. 'Thank you for asking
Marnie to take her in. I feel a lot better knowing she's in
a safe place.'

Jeremy nodded.

'Marnie's really sweet,' Lyssa continued, unable to stop

herself. 'You must like her a lot.' She glanced sideways at him, trying to gauge his reaction surreptitiously.

Jeremy smiled and nodded again.

'Have you known her a long time?' Lyssa pressed, hating herself for asking, but wanting desperately to know the answer.

Jeremy shrugged but remained silent.

They walked into the village square and Lyssa looked up at the church. She had never been inside and, for the first time, she found herself wondering what the interior was like. 'Have you ever been in there?' she asked, nodding at the ancient structure.

Jeremy shook his head.

'Where did you two meet?' Lyssa asked, breaking the silence yet again.

'School,' Jeremy said finally. 'Her family moved here just after you left. That same summer. She was incredibly shy and awkward, and she didn't know anyone. The other kids made fun of her accent and she just didn't fit in. I felt kind of sorry for her.'

'I can't imagine Marnie not fitting in,' said Lyssa a little more waspishly than she intended.

Jeremy looked down at her with raised eyebrows. 'What did that strange little man mean by the spider?'

Lyssa had expected he would change the subject. She wasn't prepared for this. 'I don't know,' she said slowly. 'But I got the strangest image of a web when he said that.'

'Me too,' said Jeremy thoughtfully. 'Beautifully woven and ornate but with rents in it, as if it had been made a long time ago and was no longer being repaired.'

'As if parts were missing as well. Like it wasn't up to date.' She frowned. 'I didn't say that very well, but I don't know how else to express it. Does it make any sense to you?'

'Yeah,' said Jeremy excitedly. 'I got the same feeling.'

'You know, I've seen the Keeper before,' said Lyssa

suddenly. 'I used to have nightmares when I was a girl, after I moved.'

After she moved. She had never understood the need for that. None of the other relatives had wanted her, so she'd been sent to boarding school. Effectively an orphan, even her summers were spent on school grounds, attending classes. No one cared if she got good grades or not. No one cared what she was going to do with any degree she obtained, so Lyssa studied to please herself.

She'd had a lot of friends but none of them close and enjoyed a number of her teachers, but had never formed bonds with any of them, so there was nothing to tie her to the school when at last it was time to leave. She went on to college and found a job that meant nothing more to her than the rest of her life had, but she was on her own, no longer beholden to a family that didn't want her, and that, at least, made her happy.

Then the call had come from her aunt, asking her to come home.

'There were only two dreams I remembered,' she mused. 'Recurring nightmares. I always thought that only one of them took place entirely in the House, but after seeing the jungle, I know both of them did. I've seen the Keeper and his companion every time I've dreamed about the jungle, and I was always afraid of them. Every time they appeared, I got a really frightened feeling and ran away and wound up in the House. I always made it back to the here and now, but when I got out of the House and onto the street, everyone was gone. Not just people: insects, birds, animals. The only things that remained were houses, trees, cars and bikes. That kind of thing. It was as if I was all alone in the world and nothing living existed anymore. I would run up and down the streets of the village, but there wouldn't be anyone there. Just as I was about to panic, I would wake up in a sweat and be unable to sleep for the rest of the night. I was certain the weird man and his little troll knew something about it, but I was too afraid to go back in and ask. I always had trouble sleeping for days after I had that dream.'

'How did the dream start?' Jeremy asked intently.

There was something in his tone that made Lyssa relax about saying these things aloud. He wasn't making fun. He was concentrating on her words as if they struck home vividly for him. 'Always the same way,' she said. 'I would be somewhere in the House. This dream started in the basement. I would be playing hide and seek with a bunch of kids, and I would open a door to hide behind: only once it was closed, I couldn't open it again, so I would have to go forward. I would find myself in the jungle, hopelessly lost and wandering for hours, badly frightened and wondering if I would ever get back to my family and friends. Then I would run into the old man and the little boy.'

Jeremy was nodding. 'I used to have the same dream. Did the other one start in the attic? Same thing? Playing hide and seek? You go through a door and once it's shut you can't get back?'

Lyssa nodded. 'Only with that one, there would be a stairway up, but most of the stairs were missing, and the ones that remained were in such bad shape I was certain they'd break under my weight and I'd fall through into the black nothingness I could see through the rotting boards. I always made it up, though, to the hallway above.'

'And there were endless doors and you had to try every knob –'

'My god,' said Lyssa. 'We were playing the Game even in our dreams!'

'Not just any game, though. Not just a tour of the House. These were two very specific scenarios,' said Jeremy with a frown. 'But there was no spider involved. Just a really huge bald eagle.'

'And an organ with bloody keys that played eerie music all by itself,' said Lyssa. 'What is going on?'

'I have no idea,' said Jeremy. 'But someone, or something

has been playing a sick joke with my life almost since it started, and I don't think you're any less manipulated by what's been happening than I am.'

'But I'm not Other!' Lyssa protested. 'I'm Family!'

'And Finder,' Jeremy reminded her. 'Maybe that makes you different.'

'How do we find out?' she demanded.

'Will you let me see the Room?' he asked.

Lyssa stopped. She didn't have an answer ready. She couldn't see the harm in it, but she wasn't sure if it was a good idea either. 'Let me think about it,' she said finally.

'What is there to think about?' Jeremy exploded. He turned on her and stood shaking, clenching and un-clenching his fists, visibly trying to restrain himself. 'You don't think you can trust me?' His eyes bore into hers. He made an oddly strangled noise and stared down at her as if he didn't see her.

Lyssa was afraid even to move. She didn't know what he might do if she stirred. No, she didn't trust him. She loved him, but she was afraid of him. He was too unpre-dictable in his rages and too quick to use violence as a means of problem-solving. Now she was certain she shouldn't show him the Room. Not until she knew what the books were for. Not until she found out what the bolts of cloth were. There were still too many unanswered questions and until she knew if Jeremy could help her find the answers, the risks were too great. She glanced up at him and was shocked to find tears slipping silently down his cheeks.

'I'm sorry,' he whispered. He reached out his hand to her.

She flinched and Jeremy looked even more pained. Lyssa turned and ran all the way back to the House, never once looking to see if he pursued.

She arrived gasping and out of breath. The stitch in her side burned against the heaving of her chest and she stood in the foyer for a long moment trying to regroup.

'Your aunt would like to see you, Miss,' said Millie from the living room doorway.

Lyssa jumped and turned, wincing as the pain deepened with her movement. 'What?' she asked blankly, staring at Millie as if she was speaking a foreign language.

'When you have a moment,' said Millie slowly.

'Oh,' said Lyssa, gathering her wits. 'Yes. Thank you. I'll go to her directly. Thank you.'

Millie continued standing in the doorway.

'Was there anything else?' Lyssa asked gently, trying to straighten up. She pressed the heel of her hand into her side to ease the cramp.

Millie opened her mouth. Then she shut it and shook her head. 'When you have a moment,' she repeated. She disappeared into the interior of the House, leaving Lyssa staring open-mouthed after her.

'What was that all about?' Lyssa wondered aloud. There were so many questions and so few answers. She shook her head and realized her thick, chestnut braid had come undone. She was sweaty and disheveled. She couldn't go to see her aunt like this so she went to her room to clean up and change. There would be more questions from Aunt Burchie, and Lyssa wanted to have her thoughts in order before facing the old lady. She didn't want to be rattled into giving Molly away. Or anything else for that matter.

'My dear,' said Aunt Burchie in her grand, husky voice. 'You look beautiful. Come in and let me look at you. You have your father's beauty and your mother's high color. Sit down.' She nodded at the chair beside the bed.

Lyssa entered the room rather shyly and sat. Why did older Family members always feel obliged to lie about her appearance, she wondered. All of them had done it when they visited the House during her childhood here. She had known they were lying by the look in their eyes. They were mouthing pleasantries they certainly didn't mean. Aunt Burchie had that look about her now. She was searching

68

Lyssa's face, but it wasn't in admiration. She was looking for information. Lyssa braced herself and hoped that whatever magic she had accidentally tapped into would protect her from the magic Aunt Burchie wielded with the ease of long practice.

'How have you been?' Lyssa asked, leaning forward to kiss the soft, withered cheek her aunt proffered. She took Aunt Burchie's hand and gave it a gentle squeeze. 'I meant to bring you something from town, but I –'

Aunt Burchie waved off her explanation. 'I don't need anything, dearie. I've told you that. It's sweet of you to think of me but it's really unnecessary. Millie tends to me quite well, you know.'

Lyssa smiled. 'I know. But sometimes a surprise is nice.'

Aunt Burchie chuckled. 'Sometimes,' she agreed. 'And sometimes a surprise isn't nice at all, don't you think?'

Lyssa gave the old woman a penetrating look, but she couldn't be certain she saw anything, so she shrugged noncommittally and sat down. 'Millie said you wanted to see me? I hope everything is alright?'

'Fine, dear. Just fine,' said Aunt Burchie a little too easily. 'You played the Game again recently?'

It was really more of a statement than a question, and Lyssa knew what was expected of her. For the next two hours, she gave as accurate an account as possible without giving any indication of her finding Molly, or meeting the Others.

'Jeremy was there, of course. The Game was much longer than it had ever been before. We finally had to take a nap after we found a strange jungle. We had the strangest dreams,' she finished. 'We really couldn't make heads or tails of them.'

'They weren't related in any way?' asked Aunt Burchie with just a hint of suspicion in her voice.

Lyssa knew she wouldn't have noticed it if she hadn't had the assistance of the old magic. 'I was in his dream, he was in mine, if that's what you mean,' she said, trying not to sound wary. 'Other than that, no, they were completely different.'

'What were they about?' asked Aunt Burchie.

There was a gleam in her eye that made Lyssa uneasy. 'Mostly jumbled images,' she replied. 'We really didn't talk about them much.'

Aunt Burchie chuckled again in her most indulgent manner. 'I find that hard to believe,' she said, smiling disarmingly.

'Well,' Lyssa admitted. 'We talked about them a little. We found the jungle in the maze of living rooms. The dreams involved being lost in it. We were frightened and finally managed to find our way out. That was it, though. It was quite a relief to wake up and find ourselves in the room just outside.'

Aunt Burchie nodded, looking satisfied with the telling. Again, Lyssa wasn't sure why, but she knew she shouldn't tell her aunt about the strange pair they had confronted in the dream they had shared. She was also relieved that the magic seemed to protect her thoughts from the old . . .

She had been about to say 'spider'.

Why? Aunt Burchie was an invalid, bedridden and helpless. She never left her room and had to be cared for by a servant.

Lyssa shuddered. There was something even more wrong here than she had suspected. Now she knew why she couldn't tell Aunt Burchie about the pair in the jungle. Aunt Burchie knew about them. She knew all about them. And they knew about her. And Lyssa was between them, knowing not much more than when she had first arrived. And the only help she had was a young man torn by rage and helplessness.

Cold fear prickled her neck and spine. She had promised to find a way home for Molly, but Lyssa was beginning to wonder if she could get herself out of here alive. She sat back in the chair and looked at her elderly aunt, as if she was seeing her for the first time. Really seeing her, not just looking at her outer appearance. What she saw made her shiver, and unfortunately Aunt Burchie noticed.

'Are you alright, dearie?' she asked Lyssa solicitously. Her eyes narrowed and she looked at Lyssa much the same as Lyssa was looking at her.

Lyssa gulped and nodded. 'I guess I'm still pretty tired from playing the Game. I told you it seemed to go on for days. I'm still not certain it didn't. What I really need is a long sleep.'

Aunt Burchie smiled sympathetically. 'Sleep as long as you like. There's no schedule around here, you know.'

Lyssa smiled back weakly, hoping her fear didn't show through. 'That sounds like a good idea,' she said, getting to her feet. 'Do you have any idea how long I was gone?'

'A couple of days,' said Aunt Burchie. 'If what Millie says about the last time she saw you is to be believed.' She made a funny sound in the back of her throat. 'Sometimes I wonder about that woman. She may be younger than I, my dear, but her mind seems to be wandering a little these days.'

Lyssa shook her head. 'She seems okay to me,' she said. 'But I don't spend much time talking to her. Or at least she doesn't talk much to me.' She bent to give her aunt another kiss. 'I'll be back in a while. Maybe we can talk a little about the estate questions you had.'

'No rush, dearie. We'll get it covered before I go, I promise.'

Lyssa grinned. 'I just bet we will.'

Millie was nowhere in sight when Lyssa went to the dining room, so she got a plate and began to fill it. It was strange knowing this food would be going to the Others when the Family was done with it. She had never thought anything about it as a child, and never wondered how the Others fed and clothed themselves. They seemed to lead a wonderfully clandestine life to the eyes of a child, and one younger than eight certainly wouldn't question how things worked.

She had played the Game. She had been telling her aunt, and the Others, all about the things she found in her travels about the House. Everyone had pumped her for information, and she had been blissfully ignorant. She had told everybody everything and never once wondered why they wanted to know.

And Jeremy had done the same.

Lyssa ate mechanically. She gulped mouthfuls without tasting them. She didn't know if she stopped because her plate was empty or her stomach was full. She left the table on automatic pilot and found herself in the shower sometime later with no idea how long she had been there. Her fingers and toes were pruned and her skin was red from the heat of the water, but she had been unable to scrub herself clean enough.

She was Family. What did that mean? Who were these people she was related to? Lyssa realized she had no idea how many Family members there were, where they were living and how. She only knew they came back here periodically. Even her father. She wondered who would come back next, and what she might be able to find out. Someone had to have the answers to her questions, especially about the Room.

Had they all been looking for it? Lyssa shut off the water and pushed open the shower door.

Jeremy handed her a towel and she jumped so violently that she slipped and almost fell. 'What are you doing in here?' she gasped. 'How did you get in?'

He smiled enigmatically. 'There are ways. I'm sorry about earlier, on the way home.'

'Yeah, well,' said Lyssa rather ungraciously, trying to cover herself.

'I'm sorry,' he repeated. 'But you have to understand, the Others have always said the Room would provide the way back to our own lives. My father might still be alive. I might have a family who still think of me, still wonder what became of my mother and me. Whether or not it's true, I have to find out. Now that the Room has been found, we all want to know. We all want our lives back. When you said you'd have to think about it, I thought for a moment that our chances were slipping away.' He looked at her. 'You have to let me see for myself'

'Jeremy, you shouldn't be here,' said Lyssa urgently, trying unsuccessfully to hide in the towel. 'If Aunt Burchie finds you –'

Jeremy laughed. 'The old lady and I go way back! She's nothing to worry about.'

Lyssa shook her head violently. 'You're wrong. I think she may be the spider the old man warned us about.'

'That's a nice thing to say about the woman who took you in and raised you,' he said, looking at her strangely.

'No, I mean it!' Lyssa insisted vehemently. She pushed past him out of the shower and grabbed her clothing. 'You have to leave now.'

'You have to answer my question first,' Jeremy said, catching her by the arm.

'What question?' Lyssa tried to stall. She tried to pull away, but he held her firmly.

'Will you let me into the Room?'

Lyssa yanked suddenly and freed herself. 'No!' she shouted. The surge of fear turned into self-righteous anger, lending her strength. She planted her hands on his chest and shoved him so hard he staggered. While he was off balance, she pushed him across the room and out of the door before he could recover. She slammed the door shut, and locked it, hoping it would be enough to keep him out. She dressed as quickly as possible, expecting a reaction. It was rather a letdown to find after long moments that he wasn't pounding on the door and demanding she take him to the Room.

Gradually, her breathing returned to normal, but she was too keyed up to sleep. She didn't dare go to the Room herself, so she sat on the bed and tried to meditate. Mental calm was impossible, what in hell was she going to do?

73

After pacing the floor for a couple of hours, Lyssa fell into bed exhausted and finally slept, but her dreams were restless fragments of the two recurring nightmares that had punctuated her childhood. She would just resign herself to one when the scene would shift and she'd find herself in the other. There were other odd images that blurred in and out of focus, which she couldn't decipher but it made her wonder; that portion of her that remained detached from the beating her psyche was taking. And throughout her agitated sleep, she couldn't help but feel there was an answer right under her nose, if only she could see it.

Dinner, that evening, was solitary except for Millie, who stood in the corner and watched Lyssa sitting alone at the large table with her plate and glass, watching Millie.

'You were going to tell me something this afternoon,' she said, almost more of a question than a statement.

Millie shook her head. 'No, Miss. Only the message I gave you.'

Lyssa thought she looked uncomfortable. 'You're sure?' she pressed.

Millie flinched and glanced about the room without moving her head. 'Yes, Miss.'

'Well, then,' said Lyssa. She returned her attention to her meal, but she had no appetite after a poor afternoon's sleep. She pushed the food around for a little while before looking up again. 'When's the last time a Family member came back for a visit?' she asked. 'I seem to remember there being more people here when I was younger.'

Millie looked relieved at the change of subject. 'That would be several years ago, now,' she said. Her gaze turned inward as she tried to remember. 'Seven or eight, I think. It was one of the uncles. I can never keep them straight. There are so many and they all look pretty much alike. They are very polite and keep to themselves and always end up fighting with Herself and leaving in a huff.'

'How many uncles are there?' asked Lyssa curiously. She

had seen mostly aunts when she was a child living here. Everyone seemed married, but no one was really attached. They all travelled separately and avoided talking to one another.

'Oh, I was never quite sure!' laughed Millie.

Lyssa was startled. She didn't think she'd ever heard Millie laugh before.

'As I said, they all look sort of alike. Let's see, there's Milton, Frederic, Hanson, James – goodness, I can't even remember all their names. I feed them and clean their rooms. I am polite and deferential. I see them come and go, but I can never figure out who's who, so I just call them Sir, and think of them as the uncles. When Herself talks about one or the other, I just lump them together in my mind, oh, he's one of the Uncles, I think to myself, and that's enough to identify them.'

Lyssa chuckled. 'That's how I always felt about the Aunts. All of them except Aunt Burchie, because I lived with her. But why did only Aunts visit when I was a little girl? Why did the uncles come only after I'd gone?'

Millie looked puzzled for a brief moment. 'I've given up wondering about what goes on around here,' she said. 'I do as I'm told and earn a decent living for me and my Bertie and no harm.'

'So curious things do happen?' asked Lyssa pointedly.

Millie came back to herself in an instant. 'Are you through with your supper, Miss?'

Lyssa sighed. 'I guess so.' She pushed her plate away, and her chair back from the table. She stood and faced Millie. 'We'll talk again.'

Millie made a strange gesture and shook her head. 'I'd best be getting on with my chores,' she said. 'Have a pleasant evening, Miss.'

'Thank you, Millie,' said Lyssa equally formally. 'You do the same.'

When she got back to her room, Lyssa flung herself down on her bed and buried her face in her pillow. She still had more questions than she had gone to dinner with.

When was the next relative due to visit, and who was it going to be? Lyssa knew she would have to ask Aunt Burchie to find out. She had to find a way to work it into conversation so her aunt wouldn't suspect why she wanted to know.

In the meantime, she went to the wardrobe and opened the door. She stepped through and opened the door at the back. She stepped through again and was safe at last in the Room.

Maybe if she stared at the books long enough – Lyssa knew it was silly, but she went to the trunk and opened it. She took out the top volume and held it in her hand for a long time before turning to the first page. 'Once upon a time, a long time ago, in a kingdom far away, there lived a beautiful princess who was very unhappy,' she said aloud. She laughed. The page was indecipherable, but the image of fairy tales was strong in her mind and she thought of the stories she had read when she was little. Stories with happy endings that made her feel like there was good in the world if she could just find it.

Why had she felt that good was such an elusive thing? A thing to be found only in tales that weren't true? With a sigh, she returned her attention to the slim volume in her hand, focusing on the open page, and the incomprehensible script. She had promised Molly a way home and it was a promise she intended to keep.

She shut the book cover with a snap and left the trunk lid standing open. She moved around to the bed and sat down, sinking into the feather ticking. She made a brief check of the various entrances to be sure she was safe, before snuggling down into the pillows and pulling the quilts over herself. Still clutching the book, she fell into a deep and dreamless sleep.

When Lyssa awoke in the morning she was disoriented. It had been a long time since she'd slept so soundly that she couldn't remember where she was when she woke up. She lay for a while staring at the ceiling before she recognized the trap-door and remembered the previous evening. She was still holding the book. She stared at it for a moment before turning to the first page.

It was a reading primer. She still couldn't understand the alphabet or language, but something told her this was the first key to understanding. She had to find the minister.

Where in hell had that come from?

Lyssa sat up and put the book on the bed in front of her. She rubbed her eyes, trying to get all the grit out. Finally, she stared at the book again. The minister?

She guessed it made as much sense as anything else around here. She got out of bed and spread it up quickly. She shut the trunk, tucked the book into her blouse and went back through the wardrobe into her room in Aunt Burchie's House. After breakfast, she would go to the church.

Millie stood by the buffet as usual. Lyssa wondered why the woman stood there while she ate. There were a great many rooms in the House that always needed cleaning. Aunt Burchie was very fond of dust-catchers. Every room was filled with knick-knacks. Surely she had better things to do than watch one woman eat. But no, Millie always stood throughout the meal and cleared Lyssa's dishes when she was through.

Despite growing up with servants, her life since leaving the House had not included them and she now found it uncomfortable having an old woman doing what Lyssa was clearly able-bodied enough to do for herself. Besides, she hated being scrutinized while she ate.

'Do you and Bertie live in the village?' she asked, trying to alleviate her own tension.

Millie shook her head. 'We have rooms here,' she said. 'That way I can look after Herself and still keep an eye on him.'

'He needs keeping an eye on?'

'He's not been well these past few years,' said Millie. 'He's been confined to a wheelchair for almost forty years now, and I think the winters are getting to be a little much for him.'

'Can't you take him someplace warmer?'

Millie shook her head, her lips pressed tightly together.

'Not even for the winter?' Lyssa pressed.

'He won't leave the village,' said Millie with genuine regret.

Or can't, Lyssa thought darkly. So Millie had married an Other? How had he managed to escape the usual two-year turnover? Maybe marrying Millie gave him some sort of immunity. She hurried through the rest of her breakfast in silence and started down the hill to the village and the church.

Jeremy caught up with her about halfway down. 'Going to see Molly?' he asked casually as he fell in step with her.

'I thought I might,' said Lyssa easily. 'I have some errands to run first. Aunt Burchie asked me to pick up a few things for her.'

'Liar!' he laughed. 'She hasn't needed anything from the village in years. Millie does all the shopping, and anything special is delivered.'

'How would you know?' Lyssa demanded, feeling shaken by the truth and his knowledge of it.

'Because I've been offering for years to bring her back stuff from the village, and she always says no. I told you, your aunt and I go way back.' He smiled smugly. 'So, what are you doing besides going to see Molly?'

'None of your business,' she snapped, trying to lengthen her stride.

He matched her easily. 'Everything you do is my business,' he said. 'Until we find out what's going on in that place, everything that happens is something I have a vested interest in, and I expect you to tell me or I'll just have to find out.'

Lyssa stopped. 'Are you threatening me?' she demanded.

She planted her fists on her hips and glared at him. 'Is that the only way you can think of to get what you want? You can be as unpleasant as you want, but do it by yourself. You won't find out anything from me that I don't want you to know. There may be magic governing the House, but I've found some that I can bend to my use, and I notice you don't have any, so I suggest you think about who you threaten, and that you leave me alone!' She resumed walking down the hill, and wasn't surprised when Jeremy fell back in step with her. 'You catch more flies with honey than you do with vinegar,' she said, wondering, as she said it, where that had come from. 'You could try saying please once in a while, you remember to with Marnie. Why do you think bullying is the way to approach me?'

'You're right,' said Jeremy. 'I'm sorry. I keep forgetting we aren't kids anymore. Guilt and threats were the only things that worked when we were little.'

'Only because you were bigger and I didn't know any better,' said Lyssa bitterly. 'I didn't have any other friends. I didn't think I could afford to lose the only one I had.' She gave a short, derisive laugh. 'What a little idiot I was to think that! And you did everything in your power to foster it.'

Jeremy nodded, looking ashamed. 'How many times do I have to apologize before you believe I mean it?'

'How many times are you going to demonstrate that your apologies mean nothing and you won't hesitate to try intimidation and threats before anything else in every new situation we encounter?' she snapped. 'You can talk all you want about changing, but until you do, no, I don't trust you. And until I trust you, I won't show you the Room, and I won't share my discoveries with you. You can tell that to the Others. You can tell them you keep blowing their chances.'

'So you won't tell me what errands you have to run?' he persisted.

'Don't you listen?' she shouted. 'Or are you just stupid?'

'I'll just follow you,' he said.

'Then I won't be finding out anything very soon, because I won't go where I need to as long as you're lurking in the bushes,' said Lyssa. 'Shall we go see how Molly is doing? Shall I tell her you're keeping me from finding a way to take her back to her parents?'

Jeremy ground his teeth. 'I'll see you there,' he said, lengthening his stride. He walked away quickly and was soon out of sight.

Lyssa tapped into the old magic and scanned the area to find out where he had gone, but she could find no trace of him. She kept her vigilance with the old magic and set out again for the church.

The sanctuary was deserted when Lyssa entered. She stood in the inner doorway, not sure if she should go any further, or wait to see if anyone came.

Lyssa knew very little about the church beyond the gossip that the building was almost a thousand years old. Built of stone without mortar, it certainly had an ancient look about it, but no one could actually credit the story. They couldn't discredit it either, so she had always figured there was no harm in believing.

Glass had been installed in the windows at a much later date: but it was plain. There were no colorful scenes of people dying, or praying, just clear panes set in lead. There was something more dignified in that, she thought, looking around. The obligatory cross, with or without victim, was also missing. The pulpit was plain, uncarved, and unvarnished. The wood had been rubbed by hand to a warm glow, darkened by oil and sweat from the people who had tended it over the years. It stood alone, flanked by two closed doors, in front of the pews which were also hand-rubbed wood. There were tapestries on the white walls and long runners down the aisles, to protect the wooden floor from foot traffic, which showed much wear, but were still beautiful. There were three chandeliers, one above the pulpit and two above the pews, which held candles and could be raised and lowered by great chains for the candles to be lit. Everything about the room bespoke great age and much loving care. Lyssa was surprised by how comfortable it all was.

She had only been in a few churches in her life, not having been raised in a particularly religious family. She had seen to her own religious education as a teenager by attending various places of worship with friends willing to indulge her interest. She had come away with the feeling that organized religion had nothing to offer her, but she thought she could be comfortable in this place. She wondered what they preached. Not that she was particularly interested in joining a church. She was just curious.

'Curious enough to come in?' asked a voice nearby.

Lyssa jumped and turned toward the sound.

'I didn't mean to startle you,' said the very pleasant-looking man. 'You look as if you'd seen a ghost.'

'Did you just read my mind?' she stammered.

The man laughed. 'No! The look on your face. Your body language.' He gestured.

Lyssa was leaning forward into the sanctuary, but her feet remained planted on the outside threshold. She had rocked forward against her toes to maintain her balance. She could only guess at her expression. She smiled and stepped forward. 'Are you the minister?'

'I am called the Speaker, but that would be an equivalent title, yes,' said the man. He stood about six feet tall and had a comfortable paunch. Clean-shaven and mostly bald, he looked very pink and healthy, very kind and open. 'Did you want to talk to me?'

'I had a question, but I don't know if you can answer it,' Lyssa said, holding out the book. 'I found this, but I can't make heads or tails of it. It's not any language I recognize, and it looks pretty old. I remembered the stories about this place, and thought they might have a connection.'

The Speaker took the volume and opened it. His eyebrows shot up as he thumbed the pages, but he said nothing.

'I realize it's pretty silly,' she suddenly felt compelled to go on. 'I've learned a lot of different languages in my studies, and seen just about every script ever used, but I've never seen this one and I want to find out more about it.'

'Where are you from?' the Speaker asked finally.

'Well, here,' she began, wondering what that had to do with anything.

'No!' he interrupted. 'I mean where did you find this? It's not the kind of thing that turns up in libraries or used-book stores. This isn't even the sort of thing that comes out of attics during spring cleaning.' He looked Lyssa directly in the eyes. 'Where did this come from?'

'I live in the House at the top of the hill,' she whispered. Never had that seemed like a more important admission, and never had she been more reluctant to tell. 'I found it in a trunk in one of the rooms in the oldest part of the House.'

'Come with me,' the Speaker said excitedly. He turned and walked quickly away. She'd have called it a run if both his feet left the ground at once. She had to run to keep up.

'Where are we going?' she called after him.

They left the sanctuary by the door to the left of the pulpit and plunged down a dark flight of stairs. 'This isn't a game, is it?' Lyssa asked, only half-joking. 'I didn't bring my leather pouch.'

'No,' said the Speaker, turning back at the foot of the stairs. 'No game.' He rummaged in the dark and switched on a flashlight. 'I do wish they'd put electricity into this place, but Miss Burch won't allow it.' He turned, gesturing with the beam, and continued down a short hallway.

'Aunt Burchie?' Lyssa was confused. 'What would she have to say about it?'

'The church belongs to your family,' he said, opening a door and stepping inside. He stood aside so she could enter, then let the door swing shut. He went to the desk and lit the lamp that stood on it before dousing the flashlight. He put the book on the desktop. 'Sit down,' he gestured at a straight-backed chair beside the desk.

'The church belongs to my family,' she repeated blankly. 'We've never set foot in the place.'

'True,' the Speaker confirmed. 'But it's yours nevertheless.'

'Is this a particularly religious community?' Lyssa asked, still feeling strange inside. 'What's your name?'

'My name is David Baker and, yes, this is a particularly religious community. Nearly everyone attends this church, and most of them come every week.'

'But you aren't a minister,' she said, almost accusingly. 'You called yourself the Speaker. There are no crosses, or stained glass. I didn't see any prayer books or hymnals in the pews.'

Mr Baker laughed. 'There are many different ways to worship.'

'True,' Lyssa granted. 'But how many churches are privately owned by people who don't attend them?'

The Speaker shrugged. 'Is that important?'

Lyssa sighed. 'I have no idea. Is there anything you can tell me about the book?'

David Baker smiled, nodded and pulled an ancient-looking scroll out of a drawer in his desk. 'I just came across this the other day while cleaning out a storeroom down here. Some boxes were covering a hole in the wall. I thought mice were nesting and I'd better do something about the infestation. I was wrong. I don't know if this helps you at all, but you're welcome to it as long as you promise to tell me if you find anything out. I'm really very curious about how this church came to be here, and why the village grew around it. Usually these things work in reverse.'

Lyssa nodded. 'Have you been able to discover anything yourself?'

The Speaker shook his head. 'It makes no more sense to

me than the book does, but I thought you should see it, especially since you told me who you are.' He looked at her for a moment. 'Actually, you never did tell me who you are.'

'Lyssa Anders,' she said, formally extending her hand.

They shook and she stood up, taking the scroll and book. 'I guess I have some studying to do,' she said. 'Thank you for your help. I'll certainly let you know if I find anything.'

They were on the front lawn playing keep away. Jeremy was in the middle. Marnie and Molly were tossing the ball over his head to each other. Marnie and Molly were laughing so hard they could barely throw the ball, let alone catch it. Jeremy was making a big noise about not being able to intercept it, even though all he really had to do was reach up and pluck it from the air above his head. It was obvious to Lyssa that Molly was in the best possible place aside from her own parents' home.

Lyssa approached the house slowly, feeling very grateful to Marnie, very happy for Molly and very left out. She didn't want to bring an end to the game, but knew her presence would do that automatically. She couldn't join in the game with the same light heart it was being played with; not and still be able to defend herself from Jeremy.

Not that she really thought he would try anything with both Marnie and Molly present, but she didn't feel she could let her guard down.

'Lyssa!' Molly caught sight of her and immediately abandoned the game. She dropped the ball and ran down the grassy slope toward the sidewalk, her arms outstretched.

The look on her face made Lyssa's heart melt all over again. She opened her arms to catch the tiny juggernaut and swung her around in circles, hugging her close. 'I've missed you,' she whispered. She stopped spinning and gave the little girl as many kisses as Molly would keep still for.

'I missed you too,' Molly announced, squirming to be put down. 'Look!' She stepped back and twirled around.

The skirt of her blue cotton dress spun out beautifully, showing yards of white lace petticoats underneath.

'Wow,' said Lyssa appreciatively. 'I always wanted a dress like that. And it's got smocking and puffed sleeves. You're really lucky. Did Marnie give that to you?' Lyssa glanced up at Marnie and Jeremy where they stood on the lawn, together, watching Molly and smiling. Jeremy had moved to stand beside Marnie and had put his arm around her shoulder. Lyssa felt a bitter stab of pain in her stomach.

'Uh huh,' said Molly. 'Isn't it the prettiest thing you ever saw?'

'*You're* the prettiest thing I ever saw,' laughed Lyssa, looking back at the little girl. Molly's eyes were shining and her cheeks were flushed with the exertion of the game she had been playing. She was a truly beautiful girl. Her parents must be frantic with worry. 'And you look like a ballerina in that dress.'

'Really?' Molly gasped. She turned to Marnie and Jeremy. 'Did you hear that?' she yelled. 'Lyssa says I look like a ballerina!'

'You do,' they agreed in chorus.

Molly pirouetted up the lawn to where they stood, and Lyssa followed reluctantly. Jeremy was watching her closely, searching her face for any clues about what she had been doing. Lyssa knew she was going to be escorted home again. She didn't want to draw out the visit, having to watch him with Marnie, but she didn't want to leave, either. She didn't want to be walked home. She didn't want to be interrogated.

'Would you like some lemonade?' asked Marnie, gesturing to the porch. 'We have cookies, too.'

'Cookies!' shrieked Molly. She ran to the porch with no further invitation.

Lyssa grinned. 'They come highly recommended. I'd love one.'

Molly kept up a steady stream of chatter, telling Lyssa

85

everything she had been doing since Marnie had taken her in, but gradually the conversation wound down, and the silences between Marnie, Jeremy and herself finally became unbearable. 'I have to go now, sweetheart,' she told Molly, announcing her intention to leave.

'Oh, do you have to?' Molly cried, throwing herself into Lyssa's arms and burying her face in Lyssa's shoulder. 'Can't I come with you, please?'

Lyssa glanced at Marnie, who looked a little hurt and embarrassed. 'Molly?' She sat the child up in her lap and turned so she could see her face. 'I can't keep you up at the big House. It isn't safe for you there. You love it here with Marnie and she's happy to have you while I find a way to take you back to your mother and father. I can't do that if I have to worry about your safety, and you do want to go home to them, don't you?'

Molly nodded, sniffling. She wiped her eyes with the back of her hand. 'I just miss you so much,' she whispered and hugged Lyssa tightly.

'Oh, baby, I miss you, too,' murmured Lyssa, hugging her back. 'And I'm doing everything I can to take you home, I promise. Now be a good girl and I'll come back as soon as I can, okay?'

'When?' asked Molly, allowing herself to be put back down.

'Tomorrow?' Lyssa looked at Marnie for permission. Marnie nodded; reluctantly, Lyssa thought. Well, she'd just have to be in the way for a while.

'Promise?' Molly wheedled.

'I promise,' said Lyssa. 'Maybe we can go to the park.'

'I'll walk back with you,' said Jeremy.

Finally he'd spoken. Lyssa flinched, even though she'd been expecting it. 'Oh, no need,' she said, as lightly as possible. 'You all seemed to be having such a good time, don't cut it short on my account.'

'It's not a problem,' Jeremy said firmly. He got to his feet and offered Lyssa his hand.

She took it and allowed herself to be pulled out of her chair. 'Marnie, it was nice talking to you. Thank you for the refreshments, and thank you again for taking such good care of Molly.'

Marnie rose gracefully and smiled. 'It's my pleasure,' she said. 'I'll look forward to seeing you tomorrow.'

As they walked down the front path, Jeremy asked, 'Did you find what you were looking for?'

'No,' said Lyssa. 'Actually I didn't. Or at least, I don't think so. I think I found more questions. I won't know until I've had a chance to study things.'

'What things?' he asked casually.

'I don't want to talk about this.'

'What things?' Jeremy persisted.

Lyssa walked on in silence and didn't open her mouth for the rest of the way home.

She slipped into the house unnoticed and went immediately to her room. From there, she went to the Room. She pulled the book and scroll from her inside jacket and went directly to the kitchen table. The lamp there was already lit, but that didn't surprise her. The thoughts in her mind had been pretty one-track. The House was very sensitive and seemed to pick up on those things.

Lyssa shuddered and stared at the lamp for a long moment. Regardless of her childhood here, it was obviously going to take some getting used to, getting to know the House on a more personal level. She put the book on the table and unrolled the scroll. She used the book to hold down the top of the parchment when it immediately tried to roll itself up again, and held down the bottom with her hand so she could study it.

She stared at it for a long time.

It was no more comprehensible than the book; than any of the books. The Speaker had said he didn't know what the writing was, but that he had found it recently.

How incredibly convenient, she thought as she leaned

back in the chair and rubbed her eyes. The scroll rolled itself back up with a snap. Staring at the symbols wasn't helping.

This is a test! she knew suddenly. She sat bolt upright, her eyes wide open. He gave me the key, now I have to solve the puzzle.

'The translation key,' she said out loud, unrolling the scroll again. A brief pain lanced her temple, but she was too excited to care. She had much more to go on than most cryptographers. She opened the book and began comparing symbols.

The wick needed adjusting. The flame had burned low by the time Lyssa realized she was trying to read by a flicker. 'I need paper,' she muttered as she twisted the wick up. 'A pen.' Then she realized she had a headache. She looked again at the materials in front of her. 'This can wait an hour if it's waited all these years.' She rose slowly and went back to Aunt Burchie's part of the House.

Supper was, of course, waiting. So was Millie. 'Good evening, Miss,' she said as Lyssa entered the dining room.

Lyssa smiled distractedly.

Millie smiled, but she looked disturbed.

'Is something wrong?' Lyssa asked.

'No, Miss,' she said quickly. She looked away, but she didn't look any less upset.

'Is Bertie alright?' Lyssa pressed.

'Oh, fine, Miss. Right as rain,' Millie looked back, her grey eyes meeting the blue of Lyssa's directly.

She wasn't lying about that, Lyssa knew, but she was definitely agitated about something. 'Millie, I don't know you very well, but I can tell something is wrong.'

Millie stood silent for a long moment. 'There's something strange about you, Miss. I haven't felt it in this House for a long time. You've stirred it up again. It takes a lot of energy.'

Lyssa found herself using the old magic to throw a

barrier around the dining room, something she hadn't known she could do until that moment. 'This magic has been lying dormant for more years than you've been alive, Millie,' she said sharply.

Millie shook her head. 'No, Miss, it hasn't. It just wasn't being used correctly, or by the right person.'

'What do you know about that?'

'You've protected us?' Millie glanced around.

Lyssa nodded impatiently.

'Your father, Miss. I don't know how he found it, or where it came from. He only had it for a short time, and it did him irreparable harm.'

'But Aunt Burchie told me he never really lived in the House!' Lyssa protested.

'He has no memory of it,' said Millie. 'It amounts to the same thing. I think she doesn't want him remembering, and I think that's best.'

'When did it happen?'

'When he was a boy. Fourteen or fifteen, I think. He'd been playing in the warrens. I guess he found it there,' Millie answered. 'The place was in an uproar for months, and then suddenly everything was back to normal, except your father. Never quite right after that. A little slow in the head, and his personality changed completely. He had been such a loving boy; kind and caring. He became quite a nasty bit of work. Herself kicked him out soon after you were born. He's only been back once or twice since.'

'Everyone has to come back eventually,' said Lyssa musingly.

'Only once during the lifetime, I believe, though most come back more often than that,' Millie affirmed. 'Everyone is born here. You are the most recent, and the only one in nearly fifty years. The rest have gotten too old to have any more children. It was hoped your father would have others, but with his nature so radically altered, he couldn't find any other woman who wanted to make babies with him after your mother left.'

'What was she like?' asked Lyssa. 'I never knew her.'

'She was very sweet and young and gullible,' said Millie with a genuine smile on her face. It made her look younger, despite the grey in her blonde hair. 'Your father told her he was rich and she believed him. He told her he loved her and she believed him. He told her she was the only one for him and she believed him. He cheated on her constantly, and she refused to see it until he gave her an embarrassing disease. Once her eyes were open, she knew she had to leave but she didn't want to leave without you. Your aunt made her, though. You are Family, and she was not. As far as Burchie was concerned she was expendable.'

'Expendable?' Lyssa echoed. 'You don't mean –'

'No!' Millie denied hastily. 'But she was threatened with that and a lot worse if she didn't go away without you, and never attempt to contact you. It broke her heart, but she did it in the end. Burchie made her. She would probably have wound up staying in that hateful sham of a marriage just to stay with you, but once she knew what was going on, it was important to the Family that she didn't find out anything more.'

'What did she know?' asked Lyssa.

Millie shrugged. 'I never did find out. I'm just the hired help, after all.'

'You're a lot more than that,' Lyssa said drily. 'Thank you for telling me about my mother. I always wondered, but no one would ever tell me anything.'

'Until now, it wasn't safe to even think about it,' said Millie. 'I'll have to put it all back into the back of my mind once you release the protection, but it was good to be able to tell you finally. There have been times I thought I would burst for needing to say something. She loved you very much. She was a good mother and she doted on you for the first few years of your life. It broke your heart when she went away, but Herself took the memories from you so she wouldn't have to hear you crying. If you look for them, they may still be there.'

Lyssa wondered. It was something that would have to wait for later. There was too much on her mind right now, and those memories were too far in the past.

Just as she was beginning to think she could stare at the symbols forever and not understand, Lyssa found a pattern.

It didn't tell her anything more than she already knew, but she found the first piece of the puzzle. She found the punctuation marks. It had taken so long because she had expected them to be smaller or irregular, or somehow different from the text symbols. They weren't. They were exactly the same size, but there was always a circle involved in the construction of the element. This didn't seem like such a big deal, but now she could eliminate them from the symbols she hoped were letters.

First, she searched for every punctuation mark she could distinguish and made a list of them and where they appeared in the text. Then she studied that until she was word-blind.

Fatigue forced her to bed, but she was up again after a couple of hours to tackle the script. She rummaged in the cupboards, hoping something had appeared since she cleaned them, but Millie didn't have access to the Room, and Lyssa intended to keep it that way. She would have to stock the shelves herself, and the middle of the night wasn't the best time to do that. Maybe in a large town the grocery stores were open all night, but not here, and she didn't intend to make a midnight foray to the kitchen and risk anyone finding out what she was up to.

Lyssa twisted the wick back up in the lamp to increase the light she had dimmed when she crawled into the feather bed. She hadn't wanted to douse it completely because she hated waking up in a new place and dealing with the moment of disorientation that always accompanied utter dark. Shadows at bay, she resumed her seat at the table before her lists and the alien books.

They're not of this world, Lyssa had finally decided.

There was a tinge of magic to them that didn't feel a part of this place. The magic of the House, and the old magic of the Room felt like they belonged here, but the magic of the books and the cloth felt different somehow. Lyssa hadn't touched the cloth since the day she'd found it, but it was never far from her thoughts. She could still feel the tingling in her hands when she thought about it, and it always made her shudder. There were so many mysteries stirred up since she came back. Lyssa wondered what game Aunt Burchie was playing, and why she had summoned Lyssa to join in.

The books were a part of the solution, and she intended to decipher them, assuming of course that transliteration was possible.

By daybreak, she felt she had made progress, having identified what appeared to be some consonantal blends, and a couple of vowels. At least, that's what she hoped they were, but she had no idea which ones they might be, or rather, which letters they might correspond to in the alphabet she was used to dealing with. Familiarity with other languages helped her a little, but it also seemed to be a curious impediment. She kept trying to apply a logic that didn't seem applicable.

A shower. This would be good. A cure-all she knew she could deal with. Something that would refresh and renew her for continued brain-bending.

Lyssa rose tiredly from her chair, unwilling to take her eyes from her work, but desperately needing the break.

'Oh, my god!' she cried, sitting back down with a thump.

There it was in front of her, and she'd been staring at it the whole time. The language was, itself, magic. These were spells.

Not actually, as in eye of newt, wing of bat, but in the most profound sense, this was the history of the magic and how it applied to this world. These were the rules!

Lyssa forgot about showers and time and where she was. She read the scroll. Then she read the book. Aunt Burchie had changed and bent the rules more than even Jeremy knew. With a sigh, Lyssa closed the book and stood, feeling the protest in her muscles and joints.

She went to the trunk and pulled all the books out, going through them and figuring out which she would need to study immediately, and which she could leave until later. She hoped she would have enough time to read them all, but she didn't think that would be possible. With the magic, she could take herself outside time, but the cost would be too great in terms of her physical and mental health. She could see what such trips outside time had done to her aunt. How the old woman had lived as long as she had in spite of such sojourns, Lyssa could guess, but she was certainly paying the price. She wouldn't live much longer, no matter what she said about choosing when she would die. No wonder she had called Lyssa back when she did. Now the only questions were *what for?* and *why?*

She looked at the mess she had created on the table, and decided to straighten it up later. More than anything now, she needed sleep.

She returned through the wardrobe to her room, making note that night had come again, before falling exhausted into bed.

Chapter Four

'The nature of the magic is such that once the spell is
begun, it will perpetuate itself until completion, using
whatever means are necessary to accomplish this
task.'

The Magic Book, Chapter Twelve

Lyssa was bleary over breakfast, but she went to the dining
room first because she was afraid she would fall asleep
before talking to Millie, and she wanted to speak to the
woman while the ideas were still fresh in her mind.

'You've put the protection back on the room, haven't
you, Miss,' Millie said without preamble. It wasn't even a
question. She wasn't asking, either.

Lyssa nodded. 'We're not from here, are we.'

Millie's eyes widened. 'So you found the books.'

'That's where I've been since yesterday. Have you been
here since the beginning?'

The old woman nodded slowly.

'Who built the church?' asked Lyssa.

'The Family,' Millie answered unwillingly.

'Are you Family?'

Millie shook her head. 'Family is mortal. Family is gener-
ational. Family is subject to the laws of this world.'

'And you aren't?' Lyssa had hoped not to hear this, but
there was no denying what she had read.

'For all practical purposes,' Millie acknowledged. 'My
life-span far exceeds yours and I am not subject to the laws
of any world but our own.'

'But you've been away from there for almost a millennium!' Lyssa objected.

'A drop in the bucket,' said Millie with a wry twist to her lip.

'Does Aunt Burchie know?'

'Of course not,' Millie chuckled. 'She suspects, I think, but she never found the Room, so she never found the books.'

'She knows about the books?' Lyssa was surprised.

Millie shook her head. 'I don't think she even really believes the Room exists. She has felt the old magic, but she's become out of touch with the House just enough that she can't pinpoint what the disturbance is. She doesn't know it comes from you, or you'd no longer be safe here. You're wise to avoid spending much time with her until you get it more under control, and certainly don't use it in her presence until you do.'

'I may have already,' Lyssa said. 'I think I've used it to mask what I'm thinking. I don't think she suspected, but I honestly don't know. Why do you serve her?'

'I serve the Family,' said Millie with a shrug. 'That's my job until the Family dies off. Then I serve another. You read the books. That's how it works. Those are the rules.'

'I've only read one book so far,' said Lyssa. 'Those rules have already been changed.'

'Only the Families can change the rules,' said Millie. 'They seem disinclined to change those applying to the long-lived.'

'You wield no magic at all?'

'None,' Millie confirmed. 'I know when it's being used, and that generally makes me very uncomfortable.'

'Really?' asked Lyssa. 'Uncomfortable? How?'

'Since magic is used by the short-lived, they seldom use it with an eye toward the future.' Millie thought for a moment. 'The distant future, that is. They don't think of the consequences of their actions in terms of the long view, and they tend to be fairly petty in its application.'

'Petty?' Lyssa asked.

'They use it for personal gain and vendetta rather than

common good,' Millie clarified. 'Those around them tend to get hurt in the backlash, even if that's not what was intended. The short-lived don't tend to think before acting.'

Lyssa nodded. 'What do you recommend?'

'That you think very carefully before you act,' said Millie promptly. 'That you look at the larger picture and consider everyone involved before reaching any decision.'

'And then?' asked Lyssa.

'And then think again,' said Millie seriously. 'There has been too little thinking and too much acting in the past. Too much damage has been done already. Don't do any more.'

Lyssa thought about what Millie said for a long time as she sat over her now-cold breakfast. Millie brought her a new plate, but Lyssa continued to sit unaware. She thought about what she had read, and what she had experienced since coming home. At last she stood up and faced Millie. 'Thank you,' she said. 'If I have any more questions, I'll come to you.'

Millie nodded.

Lyssa released the protections on the dining room and went off to the shower. By the time she fell into bed, she was so tired she couldn't see straight, but she lay under the blankets with her eyes wide open and her mind in an uproar. Finally, she gave up and went to go see her aunt.

Uncle Haskell would be the next one to come home.

Aunt Burchie had answered her question and then dismissed Lyssa immediately. 'I'm too tired today to talk much, dear,' she said. Her voice sounded gravelly and distant and she looked more drawn than usual.

'Is everything alright?' Lyssa asked with more concern than she felt. She was still distracted by what she had read. She was thinking about the aunts and uncles, and Aunt Burchie's pending death. They would each be coming home soon, one at a time, to try and negotiate the transfer.

She wondered how much any of them knew about what

96

was going on, and resolved to be around for those interviews. This time she would be old enough to pay attention. She would be able to prevent her aunt from wiping the conversations from her mind. She would finally find out how far this whole thing had gone, and maybe get some ideas on how to stop it. Mostly, she was hoping to find a way to send the Others home. Especially Molly.

Molly! She had promised she would go visit today. God, she needed sleep. Putting her hands over her eyes, she lay in the dark it created and willed her mind to shut down; insisting the voices shut up, and stilling the vortex whirling, threatening to suck her in. Slowly, she created a still spot in the center of the maelstrom and there, at last, she found sleep. Wake me at two, she whispered to her subconscious and slipped under the calm.

Molly was waiting for her on the front porch.

'She's been sitting here all day,' Marnie said softly, under the cover of Molly's vigorous greeting. 'She is truly attached to you.'

'I wish this weren't necessary,' said Lyssa, equally quietly, hugging the little girl close, kissing her hair between sentences. 'But since it is, I really appreciate your willingness to have her here with you. I know how difficult it is, especially when she acts like this –' she broke off apologetically.

'She says what she means. I know she cares for me, too, but you're the one who found her. You rescued her from loneliness and fear. You treated her with kindness when she most needed it. It is only natural for her to be so enamored of you,' said Marnie gently.

'That doesn't mean it isn't difficult for you to watch,' said Lyssa with understanding. 'If I wasn't so flattered, I'd be embarrassed.'

'Lyssa!' Molly said sternly, pushing herself from Lyssa's embrace. 'You came here to play with *me*!'

Lyssa laughed. 'So I did. What would you like to do,

and can't we include Marnie? I think she'd like to join us.'

'Well, of course,' said Molly with disdain. 'I want to go to the park like you promised.'

'Well, then, let's go,' said Lyssa with a laugh. She looked at Marnie. 'You'll come with us?' Marnie seemed to hesitate. 'Please? I'd like to get to know you better, and with Jeremy not here to dominate the conversation, I think I just might be able to!'

Marnie grinned. 'He does talk,' she said. 'Let me get the basket and I'll be right out.'

'Oh,' breathed Molly. 'The basket! I forgot! She made the most wonderful picnic, just for us. But now she gets to share.' She smiled up at Lyssa and slipped her tiny hand into Lyssa's much larger one.

Lyssa squeezed back, feeling a warmth uncoil from her middle and settle into a smile on her own lips. The incredible fact of this child amazed her. It would be a wonderful and sad thing to send her back to her parents. Lyssa knew suddenly that she would miss Molly unbearably when she went home; a feeling tinged with anger once again that Molly had been brought here, alone and afraid.

Taking a deep breath, she put the thought out of her mind, determined to enjoy the afternoon playing with Molly and getting to know Marnie.

'Here we go,' said Marnie as she pulled the front door shut behind her. She held up the basket for Molly to see and smiled at Lyssa. 'She's been looking forward to this almost as much as seeing you.'

'Well, as long as I get top billing,' Lyssa laughed. Turning to Molly she asked, 'Do you know where the park is?'

Molly shook her head. 'Close by?' she asked hopefully.

Lyssa laughed again as she looked down at Molly. 'Hungry?'

Molly nodded her head vigorously. 'Are there swings?'

'There are all kinds of play equipment in the playground, and a huge lawn where you can run without stopping until you run out of breath and still not run out of grass. And trees to lie under and lots of other kids to play with,' Lyssa assured her. 'It's just down the street and around the corner.' She turned back to Marnie. 'How heavy is that?' She gestured toward the basket. 'We can carry it between us if you'd like.'

'Thank you,' said Marnie.

They set off for the park with the basket between them and Molly dancing on the sidewalk in front of them. It was a beautiful day, sunny with a warm breeze, perfect for an outing.

'You've known Jeremy a long time?' Marnie asked, obviously trying to start a conversation and not knowing where else to begin.

'I don't remember *not* knowing him,' said Lyssa. She took a deep breath and held it for a long moment before exhaling. 'I guess we were both sort of always there, the only ones our age in the House. Until we started school, we didn't have anyone else to play with.' It was more than she intended to say, but she had nothing else to talk about. 'He said you started school just after I left.'

Marnie nodded. 'He was the only one who was kind to me for a very long time,' she said softly.

'Where are you from?' Lyssa asked. 'He mentioned the other kids teased you about your accent, but I don't hear one.'

'The Continent,' said Marnie with a hesitant laugh. 'I lost the accent as soon as I could, and that helped, but kids are cruel and it took them longer to forget. It never seemed to matter to Jeremy, though.'

'Well, of course not,' said Lyssa, trying to mask hurt and derision. 'After all, he's in love with you.'

'In *love* with –' Marnie looked at Lyssa, but Lyssa was looking at Molly. 'She's a beautiful child,' she said instead. 'I'm sorry her life is so difficult right now.'

'Jeremy has told you about it?' Lyssa looked up at Marnie, searching her face for a clue as to how much she knew.

'He probably tells me everything,' she answered slowly. 'He told me about how you found Molly, that she's not from here. He told me you're trying to find a way to get her back home. She's told me the same.'

'Turn left up here at the corner, Molly,' Lyssa called. 'Don't get too far ahead, okay?'

'I won't!' Molly promised as she darted up a lawn. She flung herself to the ground and rolled down the hill, shrieking with laughter.

'Be careful!' Lyssa admonished. 'Then you know about the House?' she asked Marnie.

Marnie laughed. 'Everyone in town knows about the House. I don't know how much they actually know about what is going on up there, but there have been stories, many of which have at least a grain of truth in them. And there are many more that are undoubtedly made up, but it's hard to escape the fact that people come and go from there all the time, and yet only one crazy old lady, pardon me, and a couple of servants actually live there.'

Lyssa shuddered when Marnie said 'crazy old lady'. 'I guess I never thought about the impact on the people here. I was only eight when I left. You don't think very much about the big picture when you're that age.'

'No,' Marnie agreed. 'But I can tell you, everyone knows something strange is going on, and they'd all like to know exactly what that is.'

'The Others don't talk?' Lyssa asked curiously.

'How much does Jeremy know?' Marnie pointed out. 'The Others have less idea than he does. He's been around longer than any of them, and he talks to your aunt. She doesn't tell him anything. Everybody figures you know. They're hoping you'll talk. They have kind feelings toward you, since you were a gregarious child. They all remember you fondly, and they're hoping you'll feel obliged in some way to enlighten them.'

'They remember me fondly?' Lyssa was genuinely surprised. She had a child's memory of the place. The adults had less impact on her than the shops, the parks and the other kids, and she didn't remember *them* very well.

'There was such to-do over your mother leaving, I think they all felt a little sorry for you, stuck up there all by yourself with the crazy old lady in that strange house. They were glad you had Jeremy, at least, even if he was a little bully.'

Lyssa almost dropped the basket. 'What?' she was dumb-founded.

Marnie laughed. 'He was a dreadful boy!' she exclaimed. 'He picked on everybody, and you suffered most. At least, this is what I'm told, and Jeremy himself admits it. He had a chip on his shoulder and a grudge against the world and he was going to get even, one person at a time, if that was what it was going to take.'

'Well, I guess some things never change,' mused Lyssa.

Molly came running back up to the two women and grabbed each by their free hand. 'Hurry *up*!' she cried, tugging on them with all her might. 'The park is *beautiful*!'

Laughing, Lyssa and Marnie allowed themselves to be pulled forward onto the grass in search of the ideal picnic spot. They finally settled in the shade of a large tree, spreading the blanket Marnie had packed in the top of the basket.

'May we eat now?' begged Molly, throwing herself onto the blanket and looking pleadingly at Marnie and Lyssa.

'I don't know,' said Marnie slowly, looking at Lyssa. 'Are you really hungry?'

'Starving!' said Molly promptly. 'Please?'

'You're sure?' asked Lyssa, trying to suppress a grin.

'I'll die if I don't eat now,' Molly said positively. 'I'll just die.'

'Well, we wouldn't want that,' said Marnie, opening the basket. 'But I don't think there's anything in here that's good for little girls. Just things like brussel sprouts and codfish cakes.'

'No,' Molly denied. 'I saw you pack muffins and apples and milk.'

Lyssa looked into the basket dubiously. 'Well, there's codfish cakes now,' she said mournfully.

Molly grabbed the basket, unable to stand the teasing any longer. 'There is not!' she shouted in delight, pulling out an apple. She took a huge bite and couldn't get her mouth closed around it.

'Slow down!' Marnie laughed.

'You'll give yourself a stomach ache,' Lyssa added, taking another apple from the basket.

'My mother always says that,' said Molly.

They sat for a while crunching apples in silence.

'Have you figured out how to get me home?' Molly asked finally, breaking the stillness that surrounded them.

'Not yet,' Lyssa admitted. 'I'm making progress, though.' She ruffled Molly's hair. 'It may take me a long time, but I'll find a way. A promise is a promise.'

Molly nodded, but she didn't cheer up as Lyssa had hoped she would. They finished their picnic and played games, joining the other children who were playing on the swings, but the sun had gone behind a cloud, and none of them really had the heart for the outing any more. Each knew the others were going through the motions, and no one had very much fun.

Lyssa left Molly and Marnie at the front door and walked home feeling guiltier than ever. This was her fault. She wasn't sure why, but the House had brought the little girl here for her.

'Your aunt would like to see you again, Miss.'

Millie stood in the same doorway as before, giving Lyssa a wicked sense of *déja vu*. She nodded. 'Thank you, I'll go directly.'

'There you are, dearie,' said Aunt Burchie as Lyssa entered the room. 'Millie told me you had gone into town. You're doing quite a bit of shopping these days.'

Lyssa kissed her aunt's cheek and sat down. 'I've made

a friend,' she said. 'I was visiting her. We went to the park for a picnic.'

'You don't seem to have had much fun,' said Aunt Burchie drily. 'You look positively funereal.'

'Oh, she's having boyfriend trouble,' said Lyssa, hoping she sounded convincing. She didn't like lying, and she wasn't very good at it. 'We had a good cry about how awful men can be sometimes.'

'On a lovely day like this?'

'You know how it is,' Lyssa grinned. 'When you want to feel sorry for yourself, the weather doesn't matter.'

Aunt Burchie nodded. 'I miss friends like that.'

'It must be hard not being able to get out now,' Lyssa agreed.

'Even if I could, most of my friends have died by now. Are you looking to have another good cry?' Aunt Burchie smiled conspiratorially. 'I can tell you all kinds of tales of woe.'

'Uncle!' cried Lyssa, twisting her arm behind her back. Are you feeling better this afternoon? Let's have some happy news!'

'Yes, I'm feeling much better, thank you. Haskell will be here next week.'

'For how long?'

'Oh, a few days, I guess,' Aunt Burchie answered reflectively. 'Their visits seem to get shorter all the time. This place used to be overrun with relatives.'

Lyssa remembered what Millie had said. 'I seem to have quite a few aunts and uncles, but I thought my father was an only child. And why don't I have any grandparents or cousins?' She hadn't really meant to speak aloud, but the funny look on Aunt Burchie's face said she'd hit a nerve. 'I mean, we're the queerest family I've ever known. Isn't anyone married? Everyone seems to be single, or at least living alone in remote parts of the world. What for?'

Aunt Burchie laughed. 'If I had the answer to that one,

honey-child –' She shook her head in amused disbelief. 'We are the darndest group at that, and I don't have any easy answers for you, except that's how we seem to like it. Or maybe that's how we've come to accept it. I don't know. I thought we might get started on this estate thing. That's why I asked Millie to send you in here when you got back. I may not choose to die for a long time, but it wouldn't hurt to get things straightened out, and it might answer some of your questions at the same time.'

'Where do we start?' asked Lyssa. 'Do I need a pen and paper?'

'I guess that wouldn't hurt,' said Aunt Burchie. 'I've got some in the drawer there.' She pointed, and Lyssa got the needed supplies.

'I've dictated my will to the lawyers already, but as you know, there are things about this House that you don't exactly share with the general public,' Aunt Burchie smiled at Lyssa, who sat with her pen poised. 'I'm not telling the Family about leaving the House to you, either. Everyone will find out when the will is read.'

Lyssa sat agape. 'Y-you can't do that, ' she stammered finally.

'Why not?' asked Aunt Burchie in surprise. 'I love dropping bombs and watching the fallout.'

'What kind of warped logic is that?' Lyssa demanded. 'The aunts and uncles will *not* be pleased to hear this. You'll be dead! You won't see anything, and *I'll* have to deal with the fallout.'

'We're not telling them,' said Aunt Burchie firmly. 'We let Uncle Haskell come pay court, thinking whatever he wants to think in that little pea-brain of his. He can tell the rest of those old farts anything he wants about how he won over the old bat and finally convinced her to see things his way, or whatever story they tell themselves to console their pride, but they can court me 'til the cows come home. I have chosen you. Well, the House and I have, and I don't intend to change my mind.'

Lyssa shook her pen and sat for a moment more in silence, drawing circles to get the ink to flow and thinking quickly. 'What will I do with the place?'

'Build,' said Aunt Burchie decisively. 'It's time to build.'

Lyssa frowned. 'Why? What do you mean?'

'I mean get in touch with the Bells and design your own rooms,' said Aunt Burchie impatiently. 'I knew the moment you got back. This place has an affinity for you. You're meant to be the next mistress of the House. You need to have your own rooms, though, and it's time, finally, to build again.'

'How often does building take place?' Lyssa asked.

'It depends,' Aunt Burchie frowned in concentration, trying to remember. 'At least every century. Sometimes two or three times in a hundred-year period. It depends on a lot of things, including turnover, and when the House is ready to expand.'

'So it is independent of us?' asked Lyssa as casually as possible.

'Interdependent with,' Aunt Burchie corrected. 'We co-exist for the most part, but we depend on each other for mutual existence.'

'Oh,' said Lyssa, nodding wisely.

Aunt Burchie laughed. 'More of this will be clear as we progress. There are many things I have to tell you, and I won't remember it all at once. That's why I thought we'd better get started. You've had enough time to settle back in again, so I'd like to devote at least a little time each day to talking about things. I want to remember to tell you everything, and you'd better write it down so you don't forget. I wish my Aunt Rennie had made me write things down. I might not be having such difficulty now if I had.'

TIME TO BUILD, Lyssa wrote on her paper. FAMILY AND HOUSE INTERDEPENDENT. 'Where do I keep these notes? This isn't something I want anyone else to run across, ever, right?'

Aunt Burchie nodded. 'Keep them in the warrens some-where. In a place that's safe. You'll know where when you find it.'

'Are the warrens safe even from the Others?' Lyssa asked, sounding braver than she felt. She must have mentioned them when she was little, but it felt like a dicey thing to be doing now.

To her relief, Aunt Burchie nodded. 'They stay put, for the most part,' she said, confirming what Jeremy had said earlier. 'There are places you go that they can't get to. Places the House won't let them go.'

'Is the House a life form?' Lyssa asked.

Aunt Burchie frowned and thought for a long moment. 'I really don't know,' she said at last. 'I never thought about it like that, but I guess it could be.'

'Well, anyway, I'll keep my notes in the warrens,' said Lyssa. IS THE HOUSE SENTIENT? she wrote. TALK TO THE SPEAKER. She had other things she needed to discuss with him anyway, and she was afraid it was going to sound like her conversation with Millie. This would give them something else to discuss. Lyssa began to wonder if the church behaved like the House in any way, and if that was what inspired the Speaker to do some house cleaning just before Lyssa showed up.

'Dearest, I'd feel better if you pretended to pay attention,' said Aunt Burchie peevishly.

'Huh?' asked Lyssa. She looked up from her notes and into her aunt's glittering blue eyes.

'I said, you've still not seen everything, and there's a good deal you've seen but forgotten. While you're looking for your hiding place in the warrens, I expect you to be looking around as well, for the patterns. I also expect you to get to know your way around the village.' Aunt Burchie smiled. 'And I don't mean just the shops. I want you to become familiar with every street and building.'

Lyssa nodded, puzzled. 'There's more at stake than an orderly transition?'

Aunt Burchie looked at her sharply. 'Write it down.'

Lyssa was fairly sure her aunt meant the instructions about getting to know the village and the House, but what made it onto paper was: THERE IS MORE AT STAKE THAN AN ORDERLY TRANSITION.

'Good,' said Aunt Burchie, leaning back into her pillows. 'Now go away. I'm tired. Come here again tomorrow and we'll cover more.'

Lyssa rose and left the room quietly. She would, of course, keep her notes in the trunk in the Room. She wondered now, how long it would be before she had to move there permanently.

Get to know the House and the village? Again, Lyssa caught a brief image of a spider in a web, but she shook her head to clear it, and when she looked again, it was gone.

Lyssa had so much to do she didn't know where to begin, but of one thing she was certain; the cabinets in the Room's kitchen were empty, and she was the only one who could fill them. A study session wasn't the same without a little junk food, and it was a good excuse to go shopping.

Lyssa left the House and walked down the hill to the village, looking around her with eyes open for the first time. Figuratively, anyway, since she hadn't honestly seen the houses and cross-streets since she was a child, and she hadn't paid much attention since she got back. She was amazed at the detail she remembered once she was truly looking. This also made the trip much quicker and Lyssa was in the center of town before she realized she hadn't given much thought to her shopping list. Instead, she wandered from one shop to another deciding what she had room for, and what would be practical given the lack of refrigeration.

By the time she had made her purchases, the sun was setting, so Lyssa turned up the street toward home.

'I'll walk with you,' said Jeremy, falling into step beside

her. 'Can I carry those?' He reached for her packages.

They were heavy, and Lyssa yielded them with a murmur of thanks, startled both by his presence, and his kindness of tone and action. 'How are Marnie and Molly?' she asked. 'We had a less than great day at the park.'

'They seem to have recovered,' he said easily. 'Molly distracts pretty well, so I was able to jolly her out of her slump. She seemed pretty happy to see me.'

'I'm glad,' said Lyssa honestly. 'I felt really bad about leaving things as they were, but nothing I said seemed to make much of a difference.'

'She sees you as her savior,' Jeremy pointed out. 'And she's got a little kid's sense of time. She misses her parents, and you said you'd find a way to take her back to them. She doesn't want to hear that it might take months, she wants to go home now.'

Lyssa sighed. 'I don't even know if I've got the ability to send her back. I'm not sure it's a promise I can keep.'

'But you're trying, right?'

Lyssa nodded. 'I'm trying. But you know, I'm really going to miss her.'

'Yeah, me too,' Jeremy admitted. 'She's a good kid.'

'You just like the excuse to see Marnie!' Lyssa teased.

'I don't need an excuse to see her,' said Jeremy, missing the joke.

His tone was a slap of cold water, and Lyssa remembered where she was and with whom. 'No, I guess not,' she said in a subdued voice.

Jeremy shrugged. 'Molly seems as lost sometimes as my mother did. It hurts me to have to watch it all over again and not be able to do anything.'

He stared down at Lyssa intently, but she pretended to be absorbed in the scenery, unaware of his silent request. 'I'm supposed to be memorizing the House and village,' she said eventually. 'Aunt Burchie almost ordered me to look for patterns. Maybe you can help me with that. Maybe there are clues here if we just open our eyes.' It wasn't much, but it was all the bone she felt she could throw him right now. Then, too, maybe it would lighten her own workload to have help and an extra pair of eyes looking at things and finding clues she might have missed.

'The two are connected somehow?' Jeremy asked eagerly. 'We played the Game for years, and I know the town inside and out by now, but I never saw anything.'

'I don't know, but since that was Aunt Burchie's order, I'd say it's a safe bet,' Lyssa answered. 'I wish we could take Molly along on the Game, but I still don't think that's safe. Maybe we could take her on walks around town. Maybe the four of us could go.' Lyssa didn't like offering that, but it felt rude to shut Marnie out just because Jeremy was in love with her. It wasn't Marnie's fault, and Lyssa couldn't do anything about it, so she might as well give in gracefully.

'She might like that,' said Jeremy slowly. 'But we don't need to be dragging her everywhere if all we're doing is memorizing. I think it would be good for Molly to get out and poke around her temporary home, though.'

'Well, we can certainly invite Marnie to join us,' said Lyssa. 'If she doesn't want to come, she can turn us down herself. What are you doing?'

'Coming in with you,' Jeremy said, holding the gate open.

'You don't use the front door,' Lyssa objected. 'You never have. Is it safe?'

'Times are changing,' said Jeremy with a mischievous grin. 'And I want to have first servings at the big table. Besides, I haven't talked with Millie in a dog's age.'

'Well, then, come on in,' said Lyssa, giving up. If he wanted to tempt fate, let him. Who was she to argue. She led the way up the front walk to the door and opened it, stepping aside for him. She made a sweeping gesture and he bowed slightly as he walked past her into the foyer.

'Where would you like your packages, Madame?' he asked in a funny accent.

Lyssa smiled. 'I'll take them to my room. Why don't I meet you in the dining room? You *do* know where that is?' She took her parcels from Jeremy and headed down the hallway. She would take them to the Room later; she couldn't risk his following her. She dumped them on her bed and went straight to the dining room.

Jeremy, who was holding a superficial conversation with Millie, looked up and grinned when Lyssa entered the room. 'Ah, there's my hostess,' said Jeremy, grabbing Lyssa by the arm and dragging her to the buffet. 'I thought I was going to starve to death. What took you so long?'

'I was gone for about two minutes,' said Lyssa. 'You couldn't help yourself to a plate?'

'Not wait for my hostess? That's very rude,' said Jeremy. 'Besides, I'm nervous.'

'Could have fooled me,' said Lyssa. She handed him a plate and took one for herself.

'That's always been your biggest problem.'

The sky didn't fall. Time didn't end. The Furies didn't descend and lay waste to the dining room.

Dinner was positively mundane. Jeremy teased Millie, who dished it back with an ease that surprised Lyssa. The two knew each other quite well and the formality with which Millie addressed Lyssa was completely lacking in the way she bantered with Jeremy. Once again, Lyssa found herself feeling out of the loop. She knew Jeremy had a life here that didn't include her. She had left at quite a young age, and he had remained to make a life for himself. Of course there were people he had relationships with that were, if not exclusive, certainly not inclusive of Lyssa.

That didn't stop her from feeling jealous.

My god, she was jealous! What a hideous thing! Green and mean, and there was nothing she could do about it but put on a happy face and try to breathe deeply to stay in control. She was jealous of Millie. She was jealous of Marnie, and the Others. The only person she wasn't jealous of was Molly. Poor little Molly. 'I'm sorry, what?' she asked.

Jeremy and Millie were both staring at her. 'What did you say?' asked Jeremy.

'I didn't say anything,' Lyssa said, frantically racking her brain to remember if she had made any noise whatsoever. 'I've been sitting here listening to you and thinking.'

'You said something,' said Jeremy.

'I don't think so,' Lyssa denied. 'I can't imagine what I would have said. I wasn't really paying much attention to the conversation. I was listening more to your voices; the tones.' She shrugged and turned to Millie. 'What did I say?'

Millie shook her head. 'It was a language I haven't heard in so long, I couldn't tell you what you said. But you did speak and I recognized the tongue.'

'The books?' asked Lyssa.

Millie nodded.

Jeremy looked back and forth between them. 'What's going on?' he demanded.

'You haven't told him?' asked Millie.

'No,' said Lyssa. 'I hadn't intended to for a while yet. I'm still not sure it's a good idea.'

'Hey,' Jeremy objected. 'You're talking about me while I'm sitting here. In most places, that's considered pretty rude.'

Lyssa looked at him, and then at Millie. 'I don't know,' she began.

'He'll find out eventually,' said Millie. 'He's a good boy, and smart. Maybe he can help you there, too.'

'You don't know everything,' said Lyssa, thinking about the threats.

'Desperation does strange things to people,' said Millie. 'And unhappiness. I think it's worth the risk.'

'Yeah, but it's not a risk *you're* taking,' Lyssa pointed out.

'You've got a valid excuse,' Millie agreed. 'You can hide

behind it forever, and probably make the situation worse, or you can take the chance.'

'Hello?' Jeremy interrupted. 'You're still doing it, and it's really irritating.'

'Oh, so sorry,' said Lyssa sarcastically.

'*Lyssa*,' said Millie sharply.

Lyssa was startled. She had never heard Millie address her as anything but Miss. 'Yes?' she looked up and met uncompromising grey eyes.

'Be polite to your guest.'

'Yes, ma'am,' she mumbled. She turned to Jeremy. 'I've got some things to tell you. Perhaps you'd like to go for a little walk. I think some of these things are best not overheard.'

Millie nodded approvingly.

Jeremy gave them both an odd look and rose from the table. 'Let's walk, then. We can begin your aunt's home-work assignment.'

Lyssa sighed. 'That's kind of what it feels like,' she said, getting up. 'Thanks Millie,' she added as they left the dining room. She went to her room and got her coat, and joined Jeremy at the front door. The evening wasn't that cool, but Lyssa felt the need of a little extra protection, physically as well as psychologically.

Jeremy held the door open for her and closed it after them. They walked down the steps and into the street. 'What language were you speaking?' he asked. 'It didn't sound familiar.'

Lyssa shrugged. 'I have no idea. I've never heard it spoken. I've only read it. I had to translate it without knowing what it was. I don't even know where it comes from, but it's not from this place.'

'Where did you find it?'

Lyssa told him about finding the trunk in the Room, and her subsequent visit to the church. Then she told him about her conversation with Aunt Burchie. 'I guess I'll find out more tomorrow when we talk again, but I honestly don't know what's going on. All I know is what she told me today, and the little I've been able to piece together.'

'May I see the books?' asked Jeremy. 'Can you teach me the language?'

Lyssa looked sharply up at him, distrust evident in her face.

'I could help you with the reading,' he clarified. 'Two sets of eyes, remember?'

Millie had told her to trust him. 'I guess,' she said grudgingly. 'But not tonight.'

'Why not?' he asked.

'Because tonight, we spend some time learning the village, okay?' Lyssa stood by her guns, and they spent the night walking, beginning to memorize the streets and houses.

'You look tired, dear,' Aunt Burchie said, looking at Lyssa's pinched face. 'Didn't you sleep well?'

Lyssa shook her head. 'I don't think I slept much at all,' she said. 'I spent the night walking around town, memorizing.'

'By yourself?' asked Aunt Burchie.

'No,' said Lyssa. 'Jeremy was there.'

'Fine boy,' Aunt Burchie said smugly. 'Someday he'll be a fine man.'

Lyssa laughed. 'He's my age, twenty,' she protested. 'Hardly a boy anymore.'

Aunt Burchie looked down her nose at Lyssa. 'You are both babes-in-the-wood as far as I'm concerned. And so much the younger because you think you're so old.' She laughed, a dry, rattling sound. 'You have much growing up to do, both of you, before you can be man and woman.'

'Fine, I'm a baby,' said Lyssa peevishly. 'Why are you even talking to me then?'

'Because you won't be one forever. Someday you'll have need of this knowledge, and I won't be here to give it to you then. So, I'm giving it to you now.'

Lyssa perched her notebook on her knee and held her pen at the ready. 'Bestow your pearls of wisdom on me.'

'I should box your ears instead,' growled Aunt Burchie.

Lyssa wrote in her notebook and looked up again. 'And?' she prompted, wide-eyed and breathless.

'And slap you silly, you goose, now let's get serious about this.' Aunt Burchie straightened herself on her pillows, trying to get more comfortable. 'Where did you go last night?'

'All over the neighborhood at the bottom of the hill,' Lyssa answered, lowering her pen. 'Why are we the only house up here?'

'We own the hill,' said Aunt Burchie. 'We don't sell off parcels of our land, because we'll need it for building later.'

'Is anyone else aware that half the hill is a covered-over building?' Lyssa had decided she would ask questions she wanted to know the answers to, and not worry about how Aunt Burchie might react to her knowledge. She was going to find out eventually anyhow, she might as well not play any more games than she had to.

'I don't think so, 'said Aunt Burchie. 'I doubt it very much. I mean, the records are all there if anyone wanted to look. Even we have to follow building codes and filing of blueprints and so on, but that doesn't mean they have to be correct, and it doesn't mean they have to be filed properly, either.'

'So we just do what we want?' asked Lyssa.

'Basically,' said Aunt Burchie comfortably. 'And it isn't half the hill, it's more like two-thirds. The growth has covered the warrens nicely, so it looks like we have just let the garden go wild, don't you think?'

'I guess,' Lyssa shrugged. 'Who are the Bell family?'

'Architects,' said Aunt Burchie in surprise. 'What kind of silly question is that?'

'And contractors?' Lyssa asked.

'Yes, they do all our work.'

'Do they do any work for anyone else?' Lyssa pressed.

'I don't know,' said Aunt Burchie. 'I guess so, why?'

'I don't know,' said Lyssa. 'I just can't imagine any place else like this existing.'

'Well, they have a special contract with the Family, but it's not exclusive, if that's what you mean.'

'Who else would they do this kind of work for?' Lyssa asked.

'No one, I'd imagine,' laughed Aunt Burchie. 'But I've been told I have no imagination, so you can't rely on me.'

'Are they here in town?'

'Of course,' said Aunt Burchie. 'You'll find them in the phone book, or I could give you their number if you're ready to contact them, but I do think you're being a bit premature.'

'Premature? You said it was time to build again,' said Lyssa.

'When you inherit,' Aunt Burchie clarified. 'You clean up the loose ends of the estate with the lawyers, then you jot down some ideas and contact the Bells.'

'Oh,' said Lyssa. 'Okay. In the meantime –'

'In the meantime,' Aunt Burchie interrupted, 'I had better do some of the talking, or we'll never get anything done!'

'Sorry,' Lyssa grinned sheepishly. 'But when you're eight, or younger, you don't think of these things. Now that I'm home, all these questions come to my mind and I don't want to be in and out of here every other thing bothering you. So, since I'm here, they're all sort of coming out at once.'

'Curiosity is good,' said Aunt Burchie. 'And these are all things you need to know. I was just hoping to approach the details in a more orderly fashion.'

'There's an order to this?' Lyssa blurted out in amazement.

'There would be if you'd let me talk!' laughed Aunt Burchie. 'Do I need to gag you to get this out?'

Lyssa made a zipping motion over her mouth and held up her pen and pad.

'Good,' Aunt Burchie looked confused for a moment. 'Now where was I? Oh, yes. Your ancestry.'

Lyssa sat for the better part of three hours, stifling yawns and trying to keep her eyes open while Aunt Burchie recited her genealogy. She smiled and tried to pay attention, jotting down things fairly regularly to satisfy Aunt Burchie, but she was so tired, she couldn't concentrate.

'I'll see you tomorrow, then?' Lyssa asked, when Aunt Burchie finally finished. Jumping to her feet, she kissed her aunt on the cheek and fled. She went to her room, flung herself across the bed and immediately fell asleep.

And while asleep, she dreamed.

The Others led her to the jungle and locked her into it. She wandered for hours, lost and afraid, searching for the way out. She was about to give up hope when she came across the strange, bald Keeper and his demented companion.

'We can help you, if you'd like,' the old man said. 'But you have to ask.'

Lyssa shook her head. 'I don't know what the question is,' she said, backing away.

'Yes, you do,' said the little red-haired boy, speaking for the first time. 'You just don't want to remember.'

Lyssa sat up screaming.

Jeremy, sitting beside her, gave her another shock and she screamed again. He was stroking her hair, murmuring gently into her ear. 'It's okay, it's alright. I'm here and it was just a dream. It's okay, I'm here. You're okay. You're okay.'

'What are you doing here?' she gasped, pushing his hand away.

'You were just having a nightmare,' he started to explain, reaching to stroke her hair again.

'That doesn't explain what you're doing in my room.' Lyssa remained adamant, ducking away from his hand. Her breathing hadn't settled down, and she was beginning to wonder whether she was having a heart attack. 'What are you doing in my room?'

'I heard you screaming,' Jeremy said defensively. 'I thought you needed help.'

'You just happened to be in earshot?' she demanded sarcastically.

'I was talking to your aunt, if you must know,' he admitted finally. 'I had some questions I thought she might be able to answer.'

Lyssa looked at him hard, trying desperately to get her breathing under control. 'Did she?'

Jeremy shook his head. 'I wasn't able to ask them. There was no way of working them into the conversation without arousing suspicion. I thought we were going to wind up talking all night, but you started screaming.'

'You heard that in Aunt Burchie's room?' Lyssa asked in disbelief.

'You'd be amazed what you can hear from there. Are you going to tell me what the dream was about?'

'The old man from the jungle. He says I have the question,' Lyssa said, watching Jeremy closely. She took a deep breath, still trying to get a handle on it, but she was inhaling the fragrance of him and it set her heart pounding so that she was having trouble concentrating. He was so familiar and at the same time a stranger. 'I don't know what he's talking about, but he still frightens me.'

'It was just a dream,' said Jeremy, reaching out and stroking her chestnut hair again. 'Just a dream.'

Lyssa shook her head irritably. His touch shouldn't be able to do this to her. 'I don't think so. I think they're down there, waiting for us, and I think we have to go talk to them.'

'Not right now,' said Jeremy. 'Right now, you need to go back to sleep.'

'You might give it a try yourself,' said Lyssa, moving on the bed so that Jeremy had to stand up. 'I'll see you tomorrow.'

*　　*　　*

She was being chased.

She ran across the long balcony overlooking the dark hall. There were no lights on, and only the gibbous moon to illuminate her flight.

There should be no light here at all, she thought in passing. The stairs were before her, and she sped down them, looking over her shoulder to see if she could catch a glimpse of who was behind her.

The shadowy figure finally walked through the door at the foot of the stairs.

She waited until the footsteps faded before going to another door and stepping through it. The long corridor beyond led to stairs that went back up, so she mounted them and began to climb.

At each landing, the stair narrowed until there was scarcely room to step, and still she climbed, coming at last to a door. There was nowhere else to go, so she opened it.

The garret was lit only slightly more than the ballroom she had come from, but after the darkness of the stairs, it felt like she had come out into broad daylight.

She slammed the door and ran as fast as she had ever run before, passing doors in the hallway that she probably should have taken, but stopping was more than she could manage right now. Her only goal was to put as much distance between her and her follower as possible.

Lyssa awoke in the morning exhausted. Sunlight filtered dimly from behind the heavy curtains, enough that she could see, but the room was still quite dark. She stretched her cramped muscles and rolled over to snuggle back into the pillows.

The door opened and she rolled back toward it. 'What –'

'Breakfast,' Jeremy announced, pushing the door shut with his foot.

He flourished the tray so that Lyssa was afraid he would spill something. 'What are you doing?' she growled, sitting up and pulling the covers over her knees.

'You had a difficult night. I thought a little treat would be nice,' he explained. 'Where shall I put this?'

'The kitchen,' she said ungraciously. Still, she made a flat space in front of her feet and shifted to a cross-legged position under the blankets so she could reach the tray more easily. 'You brought enough for an army!' she protested, picking up a glass of orange juice. She drained it in one gulp.

'Dreams are hungry work,' he defended himself, nodding at her empty glass. 'Besides, I'm hungry too, and I plan on joining you.' He sat down at the foot of the bed opposite Lyssa and grabbed the other glass of juice before she had a chance to demolish it, too. 'How about we go get Molly and spend some time memorizing that side of the town today?'

Lyssa nodded. 'Sounds like a plan,' she said through a mouthful of toast.

'Don't talk with your mouth full,' Jeremy corrected automatically.

Lyssa swallowed. 'Sorry. Think we can put together a basket of goodies to take along with us? Molly is big on picnics and I seem to recall there is more than one park over there.'

'I'm way ahead of you,' Jeremy grinned. 'I asked Millie to put together one of her special lunches for us. It'll be ready whenever we are.'

'And you've called to let Molly know we'll be there by mid-morning?' Lyssa quirked an eyebrow.

'Of course,' said Jeremy. 'So eat up and let's get going.'

Lyssa grabbed a plate of waffles and set to. Between the two of them, they decimated the entire tray of food. 'I'll dress while you take the tray back to the kitchen, and meet you in the foyer, okay?'

Jeremy nodded, gathering up the remains of breakfast. 'I'll see you there.'

He closed the door gently behind him, leaving Lyssa alone once more, wondering at the gentleness of a man who could be so angry. A boy? Was Aunt Burchie right, were they were both still children?

That was certainly the way they behaved toward each other sometimes.

Lyssa sighed and climbed out of bed. She dressed quickly and went directly to the foyer. Jeremy was waiting as promised, picnic basket in hand.

Looking at him, Lyssa couldn't help but wonder if his good mood and generosity were due to Millie making her give him what he had wanted all along. With a small sigh, she opened the door and walked out onto the front stoop. Probably, she figured, but she could live with that. Millie trusted him, and if he had what he wanted, maybe he wouldn't be a threat to her anymore.

'What's wrong?' asked Jeremy solicitously, closing the front door.

'Nothing,' she lied. 'I was just thinking what a beautiful day it is. Perfect for a walk and lunch in the park.'

'Yeah,' Jeremy grinned and took her arm. Together they went down the front walk and out of the gate.

'How much of this neighborhood do you remember?' Lyssa asked.

'I've lived here all my life!' he laughed. 'I know every stick and twig.'

'Describe it to me,' Lyssa insisted.

'Go down the hill, there's nothing but overgrown garden on each side of the street. No houses, no other buildings,' he replied.

'Nope,' said Lyssa. 'Buildings on the north side of the street, hidden in the overgrowth, buried under dirt and bushes, disguised by trees. Buildings that make up the warrens. Aunt Burchie says this entire side of the hill is built up and covered over.'

Jeremy raised his eyebrows. 'I'll be damned. I thought it was all underground.'

'For all intents and purposes,' Lyssa admitted. 'But there are places where the dirt hasn't completely covered the buildings. You can actually see outside some of the windows if you peer through the shrubbery long and hard enough. I think the House pulls the hill up over itself as each new section is built. Aunt Burchie said it was nearly time to build again. I wonder if the exposed section needs to be covered for some reason.'

'Ask her,' he said.

'I think I will,' said Lyssa. 'That's what our conversations are supposed to be about these days, anyway. I have to be back this afternoon for that very thing.' Her mouth twisted in memory. 'Yesterday, it was a history of all the people I'm descended from. I figured I'll ask Millie more about that. I couldn't really concentrate on what Aunt Burchie was saying, anyway.

'I don't know when I'm going to have the free time to sit down and read anything. Those books are going to occupy a lot of my attention until I get them read. And granted you can help,' she held up a hand to forestall him. 'But teaching you the language is going to take time also, and there are a lot of books. We probably both need to know what is in all of them, at least a synopsis.'

'What makes you think that?' asked Jeremy, surprised.

Lyssa shook her head. 'There's more to all of this than meets the eye. I think the more knowledge we have, the better armed we'll be.'

'Armed?' his eyebrows shot up.

'I get the feeling we need to be armed,' Lyssa repeated. 'Not with guns, or knives, but armed nevertheless, and I don't know any other way to do it. The more we prepare, the less likely we are to be taken by surprise.'

'Okay, then who are we fighting?' asked Jeremy, sounding a little disbelieving.

Lyssa laughed, a short and bitter laugh. 'If I had any idea, I'd know what to do. Instead, I'm taking Aunt Burchie's advice and memorizing the town and the House, as much as possible.' She looked up at Jeremy and sighed. 'I think it's time to play the Game again, too.'

'I don't think you'll be finding any more children,' he said. 'If that's what's bothering you.'

'No,' Lyssa shook her head. 'I don't know why Molly was brought here, but I'm not afraid of finding other children. I'm afraid of the old man and the little boy in the jungle. They were a part of my nightmares for too long. I don't trust what they're doing, and I don't believe they're harmless.'

Jeremy nodded. 'I know what you mean. But we have to face it eventually. Why not confront it head on and get it over with?'

Lyssa laughed again. 'Since when have we ever had control over where we go in the House?' she demanded. 'We get to the jungle when we get there, and not a moment before.'

'Well, yeah, that's true,' Jeremy acquiesced. 'And that being the case, how does your aunt figure we're going to memorize the House?'

'She seemed to think there were blueprints on file, but she didn't figure they'd be exactly representative,' said Lyssa. 'That might be a good place to start. It would give us an idea, anyway.'

'On file, where?'

Lyssa shrugged. 'City Planning? Town Hall? That would be as good as anyplace to start.' They had reached the bottom of the hill, and the nearest residential area. 'Time to start memorizing.'

Jeremy sighed and started naming the buildings and quizzing Lyssa on what they had just passed. 'Not fair turning around to check,' he protested as she started to turn back.

'We're going to be doing this again and again, at the rate we're going, so I don't think a peek is going to do permanent damage!' she objected.

'No, but we should try to be as observant as we can each time we go through a place, so we don't have to waste time on additional trips.'

It was Lyssa's turn to sigh. 'Good point. Okay, there are ten houses on this block. They are positioned exactly opposite each other, and are set back from the street fifty feet. They are the same size, but each is a different shape, color and style. There's twenty feet between each house, and the driveways go past the houses to a detached garage in back. There are no fences but each person mows his lawn differently, so the property lines are clearly delineated. There are old trees in the front and back yards and neat borders of flowers and bushes along the walks and foundations.'

'Very good,' said Jeremy, impressed. 'What else?'

'The streets here are exactly the same width as everywhere else in town, there are no cars parked on the streets, ever, and children seem to play only in the parks, not in their yards.' Lyssa paused. 'Why is that?'

Jeremy shrugged. 'That's just the way things are done here, I suppose. There are lovely parks in every neighborhood. That's where everyone gets together. Maybe they prefer it that way.'

Lyssa shook her head. 'Everywhere else in the world, where there are front and back lawns, kids play on them. *That's* how it is. This place is very strange.'

'You're just noticing this?' Jeremy demanded in surprise.

Lyssa laughed. 'Well, I haven't been back that long.' She tried to defend herself.

'Okay, I'll give you a break,' Jeremy laughed. 'Now it's my turn.' He said everything he had noted about the next block, and Lyssa quizzed him on the things she had noticed that he missed. In this manner, they walked across town to pick up Molly.

'Can Marnie come too?' begged the little girl. She looked up at Marnie, and then at Jeremy and Lyssa. 'Pleeeeze?'

Lyssa looked at Marnie and raised an eyebrow. 'Would you like to join us?'

Marnie shook her head and stroked Molly's hair. 'Not today,' she said with just a little regret in her voice. 'I have errands to run and chores to do. Maybe some other day, okay?'

'Please?' Molly asked again.

'No, sweetie,' Marnie said firmly. 'You'll have fun with Lyssa and Jeremy, and they'll have you back in time for a little quiet time with me before supper.'

'Okay,' said Molly dubiously, but she grabbed Lyssa's hand and swung down off the porch. 'Where are we going?' she demanded, quickly recovering from her disappointment.

Lyssa grinned at Marnie. 'Maybe next time?'

Marnie nodded and went back into the house. Jeremy watched her go, and with a small sigh, turned back around to Molly and Lyssa. 'We thought we'd go for a walk today, and see what we can find out about some of the streets around here. Would you like to help us play a game?'

'What kind of game?' Molly demanded, drawn to the prospect immediately.

'A game of concentration,' said Lyssa. 'We have to memorize all the streets and houses around here.'

'Why?' asked Molly. Clearly, the game, as stated, had limited appeal to her.

'Because those are the rules,' said Jeremy with a chuckle. 'The person who sees the most, and remembers it best, wins.'

'Wins what?' Molly wanted to know.

'A pretty satin hair bow?' Lyssa offered.

Molly giggled.

'What's so funny?' demanded Jeremy and Lyssa simultaneously.

'Jeremy in a satin bow!' the little girl exclaimed.

Lyssa and Jeremy laughed with her. 'Maybe he could pick a leather tie if he wins?' Lyssa suggested, pulling gently on the one he was using to hold his curls at the nape of his neck.

Molly nodded. 'That would be lots better.'

'Okay,' said Jeremy, looking at Lyssa with an expression she couldn't read. 'Now, how about we get going.'

'Yeah!' said Lyssa and Molly in unison. Molly grabbed Lyssa's and Jeremy's hands, and they set off together to play a game and search for a park.

Chapter Five

'The portals are built into random doorways of the
House, allowing access to people from other places.
The spell will determine when more energy is needed,
and bring Others to the House when appropriate.'
The Symbiosis of Builder and Family, Chapter Five

As Lyssa walked down the stairs into the warrens, she felt
as if she should be feeling a sense of trepidation, but she
didn't feel anything; no anticipation, no fear. Jeremy
walked behind her, as confident on the steps as she was.
Neither had their flashlights on.

'Do you think we'll make it to the jungle this time?'
Lyssa asked, uncomfortable with the silence between
them.

'No,' said Jeremy briefly.

'Why not?' she asked.

He didn't answer.

They reached the bottom of the steps and opened the
door. They crossed the atrium and went up the stairs to
the maze of silk brocade furniture. 'It's after this that the
organization breaks down,' said Lyssa, trying again to
engage Jeremy in conversation.

He had gone cold on her since yesterday, and by now,
Lyssa was ready to give up trying to figure out his moods.
She crossed to a door and opened it. 'I guess this is where
we start.' She stepped over the threshold and fell into space.
'Oh, damn,' she said as she fell. She wondered if Jeremy
was planning on following her, or if she was going to be
playing the Game by herself this time.

She should be used to this by now, but it was always so

disconcerting, never knowing where she'd end up, or how hard the landing would be.

'I would rather have walked,' said Jeremy from above.

'You had that choice,' she couldn't help pointing out.

'Not if we wanted to stay together,' he said drily. 'I get the distinct impression you're trying to shake me.'

'I opened a door and walked through,' she defended herself. 'The House chose to make it a free-fall.'

'You could have looked,' Jeremy replied. 'No one made you step through.'

'Did you see a bottomless pit when you looked through?' Lyssa snapped defensively. 'All I saw was pitch black. Sometimes that's a room the House hasn't quite decided on yet, sometimes it's a game of chutes and ladders. Why are you being so nasty?'

Jeremy laughed shortly, but didn't say anything.

They fell for a while in silence.

'How much longer is this going to last?' Lyssa complained.

Then they landed. Hard.

Lyssa got the wind knocked out of her. Then Jeremy landed on top of her, and forced out what little breath she had left. It took her a long time to recover and by the time she regained her breath, she was in tears, and quite red in the face.

Jeremy sat silent, letting her cry, but he didn't say anything, or touch her.

Lyssa felt the distance between them and felt worse. 'Where are we?' she asked finally.

'I have no idea,' said Jeremy. 'I've never seen this place before. Given the duration of the fall, I couldn't even tell you if we're still in the House, or if this is hell.'

'There's a difference?' asked Lyssa shakily. She took a deep, sobbing breath and looked around for herself.

Jeremy snorted. 'I've often wondered that, but since I don't believe in heaven, I guess I don't believe in hell, either.'

'What do you believe in?' Lyssa wondered out loud. She wasn't particularly interested right at the moment, but it seemed a good question to occupy them while they got their bearings.

'I believe in magic.'

'And?' She stood up slowly, stretching and testing her body on the way, finding nothing broken, or permanently damaged. She would be sore for a week, though.

'That's it.'

'Nothing else?' Lyssa looked around the room again, hoping to find something she'd missed, but the room was exactly as she had first seen it: a bare cell with no windows and no doors. The trap in the ceiling was the only way in or out. She could see that with the magic and without it. They weren't going anywhere unless they could climb out. 'You don't believe in yourself or your dreams?'

'Lyssa, what dreams could I possibly have to believe in?'

He had said her name. She stood very still, hearing it in her mind again and again. She didn't hear the derision; she didn't even hear the content. All she heard was her name. He had not called her by her name since she got back and she hadn't even realized until now.

'Do you have any brilliant ideas about getting us out of here?' said Jeremy interrupting her thoughts.

Lyssa looked around again. 'Uh, no. Not unless there's rungs back up the chute. I didn't think to check on the way down. Did you?'

'Why don't I hoist you up on my shoulders,' Jeremy suggested. 'You could check.'

There were no rungs.

'I guess we stay here for a while,' she said, as he put her back down. There was a deep rumbling sound, and a wall started to swing sideways. 'Or not.'

They stood side by side, waiting for the wall to finish moving. The sourceless light of the room couldn't penetrate the darkness of the tunnel in front of them.

'Got your flashlight?' she asked.

Jeremy reached into his pouch and pulled one out. 'Fresh batteries and everything,' he confirmed.

Lyssa found hers and they switched them on. 'Then let's go.' She shined her light into the tunnel and started walking.

Jeremy fell in step behind her and they moved through the subterranean darkness. The tunnel was like the room they had just left; cement walls with no adornment, functional. It gave no clues as to where they were, or where they were going, and nothing was visible beyond the limited beam of their flashlights. They walked, wondering where this Game would end up.

'What do you think is going on?' Lyssa asked after about ten minutes. Silence didn't usually bother her, but right now any empty space felt too much like the end of her childhood nightmares, in which she made it out of the House and found herself completely alone in a world deserted by every living thing. It bothered her to feel like that, but she couldn't help it. She had to talk to fill in the gaps, and then hated herself for blathering. 'Jeremy?' His behavior bothered her. He had been capricious as a child, but as an adult, whom she didn't know anymore, she found him fearful. She *was* afraid of him. But she could see that he was afraid, too. 'Jeremy? What do you think is happening?'

'We're walking through a dark tunnel,' he snapped.

As she had grown more verbose, he had become positively taciturn. 'No, really?' she snapped back. 'You say you want to help, then help. What do you think is going on? We need to talk about what we know, and what we suspect, in order to figure things out, and you keep threatening me to get what you want out of me. Now it's your turn to talk. What do you think?'

Jeremy grabbed Lyssa's arms and pushed her against the wall where he pinned her. She was astonished and terrified by his strength and his anger. He leaned down until his face was very close to hers. 'Until I *know* what I think, I'm not going to go blurting out every thought that crosses my mind,' he said in a taut whisper. 'I may not know anything now, but I'm not going to find anything out by talking instead of listening. Understand?' He waited, staring intently into Lyssa's eyes.

She nodded, staring back, afraid to look away. 'I understand. You expect me to cooperate, and you expect to give nothing in return.'

Jeremy let go of her arm long enough to slam the flat of his hand against the wall beside her head. When she flinched, he grabbed her upper arm again. 'You miss my point. Since I have nothing to say, I am saying nothing. You would do well to do the same.'

Lyssa felt the tears welling up in her eyes. 'I can't stop,' she whispered. 'I don't talk because I want to. The words just keep coming out. I don't seem to be able to prevent it. Like now. I really don't want to be talking to you, but I can't help myself. I –'

Jeremy's hand closed over her mouth. 'You have access to the old magic still?'

Lyssa nodded, her eyes wide with fright.

'Then use it!' He let her go, turned his back on her and walked away down the tunnel, not bothering to see if she was following.

She cried in silence, moving after him down the tunnel toward wherever they were going. What hurt the most was that his words made sense. She'd forgotten the power she had tapped into. Granted there was a price to pay for using it, but in this case it would be worth it. This was the same battle she'd had with the House over being hurried. The House was manipulating her emotions in a different way, to what end she couldn't even guess.

She reached into herself and found the strange new connection. Almost immediately, a sense of well-being suffused her, calming her and taking away the hurt and confusion. Feeling this way, she could believe everything would be okay. She tried to reach out with the energy and surround Jeremy with it, but he shook it off, perhaps without even being aware. He was interested in holding onto his anger, and there was nothing she could do about it. With a sigh, she pulled the energy back into herself, allowing it to circulate through her before sending it back to its source. She would undoubtedly need it again later.

'There's a light,' said Jeremy in a tense whisper.

His pace increased, and Lyssa moved faster to keep up. She couldn't see anything beyond him, but she didn't doubt his word. She found a peculiar sense of excitement now that the fear had gone. 'Can you see where it's coming from?'

'It looks like it's coming from around a door,' he said. 'It isn't very bright.'

'Well, let's hope it isn't locked,' said Lyssa.

Jeremy snorted. 'We've been brought here to run into a locked door? I don't think so.'

Lyssa stuck her tongue out, but since she was behind him and in the dark, he didn't see it. She didn't care. The small gesture felt wonderfully defiant even if it went unnoticed. As they approached, the door swung open, eliminating the question.

The room beyond was dimly lit and cluttered with boxes. David Baker sat on one. 'I figured there was a reason I was here,' he said as Jeremy and Lyssa entered the room. 'It's good to see you both again.'

'You know him?' Jeremy and Lyssa asked each other.

The Speaker chuckled. 'Everyone ends up here eventually.' He turned to Lyssa. 'You wanted to speak to me?'

She nodded and switched off her flashlight. Taking a seat on a nearby box, she inhaled deeply and held the breath for a long moment. 'You've been here as long as the church, haven't you?'

David nodded.

'You belong to the same race as Millie?' Lyssa asked.

Again, David nodded.

'Race?' Jeremy demanded.

'Indeed, species,' David clarified. 'We are not homo sapiens.'

'Who are you, then?' Lyssa pressed.

'You'll find those answers in your books,' said the Speaker. 'It would take entirely too long to go into that now, and we have limited time in which to discuss things.'

'Is this the only chance we'll have to talk?' asked Jeremy.

David shook his head. 'There will be other occasions, but it's still best to ask what won't be answered by the books.'

'You'll tell us where to find the answers you don't give us?' asked Lyssa.

'No,' said David. 'You have to do your own research, and draw your own conclusions. I'll tell you what I can beyond what the books cover.'

'Who wrote the books?' Lyssa asked, drawing her legs up underneath her to sit cross-legged on the box. 'Why are they in the Room? Why have they been hidden all this time?'

'The actual authors have been lost to us, but they were of the Family. The books were written hundreds of thousands of years ago; possibly millions, we don't really know. They weren't big on publishing dates back then.' He chuckled at his own joke, but since Lyssa and Jeremy didn't join in, he sighed and continued, 'They are moved to each new location when the church is built, and the Family member who builds the House starts with the Room and stores the books there. They don't start out a secret, they just aren't talked about much. Gradually, they aren't talked about at all, and the House continues to grow. In a relatively short period of time, they are forgotten.'

'How many copies of the books are there?' Lyssa asked. 'Is there a set of books for each house, and each Family?'

'No,' said David. 'Only one set. Yours is the primary Family.'

'Is the House a living entity?' asked Lyssa, changing the subject.

'Yes, in a way,' the Speaker confirmed. 'It doesn't eat,

sleep, breathe, any of the things we tend to think of as living activities, but it does possess consciousness.'

'And a sense of humor,' said Jeremy with a bitter twist to his lip.

David grinned. 'You could call it that,' he said. 'You could also call it a prankster. It doesn't mature as it grows and ages. The Bell family sees to that.'

'Okay, so who are the Bells?' asked Lyssa.

'They are Family,' said David. 'Family as in race, not relatives. They have some magic, but it's focused and directed differently. They build, you destroy.' He looked Lyssa intently in the eyes when he said this.

'And what do the long-lived do?' she asked him, staring back, willing herself not to look away.

'We maintain balance. We keep the church and the House. We serve the Family.'

'You possess magic?' asked Jeremy, trying to edge his way back into the conversation. He didn't like feeling odd man out, and he particularly didn't like the fact that he understood so little of the conversation he was listening to.

The Speaker shook his head. 'Not anymore, no. Not really. Oh, a few simple things to help make tasks easier, but our magic was taken from us, and now we serve the Family.'

'Who took the magic from you?' asked Lyssa.

'You did.'

'*I* did?' She gaped in disbelief.

'Well, not you personally,' David admitted. 'The Family. *Your* branch of it. Generations ago. Too many generations to count. You people breed like rabbits.'

'How was it taken?' Jeremy asked quickly, seeing Lyssa's hackles rise over a comment that was obviously untrue. She was the last Family member born, and there were certainly few enough of them before her. Maybe there had been a time when they were prolific, but no longer.

'We were tricked,' David admitted grudgingly. 'A

particularly clever Family member outwitted a particularly slow long-lifer, and ever since, we have had to serve the Family.'

'Why haven't you tricked the Family and gotten it back?' asked Lyssa. 'How hard could it be? I mean, it was done once, can't you do it again?'

David shook his head. 'Safeguards were taken immediately, once the Family realized what had been done. They have guarded the secrets jealously ever since. I don't have the particulars, but it's said there's a talisman of some sort kept in the Room, which, if discovered, would return the balance of power to us, and so to our world, but as long as church and House are built, we will be forced to remain subservient to the whims of the Family.'

Jeremy looked long and hard at Lyssa. 'So you're no different from the Others, in that respect,' he said to the Speaker. 'Where do we come in?'

David shuddered. 'The books will tell you that.'

'So no one goes home again?' he demanded.

The Speaker shook his head, lips clamped tight. It was evident he would say no more on the subject.

'What about the little girl?' Jeremy insisted.

David looked puzzled. 'What little girl?' he asked. 'The Others are older, with no family. So they won't be missed.'

Jeremy leaned forward. 'Who told you that?' he asked in a dangerous voice. 'We all have family, and we miss them very much. That's the most significant thing about us. We all had stable family relationships before being brought here. The only exceptions have been me and my mother, and the little girl.'

'Tell me about this,' said David, leaning forward on his box, obviously agitated.

'My mother and I were brought here when I was an infant. She took me into the nursery, but never made it there. She died here, years later, still hoping to see my father again one day. She lived long enough to see me safely grown up and able to take care of myself before giving up her dream and dying. I've been here since and the only thing I've ever known is that I was brought here for Lyssa.'

'And I found the little girl,' Lyssa broke in, not wanting to explore Jeremy's purpose too closely. Not yet. 'Molly was in a room and the House led me to her while I was playing the Game. She's only four. She was going into her bedroom to get her doll. She wound up in the House, and can't get back.'

'She's not still in the House?' David looked alarmed.

'No,' said Lyssa and Jeremy simultaneously.

'She's staying with a friend of mine in town,' said Jeremy.

'This isn't right,' the Speaker muttered. 'The Others always came from no one, from nowhere. They had no family to miss them and they were always at least eighteen. Something has gone wrong. Millie knew of this?'

'Millie knows about me and my mother,' said Jeremy. 'I don't believe she knows about Molly.' He looked at Lyssa for confirmation.

She shook her head. 'Only you and Marnie and I know. And now the Speaker. I guess we're not the only ones with questions now,' she said.

'You're right,' said David. 'I need to talk with Millie.'

'You knew about Jeremy, though, didn't you?' Lyssa asked. 'You knew something wasn't quite right?'

David shook his head. 'Your mother was a very private person,' he said to Jeremy. 'I only knew what she told me, and evidently that wasn't much. She said she had been widowed and came here to start a new life for herself and her infant son. She said she was staying with family while she pulled her life back together.' His voice trailed off as he repeated the few facts he had been told. 'It was right in front of me and I never even saw.'

'It went against the rules,' Lyssa reminded him. 'You just said the Others were supposed to be young adults and alone in the world. How could you know the House was no longer playing by the rules?'

The Speaker shook his head. 'I don't think this is the House bending the rules.'

'What are you saying?' Jeremy demanded.

Lyssa knew what was coming next. The color drained from her face, but she had to hear it said.

'Burchie has twisted the balance.' David turned to Lyssa. 'Do you know who she's picked as her successor?'

Lyssa nodded, feeling oddly disjointed and very far away. 'Me,' she whispered.

David nodded. 'That explains why you're back here. I never realized you knew about the warrens. I've never seen you here before; at least, not until the other day.'

'All warrens lead to the church?' Lyssa asked facetiously.

'Most players end up here several times during the course of the Game,' said the Speaker in a slightly admonitory tone. 'When did you start playing?'

Lyssa made a noise. 'I don't remember not playing. It was just something Jeremy and I did to amuse ourselves before we were old enough to start school, and to avoid homework once school started. We played in the afternoon, and sometimes at night.'

'How many times at night?' David asked, looking at both of them intently.

Lyssa looked at Jeremy and shrugged. 'What would you say? Five or ten times? Not very often. We were afraid we'd get caught, and we were pretty young at the time. Seven or eight. I was sent away to school shortly after, so we never did it again until I came back.'

'Did you play alone after Lyssa left?' David asked Jeremy.

Jeremy shook his head slowly. 'Only once. It really wasn't very much fun.'

'Well, you're right about that,' said David. 'You might have been killed.'

'I thought the House didn't do that,' Lyssa objected. 'I thought the Game was pretty benign. We certainly never seemed to be in danger.'

'Not as long as *you* were playing,' David confirmed. 'Did any of the Others ever play?'

'No,' said Jeremy. 'Lyssa and I talked about this the other day. Why don't they play?'

'Because it's not a game. They would have died. The warrens aren't for the Others to be wandering around in.'

'Then how did they meet us in the dining room?' Lyssa wondered out loud. 'We were playing. We'd just found Molly. They ambushed us and demanded that I tell them what was happening.'

'Was the dining room familiar to you?' asked David gently.

'Yes,' said Lyssa, thinking about it. 'I guess we'd been there before.'

'It was part of their area; the parts of the House the Others are allowed to occupy. You probably approached it in a direction you weren't accustomed to.'

'What is the Game about?' asked Lyssa.

'Getting to know the layout of the House,' said David in a tone that clearly said he wasn't telling her the truth, and couldn't believe she hadn't figured it out for herself.

'Why does Aunt Burchie want me to memorize the town as well?' Lyssa asked, leaning forward slightly.

'Ask her,' said David.

'Will the books tell me?'

David shrugged. 'I've never read them. All I know is what I've been told.'

'Are you actually competent to answer any of our questions?' asked Lyssa.

This time, Jeremy leaned forward. 'And are your answers the truth?'

The Speaker shrugged. 'You can believe me or not,' he said. 'I am telling you the truth as I know it. I don't know why your aunt told you to memorize the town, but she must have had her reasons. I may not like her, but that doesn't mean she doesn't know what she's doing.'

'She's breaking the rules, is what she's doing,' said Lyssa.

'The rules are changing,' said Jeremy.

Lyssa looked at him sharply. 'True enough,' she admitted. 'But that doesn't help us much now, does it?'

David laughed. 'Immeasurably,' he said.

'How?' asked Lyssa.

'That's for you to figure out,' he answered sharply. 'Do the work assigned you and stop looking for other people to solve your problems. That's always been the way you deal with things. Auntie, do that for me. Millie, please?' He whined in a fair approximation of a tiny girl wheedling favors from her elders.

Lyssa shuddered listening to him. 'I never sounded like that,' she objected. 'How would you even know?'

The Speaker looked at her and said nothing.

Jeremy laughed. 'It was smack-on,' he said. 'I've heard that tone from you a thousand times, and not all those times were years ago.'

Lyssa glared at Jeremy, but remained silent. She was outnumbered. There was no point in arguing. But she would definitely think about the words coming out of her mouth from now on.

'So we go ahead with our street by street inventory?' Jeremy confirmed.

'That makes the most sense,' said David. 'Especially if Burchie has managed to tap outside the House.'

'What do you mean?' asked Lyssa sharply.

'Read the books,' said David.

Lyssa sighed. 'We're not going to get much more out of you today, are we?'

David shook his head.

Lyssa slid off her box. 'Do we leave the same way we came in? Or do we walk back through town?'

'Have you ever gone back the way you came?'

Jeremy grinned. 'Lead on.'

They followed the Speaker up the stairs and into the sanctuary. The Game was the shortest they had ever played and, as they left the church by the front door, they decided to use the opportunity to memorize a few more streets on the way back through town.

'When are you going to show me the books?' asked Jeremy as they climbed the hill toward the House.

'Now is as good a time as any,' said Lyssa. 'Wait for me outside.'

'I'd rather come with you,' Jeremy said. 'I'd like to see the Room.'

'No,' Lyssa said a little too loudly, a little too quickly. 'No,' she repeated the way she would have liked to have said it to begin with. 'I'm not going to show you the Room. I also don't think it's safe to have the books anywhere in the House where Aunt Burchie might be able to see them. I'll bring one to you outside, and we can study it here. If the Speaker doesn't know whether or not my aunt has tapped outside the House, we'd better be more than careful.'

'Why only one book?' asked Jeremy a little sullenly. 'How many are there?'

'Quite a few,' said Lyssa, thinking. 'I haven't counted them, but there are at least twenty. Probably more. Only one, because we can't read more than one at a time, and you'll be learning a new language with the first one. I doubt we'll cover the whole thing in an afternoon. The rest are safest where they are. I'm not denying you access to them, I just think we'd better be cautious.'

Jeremy shrugged but Lyssa could tell he wasn't happy with what she was suggesting, even if he thought she was right. 'Wait here.'

Lyssa ran up the front walk and turned to make sure Jeremy hadn't moved before shutting the door. She darted to her room and was through the wardrobe as quickly as she could. She snatched the book, scroll and her notes from the table, stuffed them into the front of her coat and went back through the wardrobe. She shut the wardrobe door and ran to the door of her room just as she heard the tread of Jeremy's shoes in the hallway. Bastard, she thought as she opened the door and stepped out into the hall. 'I said wait outside, you jerk.' She belted him across the chest with the back of her hand in frustration. It felt entirely too good to do that. Grabbing him by the arm, Lyssa swung Jeremy around and gave him a shove down the hall and back toward the front door. 'Move!'

'Okay!' Jeremy protested in surprise.

When he didn't move fast enough, Lyssa darted around him and took off for the front door. Let him catch up. He'd be reading by now if he'd done as she instructed. She pulled the door shut as she ran through, was down the front steps, and out the gate before Jeremy got the door open again. She stopped on the exact spot where she had told him to wait and caught her breath.

Jeremy didn't run, but was still red-cheeked when he finally caught up with her. 'You could have waited,' he said.

Lyssa raised an eyebrow, giving him a scathing look. 'So could you. What were you trying to do, force your way into a place I don't want you to go?'

Jeremy looked a little uncomfortable. 'No,' he started to protest.

'Then why couldn't you handle a task as simple as standing here?' Lyssa shot back. 'You are a liar and a bully, and I've just about had it with you. I didn't bring you here, and I'm not going to allow you to continue punishing me for the way your life has turned out. It's not my fault, and I refuse to allow you to make me feel guilty anymore.'

'But –' he began.

'Shut up!' Lyssa shouted. She took a deep breath and lowered her voice. 'I'm not done. I have magic at my disposal that I'm just learning how to use. If you don't want to wind up being my guinea pig, I suggest you start behaving yourself. Understand?'

Jeremy's eyes widened. 'You wouldn't.'

Lyssa glared at him. 'How angry do I look to you? Push me, Jeremy, and see if I'm making idle threats.'

He nodded, somewhat subdued. 'I'm sorry.'

'No you aren't,' she snapped. 'You're afraid you'll wake up with parts of you missing. You're afraid I've been reading other books with lots of good ideas in them. If fear is what you respond to, then I'll use it. I'd rather not have to, but you force me into it. Now, where can we go to sit down and concentrate?'

Jeremy gestured and they began to walk. 'I really am sorry,' he said.

Lyssa snorted. 'You're such a suck-up. I'm still going to let you read the books. I believe we need to pool our time and knowledge, but I don't trust you, and I'm going to keep my eyes on you.'

Jeremy sighed, but said nothing more as they walked back down the road to a small path Lyssa had never noticed before.

'Where does this lead?' she asked as they turned onto it.

'Into the warrens,' he said. 'This is the Others' entrance. I thought we'd go to my room. It's quiet enough there.'

'No,' said Lyssa, turning back toward the road. 'I said outside. Aunt Burchie may have your room wired, or tapped, or whatever it is she's doing. You're not hearing what I'm saying to you. The House isn't safe. The House includes the warrens. Any or all of it may be under her observation. She doesn't know about the books and we need to keep it that way. Am I making myself clear, or shall I find words of one syllable?'

Jeremy made a face at her, and turned back toward the road to follow her. 'What do you suggest, then?' he asked petulantly.

'A rock to sit on,' said Lyssa impatiently. 'A place off the road, away from the House where we can talk unobserved.'

'Fine,' snarled Jeremy, brushing past her. 'Follow me.'

With a sigh, Lyssa did.

*　　*　　*

141

Jeremy learned frustratingly slowly.

Lyssa knew it was an alien language and he didn't have the magic to help him, but she had a hard time concealing her impatience, and he was unfortunately aware of it.

She was certain it was only his grim determination to solve his own mystery which kept him from throwing the book in the dirt and stomping away. Instead, he ground Lyssa over and over again on the ins and outs of the alphabet, grammar and punctuation. It was almost dark when he had his first real breakthrough.

By that time, Lyssa was exhausted and wanted to quit on a good note.

Jeremy wanted to go get a flashlight and keep ploughing through until he had achieved mastery.

'We need a rest!' Lyssa protested. 'Don't you know the best breakthroughs occur when you're asleep and your mind has time to assimilate all the information and come to its own understanding? The subconscious needs to worry things for a while before accepting them.'

Jeremy snorted.

'You don't think so?' asked Lyssa. 'Look at your dreams.' She stood up and reached for the book.

Jeremy snatched it away from her. 'I want to keep working.'

'Fine,' said Lyssa tiredly. 'I've already read that one. Just promise you won't take it into the House, or get it messed up.'

Jeremy shifted on his rock.

'Promise,' Lyssa demanded, holding her hand out again. 'Or give it back to me. If Aunt Burchie finds out about it, you can kiss your home and your father good-bye. Don't you understand that? She'll blow us out of the water before we even find the boat. You heard the Speaker. You should know what's at stake more than anyone. She's not playing by the rules anymore. She might never have been. Oh, god,' Lyssa stopped, clapping her hand over her mouth. 'I didn't go to her this afternoon.'

Jeremy grinned. 'Forgot to answer the old lady's summons?'

'Oh, shut up,' Lyssa growled. 'Just promise you won't do anything stupid with the book?'

'Okay,' said Jeremy grudgingly. 'I promise.'

'Thanks,' Lyssa called over her shoulder as she sprinted back toward the House. She would have just enough time to visit Aunt Burchie before dinner.

'There you are,' said the old woman as Lyssa arrived breathless in the room. 'I was beginning to wonder if you'd forgotten.'

Lyssa grinned sheepishly. 'I did,' she admitted. 'Jeremy and I were out exploring the town, memorizing the streets and stuff, like you said.'

'And stuff?' Aunt Burchie echoed disdainfully. 'Really, dear. Your language is atrocious sometimes. Like I said? *As* I said!'

'Yes, ma'am,' said Lyssa as she slid onto the chair beside the bed. She pulled a pen and some paper out of her coat, materials left over from her notes on the translation. She hoped her aunt wouldn't want to look at what she was writing down, since there were scribbles on the page that would undoubtedly have nothing to do with what they would be discussing today.

'Have you ever been to the church?' asked Aunt Burchie.

Lyssa jumped. 'Uh, not to worship,' she said, casting about for what would be safe to tell. 'I've poked around a bit during off hours to see what the place was like. I've studied other people's religions since I didn't grow up with one of my own. Curiosity mostly. It's a pretty place. Why?'

'Just pay attention to where it is, and how it relates to the buildings around it. Study it a bit more closely. Just keep it in mind.'

'Okay,' Lyssa shrugged. She jotted it down to make her commitment to the task seem more real. 'Is there truth in the rumor that the church has been around longer than the town?'

Aunt Burchie laughed. 'I'm old, but I'm not *that* old.'

Lyssa blushed. 'You know what I mean!' she protested.

'Yes, I just like to see you flustered sometimes. It's a nice change from the smart-aleck, sure-of-yourself kid you've become. Honestly, I don't know if the rumors are true, but I wouldn't have any reason to doubt them. Why?'

'I just figured since we own it,' said Lyssa slowly. 'Well, *you* own it, that you might have some idea of its age and worth.'

'You're planning on selling it once you inherit?' Aunt Burchie smiled a little thinly. 'This place is tied up in trusts so tight no lawyer could break them.'

'No! Of course not!' Lyssa protested, disconcerted again. 'But I've heard people speculate and pass on the rumor, and I just wondered, is all. It's rather a historical building and I'm sure a preservation society would love to get their mitts on it. Give tours and lectures, that kind of thing.'

Aunt Burchie made a dismissive gesture with one hand. 'Never happen. Just remember to keep your eyes peeled and your thinking cap on.'

'Okay,' said Lyssa, relieved to have talked herself out of that one. She wasn't even sure why she was asking. The questions just kept coming out, and getting more stupid. Maybe Jeremy was rubbing off, she thought wryly. Then she felt guilty. That was a pretty mean thing to think. 'Is there going to be a test?'

'You're in a foul mood this evening,' said Aunt Burchie. 'No. No test. Nothing that formal. But that doesn't mean you don't need to do the work. You won't know until you need it, just how important that information is.'

'I'm sorry,' Lyssa said contritely. 'I am pretty crabby. I don't mean to take it out on you. Jeremy's getting pretty awful to be around.'

'You have to learn how to handle a man,' said Aunt Burchie with a knowing look. 'Maybe that's something else I could teach you.'

Lyssa tried not to let her aunt see her shudder. That's

all I need, she thought. 'I think I'll try to do this myself for a while, first,' she said aloud. 'Thanks for offering, though.'

Aunt Burchie smiled. 'I wasn't always a silly old woman, you know.'

'I don't think that!' Lyssa objected.

'Indeed,' said Aunt Burchie drily. 'Go get yourself some supper. Your mind is wandering something fierce. Come back to me when you're done and we'll try this again.'

The evening finally ended.

Lyssa shut her bedroom door and leaned against it, breathing a sigh of relief.

'Are you ready?' asked Jeremy from the chair in the corner.

Lyssa jumped a foot and yelped, 'Go away!'

Jeremy held up the book. 'We need to work. There's still time left before bed, and I'd like to get a handle on this.'

Lyssa's eyes widened. She shook her head in disbelief. 'You promised,' she whispered.

Jeremy made a dismissive gesture. 'Come on. I think I'm getting the idea –'

Lyssa leaped across the room and snatched the book from him. 'You are too stupid for words! I don't know why you're defying the advice other people are giving you, but I'm telling you flat out: I'm not going to show you anything more. Nothing! Now get out of my room.'

She grabbed him by the shirt-front and dragged him out of the chair, surprised at the strength anger lent her. 'You can whine to Millie all you want, but I'm not relenting on this. I'll talk with her myself.' She propelled him across the floor and opened the door.

Aunt Burchie stood in the now-open doorway. 'I'll take that,' she said, holding her hand out for the book Lyssa clutched.

Lyssa screamed and thrust Jeremy at the old woman

*instead, pushing them both out the door. She slammed it
shut –*

And woke with a start.

She lay in the dark, gasping for breath, clutching the
covers to her chin in a half-remembered gesture from childhood that had something to do with protection from the
monsters under the bed. Did Aunt Burchie really represent
that much of a threat? Did Jeremy, through his controlling
behavior? Or was she just getting paranoid?

She shook silently. There's certainly good reason for
paranoia, she thought, relaxing her grip on the blankets.
She shifted to a more comfortable position, but after a
couple of minutes, realized she was much too tense to fall
back to sleep. Looking at the clock, she decided a couple
of hours of reading might be the thing to unwind her. It
certainly couldn't do any more harm than lying in the dark,
thinking of all the things she didn't have answers to. She
might even find a couple.

With a sigh, Lyssa climbed out of bed. On a hunch, she
turned on the light, but there was no one else in the room.
She wasn't sure if she was relieved or disappointed. Yelling
at Jeremy would have made her feel better, even if he didn't
deserve it.

She turned out the light again and made her way across
the room in the dark. No one would see a light under the
door, but Lyssa felt better with it off. Silently, she went
through the wardrobe and into the Room. She shut the
doors quietly behind her and pulled another volume out
of the trunk. She settled into one of the rocking chairs in
front of the window, and turned up the lamp on the table.

She glanced around again, reflexively. She knew the lamp
was on because the House had known she was coming, but
it still felt kind of creepy, and she wanted to make sure
she was alone.

Finally, she settled back and opened the book.

It turned out to be a history like the one Aunt Burchie
was telling her, but much more ancient. Aunt Burchie could

remember only what had happened during her lifetime, and what had been told her of the previous generations. This book had no information that recent, but it uncovered a past Lyssa felt was best left alone.

The picture painted was that of a predatory species, devoid of conscience and as manipulative and power-hungry as she could have imagined. Aunt Burchie was a perfect specimen. She was indeed dangerous, and extremely well-informed.

Lyssa was brought back to the present by a throbbing head. She glanced at her watch and was shocked to discover it was morning already. She closed the book and went back to her room to dress.

Her mind was still spinning with images from the text as she sat down at the dining room table for breakfast. She stared at her plate for a long while as the food got cold, but she didn't pick up her fork.

'Is that what we're really like?' she asked finally.

Millie's eyes darted around the dining room uncomfortably.

'Sorry,' Lyssa said, putting up the protective barrier. 'I was reading all night. I guess my brain is a little fuddled.'

'You were reading one of the histories?' Millie guessed.

'How do you know so much about the books if you've never read them?' Lyssa asked sharply.

Millie shrugged noncommittally. 'There's always talk.'

'Yes, it was one of the histories. One about the Family. It wasn't very flattering.'

Millie almost snorted. 'There's not much flattering to be said about the Families.'

'How many are there?' asked Lyssa, worried.

'I'm not sure,' Millie answered slowly. 'Several hundred, I think. We tend to lose track of each other between moves. Sometimes in the interim, whole branches die off.'

'Is there some kind of central meeting place, then?' Lyssa asked curiously.

'There is a general check-in during transition.' said Millie. 'The long-lived gossip and catch up with the news. The Families plan their next locations, but since they don't know each other, and don't care to, they don't stay very long.'

'And yet, it's the long-lived who do all the work?' Lyssa confirmed. 'How do you have time to socialize and still get everything done?'

'Those who build the churches and Houses are Family. The long-lived have always followed sometime after the Families set up housekeeping. You may control our purpose, but you do not control our time. It's a small defiance, but one which makes us feel better.'

Lyssa nodded. 'That I understand,' she grinned. 'Is there a purpose to all these transitions?'

Millie remained silent for so long, Lyssa finally prodded again. 'Was there a purpose before the Families tricked the long-lived out of their magic?' she asked, looking closely at Millie.

The woman started almost imperceptibly, but recovered so quickly Lyssa wasn't sure she'd actually seen it. 'There was something besides transition,' she said softly. 'But I can't tell you about it right now. Transition was introduced after the magic was stolen. We had to do something fast. In retrospect, we probably would have done something different, but this was the choice we made at the time.'

Millie took a deep breath and held it for a long moment before exhaling slowly and looking Lyssa in the eye. 'The long-lived created a cycle you would have to live by, that would bring you back together periodically. Unfortunately, I can't tell you why just yet,' she said softly.

'Why not?' asked Lyssa in an equally soft voice.

'Because you aren't ready to hear the answer.'

Lyssa looked up sharply. 'The Speaker said there were questions he could answer, and questions the books would answer. Is this like that?'

'No,' said Millie definitely. 'This answer isn't in the

books. You won't find it written anywhere, and I'm unable to tell you right now.'

'You will tell me when the time is right?'

Millie nodded. 'But not until then,' she said a little defensively.

'I won't say I understand,' Lyssa grimaced. 'But it makes as much sense as anything else around here.'

'With that, I'll agree,' Millie grinned. 'Now, would you like a fresh plate of hot food?'

Lyssa looked down at her plate. 'Uh, yeah,' she said getting up. 'That's sort of why I came here.' She started to clear her cold breakfast, but Millie took the plate.

'I'll give this to the cat,' she said.

'We don't have a cat,' said Lyssa.

'Then we should get one,' said Millie, leaving the dining room.

Lyssa frowned and stared after her for a long moment before getting a new plate and serving herself from the still-hot dishes on the buffet. She ate alone and in silence. Millie didn't return. When she was done, Lyssa brought her plate into the kitchen and packed a basket of goodies to share with Molly. She was feeling guilty for not having visited the little girl much recently and it was time to remedy that.

'Where have you been?' Molly demanded as she flung herself off the porch and hurtled toward Lyssa at top speed.

Lyssa dropped the basket and caught the little girl, swinging her up in the air, laughing. 'I missed you, too!' she exclaimed. 'So I came to play with you today.'

'Are we going to take another walk?' asked Molly.

Her voice sounded strange and Lyssa wasn't sure how to read the tone of voice and body language. 'We can if you'd like,' she said hesitantly.

'Maybe a little later,' said Molly, nodding. 'Can I show you something?'

'Of course,' said Lyssa. She picked up the basket and held out her hand to Molly. 'Where is it?'

Molly grabbed the outstretched hand and pulled Lyssa in the direction of the house. 'Up in the attic,' she said mysteriously. 'Come with me and I'll show you.'

Lyssa followed, laughing. '*What* is it?'

'You'll see,' was all Molly would say. She dragged Lyssa up two flights of stairs to the attic, and across the floor to the far side by the window. 'Look,' she said, sweeping her arm dramatically.

'Ooh,' said Lyssa, sinking to the floor, staring in wonderment. 'I always wanted one like this when I was little.' She looked up at Molly, who was beaming with pride. 'May I touch it?'

'You have to be very careful,' said Molly in an important voice. 'It's very delicate.'

The doll's house was incredible, and Lyssa was sure these were the same admonitions Marnie had given Molly when she showed the house to the little girl. As Lyssa explored, she discovered doors that opened and lights that turned on. 'Was this Marnie's when she was a girl?' Lyssa asked.

'Uh, huh,' said Molly, crouching beside Lyssa. 'It's still hers. She's letting me be very careful with it. Look.' She gently opened a cupboard in the kitchen and revealed tiny dishes and cups on the shelves.

'Are there any dolls?'

'Of course, silly,' said Molly. She pointed to a box beside the doll's house. The large doll Molly had brought with her from the warrens sat next to the box, as if keeping the smaller dolls company.

Lyssa reached out to finger the material of her dress. It was a beautiful doll and didn't belong in an attic. 'Doesn't she get lonely up here?'

Molly laughed and shook her head. 'Sometimes, but I spend a lot of time up here, so she doesn't have to be lonely.'

Lyssa smiled and took a smaller doll out of the box. As

she placed dolls on beds to sort them out, Molly told her their names and ages. 'Did you make those up? Or did Marnie tell you who they were?' asked Lyssa. 'They had rather a lot of children, didn't they? There are more children than beds.'

Molly giggled. 'Children need friends,' she said. 'They don't all live here.'

'Where do the other dolls live?' asked Lyssa, looking around. 'Is there another house for them?'

Molly shook her dark head solemnly. 'They live in the box.'

'And their friends live in a mansion? That's not fair,' said Lyssa. 'Maybe there's stuff up here that we could use to make a house for the other children.'

Molly leaped eagerly to her feet and began rummaging around the attic.

'Find a big box,' Lyssa instructed. 'That'll do for the structure.' She stood up and looked about. 'Do you think Marnie might like to help us?'

Molly nodded, distracted by her search. 'Here's a box,' she said. 'But it's full of stuff.'

'Maybe it's stuff we can use,' said Lyssa, making her way to the attic door. 'Marnie?' she called down the stairs.

'Yes?' came the distant reply.

'Oh, Lyssa, look!' squealed Molly.

'Could you come up here, please?' Lyssa called back to Marnie. She turned to Molly, who had swathed herself in veils and was dancing around the attic. 'Very pretty,' she laughed. 'Would you rather play dress-up?'

'No!' Molly fingered the veils. 'I want to build a home for the lonely children.'

'Are they lonely?' asked Lyssa gently, suddenly hearing in Molly's voice the loneliness she must feel.

Molly nodded. 'They're all by themselves. That's why I brought the big doll up to keep them company. They don't even have a home.'

'They've always lived in a box,' said Lyssa. 'They don't even know that a home is like.'

'Yes, they do,' said Molly vehemently, 'They go visit their friends in the mansion all the time. They know what mummies and daddies are, too.'

Lyssa went to Molly and hugged her tightly. 'I'm working to find a way for you to go home,' she whispered. 'I'm trying very hard.'

Molly nodded solemnly.

'What's this?' asked Marnie from the top of the attic stairs. 'Are you a gypsy dancer?' Her blue eyes sparkled and she smiled at Molly.

Molly shook her head. 'We want to build a home for the children who don't have one.'

'You mean the extra dolls?' asked Marnie.

Molly nodded again. 'They need a home. They can't keep living in a tiny box like that.'

'You're right,' said Marnie. 'I never thought about them out in the cold all night by themselves, getting to visit the mansion only during the day.'

'We were looking for a box we could use to make the house,' suggested Lyssa.

'I know just the thing,' said Marnie. 'And we can use extra cardboard to make floors and walls for the rooms, and some of these scarves for wallpaper and curtains and bedclothes and –'

'And everything!' sighed Molly, removing the scarves.

They never took a walk. They spent the morning and early afternoon creating a doll's house which, while not as fancy as the original, was certainly made with love and care.

'Isn't it the most beautiful thing you've ever seen?' Molly breathed, rocking back on her heels to view it.

'It is,' said Marnie and Lyssa together.

'And it's all yours,' said Marnie. 'You may take it when you go home, along with the lonely children.'

But Molly shook her head. 'Then the children of the

mansion would be lonely without their friends. This is for them, not me.'

Marnie hugged the little girl. 'You are kind and generous. Thank you.'

Molly beamed up at Marnie, and then over at Lyssa. 'Now, let's play!'

They gathered up the new house and all the dolls and moved back over to where the mansion stood. They played dolls for the rest of the afternoon.

When she noticed the shadows growing long outside the attic window, Lyssa stood. 'I have to go,' she said with regret.

'Do you have to?' Molly cried, leaping up and wrapping her arms around Lyssa's waist.

Lyssa gave her a big hug. 'I'll come back soon, I promise.'

'Can't you spend the night here?' Molly begged.

'I wish I could,' she said. Looking at Marnie, she found she honestly meant it. Marnie was really nice, and Lyssa enjoyed her company. It was a shock, and she had wanted very much to be justified in disliking her, but she couldn't. Instead, she found she wanted to get to know Marnie better, and spending the night would have been a perfect excuse. Lyssa crouched down and took Molly's face between her hands. 'I have too much to do trying to find a way home for you. If I stayed here tonight, I wouldn't be spending the time looking. You understand, don't you?'

Molly tried to look away, but Lyssa held her firmly. 'Please tell me you understand, Molly. Because I really hate to tell you no. I'd rather spend time here with you and Marnie, but it would be selfish of me. I wish I could keep you for my very own, but your mommy and daddy are worried sick about you, and you miss them terribly. I don't want to delay getting you back together any longer than I have to. Do you understand?' Lyssa let go of Molly's face, still searching her eyes for the answer.

Molly nodded slowly. 'I wish you could keep me, too. But I want to go home even more.'

Lyssa hugged the little girl again. 'I know you do,' she whispered. 'I'll find a way. Somehow, I'll find a way.' She stood again and looked at Marnie. 'It was a lovely afternoon.'

Marnie grinned. 'I haven't played like that in years. We'll have to do it again sometime.'

Lyssa grinned back. 'As soon as my body recovers from sitting on the floor like that.'

Marnie laughed and rubbed the small of her back with one hand. 'Come on, I'll walk you down.'

'Me, too,' said Molly, taking Lyssa's hand.

Lyssa had to stop in town and purchase a few additional things she thought she'd need in the Room. They weren't much, but by the time she had gotten to the bottom of the hill, she was wishing she had brought a wagon or cart to haul the bags.

'Let me give you a hand,' said Jeremy behind her.

Lyssa jumped, but for the first time in days, she was glad to see him. 'I like Marnie a lot,' she said, surrendering a bag.

Jeremy smiled slightly. 'What brought that up?'

'I just spent the day playing with her and Molly. We had fun. She seems like someone I'd like to get to know better.'

'She'll be happy to hear that,' said Jeremy laconically. 'She thinks you don't like her.'

'I didn't want to,' Lyssa admitted slowly. 'Sometimes I'm an idiot.'

Jeremy laughed. 'I won't disagree with you, but I think you're too hard on yourself.'

'How goes the reading?' Lyssa asked.

Jeremy grimaced. 'Slowly. This language of yours is impossible.'

'It's not mine,' Lyssa denied. 'I'm just trying to decipher it. The begats were boring when Aunt Burchie was telling them. When they're written, they're terrifying. There are a couple of volumes I've set aside that look interesting. I'm going to tackle them next.'

'What are they about?' asked Jeremy.

'Spinning and weaving,' said Lyssa. 'Cottage craft, I think. Ways to support yourself while getting on your feet on a new planet. Something like that. In this day and age, it doesn't make much sense, but a thousand years ago, it would be perfect. Make money without having to leave home to work. Anyway, it should be interesting, and there's equipment in the Room to try out the techniques if I get bored or hung up on a point I can't visualize.'

'You like to try out stuff like that, too?' asked Jeremy in surprise.

Lyssa nodded. 'If I can't make sense of something, it helps me to try it out in the real world to see how it works. That's how I know for sure.'

'You'll let me know how it goes?' Jeremy held the front gate open for Lyssa and followed her up to the door.

'Yeah,' she said, taking the bag from him. 'Thanks for the help.'

'Sure,' he said, leaving her standing alone on the porch.

Lyssa watched him leave, wondering where the gentle streak fit into the angry young man. At last, she shook her head and went inside. She had a lot of work to do that evening, and too many other things to worry about. When she found a way home for Molly, Jeremy could go home too. Then she wouldn't have to worry about him anymore.

Chapter Six

'You will follow the rules. There are no exceptions.'
The Book of Rules, Chapter Four

Lyssa never made it back to her books that night.

Instead, she found herself playing the Game. She didn't have her leather pouch with her, and felt naked and vulnerable. And there was danger here she had never felt before.

Lyssa wasn't comfortable with the old magic, and hadn't had any time to practice with it unobserved. Since she couldn't guess how much of the House Aunt Burchie had under surveillance, now didn't seem like the time to start.

So she walked the corridors and studied the rooms as she went where the House led her, wondering what was really going on. Tonight, there were no doors to try, and no sense of urgency, but dread settled into Lyssa's bones as she tried to memorize the layout of this portion of the warrens.

Without an overview, she felt the task seemed pointless. She couldn't visualize a whole out of the parts she was being given. There seemed to be no order to the way they were presented, and the magic kept shifting everything around, so that even when she thought she might have been in a particular section before, she couldn't be certain.

There had to be blueprints on file somewhere, and she had to take a look at them. Even if they were inaccurate, they would still provide some sense of the whole.

The night wore on, and Lyssa grew tired, but she moved from room to room, down the endless corridors, making mental notes and searching for any clues that might be hidden from casual view. There was a sense of enormous space here, and the decor, while beautiful, was surprisingly casual. The furniture looked like it was meant to be used, and the atmosphere was pleasant, at odds with the sense of foreboding Lyssa carried with her.

Searching inside herself, Lyssa found the fear was hers, and not any doing of the House. She tried to shake it off, but it clung to her, planted by the Speaker, David Baker. Deep breathing helped a little, but Lyssa didn't enjoy the Game; it was a chore. She was jumping through hoops of someone else's devising, for no apparent purpose. She was walking a pattern of the House's choosing.

She was walking a pattern.

'Oh dear god,' she stopped in her tracks. Was this a spell that had been set up over the years or was it something she was setting in motion only now? 'I can't go on,' she said, again speaking out loud.

You must, said a voice in her head. *Walk on.*

Lyssa shuddered and looked around her, wondering what she could do. To go on meant to continue a pattern whose purpose she couldn't even guess. To go back violated the rules of the Game and would surely put her in grave peril.

But there was no other way to go. Then she thought of the old man in the jungle. Frowning, she shook her head, but she couldn't get his image out of her mind. What good was this doing, she wondered as she sat down in the middle of the hall. He wasn't here, and she couldn't get to him. Even if she could, she wasn't sure she wanted to. He and his strange companion frightened her almost as much as Aunt Burchie.

She had no knife and no light; no means of defending herself. She couldn't go back. She sat with her eyes closed and reached into herself for the old magic, feeling where it had taken root in the core of her being. The hard knot was growing, pulsing with a life of its own and she touched it, wondering what was going to happen. There had to be another way out of here, and she was going to have to find it on her own.

Opening her eyes, Lyssa looked around, hoping to see more than was actually there. The hallway was unchanged, but a door nearby had opened. Rising slowly, she walked toward it.

The room was not much different to the others she had been looking into all night, but she could see more in it than she had in the rest. Much like the Room after she cleaned it, she could see what the magic had been hiding: another way out.

Holding her breath, Lyssa stepped through the door and into a blinding light. Unable to see, she stood, holding the door with both hands.

Shut it, snapped another voice in her head. Her hands obeyed before her mind could respond.

The light dimmed and she quickly realized she was in the church. David stood in front of her with his back turned.

'Oh,' she blurted.

The Speaker turned quickly, startled. 'Lyssa!' He started toward her. 'Are you alright? What are you doing here at this time of night?'

'I came through a door,' she began, not sure exactly how to explain.

He nodded. 'Playing the Game?'

'Yes and no,' she said. 'I just realized I've been walking a pattern. Do you know anything about this?'

David gestured toward a pew and Lyssa moved to sit down. The Speaker sat beside her and took a deep breath.

Finally he exhaled and shook his head. 'How did you figure that out?'

'It's the second time this has happened,' Lyssa explained. 'I had an intuitive leap, rather than actually arriving at the knowledge logically. The first one disappeared almost as soon as I saw it, and I'm still not sure what I understood in that moment. This one stuck with me, though, and brought up a bunch of questions. I guess subconsciously I thought you'd be the best person to ask, so here I am.'

'You finished the Game and came here at this hour?' he asked.

'Uh, no, I didn't finish,' said Lyssa. 'I tapped into the old magic and it brought me here. I've never left the Game before finishing. I thought I'd better find out more about what the House was making me do before I continued.'

'You broke the pattern?' David demanded in disbelief.

'I guess so,' Lyssa stammered, embarrassed by his tone, and beginning to see the implications. 'Yeah, I did.'

The Speaker stood and began pacing in the aisle agitatedly and muttered continually under his breath.

Lyssa sat watching him and turning the fact over in her mind. She had broken the pattern. 'Is this the first time it's happened?' she asked, thoughts churning in her mind.

'Yes,' the Speaker said.

He continued talking, but Lyssa had difficulty following what he said. Searching her memory, she thought about all the times she and Jeremy had played the Game as children. They had always played by the rules. Not to do so was foolish.

'. . . the pattern,' he continued. 'Transition is . . .'

Especially as children, they had understood the necessity of playing by the rules. Games always had a formula, or they just didn't work; they weren't any fun. Always go forward, never back. When the House said hurry, they did. When the House said check every door, they did. They played by the rules. They never influenced the outcome.

'. . . what Millie told you is essentially true,' he finished.

'So what happens now?' she asked faintly.

The Speaker shrugged. 'We're going to have to . . .'

Lyssa couldn't hold on to anything he was saying. She thought about what had happened since coming back. The House had told her where to go, and she had obeyed. The habits of childhood were too firmly ingrained for her to have done otherwise. She had fought against the order to hurry, but never questioned the direction of travel.

'So what you're saying is . . .' she prompted automatically when his voice stopped.

'What I'm saying is . . .'

She had walked the pattern, but she couldn't trace her footsteps in her mind. She needed the overview. She needed to read the rest of the books. She had to find out what she had been doing all these years.

The Speaker stopped in front of Lyssa, jolting her back to the present. 'If I could tell you not to go back to the House and reasonably expect you wouldn't . . .' He rubbed his chin and thought again for a moment. 'But you have to, don't you?'

Lyssa nodded, wondering what he was driving at.

'Watch your back.'

Lyssa sighed. 'What does this all mean?'

'I'm not sure,' David said slowly. 'But the danger has increased and you had better find the answers fast.'

Lyssa made a gesture of frustration. 'How can I do that if all my questions are answered with more questions and cryptic little things like "watch my back"? Has the pattern *ever* been broken before?'

He looked at her oddly, and shook his head. 'No, it hasn't.'

'How many years has the pattern been maintained?' she pressed.

'I couldn't even begin to tell you. Thousands? Hundreds of thousands? The pattern has never been broken since the Families seized power.'

Lyssa shuddered. 'I'm the first? The only one? Why?'

'You'll have to find that out on your own.'

'Do you know?' she demanded, leaning toward him.

'I can only hope,' he said. 'But I can't sway the outcome any more than the others could change the pattern.'

Lyssa made a moue of exasperation and stood up. 'I've got a long walk home,' she said, brushing past him and starting up the aisle.

'Why don't you just go back the way you came?' he asked.

Lyssa turned and stared at him incredulously. 'I've got some thinking to do,' she said, moving away again. She wasn't comfortable experimenting with the old magic in the church or in front of the Speaker. Unsure why, Lyssa went out the front door and into the dark of early morning. Cold and inadequately dressed, she headed through the silent town toward the House.

Lyssa warded the dining room as she entered and nodded for Millie to sit at the table with her.

'Let me tell you what happened last night,' said Lyssa as she sat down.

'I've got a pretty good idea already, if Herself is to be believed,' said Millie.

'What did Aunt Burchie say?' asked Lyssa, taken aback.

Millie shook her head. 'Quite a bit I won't repeat, but she is very disappointed in the way the Game went last night.'

'So she knows,' said Lyssa slowly. This wasn't a big surprise, but she wasn't comforted by the thought that Aunt Burchie was so aware of what happened in the House. 'What does she know?'

'She knows you disappeared in the middle of play,' said Millie cautiously. 'What actually happened?'

'I stopped playing. I stopped walking the pattern. I went to the church.' Lyssa smiled slightly. 'I spoke with David Baker. He was pretty excited, but couldn't tell me anything about the ramifications of what I had done.'

Millie nodded slowly. 'So it's true.'

Lyssa shrugged. 'Can you tell me any more?'

'Well, let's start with you aren't safe in the House anymore.'

'Was I ever?' asked Lyssa.

'As long as you played the Game, you were safe,' said

Millie. 'As long as the transition went smoothly, everything was fine.'

'David said I should watch my back,' Lyssa admitted. 'Should I find another place to stay?'

Millie shook her head. 'There isn't any place that will be safer now that you've broken the pattern. You'll just have to stay on your toes.'

'What about the Room?'

'That would raise your aunt's suspicion even further,' said Millie. 'Avoid the Game for a while and concentrate on what your aunt has brought you here to tell you about the estate.'

'How can I pretend this hasn't happened if she knows and is angry?' asked Lyssa, beginning to feel a little desperate about the whole situation.

Millie shrugged. 'Follow her lead and talk about only the things she brings up. Volunteer nothing and maybe that will be enough. Just be sure to keep yourself warded, and any room you are going to spend time in.'

'Except hers,' mused Lyssa. 'Anything I do there she'll immediately pick up on.'

'That sounds reasonable,' said Millie. 'I wish you'd had more time to read and study before discovering the pattern.'

'I have no idea about the pattern!' exclaimed Lyssa in frustration. 'I have no idea what pattern I've been walking. I don't know when it started, or what it's for. I don't even know what it looks like.'

'The books will help you with that,' said Millie.

Lyssa looked up sharply. 'You seem to know an awful lot about them, given that you insist you've never seen them.'

'You're around a while, you pick things up,' said Millie. 'I haven't ever read them, but I know what's in them. The House is always built according to the pattern. It's necessary for the survival of the Family. Your aunt walked the pattern, and her grandmothers before her. Always women. The uncles don't know this, that's why they keep coming back.'

Lyssa frowned. 'How can they not know?'

Millie raised an eyebrow. 'People often see only what they want to.'

'The Speaker said the pattern had never been broken,' Lyssa tried prompting.

'To my knowledge, that's correct. Not from the very beginning.'

'Has anyone besides my father accessed the old magic?' asked Lyssa. '*How* did my father access the old magic? He's not a woman.'

'The House was still trying to keep up with the changes Burchie was making. She threw everything into chaos for a long time and your father fell through a crack. Literally, as I understand it.' Millie shook her head. 'Anyway, no one else has accessed the old magic during this cycle. It's the old magic that takes us to the meeting place in between cycles. Your father found it accidentally. You found it by design.'

'I'm supposed to take us to the transition site?' Lyssa protested. 'I thought I was supposed to build onto the House again.'

'Eventually we will leave this place,' Millie acknowledged. 'But first, the building. There is a great deal more energy needed before we can return to the meeting place.'

'Energy?' Lyssa echoed.

Millie pursed her lips. 'You had better talk to your aunt. The longer you put it off, the worse it will be.'

Lyssa sighed. Getting it over with was the best thing, but she wasn't looking forward to discovering what her aunt actually knew. She stood up. 'Now is as good a time as any.'

'Breakfast?'

Lyssa shook her head. 'My stomach is in knots. I need to get this handled.' She looked down at Millie. 'Hopefully

I'll see you later,' she said with a bitter twist to her mouth. Warding herself, she left the room.

Lyssa could feel the vibrations as she walked down the hall toward Aunt Burchie's room. The very walls seemed to be humming, and Lyssa felt very much like a fly on a web. The silk strands were telling on her, announcing her coming, and Aunt Burchie lay in wait at the center.

Lyssa shuddered, trying to shake off the imagery, but she could feel the magic singing around her as she approached. It was the only analogy that felt right. The Speaker and Millie were both right: she was in grave danger and there was nowhere safer for her to be.

She thought longingly of the home she had left behind. It wasn't much; a small two-bedroom house on a half-acre of garden Lyssa had landscaped herself. The place was simple, but it suited her needs and the rooms never rearranged themselves. Everything was always as she had left it, since she didn't have a room mate.

Oh, god, she thought. She was as solitary as the rest of her peculiar family.

Lyssa had never thought of it in those terms before. She'd never had a boyfriend, and didn't date much. She worked, and went to school, and got together with friends on the weekends, but she wasn't close to anyone, and this was the first time she had realized it. If she never returned to her little house, would anyone even notice? She had taken leaves of absence from work and school. Eventually, they would try to contact her, but receiving no answer, would give her positions to other people and think no more about it. What if I never get home, she thought as she neared Aunt Burchie's room.

Checking the wards, and shaking off her self-pity, Lyssa squared her shoulders and reached for the knob.

The door swung open before she could touch it. Taking a deep breath, Lyssa entered the room and faced her aunt. 'How are you this morning?' she said, rather too brightly.

She came to the bedside, studying the aged face on the pillow while trying not to appear anxious.

'Sit down,' said Aunt Burchie unceremoniously.

Lyssa pulled the chair over to the bedside and sat. 'Yes, ma'am?'

Aunt Burchie shook her head. 'You make me feel ancient sometimes,' she said.

Lyssa could feel the tension in the room ease. 'I'm sorry.'

Aunt Burchie waved her hand dismissively. 'It's not something you do on purpose,' she said. 'I just look at you and hear the word "ma'am" and it makes me cringe. It doesn't feel like so very long ago I saw your face when I looked in my mirror.'

'I don't think I've ever seen pictures of you at my age,' said Lyssa. 'Do I look like you?'

The old woman grinned. 'I like to think I was that pretty.'

Lyssa looked down at her hands, folded in her lap. 'I'm considered quite plain, actually.'

'Nonsense,' said Aunt Burchie. 'You just don't know how to flirt. That makes all the difference.'

Lyssa grinned now, looking back at her aunt. 'That's your answer to everything, isn't it?'

'If the shoe fits, darling. Now, are you ready to tell me about last night?'

The atmosphere in the room remained the same, but Lyssa could feel her guard rise instantly. She had let the banter lull her. What in the world could she say about what had happened? 'What do you want to know?' she asked carefully.

'Well, you played the Game, didn't you?' Aunt Burchie asked impatiently.

Lyssa nodded.

'Then tell me where you went. What did the halls and rooms look like? Where did you end up? Did Jeremy play with you?'

She seemed genuinely not to know the answer to the last

question. Lyssa thought for a long moment. There were holes in the web. Aunt Burchie quizzed her on the Game because she couldn't go into the warrens herself and keep up with the changes in the House.

She couldn't see everything.

This was good to know, but since Lyssa had no idea what parts of the House Aunt Burchie had no knowledge of, it didn't really help her much. All the old woman knew was that Lyssa had been walking the pattern and then stopped. She knew the pattern had been broken, but not where or how. The web wasn't fixed in that place, and Aunt Burchie was going to have to find a way to make Lyssa finish the job.

As long as that possibility remained, Lyssa felt she would be safe. 'No, Jeremy wasn't there last night,' she said, trying to edit as she spoke. 'This portion of the warrens seemed more modern than the others I have been through. Things looked like they would be used by people today, instead of the more formal, antiquated trappings of the rest of the House. The rooms were large and the furniture looked like it was meant to be sat on, not just admired.'

'Did you look in any of the closets?' asked Aunt Burchie.

Lyssa shook her head. 'I didn't even think to.'

'You used to love playing in the closets,' the old woman chuckled.

'It made me feel closer to the people who lived in the rooms I was playing in,' Lyssa admitted.

'Maybe you should go back and do that,' Aunt Burchie suggested casually. 'It may give you a clearer picture of what they were like.'

Lyssa shrugged noncommittally. 'You know the House,' she said. 'You have no say in where you go.'

'That's often the case.'

'Of course, it couldn't hurt to try,' Lyssa offered.

'Try,' Aunt Burchie repeated. 'Now tell me about the rest of the area.'

* * *

City Hall only had plans on file for the portion of the House Lyssa had grown up in. There was no record of any renovation, remodelling or extension to any existing structure, and the clerk couldn't imagine why Lyssa would be searching for other buildings on the property.

'This is what we have,' was all he said. 'I'm sorry we couldn't be more help.'

'Thank you,' said Lyssa. She knew where she had to go next.

'Is it that time already?' asked the old man as Lyssa entered the office.

She blinked and focused on him again. He was completely unprepossessing, and she was sure she had never seen him before, but he knew who she was, and obviously thought it was time to build again.

'I hadn't heard that old Burchie had died, but that must be the reason you're here?' He stood up and came out from behind the desk, hand outstretched.

Lyssa shook his hand and her head. 'Aunt Burchie is still alive,' she said. 'I was hoping you could help me with another matter.'

He gestured to the chair beside his desk and resumed his own. 'How can I help you?'

She studied him again, noting the pale face and thin hair. His glasses seemed to be his most prominent feature. 'I was hoping you might have blueprints of the House. I'd like to see them.'

'Certainly!' He jumped up and went to a file cabinet. Rifling through the papers, he finally produced a set that he brought over to where Lyssa sat. 'Here,' he said, spreading them out on his desktop.

'These are of the portion Aunt Burchie lives in,' said Lyssa. There was a sinking feeling in her gut as she looked at the same papers the clerk at City Hall had shown her.

'Portion?' the old man asked.

'Are you Mr Bell?' asked Lyssa.

'Yes, yes, I am,' he said.

'Then you know exactly what I'm talking about,' Lyssa said, glaring at him, willing him to give her what she wanted.

He nodded slowly. 'You don't think there are any other plans, do you?'

'There must be!' Lyssa exclaimed impatiently. 'You did all the building. You must have drawn up plans for the workers to follow. Where are those plans?'

Mr Bell shook his head. 'Even if those plans still existed, don't you think the House has reconstructed itself to the point where they wouldn't have any accurate information anyway?'

'I just want an overview,' Lyssa objected. 'I only want an idea of what I'm dealing with.'

Mr Bell shook his head again. 'This isn't the place to find those answers.'

Lyssa sighed. 'Can you tell me where is?'

'No.'

She stood up. 'This is all the help you can be?'

'Until Burchie dies and it's time to build; then you come to me and I can help. Until then, you're on your own.' Mr Bell stood up and gathered the papers together.

Lyssa returned to the street. As the door closed behind her, she turned and started walking.

'Any joy?' asked Jeremy.

'No,' said Lyssa glumly, not even caring that he must have been following her. 'No joy, and no ideas. I broke the pattern last night, and Aunt Burchie is pretty angry, but since I can't find any plans on the warrens, I don't know what pattern I was walking, or how to change it to do what I want it to.'

'What do you mean?' asked Jeremy. 'What's walking the pattern?'

'The Game,' said Lyssa. 'It was all about walking the pattern. The House was using us to work a spell by having us trace a pattern with our footsteps. Either that, or Aunt

Burchie was doing it. I'm not sure which, but the important thing is that, last night, I broke the pattern. The spell has been interrupted.'

'Wouldn't something like that terminate it?' asked Jeremy, catching on quickly. 'Wouldn't you have to start again from the beginning?'

Lyssa shrugged. 'Aunt Burchie really wants me to go back to that part of the House again, so I figured I only have to redo that part in order for everything to start working again.'

'Are you going to go back?' Jeremy asked.

His tone was casual, but Lyssa could feel the tension in his body as he walked beside her. '*Can* I go back? I don't know how much control I have over any of this. It may be that I have to, but until I find out what the pattern is, I don't think I want to keep weaving spells.'

'We have to go back to the jungle,' said Jeremy.

Lyssa nodded. 'I think you're right. I really want you to be there. Those two scare me.'

Jeremy laughed briefly. 'I don't find them very reassuring myself. Are we walking a pattern when we explore the town?'

Lyssa stopped short and looked up at him. 'I have no idea. I never even thought about it.' She resumed walking. 'Probably not, because we determine where we go, but even then, I couldn't say for sure.'

'Well, we seem to have enough to worry about for now, so why don't we just make a date to go into the warrens tonight and leave the rest of it for later?'

'A date,' Lyssa echoed. She knew that wasn't what he meant, but it was still nice to hear. 'Shall we go see Molly and Marnie?'

'Sounds like a plan.'

Night came all too quickly, and Lyssa found herself standing next to Jeremy, preparing to enter the warrens, hoping to find the jungle but terrified of finding the two people inhabiting it. She took a deep breath and turned the knob. 'Here we go again.'

'Can you take us there?' asked Jeremy as they stepped through the closet in the bedroom Lyssa had occupied as a girl, and started down the hallway to the stairs.

Lyssa put wards around them. 'I can try, but let's at least get to the atrium. I feel like Aunt Burchie is watching us in here.'

'It won't be any different there,' Jeremy objected.

'I know,' said Lyssa. 'But it feels like it would be safer.'

'Then that's what we'll do.'

Lyssa frowned, wondering why Jeremy was being so cooperative. She felt guilty being suspicious, but she was glad not to be arguing with him right now. Once the door to the stairway was shut and they stood in the teak and marble atrium, Lyssa stopped and closed her eyes. Reaching into the core of old magic, she took Jeremy by the hand and willed a doorway to take them to the jungle.

'Wow,' said Jeremy beside her.

Lyssa opened her eyes. 'Takes some getting used to. What happens if we get lost?'

Jeremy laughed. 'What difference does it make when you have that trick to get us where you want us to go? Even if we get lost, we can still get out.'

'You think the magic works in there?' she nodded toward the jungle. They stood in the room outside, where they had slept the night of the awful dreams.

'It works in the House. The jungle is part of the House,' said Jeremy impatiently.

'Is it?' asked Lyssa.

'Don't you remember the floorboards?'

'Well, I guess we take our chances,' said Lyssa, starting forward. 'Here's hoping.'

Jeremy followed her into the foliage, and they began their search for the old man and his peculiar companion.

* * *

'We should have brought machetes,' Lyssa gasped as they cut their way through the dense tropical growth with the knives from their leather pouches. The blades had grown dull quickly, but they were still better than nothing. There were no paths to be found, and they had been slogging through the jungle for hours, trying to find the elusive pair who lived here.

'You'd think they'd need a way to get around in here,' Jeremy complained, wiping sweat from his eyes. 'When did it get so hot?'

'About the time we started exerting ourselves?' Lyssa suggested. 'Maybe they don't travel. Maybe they have a place they stay and that's it.'

'Could be,' said Jeremy, stopping for a moment. 'Can you try again to locate them using the old magic?'

Lyssa sighed impatiently. 'I've tried twice already.'

'Third time's the charm?' he grinned engagingly.

Lyssa twisted her mouth and shrugged. 'This is the last time I try,' she warned.

It was no use. The magic was there, but the strange duo were not. 'They either don't want to be found, or they want us to have to work for it.'

'Which is it?' asked Jeremy.

'If I knew they didn't want to be found, don't you think I'd have gotten us out of here by now?' Lyssa demanded. 'I'm not enjoying this either. I could be asleep right now, and . . .'

'That's it!' Jeremy exclaimed, interrupting.

'What?' asked Lyssa, annoyed.

'The last time we found them was in our sleep,' he said excitedly. 'Maybe what we need to do is dream.'

'They don't exist on this plane?' Lyssa suggested.

'What gave you that idea?' asked Jeremy.

'When I look for them, they're not here.'

Jeremy shook his head. 'I don't think so,' he said slowly. 'I think maybe this is one of the places your aunt has access to.'

Lyssa glanced around involuntarily and shuddered. She'd be a lot happier when this was over.

'Do you want to try it?' Jeremy pressed.

'What?' asked Lyssa, still searching the jungle for signs of Aunt Burchie.

'Sleeping?' Jeremy asked. 'Dreaming?'

'I guess it couldn't hurt to try. Do you want to make a place here to lie down, or do you want to go back to the room just outside?' They both studied the area around them and then looked at each other.

'Let's go back,' they said in unison. Then they laughed.

Lyssa reached for the old magic for the fifth time that night, and took them to the room where they had first made contact with the odd pair from the jungle. Somewhat self-consciously, they lay down on separate couches, but they were both tired and fell asleep almost immediately. Once asleep, they began to dream.

This time the path through the jungle was clear, and Jeremy and Lyssa had no trouble following it.

'Does this mean we'll be welcome?' Lyssa wondered out loud.

'At least we won't actually get killed,' said Jeremy fatalistically.

'How do you know that?' Lyssa laughed. 'Have you ever been killed in a dream?'

'You can't be killed in a dream,' Jeremy scoffed.

'Don't be so sure,' said a raspy voice.

Jeremy and Lyssa stopped short and looked around. They could see nothing through the riot of green surrounding them.

'Hello?' Lyssa asked timidly, remembering the wickedly-curved knife.

The Keeper emerged from the undergrowth and stood before them. His companion was nowhere to be seen. 'Dreams can kill, and no place is safe in this House.' He gestured for them to keep walking.

'Where are we going?' asked Jeremy.

Silence met his question, and they walked on for some time before reaching a clearing. The odd, red-haired child awaited them. 'Be seated,' he squeaked.

Lyssa and Jeremy sat down in the dirt, and looked expectantly at their hosts.

'You have questions?' asked the old man finally.

'May we speak freely here, or shall I ward the clearing?' asked Lyssa.

The old man frowned slightly. 'It couldn't hurt. This place is as safe as I could make it. I don't think the old woman can see in here, but you never know just what she has access to.'

Lyssa placed the protective barrier around them. 'I think she only has knowledge of the places she's been that have remained unchanged, and the places I have described to her after I played the Game,' she said. 'I didn't know why she was asking me about the details of where I'd been until recently.'

The old man nodded. 'I felt a tear in the web. Was that you?'

'I broke the pattern,' said Lyssa. 'Can you tell me anything about what the pattern is, and what spell it's weaving?'

The old man shook his head. 'The pattern is too complex to explain. It is centuries in the making, guided by the intelligence of the House, and walked by many individuals over the years. You are right about your aunt, though. The less she knows about the areas she doesn't have access to, the safer you will be.'

'Keeping that information from her won't be easy,' said Lyssa. 'She knows about the pattern, but hasn't admitted it to me yet. She wants me to go back to that area again and pick up where I left off.'

'Of course,' said the old man impatiently. 'The transition can't be completed until the pattern is. Each transition is accomplished after the pattern is walked. Each matriarch is responsible for walking a portion of the pattern, but Burchie was too busy changing things around to complete her part of the spell. She needs you to do it for her. She won't die until that happens, and you can't take over until she dies. When you take over, you begin walking the final part of the pattern and when you finish, the spell will be cast. Then transition will occur.'

'You know that?' Lyssa asked, surprised.

'There is very little I don't know,' said the Keeper smugly. 'I, too, have my network and my successor.'

'Your companion?' asked Jeremy.

The Keeper shook his head. 'You.'

'No!' Jeremy stumbled to his feet. 'I was brought here for Lyssa,' he said, hands in front of him as if to ward off something.

'To balance the power,' the old man agreed. 'Sit down. This won't take place for a while yet, and you will quickly learn what you need to know. Hers is the difficult task,' he nodded at Lyssa.

'How is that?' she asked.

'You've broken the pattern. You have to decide if you are going to resume and complete the spell, or weave a different one. If you choose another path, you must decide where you want it to go. These aren't easy choices. It would have been simpler if you had stuck to the rules, but it may be better if you follow your own mind.'

Lyssa laughed shortly. 'My own mind is so confused, I don't even know where to start sorting it out. How can I make a wise decision when I have so little information?'

'Educate yourself,' he said. 'You have the means already. Just finish your research and ask the right questions of the right people.'

'Sure, no big deal,' said Lyssa sarcastically.

The Keeper chuckled. 'It only seems like it is. Now,' he stood up. 'It's time for you to leave.' His companion stood as well, leaving Lyssa the only one sitting.

Reluctantly, she rose and faced Jeremy. 'I'm going to need your help.'

The old man nodded approvingly. 'This is a good start. Now get out of here.'

Lyssa turned and headed back the way they had come. She could hear Jeremy behind her, and was relieved. She had been afraid since the old man's revelation that Jeremy would further close himself off from her. She realized as she walked, that she had been afraid he might stay, leaving her completely alone in this strange quest for information.

After a time she asked, 'Are you okay?' but Jeremy said nothing.

When she awoke, Jeremy was still asleep, so Lyssa helped herself to some fruit and sat waiting for him to wake up.

She was being chased.

She ran across the long balcony overlooking the dark hall. There were no lights on, and only the gibbous moon to illuminate her flight.

There should be no light here at all, she thought in passing. The stairs were before her, and she sped down them, looking over her shoulder to see if she could catch a glimpse of who was behind her.

No one was there. It felt like a panic manufactured by the House, but she knew it wasn't. Someone was in the darkness behind her, and the chase was quite real. There was a door near the base of the stairs.

Her breath came in gasps, and she desperately tried to quiet down so as not to give away her hiding place. Her heart pounded so loudly in her ears, she was certain the sound filled the room. There were doors at intervals along the wall stretching away from her, and any one of them would do once she was certain her ruse had worked, but her pursuer paused on the stairs for what seemed an eternity.

Then she heard the footsteps on the stairs above her. Unexpectedly, she started violently. They were right beside her ear, as if the person following her was right next to her under the stairs. Then she realized what had happened, and hoped she hadn't made a noise that would betray her location. By now she was holding her breath.

The shadowy figure finally walked through the door at the foot of the stairs.

She waited until the footsteps faded before going to another door and stepping through it. The long corridor beyond led to stairs that went back up, so she mounted them and began to climb.

At each landing, the stair narrowed until there was scarcely room to step, and still she climbed, coming at last to a door. There was nowhere else to go, so she opened it.

The garret was lit only slightly more than the ballroom she had come from, but after the darkness of the stairs, it felt like she had come out into broad daylight.

The maze of rooms looked familiar, but she couldn't place it. Somewhere here was her pursuer. She moved carefully, using the furniture as cover, crouched on hands and knees in order to move more surreptitiously through the rooms.

How had the person chasing her found her here? she wondered as she crept from behind a couch. She caught a flicker of movement out of the corner of her eye and froze, searching the area. Her heart was in her throat as she waited, crouched against the couch, hoping her own movement hadn't been detected.

She stood up and sprinted for the door, getting through it only moments before the person she was trying to evade. She still had no idea who it was chasing her, only that if caught, she was as good as dead.

She slammed the door and ran as fast as she had ever run before, passing doors in the hallway that she probably should have taken, but stopping was more than she could manage right now. Her only goal was to put as much distance between her and her follower as possible.

Finally, a door loomed in front of her, and the end of the hall. She found a large kitchen beyond. The tile floor was slick and she felt like a poodle scrambling for traction as she rounded the corner of the long counter and headed toward the pantry. There had to be a way out.

The dumbwaiter beckoned as she looked wildly around the room. Shelves lined the dead-end, but promised a way her pursuer might not think of.

Glancing over her shoulder, she climbed into the dumbwaiter and shut the door. The platform on which she sat moved smoothly down into the depths of the warrens and she wondered where she would finally emerge.

Lyssa sat up with a gasp and realized she had fallen asleep again, slumped against a corner of the couch. She had a wicked crick in her neck and her heart was beating hard and fast in her chest.

Jeremy stirred on the couch nearby.

Lyssa breathed deeply several times, standing to stretch and pull herself together before he awoke and started asking questions. She didn't think she was prepared to share this dream with anyone just yet. She readjusted her clothing and sat back down before he opened his eyes and saw her.

'Have you been awake long?' he asked, voice thick with sleep.

Lyssa shook her head. 'I woke up earlier, but I fell back to sleep while I was waiting for you. I left you some fruit,' she gestured to the small pile she had placed by him after her own meal.

'Thanks,' Jeremy said briefly. 'I think we should go outside.'

Lyssa nodded. It was probably the safest place to talk. 'When you finish.'

'Do you want any more?'

'No,' she said, thinking of her dream and trying not to shudder.

'Then why don't I just take these with me,' Jeremy suggested, starting to gather up the fruit.

'No,' Lyssa said, a little too quickly. Jeremy gave her a funny look, but she waved him off. 'We aren't in that big a hurry,' she said. She didn't want him to see how shaken up by the dream she was.

At last Jeremy stood. 'Let's go,' he said.

Lyssa joined him and transferred them both outside the House, onto the road leading down the hill into town. It was still dark out, but she had no idea what time it was. 'Shall we walk?' she asked, pointing. The road was dimly lit by a gibbous moon. Lyssa shuddered, remembering.

'Are you okay?' asked Jeremy, noticing.

'It's a little chilly,' she said, wrapping her arms around herself. 'I'll be okay once we're moving.'

'I guess we'd better step up the reading,' Jeremy said as they walked down the hill.

Lyssa nodded. 'There seems to be so much to do and so little time in which to do it.'

'What gives you that idea?' Jeremy wanted to know.

Shaking her head, Lyssa could only say, 'I just feel like we don't have much time.'

'Hmm,' he said. 'I guess you know more about this than I do.'

'Maybe,' she responded. 'What did you make of our conversation in the jungle?'

Jeremy shook his head. 'Either the old man is crazy, or things are stranger than we thought.'

'Probably both,' said Lyssa fatalistically. 'I was surprised by what he had to say about you.'

'I am *not* turning into a crazy old man in that jungle!' Jeremy said vehemently.

'Well, I'm not going to turn into Aunt Burchie, either,' said Lyssa hotly. 'Somewhere in those books there has to be an answer about the patterns and what we have to do to prevent this.'

178

'I don't know how much help I'm going to be with that, either,' said Jeremy, somewhat subdued. 'I can't seem to get a real grip on the language.'

'You just don't have the magic to help you,' said Lyssa, trying to be encouraging.

Jeremy shook his head. 'It's not that. I've never been good with other languages anyway, but this one just doesn't seem to want me to learn it.'

'So it'll take a little more time,' she said. 'Every little bit helps, and it's your mystery to solve as well as mine. I've never known you to quit.'

'I'm not talking about quitting,' he said, raising his voice in frustration. 'I've been working on that damned book since you gave it to me, and I've only gotten a few pages translated. I just can't seem to make any headway on it!'

'How long have you been trying?' Lyssa asked. The walk was beginning to help warm her up, but she still shivered in the cool night air.

'Since you gave it to me,' he repeated impatiently.

'I mean hours per day,' she said. 'How much time have you been putting in on it?'

Jeremy shrugged. 'I guess an hour or so.' They walked in silence for a moment. 'I don't *have* much time!' he protested.

'And the less you put into it, the less you get out,' Lyssa said sarcastically. 'I put hours into it in one evening alone. I slept, ate and breathed it for a couple of days before things suddenly made sense. Yes, some of it was magic, but the rest was plain hard work. You have to be willing to make the same effort.' She thought about the time he spent with Marnie, and wondered what occupied the rest of his days. She certainly hadn't seen much of him lately. She had assumed he was spending time translating the book she had given him. 'Where do you keep it, anyway?'

'There's a tree near where we started reading it together. There's a hole under the roots. I wrapped it in cloth and stashed it there.'

Lyssa nodded approvingly, relieved that he was taking her warning seriously and keeping the book out of the House. 'Do you want me to give you any more help with the language?'

'Yeah, that would be good. When?'

'Sometime today, I guess.' Lyssa thought about it. 'I'm not sure when I'll have time, but I'll definitely make some.'

'So I just stay at your beck and call?' he demanded.

Lyssa grimaced. 'Look, it was bad enough to break the pattern the other night. Last night, I took us to the jungle instead of going back to the place Aunt Burchie wants me to do over. I don't know how angry she's going to be or how much trouble I'm going to be in. I don't know how much time I'm going to have to spend with her trying to cover myself. I know I won't be able to see Molly again and I already feel guilty about that. Do you think you could manage to cut me a little slack and maybe spend some of the time waiting for me reading the book?'

'I guess,' he said ungraciously.

Lyssa wanted to slap him, but resisted the impulse. 'Thank you,' she said instead. 'Do you want to keep walking, or shall we go home and try to get some sleep?'

'Well, since the stores are closed, you won't be able to do much shopping,' Jeremy said slowly, teasing.

'Home it is,' said Lyssa, pulling a U-turn and starting back up the hill. Home didn't seem like the right term to use, referring to the House. Looking up, it seemed to crouch on the hilltop, menacing and aware. Lyssa shuddered.

'I know,' said Jeremy, putting his arm around her. 'I've felt that way all my life, even though I've never really lived anywhere else.'

'I never saw it that way before,' she said. 'Is that how the town sees it?'

Jeremy shook his head. 'I think you have to know some of what goes on inside to understand.'

'The Others don't talk?'

'To whom?' he wanted to know. 'Who would believe us? And even if they did, what could be done about it? No, the Others don't talk.'

When they reached Jeremy's turn-off, the Others' entrance to the House, Lyssa stopped. Jeremy reluctantly stopped with her. 'Are you sure you'll be okay?' he asked. 'Do you want me to come up with you?' He didn't let go of her shoulders, still holding her against the chill of the night.

Lyssa nodded. 'I'll be fine,' she said. 'Thanks.' Still, she didn't move, feeling safe in his arms for the first time. It was impossible to reconcile his current mood with the anger she usually felt from him.

'Well, good night,' he said.

'Good night.' Lyssa finally moved to disengage. 'I'll see you in the morning.' She walked up the hill to the front door, afraid to look back, knowing Jeremy was still watching her.

She fell into bed without bothering to undress and slept dreamless the rest of the night.

The House was in an uproar when she awoke in the morning.

It wasn't sound that roused her. There were too few people for that. Aunt Burchie wasn't yelling, and no one was throwing things.

Lyssa lay for a while, trying to sort out just what was jangling on her raw nerves. Yes, Aunt Burchie was furious. Lyssa could feel that vibrating through the air, but it was the House itself that felt angry.

No. Not angry, betrayed. Lyssa was supposed to weave the spells just as her ancestors had. This was supposed to be another orderly transition, only things were going wrong. It began with Aunt Burchie breaking the rules, and her father slipping into places he shouldn't have been. Now Lyssa had broken the pattern.

The House had lost control.

'Oh, god,' Lyssa sat bolt upright. 'Oh, my god.' She ran to the closet and through the back panel. She had better do some serious reading. There was even less time than she had thought.

The Room was the only peaceful place in the House, as far as Lyssa could tell. The lamp was lit, and the air was clear. The vibrations affecting the rest of the warrens, and Aunt Burchie's quarters, were conspicuously absent here. It was a relief to Lyssa to step through the cupboard and shut the door on the chaos she woke up to. She went immediately to the cache of books she'd left on the table and took the first one off the stack. Sitting in one of the rocking chairs, Lyssa opened the cover and settled in to read.

By mid-morning, the adrenaline had worn off and Lyssa stopped long enough to eat before returning to the book. By mid-afternoon, she had finished. She returned to her bedroom, and ran to the kitchen for a couple of apples.

Millie stood at the sink. 'Miss?' she asked, looking searchingly at Lyssa.

Lyssa shook her head and ran to the front door, knowing she would find Jeremy outside near the tree where he was hiding the book.

He looked angry and frustrated. 'Where have you been?' he demanded as she handed him an apple and sat down.

'Reading,' she said briefly. 'How are you doing with this?' She bit into her apple and nodded at the book he held.

'It's slow going, but I think I'm starting to make progress,' he admitted.

'Good. What can I help you with?'

'Calming down the Others?' he suggested, only a little facetiously.

'How are they doing?' she asked, feeling a sudden stab of guilt. She hadn't even considered the impact on them.

'Not great,' said Jeremy. 'Several of them were missing this morning. They are even more helpless and afraid than they were before. I couldn't tell them anything about last night, since I figure your aunt has their quarters pretty well bugged.'

Lyssa nodded. 'Good assumption. At this point, I don't think there's anything reassuring we *can* say. Especially after what I read this morning.'

Jeremy looked at Lyssa sharply.

Lyssa looked back unhappily. 'The Others don't go home,' she said slowly. 'Their souls, their emotions are sucked out of them, and distilled. The energy this creates is what powers the whole thing; the House, the magic, the transitions, all of it. From one world to the next, this has been going on for millennia, and this world is just one more in the chain.'

She paused a moment as Jeremy absorbed the information. 'I think that's why Aunt Burchie changed the rules and started gathering people who had families they longed to return to: more emotion, deeper feelings, greater power.'

'This is sick,' whispered Jeremy. He had turned pale, and looked like he might throw up. 'All those years . . . all those people I grew up with . . . my mother?'

Lyssa nodded miserably.

'Dear god,' he murmured. 'You're right. There is nothing we can tell them.' His head jerked up and he stared at Lyssa. 'And you're Family.'

She nodded.

'Are you learning how to do this?' he brandished the book.

'No,' she denied. 'I'm as sickened by this as you are. I think that's why I've been able to break the pattern. I've always known there was something wrong here.'

'And there's even less time than you thought.'

'What are we going to do?' asked Lyssa, nodding.

'Study,' said Jeremy with grim determination.

'I think it's time you saw the Room.' Lyssa's eyes widened. She couldn't believe she'd said that, and it was certainly not possible to take it back. It was the only place the two of them would be safe.

He stood up and held out his hand to her. 'Now,' he said, pulling her to her feet.

Lyssa took the book from him and slipped it under her shirt. She warded them both, and started to run back to the House.

'Can't you just take us there?' Jeremy asked, resisting.

'No!' She grabbed his hand and pulled. 'There's a price for using the magic, and I don't know what it is. Quickly!' she cried, pulling Jeremy along behind her.

Only once the cupboard door was shut behind them did she feel she could breathe again. 'We have to find another way in and out of here,' she gasped. 'We can't keep risking going through Aunt Burchie's rooms to get outside.'

'Can we dig through the dirt outside the door?' Jeremy gestured.

'In some fashion, I guess we'll have to,' said Lyssa. 'In the meantime, let's find out what we're up against.' She gestured at the books on the table with her free hand and realized she still held Jeremy's hand tightly in the other.

Gently he pulled her to him and enveloped her in his arms. 'We'll find a way,' he murmured into her dark auburn hair.

Lyssa surrendered herself to his embrace, feeling safe and protected, knowing it was only an illusion. Finally, taking a deep breath, she pulled away. 'Come on,' she exhaled. 'We've got a lot of work to do.'

With a sigh, Jeremy followed her to the table and sat down. 'I'll just ask questions as they come up. We should get more done that way.'

Lyssa handed him back the book he'd been working on and nodded. She sat and reached for another volume. 'Here's what I've already read,' she said, pointing to two other books off to the side. 'I don't think we have the time or the luxury of each of us reading all of the books. We'll have to summarize for each other.'

'I agree,' said Jeremy, opening his book.

They both began to read.

* * *

184

'Lyssa.' Jeremy shook her gently by the shoulder. 'Lyssa, why don't you go lie down?'

Lyssa came to with a start, wondering fuzzily where she was. Her face hurt and she had a terrible crick in her neck and back. 'Huh?' She pushed herself into a sitting position and realized she had fallen asleep on her book. She looked around the Room, then focused on Jeremy. 'What?'

'You need to sleep,' he said. 'Go lie down.'

'What about you?'

Jeremy laughed. 'If I fall asleep, the stuff I've been reading will give me nightmares. I'm better off staying awake.'

Lyssa stood up. 'I know what you mean,' she said, stretching. She could feel her vertebrae popping back into place. 'But you're right. I need some rest.' She moved to the bed and lay down. 'Just shove me over if you change your mind,' she mumbled, closing her eyes. She was instantly asleep again, but her dreams kept her from peace. Sometime later, she was aware of Jeremy beside her.

When she woke up, Lyssa was careful not to disturb him as she got out of bed. She grabbed breakfast and went back to work on the book that had put her to sleep. She had been right about cottage industry as a means to support the Family until it could better establish itself on each new world. The loom had been the most practical method this last time, but there were many possibilities outlined in the volume she was working on, and suggestions for finding other ways depending on the primary culture of the new world.

She shuddered and glanced up at the stack of finished books. Jeremy had finished the first one and had moved on to the next. Lyssa was impressed by his progress and tenacity. He'd had few questions as they worked, and seemed to pick up speed as he became more familiar with the language. Lyssa felt he was selling himself short saying he had no aptitude, but it was clear she would be doing the bulk of the work. She didn't mind, but the work was so tedious. Most of the books seemed to deal with Family history, or setting up housekeeping. Each transition took the members to different worlds, where the cycle began all over again.

Every thousand years. There seemed no point to it. At least, there was no point Lyssa had been able to find. The stack of unread books was slowly diminishing, but she could find no purpose for the cycles. With a sigh, Lyssa returned to her work.

'No!' Jeremy shouted. He was wrestling with the covers, tossing pillows on the floor. 'No, that can't be true!'

Lyssa was up and across the Room in a moment. 'Jeremy,' she said, putting a hand on his shoulder.

He flailed his arms and backhanded her in the mouth. 'We've got to make it stop!' he mumbled, rolling away from her.

'Jeremy,' Lyssa tried again, reaching for him and ducking at the same time. She grabbed his shoulder and shook him. 'Jeremy, wake up, you're having a nightmare!'

A pillow sailed over her head and knocked the lamp on the table over. Glass shattered and oil pooled on the floor. Lyssa sighed. 'Jeremy!' She shook him harder.

He sat straight up, looking wildly around, his eyes still focused on his dream. 'Lyssa?'

She could hear the panic in his voice. 'I'm right here,' she said, trying to sound reassuring. 'It was a dream. You were having a nightmare.'

He shook his head. 'It was no dream.'

'Well, whatever it was happened in your sleep. Right now we have other work to do,' she said, hoping practicality would jolt him out of the state he was in.

He looked at her as if seeing her for the first time. 'What happened to your mouth?' he asked.

Lyssa laughed shortly. 'Your aim is as good asleep as it is awake.'

Jeremy reached out and touched her lip gently. 'I'm sorry,' he said.

When he drew his hand away, Lyssa could see blood on his fingertip. She put her own hand to her mouth and was surprised by how much it hurt. 'It'll heal,' she said. 'Do you want something to eat?'

'Just let me clean up here a little,' Jeremy said, climbing out of bed. 'Why don't you get back to your book?'

'Are you sure you're okay?' Lyssa asked, rising to her feet.

Jeremy snorted. 'You're the one who's hurt.'

'I'll get over it,' she said. 'You're the one who had the nightmare.'

He laughed. 'I'll get over it.' He started straightening the sheets and quilts. 'I know where the kitchen cupboards are,' he looked around. 'I'll even clean up the lamp. How's that?'

Lyssa grinned. 'You're hired.' She returned to the kitchen table to resume her work. Watching Jeremy clean up, she thought if they could just maintain their sense of humor, they might make it through this. Then she looked at the door and wondered how they were going to get out. 'If we dig,' she said, 'there's no place to put the dirt.'

Jeremy looked at her quizzically.

'The entrance,' Lyssa nodded at the door. 'We don't know how much dirt there is between us and the outside.'

'What about the old magic?'

'We can get back outside that way, and dig from there, I guess,' she said, feeling a little silly for not having thought of it. 'But I don't think I should be using it too much.'

'Why?' Jeremy asked.

Lyssa shrugged. 'Just a hunch, but I get the feeling I'm not supposed to have access to it yet. Using it too much will do damage in the long run.'

'To what?'

'To whom, I think,' she said. 'To me, and to whomever is supposed to be using it instead.'

'Well, you know more about it than I do,' Jeremy said. 'But I don't think digging from inside is the best approach.'

Lyssa grinned. 'We'll think about it.' She nodded at the stack of books still confronting them. 'We've got some time before it's an issue.'

Jeremy groaned. 'We have to stay here until we finish?'

'I want to know what I'm up against before I stick my nose back out there,' she said.

Jeremy nodded, resigned. 'What do I use to clean up the oil?' he asked.

Chapter Seven

'Balance is a circular thing. When it is time for transition, the spell will have come full circle, and the Family will be back where it started.'

The Way Things Are, Chapter Ten

There was no light in the Room, beyond the lamp which burned constantly without additional fuel. Day and night had no meaning. Jeremy and Lyssa read, ate and slept, barely talking, vaguely aware of the passage of time. The issue of leaving the Room remained unaddressed as long as there were books still to be read.

The twenty or so volumes Lyssa had found had seemed like such a daunting task until they became familiar with the language. Once they began to read, it seemed impossible.

'Where does the eagle imagery fit in from those dreams we had as children?' Jeremy asked, during one of the few breaks they took during this time. He sat back in his chair, rubbing his eyes.

Lyssa squirmed on her seat, trying to find a comfortable position. 'I hadn't even thought about that,' she said, giving up and going over to the bed to lie down for a minute. 'It wasn't an active part of the dream. Just a huge eye glaring through the window from outside while the organ with bloody keys played.'

'The organ music drew us into the room, the eagle drove us from it.' Jeremy yawned and stood up to stretch.

'All in a fairly short time,' said Lyssa. 'Did he represent the House, or Aunt Burchie?'

'What makes you think it was a he?' asked Jeremy.

'I don't know,' said Lyssa through a yawn. 'That's just

always how it seemed. I guess I never really did think about it.'

'Burchie seems more spiderish in her representation,' said Jeremy. 'Maybe the eagle was the House.'

'But why would we be rushed from a room we had just been lured into?' Lyssa asked sleepily.

'Think about it,' said Jeremy, going over and sitting on the bed beside Lyssa. 'What did the room look like?'

'Pretty barren,' Lyssa responded, sitting up and trying to concentrate on a dream that was more than a decade old. 'I walked through the door and directly opposite it was the open window. A tremendous wind was blowing through it, gusting tattered curtains. The organ stood on the right wall, and an open closet was set into the left; the door was half-off. The lath and plaster could be seen through holes in the walls, and the floor was wood, slivered and splintery. The ceiling never really registered. The room was empty other than that.'

Jeremy nodded. 'What music was playing on the organ?'

Lyssa shook her head. 'I dream in color, with no sound. I never actually heard the music, I only knew that there *was* some. I could see the keys moving, like on a player-piano, but there was no sound. What did you hear?'

'Nothing,' Jeremy said softly. 'I dream in color, with no sound.'

'Why would an auditory cue be used on two people who couldn't hear it?' Lyssa leaned forward.

'Maybe it was just a distraction,' suggested Jeremy.

'There was something else we were supposed to see that the House didn't want us noticing?' Lyssa could feel the excitement rising inside her. This line of questioning made sense to her on a gut level. 'What did you see during the dream?'

'No more than you did,' Jeremy said slowly. 'But you always had a passion for the closets in this place. Take a closer look at the one in the dream. Are you sure it's empty?'

Lyssa frowned, turning her vision inward, straining to find anything she might have missed. 'I give up,' she said finally. 'I'd have to dream it again and pay specific attention in order to answer that. I can't remember details after so many years.'

'Can you make yourself dream it?'

'Do I *want* to make myself dream it?' said Lyssa. 'I hated those dreams. The attic ones in particular.'

'Why?' Jeremy wanted to know.

'After the organ room, there were all those floors and floors of endless bright white with those holes and ladders, only one of which went to the next floor, which was exactly like the first, ad infinitum. It was more tedious than scary, but the idea of accidentally going too far down a ladder that didn't make it, and never coming out –' Lyssa shuddered slightly. 'It's like when we play the Game and have to open a million doors before finding the one the House wants us to take. I mean, what's the point?'

'Maybe the pattern isn't set ahead of time. Maybe the House has to design the spell according to who's doing the walking and when it's being done?'

'My head hurts,' Lyssa complained, flopping back down on the bed. 'Why can't this all just make sense?'

Jeremy laughed drily. 'It probably does, and we just haven't figured out how, yet.'

Lyssa grabbed a pillow and smacked him with it. 'You're no help,' she said. 'And you're not going to let me sleep, are you?'

'Nope,' he said comfortably. 'We've got too much work to do still.'

Lyssa sighed and sat up. 'You're right.' She picked up her book and went to a rocking chair. Silence settled back over the Room as Jeremy returned to his work as well.

'So what's the cloth for?' asked Jeremy.

The contents of the trunk lay spread across the bed, rocking chairs and both tables. Clothing from the cupboard festooned the loom and the books were neatly stacked on the kitchen table.

'I have no idea,' Lyssa admitted. 'Most of this still makes no sense. When I first handled it I actually opened one of the lengths. Both my hands fell asleep.'

Jeremy gave her a quizzical look.

'The magic numbed my hands and forearms,' she clarified. 'I don't know what it's for, but we'd better ask before we do anything with it. Messing with magic in this House is unwise when you don't know what you're doing.'

He nodded. 'What about the jewelry?'

'Nothing,' she said, pulling the necklace she wore out from under her blouse. 'I found this one in the pocket of the bathrobe instead of with the other pieces in the trunk.'

'They were separated?'

Lyssa nodded. 'I wonder why. Suppose someone just forgot to put it away?'

Jeremy shook his head. 'These days I don't take anything for granted. Why don't you try putting them all together.'

Slowly, Lyssa put the necklace down with the other items. She and Jeremy withdrew, unconsciously trying to protect themselves from whatever might happen. Minutes passed by and Lyssa realized she was trying to hold her breath as well.

'This is silly,' she said, turning toward the loom. 'Nothing but the cloth seems to have any special potential, so why would these things be saved?' She gestured toward the odd assortment of clothing hanging from the frame. 'There can't have been this many people living here, and if there were, there should have been a *lot* more garments left behind when they began adding on to the House. Every other closet was left pretty much intact as far as I could tell.'

'There could have been several generations who lived here before they could afford to build,' Jeremy suggested. 'Maybe they saved a garment from each person to remember them by?'

'If they were doing that, don't you think they'd have saved things in better condition?' Lyssa gestured. 'These things are all ratty and old. I wouldn't buy any one of them at a flea market.'

Jeremy laughed. 'Maybe they're so ratty because they were so well worn. If you wanted to remember someone, you wouldn't pick the nicest item, so much as the one that most reminded you of them; an item they wore all the time.'

Lyssa picked up the stained baby shirt. 'Then this would be pretty tragic.'

Jeremy nodded. 'Infant death was very common then.'

With a sigh, she put the shirt back down. 'I don't know about any of this, but I think we need to talk about how we're getting out of here. We've been gone a long time, and out of touch with the rest of the House. Who knows what we'll be going back to.'

'Have you explored all the trap-doors and other entrances?' Jeremy asked, looking around. He couldn't see them, but Lyssa had told him about finding them after cleaning the Room.

'Uh, no,' Lyssa said, wondering why she hadn't thought of that. 'Do you think it's safe?'

Jeremy grinned. 'Has that stopped us yet?'

'Well, let's at least put away these things. I hate coming back to a messy room.' She put the cloth back into the false bottom of the trunk, and stuffed the jewelry back into the sock, stowing it beside the cloth. She put the top back on and refilled the trunk with the books.

They had finally finished them all and some of their questions had been answered.

Among the more useful bits of information they had come across were descriptions of the portals built into random doorways in the House. Since it was impractical to roam the countryside in search of young, healthy, solitary individuals, the Bell family magic constructed gateways that would monitor the movement and habits of the people living on the world being settled. When specific portions of the pattern were being walked, it activated the portals, bringing the needed individuals to the House to be kept until their energy was optimum. Then they would be consumed and more would take their place.

Because the rules had changed, the pattern being walked was no longer anything like the one described in the books. The goal, it seemed, was no longer transition only. It had become something more, but Jeremy and Lyssa had no way of knowing what.

Lyssa only knew she wasn't interested in walking either pattern, and there was no information in any of the books to help her determine what other pattern she should create, or what such a pattern might do.

There was so much in the books that no longer applied to their situation, both agreed they needed to talk to David Baker.

Then they needed to go and see Molly.

Lyssa had no better idea about how to get her home, but they had been away for several days at least, and were sure both Molly and Marnie were worried by now.

Jeremy put the clothing back into the cupboard and washed the few remaining dishes in the kitchen. By the time he was done, Lyssa had finished straightening the rest of the Room.

'Ready?' she asked.

He nodded. Then he shook his head. 'I don't know if I've ever been so scared in my life,' he admitted.

Lyssa smiled weakly. 'I know.'

During their time together, she had been surprised by his behavior. Gone was the hostile antagonist; in his place was the funny, sensitive, caring person she had seen only glimpses of when he was with Marnie. Lyssa was afraid to leave here, too, but much of her fear came from thinking that the Jeremy she knew in this Room would change once they left it.

'Well, soonest begun,' he said.

Lyssa nodded, and pointed out the first possible exit. They agreed to check each of them before taking any one.

Opening a door, they found only darkness. 'Oh, god, not this again,' wailed Lyssa. 'I've had it with blind leaps of faith!'

'That was only one door,' said Jeremy practically. 'How many are there?'

'Three more,' she sighed, knowing he was right. She opened the next door, and again found only darkness. The last two doors proved equally unhelpful.

'Eeny, meany, miney, moe,' said Jeremy, spinning in a circle. 'We take this one.' He stopped and pointed.

Lyssa pulled the door open and stepped through. Jeremy followed her.

'The gods are kind today,' he observed, looking around the church.

'Maybe there's something to be said for intention,' Lyssa grinned. 'Let's go and find the Speaker.'

David Baker was in his office. He jumped when they walked in. 'I'd given you up for lost!' he said, rising quickly and coming out from behind his desk. 'Are you okay?'

'Yes,' said Jeremy and Lyssa simultaneously.

'Why?' Lyssa added.

'You haven't been in the House?' David asked.

'We've been in the Room,' said Jeremy. 'Reading the books.'

The Speaker's eyes widened. 'You read them all?' he asked eagerly. 'All of them?'

'All of them,' Lyssa confirmed. 'What's going on at the House?'

'Miss Burch is very angry indeed,' he said.

'She thinking of changing her will?' Lyssa asked, only half-joking.

'Transition had already begun,' the Speaker said seriously. 'Besides, something she may not have told you is that the House must be passed on to a Family member who is relatively young. There are no others who fit this description.'

'How do you know this?' asked Jeremy.

'They've all come home,' David answered.

'All of them at once?' Lyssa gaped in disbelief. 'Even my father?'

'He was the first one to arrive,' David chuckled bitterly. 'He was hoping to convince Miss Burch to name him for the transition.'

'She'd never do that,' said Lyssa emphatically.

'Even if she wanted to, she couldn't change her mind. The House chose you, and you've been walking the pattern for years. For someone else to start now would delay transition for decades, and your aunt doesn't have that kind of time. Playing fast and loose with the rules has cost her dearly, and now she's paying the price.'

'How do you know all this?' asked Jeremy.

'The church and House are connected,' said the Speaker slowly. 'But Millie comes to see me when she is in town to do the marketing and such. She has been here a lot in the last two weeks.'

'Two weeks?' Jeremy and Lyssa exclaimed together.

David nodded. 'How long did you think you'd been missing?'

'Not as long as that,' said Lyssa. 'Molly must be very frightened.'

'Marnie brought her by a couple of times,' David said. 'I think I was able to provide some comfort, but she thinks you've abandoned her. After what she's been through, I'm not surprised. You should go over there as soon as you can.'

'When we finish here,' said Jeremy decisively. 'We have so many questions after what we've read. So much of it is moot, now that Burchie has messed with the order of things.'

David nodded. 'And then Lyssa started messing with them, and things got even farther out of whack.'

Jeremy grinned. 'It's made figuring out what tracks and what doesn't that much more difficult.'

'By now, the best advice I can give you is that since the rules are being made up as you all go along, don't worry too much about what's in the books, and concentrate instead on where the next step leads you.' He paused a moment to consider. 'Above all else, defend yourselves.'

'But what about . . .' Lyssa began.

The Speaker held up his hand. 'I told you, I don't know any more. Before all this happened, there were questions I could answer. Now,' he shook his head. 'Now, I just don't know. There are three ways this could go, and I can't say anything to influence your choices.'

'Even if I ask you to?' Lyssa pleaded.

'I'm sorry,' David said, looking genuinely regretful. 'I can't help you any more.'

'With anything?' asked Jeremy.

David shook his head.

Lyssa took Jeremy's hand and turned to walk down the aisle. She stopped at the door and looked back at the Speaker, but she couldn't read his expression. As the door closed behind them, it had a sound of finality to it that was depressing.

Jeremy sighed. 'We're on our own.'

They walked down the steps and onto the village green, turning toward Marnie's without saying another word.

Marnie opened the door and stood staring blankly at them for a moment. Then she smiled radiantly and turned to call, 'Molly!' up the stairs. 'Come in,' she said, stepping aside and opening the door wider. 'We've been so worried, Molly?'

Lyssa stepped into the foyer and turned to see Marnie give Jeremy a long hug. She whispered something Lyssa didn't catch, and Lyssa felt the familiar knot in her stomach at seeing the two of them together. She had grown so used to having Jeremy to herself, she'd almost forgotten he basically disliked her.

'Lyssa?' asked a small voice at the top of the stairs.

Lyssa turned and held her arms out to the little girl.

Molly hurled herself down the stairs and into Lyssa's open arms. 'Where have you been?' she demanded. Then she buried her face in Lyssa's shoulder and burst into tears.

Lyssa walked to the stairs, holding Molly tightly and murmuring into her hair, and sat down rocking back and forth gently.

Jeremy and Marnie withdrew.

Lyssa felt a brief stab as they left, but her primary concern was with the tiniest victim of this mess. Molly cried for a long time before subsiding to whimpers, but her grip on Lyssa never diminished.

When Molly was at last quiet, Lyssa whispered, 'I'm so sorry, sweetheart. I had so much to do I wasn't able to come see you, or send word. When I make a promise, I do everything I can to keep it, and I've been doing everything I can to find out how to get you home.'

'Did you find a way?' Molly asked in a choked whisper.

'Not yet,' said Lyssa. 'But I know more now, and that will help us.'

'I want to go h-home,' Molly hiccoughed. She lifted her tear-stained face to look at Lyssa.

Lyssa brushed the tears from the little girl's face. 'I know. I'm trying my best.' She kissed Molly's cheeks and hugged her again. 'I'm sorry I was gone for so long. I didn't mean to frighten you.'

'I was really scared,' said Molly. 'I didn't think I'd ever see you or my mommy and daddy again.'

'Well, I'm here now,' said Lyssa, looking Molly in the eyes. 'And I don't want your mommy and daddy to worry any longer, so I've got a lot more work to do. I may be gone again for a while, but I'll come back for you, I promise.'

'You look like her,' said Molly, reaching out to touch

Lyssa's hair. She ran her fingers through the thick, chestnut strands. 'Her eyes are blue, too.'

Lyssa smiled. 'Shall we go find Marnie and Jeremy?'

Molly shook her head. 'Will you sing to me?' she asked. 'Rock me again?'

So Lyssa dug into her memory and found a song. Holding Molly, she rocked and sang to the little girl as the house darkened and night fell. Lights came on in the other room and Molly's breathing evened out into sleep. Finally, Lyssa stood and carried Molly up the stairs to her bedroom.

She covered the little girl and kissed her forehead, stroking the black curls from her face. Leaving the door open, Lyssa turned on the hall light in case she woke up, and returned downstairs to find Jeremy and Marnie.

As she came around the corner and into the living room, Lyssa saw Jeremy and Marnie sitting with their heads together, talking. Marnie looked up, and for a moment, Lyssa thought she saw a flash of anger and hatred in her eyes. She blinked and the look was gone, leaving Lyssa to wonder what she had actually seen.

Jeremy looked up and then stood. 'We've been talking,' he said.

Lyssa nodded.

'We should probably go,' he said, sounding a little guilty.

Lyssa nodded again.

Marnie stood also. 'You'll come back again soon?'

Jeremy looked from Marnie to Lyssa and back again, with a helpless expression on his face.

Lyssa looked at Marnie. 'If we can,' she said slowly. 'I talked with Molly. She knows I might not be able to come here for a while. Are you still able and willing to keep her for us?'

'Of course!' Marnie said brightly, putting her hand on Jeremy's arm. 'She's no trouble at all. I'll miss her a great deal when she goes home.'

'Thank you,' said Lyssa, inclining her head slightly.

'We'll be back as soon as we can.' She turned and left the room, hoping Jeremy would follow quickly. She was out the door and down the walk before he caught up with her.

'I didn't tell her anything about what we read, or anything like that,' Jeremy said as he jogged up to her.

Lyssa shook her head. 'What were you talking about?'

'Stuff,' he said uncomfortably.

They walked in silence for a few moments before Lyssa stopped and looked up at him. 'I don't think it's a good idea to mention anything about any of this to her.'

Jeremy spun back toward her as if jerked by a string. 'Huh? Why not?'

'I don't know.' Lyssa frowned. 'I caught some weird feelings off her as I came into the living room just now. She looked at me – I don't know. I'm probably being paranoid, but I'm beginning to think there's really no one we can trust.'

'Do you trust me?' asked Jeremy.

Lyssa barked a laugh. 'No, but you're all I've got.'

'So, shall we study more of the town's layout before trying to find the entrance to the Room from outside?'

Jeremy sounded a little too blithe, but Lyssa decided to ignore it. 'That was one of Aunt Burchie's assignments. I guess by now it's probably a moot point.'

'Why?' asked Jeremy. 'There might be information there we'll need to know. We read all the books, even after it became evident that a lot of what they talked about no longer applied. We might as well assume that somewhere in this twisted mess, your aunt has a purpose we need to know about. There may even be an advantage, especially if she thinks we stopped her lessons when we stopped seeing her.'

Lyssa sighed. 'You're right. We know this part of town. Where haven't we been looking?'

'Up the hill,' said Jeremy softly. He pointed.

Lyssa followed his gaze and inhaled sharply. 'My god,' she breathed. The House was almost glowing. Every window was lit, but the strange brilliance seemed to shine beyond that, giving the House an aura radiating into the night. 'What are they doing up there?'

Jeremy shook his head. 'All the aunts and uncles have returned?'

'That's what the Speaker said.' Lyssa shuddered and closed her eyes. 'What are we going to do?' she whispered.

'We're going to take a walk,' said Jeremy, taking Lyssa by the arm and moving purposefully down the street. 'We're going to memorize the town and find a way back into the Room that avoids *them*,' he jerked his head back toward the hill. 'And we're going to find out how to make the pattern work for us.'

Lyssa smiled weakly. 'Okay, so I trust you a little.'

Jeremy laughed. 'You trust me completely. Now come on.'

By dawn, they had walked every street in town that they had never walked before. They carried in their heads a map of the entire area, from the orderly grid of downtown, to the meandering streets of the outlying neighborhoods. They knew where the parks were, and the schools. They knew there were only three ways out of town, and realized they only knew where one of those ways went.

By dawn, they were exhausted.

'How are we going to find the door to the Room?' Jeremy asked as they approached the road leading up the hill to the House.

'I guess I use the old magic and hope no one up there notices,' said Lyssa. 'Do you think they're even paying attention?' The glow had subsided during the night, and at daybreak it was almost unnoticeable, but, Lyssa was still unnerved by it. This was her home and her family, and she was finding she knew almost nothing about the strangers she had grown up with.

'I'd say we have to risk it, regardless,' said Jeremy, sounding none too thrilled by the prospect.

Lyssa took a deep breath and touched the old magic, using it to enhance her senses as she looked at the area around her. Somewhere here was the door she sought.

They looked for the better part of the morning, circling the hill slowly, stumbling through the dense growth that covered the hill. There was no path to follow, and they had no idea where they were actually going, so it was a surprise to stumble across the entrance on the far side of the hill, away from town.

'I'd have thought the place would be more accessible to where the church and town were,' said Lyssa, stepping closer to examine the area.

Jeremy shrugged. 'Nothing these people do makes any sense to me,' he said, looking back up the hill. The House was out of sight from where they stood.

'I know,' said Lyssa.

Jeremy looked at her questioningly.

She nodded up the hill. 'It makes me feel better to be out of sight, even if I'm not actually safer.'

Jeremy grinned. 'Do we have some digging to do?'

'It would appear so,' said Lyssa. 'Do we go buy shovels in town, or find clam shells in the dirt?'

Jeremy laughed. 'I don't think the sea ever covered this area. Let's pull out a few bushes first and see if that helps. Then we'll have a better idea what we're trying to accomplish.'

Lyssa bent and grabbed a weed by the base stem. Putting her back into it, she gave a mighty pull. The plant gave way immediately, and Lyssa found herself sitting hard on the ground. 'It's not as tough as it looks,' she said. Standing, she rubbed her butt gingerly, brushing the dirt from the seat of her pants.

They settled into the work, and shortly had a large area cleared up the hillside.

'Can you see if the door is any more accessible?' asked Jeremy, surveying what they had done.

'We need a shovel and a pick-axe,' said Lyssa. 'And we'd

better get this finished before dark, or we'll be spending the night out here.'

'I need to sleep in a bed,' said Jeremy emphatically.

Lyssa grinned. 'Then we'd better get to town and back quickly.'

They made quick work of the dirt covering the door and, by dusk, had cleared the entrance to the Room.

'What if the door's locked?' asked Jeremy as they cleared the last of the unstable ledge above the door.

Lyssa grinned. 'They didn't have locks way back then,' she said, reaching for the latch. She pulled the rusted metal, surprised at its integrity, and felt it lift from its housing. The door swung open and they stepped inside. 'God, I need to sleep.'

'I'm almost afraid to,' said Jeremy, pulling the door shut behind them. He sat in one of the rocking chairs and put his feet up on the table. 'After everything we read, and what we saw last night, I don't know if I'll sleep without nightmares ever again.'

Lyssa sat facing him, pushing against the floor with her toe to rock. 'At least it's not your people doing these things.'

'No, I've just lived with it all my life, and evidently, I'm either part of the problem, or the solution.'

'We don't know what the solution is,' Lyssa protested.

Jeremy shook his head. 'But you've been told you know the answer.'

'I can't access it!' Lyssa cried in frustration. 'There was a moment when I knew everything, way back when I first came home, but I couldn't hold onto it, and I haven't been able to reach it since!'

'Maybe you need to set up the magic to help you remember while you dream,' Jeremy suggested.

'Sounds like a perfect way to guarantee a nightmare,' Lyssa said, with a grim twist of her mouth. 'But I think you may be right. Is there anything left in the cupboards?

I didn't think to check before we left, and I could use some dinner before I run out of gas.'

Jeremy lifted a hand and dropped it back onto the arm of his chair. 'That would mean moving,' he protested.

Lyssa grinned weakly. 'I know. That's why I asked instead of getting up. What do you think they were up to last night?' she asked, changing the subject.

Jeremy shrugged. 'Who knows how long they've been up to it. I wish we could talk to Millie.'

'I've never seen lights like that before,' Lyssa mused. 'Were they trying to repair the pattern?'

'I doubt it,' said Jeremy, rising slowly. 'They didn't seem to be in the warrens, and besides, the Speaker said they were too old, and the House had already chosen you.' He walked to the kitchen and began rummaging the shelves to see if he could make a meal out of what they had.

'Millie has been coming into town more recently,' Lyssa said, reluctantly getting up and following him. 'Maybe we could find her in the shops or at the church. David said she'd been to see him several times.'

'We have to find out what's going on in the House,' Jeremy agreed. 'That's the best way. What about the warrens?'

'Maybe we could do the same thing with them that we did with the town,' Lyssa suggested. 'We don't have to walk the pattern anymore. We could just go from one area to another and map our way directly. We can't find any blueprints, so that may be the only way to get the overview we need.'

'What about the magic changing the configuration of things?' he asked, surveying the items he had pulled from the cupboards. 'What do you think?'

Lyssa looked at the proposed dinner. 'Could be worse,' she grinned. 'I wasn't shopping with living here in mind. I don't think the magic will be changing things right now. I think the House is waiting to see what we'll do. If we resume walking the pattern, then it can take control again and do whatever it was doing. For now, it has to stay where it is in order for us to pick up where we left off.'

'You sound pretty sure of yourself,' said Jeremy, pulling a pot out and putting it on the stove.

Lyssa shook her head. 'Not even remotely. It's just the only thing that makes sense. If you wanted someone to do something, wouldn't you play a waiting game if that was the best chance for success?' She leaned against the counter, watching Jeremy cook.

'I guess,' he said. 'But what I think is less important than what you seem so sure of. Do you think it's safe to go into the warrens while the aunts and uncles are magicking up a storm at the top of the hill?'

'I guess we'll find out tomorrow,' said Lyssa. She pulled open a drawer, grabbed forks, knives and spoons and started setting the table. 'But for tonight, we eat and sleep.'

'Sounds good,' Jeremy grinned, stirring the contents in the pot. 'But before we enter the warrens, we go shopping. Maybe we'll run into Millie. At least we can leave word with David that we're looking for her.'

'Agreed. Is there anything I can do to help?'

Jeremy shook his head. 'I'm just about done.'

After they finished supper and washed the dishes, they crawled into bed and fell instantly asleep.

Nightmares chased them until dawn.

'Oh, god,' Lyssa lay staring at the trap-door in the ceiling. 'Why did we bother?' Her eyes burned and her mouth felt sticky and thick. Her arms and legs were leaden and her head throbbed.

'I think we were out in the sun too long yesterday,' said Jeremy. 'I feel hung-over. Did you sleep at all?'

'Yeah,' said Lyssa, trying to swallow. 'But I didn't get any rest. You?'

Jeremy sat up and swung his legs over the edge, placing his feet on the floor. 'Ooh, don't try this yet. I slept. What were those dreams about?'

'I don't remember,' Lyssa said, ignoring his advice and sitting up. 'Ooh, why don't I listen?'

Jeremy slumped, face in hands, rubbing his eyes gingerly. 'You never did, why should you start now?'

'Could we not fight this morning?' she asked, leaning back against the wall. 'I'm tired of fighting. I was fighting all night long.'

'You do remember the dreams?' Jeremy looked back at her. The effort cost him, and he slowly turned his whole body so he could continue looking at her without pain.

'No. I don't know where that statement came from,' Lyssa denied.

Jeremy gave her a look, as if trying to decide whether or not she was telling the truth. Finally he turned around again and stood. 'I don't want to fight either,' he said, walking gingerly away from the bed. 'I don't like fighting with you.'

Lyssa resisted the urge to comment, easing herself across the bed to stand as well. 'We might as well go into town first thing. The sooner we get our errands run, the sooner we can go into the warrens.'

'Now there's something to look forward to,' Jeremy said darkly.

'Are you always this cheerful in the morning?' Lyssa searched her memory, but couldn't remember a morning she'd spent with him just out of bed. As children, they'd slept in their own beds at night: he in the quarters he shared with his mother, she in the quarters she shared with Aunt Burchie. Most recently, they had slept in shifts and concentrated more on the books than each other.

Jeremy made a face. 'You should talk?'

'So neither of us is a morning person?' Lyssa grimaced. Standing was worse than opening her eyes had been.

'Make a list so we don't forget anything.' Jeremy was finger-combing his hair, trying to tame the curls sufficiently to get them tied back.

'Your hand is broken?' she demanded. 'You can't write?'

'I'm going to see what I can do about fixing us breakfast,' Jeremy said patiently, tying a strip of green leather around the resulting ponytail. 'For someone who doesn't want to fight, you sure are spoiling for one.'

Lyssa pulled a face. 'I'll write a list.'

By the time they started for town, both were in somewhat better spirits. They went first to the church to leave word with the Speaker for Millie. Then they did their shopping, half-hoping Millie would be in town as well.

She wasn't. Even though the possibility was slim, Jeremy and Lyssa were still disappointed. They returned to the Room with their purchases and prepared to re-enter the warrens.

'I'm scared,' Lyssa confided, putting her hand against the door they had agreed to try.

'Me too,' Jeremy admitted. 'Have you warded us, just in case?'

Lyssa nodded, checking for the hundredth time to make sure the wards were in place and hoping they were strong enough. 'Here goes.' She pushed the door open and stepped through. 'You have the pen and paper for mapping?'

'And the knife and flashlight,' he said with an unsteady chuckle.

They moved down the corridor toward a long flight of stairs visible in the distance. 'Why do I get the feeling I'm going to wish they'd had elevators way back then?'

The stairway wasn't as long as it had appeared. The House it led them to was only moderately larger than the Room they had just left. It was clearly a step up from the one-room cabin the Family had started in, but no more than would have seemed right for the times.

The living room was more formal, with pictures of flowers and landscapes on the walls, but all the chairs were rocking chairs still, and there were two tables instead of just one. The kitchen and dining room shared the same space, and there were two separate bedrooms. There were two floor-looms in the loft above the bedrooms, overlooking the living room and dining room, and another spinning wheel had been added as well. They were becoming more prosperous, but the industry was the same.

'This place is as clean as the rest of the warrens we've been in,' Lyssa said as she poked around, looking in the cupboards and drawers. There was one large bed in one room and two trundle beds in the other.

'Why is that remarkable?' asked Jeremy, calling down from the loft.

'The Room was filthy when I first found it,' Lyssa called back. 'I cleaned for hours before I could really see what the place looked like.'

'But the House sent you there deliberately?'

'There was a lamp burning when I got there,' Lyssa confirmed.

Jeremy frowned and came back down the stairs. 'Might as well start drawing the map,' he said, pulling paper out of his leather pouch and spreading it on the dining room table. 'Do we attempt to draw to scale? How long was that corridor?'

'I don't think exact measurements are necessary,' said Lyssa, bending over the empty page. 'All we need is an approximate overview.'

Jeremy drew the Room, the corridor and stairs, and then the House they were in. Then he folded up the paper and tucked it back into his pouch. 'Do you see doors I don't?' he asked, looking around.

Lyssa grinned. 'I thought we'd give this one a try,' she said pointing at a wall.

'Lead on,' said Jeremy. 'Do we have to try all of them eventually?'

'I don't know if they all go somewhere,' said Lyssa, pulling the door open. 'It may be there are others just to give the House options in playing the Game and walking the pattern.'

'Yeah, but what if we're missing an important piece of the puzzle by not checking them all?'

Lyssa shrugged. 'How many doors do you want to open today? This exploration could take weeks if we're not careful.'

'Do we have weeks?' asked Jeremy.

'I don't know if we even have hours,' said Lyssa sourly. 'We just have to hope there's enough time to find out what we need to know. Otherwise, we're flying blind.'

'Charming thought,' he said, following her through the door and into another long hallway. 'More stairs,' he observed as they started walking. 'They believed in climbing up the hill as quickly as possible back then?'

'It's a big hill,' said Lyssa.

'Yeah, but they had hundreds of years to cover it,' he protested.

'Look, don't ask me to make any sense of this. I'm their descendent, not their apologist,' Lyssa said impatiently.

They climbed the stairs and found themselves in a new building; nicer than the one they had just left, but not a huge leap forward in opulence. This was a completely two-story structure, with the weaving room taking up the entire back of the first floor. Living room, dining room and kitchen were separate rooms, and much larger than in the previous House, and a parlor had been added. Upstairs there were four bedrooms, two on each side of a short hallway that went from front to back down the middle of the House.

'The map is beginning to look seriously linear,' said Lyssa as they went from one room to the next. 'I wonder why these buildings aren't part of the Game.'

'There's not much pattern to a straight line,' said Jeremy. 'Maybe there's no magic here.'

'No,' Lyssa denied. 'There is magic to get from one section to another, and each of these homes is clean and neat, just like the portions we've always played in. There just don't seem to be answers here.'

'When we have a better idea of the whole, we may find there are answers here that we didn't know we were looking at.'

'Maybe,' said Lyssa doubtfully. 'Shall we look for the next long hallway and flight of stairs?'

Jeremy laughed. 'Lead on.'

The weaving room in the next House was a tiny factory in its own wing. An entire wall was given to folds and bolts of fabric, and an area had been added for sewing and fitting garments.

'This is becoming quite an industry,' Jeremy whistled, looking around. 'The town must be growing as well, in order to support the Family so richly.'

'I wonder how long it took to get to this point,' Lyssa mused, pulling open drawers and rummaging their contents. 'It must have been decades for each House to get to the point where building became necessary.'

'We don't know how many add-ons there have been,' said Jeremy. 'But it's safe to assume things probably started off slowly, gathered speed and finally slowed again. One hundred years for each build would mean only ten separate areas. We know there are more than that because we've walked the pattern in more than that. We also know that your aunt has been living in the section her mother built, so the pace definitely slowed in there somewhere.'

'I don't recall any industry to support the Family evident in any of the areas we've played in, do you?' Lyssa finished with the drawers and moved on to the cupboards. 'Did they move the equipment off site?'

'Maybe they've been living off investments,' Jeremy suggested.

'That happened eventually,' said Lyssa. 'But how do you get that rich weaving fabric and making clothing?'

Jeremy shook his head. 'If the fabric in the chest in your Room is any indication, it was no ordinary stuff.'

'Well, and what is *that* for?' Lyssa demanded impatiently. 'Why is it every time I turn around I have more questions?'

Jeremy laughed. 'Let's do some more mapping.'

They walked from the spacious workroom into the House and began exploring the Family's rise in status. This House finally began to show some of the opulence familiar to Jeremy and Lyssa from the warrens they had grown up in. A music room had been added to the downstairs complement. All of the rooms were huge and richly decorated, and none but the kitchen looked like they were designed for family living.

Upstairs was still nothing but bedrooms, and there were a lot of them. 'These people were prolific,' Lyssa commented as they looked into one after another.

'Got to have lots of weavers and spinners if you're going to support this kind of living,' said Jeremy facetiously.

Lyssa shuddered. 'Sure goes along with the image of Aunt Burchie as a spider, doesn't it?'

Jeremy stopped short and gave Lyssa a strange look. 'How odd and appropriate.'

'And totally creepy,' Lyssa agreed.

'Creepy crawly,' Jeremy laughed.

Lyssa groaned. 'Oh, stop it. Why do I feel like we should be turning over rocks and poking around with sticks?'

Jeremy grinned. 'Come on. We've got a lot more mapping to do.'

The next level was the one in which the industry was moved out of the home. There were no traces of loom or wheel, needle or thread in the House.

The bedrooms and living area had been moved into a wing to one side of the area Lyssa thought of as the showcase. The kitchen and dining area had been moved to a wing on the other side.

The showcase had two-story ceilings, and a large balcony with doors that led to smaller rooms for private entertaining. One room was clearly for drinking ports and fine wines, another was set aside for pipes and cigars. A large library took up the middle third of the balcony, and two smaller rooms for ladies' entertainment occupied the other side. One had chairs politely set in rows before a lectern, the other contained small, curved sofas set in circles about low tables, probably for intimate conversation over tea.

Downstairs was a great hall which functioned both as foyer and dance floor. On the left was a parlor decorated in ornate fashion with pink velvet curtains and gilded furniture. On the right was a formal living room done in dark woods and heavy fabrics.

'They sure believed in segregating their entertainment,' Jeremy said as they moved from room to room.

'Gives you a good idea of customs and practices, though,' said Lyssa. 'Must have been a pretty sterile environment for kids.'

'On the contrary. The kind of entertaining these people must have done would be perfect for kids to spy on. Can you imagine finding hiding places here and watching what the grown-ups were doing?'

Lyssa was amazed at how boyish he looked, and how handsome he could be when there was no trace of anger in his face. 'Yeah, I can see it,' she said with a sigh. 'And this is beginning to look familiar.'

'Have you been here before?' Jeremy asked, focusing intently on her.

'No,' Lyssa shook her head. 'But I'd be willing to bet we're about to start mapping the parts of the warrens we *have* been in.'

'You're probably right,' said Jeremy, reaching for the map in his pouch. 'Are we still going in a straight line?'

'I don't think there will be a whole lot of zigzagging,' said Lyssa. 'I think they just began building huge and sprawling buildings across the hill, and that's where the patterns come in. They still seem to have gone pretty much straight up the hill from one add-on to the next.'

'And the buildings got closer together,' Jeremy offered. 'I'm starting to notice the hallways and stairs in between are getting shorter.' He spread out the paper and began to draw the current layout. 'Are you feeling anything from your aunts and uncles?'

'The wards are pretty strong, but I don't think any of them know about this area. I don't sense any activity from them yet.'

The sixth level was familiar to them both.

As Lyssa opened the door, she could feel a tingling in her veins and knew also that the magic her aunts and uncles were working was present here.

'What?' asked Jeremy, following her into the warrens.

Lyssa glanced back at him. 'Huh?'

'You inhaled like you were about to say something,' he clarified. 'I know this place,' he added, looking around. 'We've been here before.'

Lyssa nodded. 'We've got to be careful, though. The Family is strong here. Try not to disturb anything, or they may be able to trace us.'

'Are they here?' Jeremy glanced around reflexively.

'Yes and no. I think this is one of the places Aunt Burchie still has unchanged in her memory. I don't know if the rest of them played the Game, but we'd better assume that all of them have. That being the case, everyone knows this area as well as we do.'

'We'd still better map it,' said Jeremy.

'I agree,' said Lyssa. 'We need every hallway and room of every building we can find, but there's a possibility of running into someone down here.'

'Significant?' asked Jeremy.

Lyssa shrugged. 'I can't imagine the old folks poking around down here if they don't have to, but we still don't know what the stakes are. It may be worth their while. All I'm saying is we have to stay on our toes and be careful from now on.'

'Best to draw as we go, then?' Jeremy suggested.

Lyssa nodded. She checked her wards again, but since she had so little practice with the old magic, she had no idea if she was accomplishing anything in trying to strengthen them.

They set off down the hall, opening doors as they went. Jeremy drew, using the palm of his hand for a table, gripping a flashlight between his teeth. Lyssa kept her eyes peeled for relatives and dictated notes for the map.

She was surprised that being familiar with the layout was no help really. Some of the rooms she had no recollection of, and others had been misplaced by her memory, so that what was drawn on the map was not what she would have drawn from memory. As they finished exploring, Lyssa looked at what Jeremy had done and frowned. 'This looks familiar, too,' she said, circling the entire drawing with a finger.

Jeremy frowned. 'I doubt it,' he said sourly. 'Where to next?'

Lyssa pulled a face. 'I saw a door back this way,' she said, turning.

Uncle Haskell stood in the hallway behind them. 'I was hoping to run into you,' he said pleasantly.

Lyssa inclined her head slightly, moving to put Jeremy behind her. 'How have you been?' she asked. 'I haven't seen you in a long time.'

Uncle Haskell smiled graciously. 'You have become quite a lovely young lady in the intervening years.'

'What brings you back?' Lyssa asked, keeping her tone even. Her heart was racing so that she could scarcely hear her voice in her ears.

'Oh, that's right,' said Uncle Haskell, too innocently. 'You haven't heard. Burchie has had a stroke.'

Lyssa started, feeling the warmth of guilt flush to her limbs from the tingling in her chest. 'Will she recover?'

Uncle Haskell shook his head. 'It's touch and go right

now. We all came as soon as we could. We've been looking for you to tell you, but you had disappeared.' He shook his head disapprovingly. 'And here we find you playing the Game.'

'Just doing my homework,' said Lyssa. 'We've been going where the House tells us to for a very long time now. We weren't sure how long it had been.'

'Quite long enough for us to become very worried indeed,' said Uncle Haskell.

The disapproval in his voice seemed to abate somewhat, but Lyssa was sure he didn't believe her story.

'Well, here I am in any case,' said Lyssa. 'You can tell the others I'll be along as soon as I'm released from the Game.'

Uncle Haskell shook his head. 'I'm afraid I'll have to ask you to come back with me now. Burchie needs to know you're safe. Without that peace of mind, I'm afraid her recovery can't be effected.'

Lyssa smiled. 'You know the rules, Uncle Haskell. I can't go until I'm released.'

'I think we both know there are no longer rules, dear,' said Uncle Haskell, advancing toward them for the first time.

'Please don't come any closer,' Lyssa said softly.

He took another step.

Lyssa held up her hand and felt the old magic crackling in her palm. 'Please stop.'

As Uncle Haskell picked up his foot, the energy exploded from Lyssa's hand and struck the old man squarely in the chest, sending him flying backward down the hall.

'Damn,' said Jeremy from behind her. 'Remind me not to make you mad.'

'We've got to get out of here,' said Lyssa, tugging urgently on Jeremy's arm. 'He got past my wards like they weren't even there.'

'Are they?' asked Jeremy, allowing himself to be pulled down the hall.

They stepped over Uncle Haskell. Lyssa couldn't tell if he was stunned or dead, and wasn't sure she wanted to know. 'I guess I can't be certain. I have no idea what I'm doing. I didn't mean to hurt him, even. He threatened, I struck. It isn't as if I thought about it, it just happened.'

'Maybe you'd better do some practicing while we make our map,' Jeremy suggested.

Lyssa opened the door and stepped through. 'I don't know how,' she protested. 'All I can do is keep my eyes and ears open and hope for the best.'

'I don't find that comforting,' said Jeremy, looking around at the next level.

'Well, it's what we have to work with,' said Lyssa. 'So it'll have to do.'

'Are we going to have enough paper?' Lyssa asked as Jeremy pulled out yet another sheet. The map now sprawled over several pages and had gone from linear to rambling.

'Too bad your relatives were so wealthy,' Jeremy observed drily. 'By the way, where did the textile industry go?'

'What do you mean?' asked Lyssa, opening yet another door. If she'd thought it was tedious to do while playing the Game, doing it for cartography was even more so.

'I mean, there is no textile mill in the town. There isn't one anywhere near here that I know of. This place isn't known for its fabrics, or even its garments. Where did all those looms go?'

'Investments,' said Lyssa. 'What little I got from Aunt Burchie before our talks ended was that money makes money, and we are very good at it. If you invest in other people's successful businesses, you don't have to run your own.'

'So you've been parasites for a long time?'

Lyssa knew he meant it as a joke, but her humor was wearing thin. 'I am not a parasite,' she said sharply. 'I can't vouch for my relatives, but I've had little contact with them and evidently that's a good thing.'

'Sorry,' said Jeremy briefly. 'What do we do when we run out of paper?'

'I guess we find more here, or go back to the Room for some.' Lyssa thought about it. 'We could use a break, but I don't think it's such a good idea to rest here. I don't feel like we ought to stop until we're done.'

'I know,' Jeremy agreed. 'I keep expecting to run into another aunt or uncle.'

'I think I must have done real harm to Uncle Haskell, or we probably would have by now,' said Lyssa.

'Harm?' Jeremy gaped. 'You killed the guy! How much more harm can you do?'

'Did I?' Lyssa felt oddly detached from the action. 'We didn't stop to examine him. I wasn't sure.'

'Oh, man,' Jeremy muttered under his breath. He continued drawing the map.

Lyssa had long since stopped searching every drawer and cabinet, but when they came to the next room with a desk in it, she went through it and found more paper. 'Would you like me to do some drawing for a while?' she volunteered, showing him the sheaf, but not actually giving it to him.

'I feel safer with you keeping an eye out,' Jeremy admitted, reaching for the paper. 'I don't mind drawing.'

Lyssa nodded and turned to the next door.

On the next level, they found themselves in the endless living rooms.

'This shouldn't take as long,' said Jeremy with an obvious sigh of relief. 'There are no closed doors. We can walk two rooms apart, keep an eye on each other and do six rows of rooms at a time.'

'Are you sure you feel safe splitting up that much?' Lyssa asked dubiously.

Jeremy nodded. 'I also really want to be done with this.

I don't remember how long it took us to get back to Burchie's from here, but we must be getting close to the top of the hill.'

'Well, since the House kept changing itself, it's pretty much impossible to know where we were sent after we left here, or where this area is in relation to the rest of the structure,' said Lyssa. She was impatient as well, and after the poor night's sleep, eager for rest. 'At least we know the jungle is near here. I could use some fresh fruit.'

'So let's make quick work of this area, stop for a break, and then continue.'

Breaking up the task made the area seem much smaller than it had appeared the first time they walked through it. Also, having Molly with them colored their perception. They could cover much more ground without her, but missed the awe with which she regarded the gaudy decor.

They counted the rooms in their rows, accounted for the rooms between and beside them, and Jeremy drew hurried lines at the end of each segment. By the time they reached the crystal ballroom in the center they were surprised by the amount of ground they had covered.

'Is the jungle on the other side?' Lyssa asked. 'I thought it was that way.' She pointed in the direction they had just come from.

'I thought so, too,' said Jeremy slowly. 'We could have gotten turned around, or the House might have moved it before you stopped walking the pattern.'

'We probably got turned around,' said Lyssa hopefully. 'Come on. Let's finish this.'

It was a relief to discover the jungle on the far side. In a place where nothing was as it seemed, and the structure itself kept changing, it was almost necessary for them to find something where it was supposed to be.

They picked some fruit and sat down.

'I didn't realize we'd been on our feet this long,' said Lyssa, stretching out on one of the couches to put her feet up.

'Why don't we ever think to wear a watch?' asked Jeremy.

Lyssa laughed. 'It'd be too depressing. Then we'd know we'd been awake and plodding in this awful place for days and days with no rest and lots of danger. Time and adrenaline don't mix.'

'I haven't had a real rush since we ran into Haskell,' said Jeremy. 'I could use a little more excitement, or a good cup of coffee.'

'Be careful what you wish for, little boy,' said Lyssa with a grin.

Jeremy made a face at her and bit into a peach. 'Weird choices for fruit trees. I wonder why they're only here near the door.'

'I'm just glad they are.' Lyssa snuggled down into the sofa and closed her eyes.

'Don't get too comfortable,' Jeremy warned, throwing a pillow at her.

Lyssa sat up and made a face, tossing the pillow back. 'Are you ready to get going again?'

'Is there anything else on this level that we haven't mapped yet?' Jeremy asked, wiping his hands on his pants.

Lyssa nodded toward the jungle. 'What do you think?'

'I think that's even more dangerous than walking in the front door of Burchie's place and yelling, "I'm home!"'

'Oh, come on,' said Lyssa. 'Where's your sense of adventure?'

Jeremy laughed. 'I have no sense of adventure. I've lived all my life in the same place.'

'Haven't you ever read books about other places?' asked Lyssa, genuinely curious.

'Yeah,' Jeremy nodded. 'But unless you can actually go to them, those places are no more real than the made-up places in fiction.' He stood up. 'So this is my adventure. Playing the Game; mapping the House and warrens.'

'We'll see if we can't change that,' said Lyssa, standing

as well. 'Come on. I want to get this finished as much as you do.'

They trudged up stairs and down hallways. They opened doors and drew lines on paper. They went from one level to the next, always climbing, always finding areas they had never seen before mixed in with the familiar.

Gradually the map took shape, but they were so tired and mentally stunned by the enormity of the task, neither could do more than open the next door and make the next notation.

Lyssa began to relax her guard. Uncle Haskell faded from memory, and exhaustion clouded her senses. 'We're never going to reach the damned atrium, are we?' she asked, opening yet another door.

'Atrium?' Jeremy asked blankly, scribbling on the paper and following Lyssa on down the hall.

'The one at the base of the stairs leading up to Aunt Burchie's?' Lyssa jogged his memory.

'Eventually,' he shrugged. 'Are you getting anything from the folks above?'

Lyssa checked, guilty about her lack of vigilance. 'Nothing,' she said shortly, wondering if she could in fact count on that.

'They've been too quiet since we ran into your uncle,' said Jeremy. 'When we finish this, we should try to get in touch with Millie and see if she has anything to tell us.'

'When we finish, I'm going to sleep for a week,' said Lyssa. She knew they wouldn't have that luxury, but it felt good to say it anyway.

'I'm going to prop your eyelids open with toothpicks and make you see the patterns in these rooms and halls,' Jeremy laughed.

'Ow,' Lyssa cried in mock pain. 'You are truly a cruel man.'

'Count on it,' he grinned. 'Now, let's pick up the pace and we may be done by next week.'

'Don't count on it.'

Lyssa stopped short and Jeremy bumped into her. They stood in the hall and stared.

'You can't think we would allow you to finish,' said the old woman who stood in front of them. Her face shifted, and her body moved in and out of focus, as if several women had been superimposed over each other in poor holography.

'W-what happened to Uncle Haskell?' Lyssa quavered, backing a step into Jeremy, even though he hadn't given way after bumping into her. She stepped on his foot, and stood there leaning against him.

The old woman's face twisted and wavered, but remained intact. 'He's dead, you little brat. You killed him.'

'You don't seem terribly broken up about it,' said Jeremy.

Lyssa elbowed him, but the old woman laughed. 'He was sort of a sacrificial lamb, even if he didn't know it,' she said. 'We had to have some way of finding out what you were doing, and what you might be capable of.'

'Well, now you know it's murder,' said Lyssa. 'Doesn't that worry you at all?'

The old woman shook her head. 'You can't kill a projection.'

'And a projection can't kill us,' said Lyssa. 'What are you doing here?'

'Testing you,' the old woman hissed. Her apparition shivered and swayed a moment, and energy sparked around it.

Lyssa felt Jeremy backing away from her, and backed up with him, unsure of what was happening. The whip struck before she could react, lashing them in spite of her protections. They went down, and the last thing Lyssa saw before losing consciousness was the old woman disappear.

Chapter Eight

'The symbols of power are not yours, but you will draw from them for the magic you use. You will keep them hidden, and apart in order to preserve them.'

Power and Responsibility, Chapter One

They awoke in the jungle.

Lyssa opened her eyes and lay very still, but her mind was busy checking every part of her to assess damages. There were bad burns on her face, arms and torso, and her head ached fiercely, but her legs seemed fine, and her insides didn't seem to hurt. There would be no permanent internal damage. She moved experimentally, and instantly regretted it. 'O-oh,' she whimpered, wishing she could take back the movement.

'Hmm?' Jeremy stirred beside her and then groaned. 'My god, what was that?'

'An attack,' Lyssa panted, trying to steady herself against the pain to see if she could find where it hurt most.

'How did we get here?' Jeremy sat up, apparently doing the same inventory on himself.

Lyssa shook her head slightly, experimentally. 'Your guess is as good as mine.' She tried to sit up, and found she couldn't. The pain seared in her chest and brought tears to her eyes.

'My god!' Jeremy exclaimed again, bending over her. 'We need to get you to a doctor.'

'That you can't do,' hissed a voice nearby.

'I'm getting t-tired of this,' Lyssa sobbed. 'Too damned many voices coming out of nowhere.'

Jeremy turned away from her. 'She needs a doctor.'

'She'd be dead already if not for the magic, and you along with her.' The Keeper and his companion came out of the dense foliage and stopped in front of him. 'Apply this to the burns. It will help.' He handed Jeremy a small white jar with a silver lid.

Jeremy looked at the size of the jar, and at the extensive burns on Lyssa's body. 'This will never cover all of those.'

'Is it that bad?' Lyssa whimpered. She hated hearing her voice like that, but it hurt so much, and Jeremy seemed really concerned.

'Yes,' he said briefly. He turned back to the old man. 'She needs a doctor,' he repeated. 'You have to help me get her to one.'

The old man shook his head. 'I can't do that. I can't leave here. You don't have time for her to recuperate. The salve will work with the magic to hold her mind and body together, and you will be able to finish your task. You must finish while they still think she is dead.'

'But –' Jeremy began.

The old man cut his protest short. 'Now! There is no time to argue.' The strange pair turned and disappeared back into the jungle, leaving Jeremy and Lyssa alone again.

Jeremy turned back to Lyssa and held the jar, looking from it to her and back again, as if boggled by the enormity of the task. Then, slowly, he began to pull the shreds of Lyssa's clothing from her body, trying not to touch the burns.

Lyssa couldn't help flinching as he removed bits of fabric that had been burned into the wounds. She tried instead to watch his face as he concentrated on his work. His expression was difficult to read, but she was certain she saw pity mixed with the concern, and no small amount of horror at the damage that had been done.

Shortly, she was naked. The burns had covered more area than Lyssa had thought while doing her self-inventory. Jeremy took the lid off the jar and began gingerly dabbing ointment onto the wounds.

Lyssa's breath hissed inward at his touch and Jeremy snatched his hand away, apologizing. She shook her head slightly. 'You have to do it,' she said. 'I'll try to be quiet and hold still.'

Jeremy shook his head and bent to his task again, trying to be gentle and work quickly. 'This one on your cheek is going to be quite a rakish scar when it heals,' he said, trying to make her feel better.

Lyssa understood what he was doing, but it didn't help. She would bear these scars for life, and didn't feel like making jokes about it while the burns were raw. She was amazed at how light his touch was, but it was a relief to have him finish. The salve helped, but the burns throbbed, and Lyssa found she could sit only with difficulty. 'I have nothing to wear,' she wailed, suddenly realizing her state. That seemed more than she could handle, and she cried as she had not over the pain of her wounds.

Jeremy looked around helplessly and then began unbuttoning his shirt. 'Here,' he said, putting it around Lyssa's shoulders. 'It's better than nothing. Maybe you'll find something else in one of the closets when we get back upstairs.'

Lyssa put her arms into the sleeves, but she shook her head. 'I can't go back up there,' she whispered. 'We have to go back to the Room.'

Jeremy shook his head and started buttoning the shirt for her. 'We have to finish mapping the House before they realize you're not dead,' he said. 'You heard the old man.'

'He's crazy,' Lyssa protested. 'I need a doctor. You said so yourself.'

'No,' said Jeremy insistently. 'I believe him. We have to go back upstairs.'

'They tried to kill us,' Lyssa cried. 'They aren't going to be fooled for very long. Next time they might succeed. Are you willing to take that chance?'

'To find out what it is they're trying so hard to keep us from?' he asked. 'Yeah, I'll take that risk.'

'It's easy for you to say,' she answered bitterly. 'I'm the one who got hit. You don't have a mark on you,' she nodded at his bare chest and arms.

'I still got hit. It still knocked me out, and I have the headache to prove it,' Jeremy said. 'We have to go back up.'

'A headache?' Lyssa demanded in disbelief. 'You've got a headache?'

Jeremy put his finger under Lyssa's chin, and tilted her face up to look in her eyes. 'I know you're hurt. I know you got hit a lot worse than I did. I know there are a hundred reasons why we should just go back to town and have the doctor treat you. I also know the old man is right. We have to finish this.'

Lyssa searched his eyes for a long moment, seeing the hope and pain and frustration in them, and finally she sighed. 'You're right,' she said. 'Help me up, and I'll see if I can't get us back to where we were. Do you still have the map?'

For a moment, Jeremy looked frantic, but the map lay on the ground beside where he'd woken up, dirty, but intact. He snatched it up and smoothed out the sheets. 'Here,' he said. He held out his hand, and helped Lyssa to her feet. 'Are you going to be okay?'

'The crazy old man says I will,' she laughed nervously. 'If you believe he's right, I guess I have to also.' She reached for the old magic deep inside her, took Jeremy by the hand and thought about where they had been when they were attacked. Then they stood in the hallway again. Lyssa looked around quickly, but they were alone. Burn marks scored the walls near where they stood, and she shuddered when she saw them. She still hadn't the courage to look at her own. 'Come on,' she said in a low voice. 'We'd better get started.'

They tried to move quickly, but Lyssa slowed them down. She could walk, since her legs were undamaged, but the throbbing of her wounds and the ferocious headache caused by the backlash of the energy surge made it difficult for her to remain upright and focused.

Jeremy's headache wasn't much better, and both found it difficult to concentrate, but the sense of danger kept goading them. Doggedly, Jeremy drew new rooms and halls onto the map, glancing into the rooms beyond the doors Lyssa opened, but neither of them took the time to do more than a cursory look.

'I wish I could appreciate the beauty more,' Lyssa complained, trying to focus on the rooms around them. The woods and fabrics were so rich in color, texture and detail, they would have taken her breath away, but all her effort was concentrated on putting one foot in front of the other, and trying to maintain enough vigilance to prevent another attack.

'We've seen all this before,' said Jeremy shortly. 'I just want to finish this and get back to the Room.' He looked at her closely. 'I still think you should see a doctor.'

Lyssa nodded gingerly. 'I'd like a lot of painkillers,' she admitted. 'At least we got some sleep in the jungle.'

Jeremy snorted. 'That's not really very funny.'

'I can laugh or cry. You choose.'

'I don't think either one would be very good for your cheek,' he said, not thinking.

Lyssa put her hand to the burn on her face. The ointment had been absorbed, and now the raw flesh was blistered, hot and swollen. She must look really awful, she thought, dropping her hand to the knob of the next door. She could feel tears welling up in her eyes, but blinked them back hard, not wanting the salt to get into her wounds.

'It's the ballroom,' she whispered, stepping back so Jeremy could see to draw.

'I've never been here before,' he said, stepping out onto the grandparents' balcony overlooking the dance floor. 'You know this place?'

Lyssa nodded. 'I was playing the Game by myself that

day. I found Molly behind one of the doors down there.' She pointed.

'Have we mapped them yet?' Jeremy asked, consulting the map.

Lyssa looked over his shoulder. 'Yes, here,' she indicated where the rooms were already drawn. 'I guess we thought the other doors were closets, or bathrooms, or something. We should have checked to make sure. We missed drawing the ballroom from down on the floor.'

'Do you think we've missed anything else by not opening enough doors?' Jeremy almost groaned at the thought of having to backtrack and recheck.

Lyssa shook her head. 'We *didn't* miss this, but by now, I almost don't care,' she said. 'When I look at what you've done, I don't think we're missing anything. Eventually, most of this interconnects anyway. What we missed the first time, we get again later,' she indicated the ballroom. 'Here's where I found Molly,' she said, pointing to a room on the map.

'How can you be sure?' he asked, giving her a strange look.

Lyssa shrugged, then winced. 'I just am,' she said. 'Come on, we've got to keep going, or I'm going to collapse where I stand.'

Jeremy nodded, finishing his notations and pulling the door closed behind him.

'Look!' Lyssa breathed.

Jeremy craned past her to see what she was seeing. 'The maze?' he asked in disbelief.

'The maze,' she confirmed. 'We've made it! You can draw the rest from memory, can't you?' She gave Jeremy a pleading look.

He shook his head. 'Even though I want to, I don't think that's such a good idea. We haven't been here in a while, and you never know what the House has changed in the meantime.'

'But the rest of this never varies,' Lyssa protested. 'There's the maze. You go down the stairs to the atrium and across the floor is the door that goes upstairs to Aunt Burchie's quarters.'

'So it'll only take us a moment to check and be certain, yes?' he insisted.

Lyssa sighed and started across the floor, threading her way between the huge, overstuffed cream-colored couches, chairs and ottomans, trying not to bark her shins on the hardwood of the tables. Jeremy followed her. She was right. Down the stairs was the atrium, and across from where they stood on the balcony was the door they had always come through on their way from the House into the warrens.

'Do we check that to make sure?' Lyssa nodded at the door.

Jeremy shuddered involuntarily. '*That* I don't think is such a good idea,' he admitted. 'Do you see any other doors?'

Lyssa shook her head.

'Good. Then let's get out of here. I'll draw the rest when we get back to the Room.'

With no further prompting, Lyssa got them out of there. When they arrived back in the Room, Lyssa ran out of whatever had been keeping her going and she slumped to the floor, unconscious.

Jeremy stripped off the leather pouch, stuffed the map pages inside and tossed it onto the table. Then he picked Lyssa up and strode from the Room, intent on getting her to the doctor.

'Why in heaven's name didn't you get her here sooner?' the doctor demanded. He was large; both tall and broad, towering over Jeremy and making full use of size and station. 'You should have gotten her to me as soon as this happened.'

Jeremy held his hands out in a placating gesture, but the doctor was having none of that.

'She could have died!' he roared. 'What did you have to do that was worth more than her life?'

'It was necessary,' Lyssa croaked, having finally come to. She lay on the table, disoriented from the pain, but she knew Jeremy would never be able to defend himself adequately for this.

The doctor turned on her, but couldn't unleash the same ferocity on an injured patient. He shook his head. 'The two of you are crazy,' he said. 'Now, let me see what I can do.' He turned back to Jeremy. 'Get out!'

Jeremy almost ran from the room in his relief.

Lyssa watched him go. She understood his eagerness to be gone, but wished he'd stay and hold her hand while the doctor treated her wounds. He unbuttoned her shirt and began examining the burn marks on her arms and body.

'What did you put on these?' he asked her in a much quieter voice.

'I don't know,' she whispered. 'An ointment of some kind.'

He shook his head. 'I should have guessed.' He cut the shirt from her and began to clean and dress the raw, swollen flesh.

Lyssa winced and gritted her teeth, wishing he had given her something for the pain first, but he worked quickly, and soon she was bandaged and wrapped in a hospital gown.

'I'll send your boyfriend home to fetch your clothes,' the doctor said, leaving the room.

Lyssa lay alone on the table, and finally let herself cry. Pain, anger, fear, loneliness, humiliation and exhaustion all combined to overwhelm her. The misery of being alone fed her self-pity and she sobbed until she couldn't keep silent any longer. Hoarse cries wrenched from her throat and tears rolled into her hair because she couldn't move enough to roll onto her side.

The doctor came back into the examining room with a

syringe. 'I'm sorry,' he said softly. 'This will make it better.'
He swabbed her arm and gave her the shot.

Lyssa felt better almost immediately, and then she fell
deep into a drugged sleep.

Slowly her eyes opened. Reluctantly they came into focus
and Lyssa gave up fighting against the awakening. She
didn't want to leave the soft, dark place she had been
in; she hadn't felt so safe for months. Jeremy came into
view.

'Where am I?' she whispered.

'Back in the Room,' he said softly, sitting down in a
rocking chair he had pulled over by the bed. 'How do you
feel?'

'Pretty grim,' she said after a moment. There wasn't a
part of her that didn't ache. 'How long was I out?'

'Only a few hours,' he said. 'I have some painkillers to
give you if you want them.'

Lyssa tried to chuckle, but it hurt too much. 'Yes, please,'
she said.

Jeremy brought the medicine and a cup of water, which
Lyssa obediently swallowed. 'Do you feel like talking, or
shall I let you sleep some more?' he asked when she was
done.

'Do you have something to tell me?' Lyssa asked, settling
back into the pillows.

'Something to show you, if you feel up to it,' he said.
She nodded.

He got up and went to the kitchen table, fetching back
the papers stacked there. 'I've had some time to clean
up the maps and get the pages organized,' he said, holding
up the much-taped collages. 'What do you think?'

'You drew up a map of the town as well?' she asked,
frowning in concentration. She was still fuzzy with pain
and fatigue, and the drug was beginning to work.

Jeremy shrugged. 'I figured if your aunt had told you to
memorize the town, there must be a reason.'

Lyssa studied them as best she could. Then her eyes widened. 'The shape –'

Jeremy grinned and superimposed the pages.

'They almost match!' She tried to sit up, but couldn't. 'O-oh! Why didn't I duck?' she moaned, collapsing back onto the pillows. 'Bring those closer.'

'If you had ducked, I'd have got hit,' Jeremy reminded her as he brought the maps to her. He helped her sit enough to prop the pillows behind her so she could see them better.

'Oh, better me than you?' she asked sarcastically as she pulled the pages closer to her.

'I'm not glad you got hurt,' Jeremy said defensively. 'I know it's selfish, but I'm glad I wasn't hurt as well. The aunts could have gotten us both if you had been standing beside me instead of in front. If they had, we'd be in a lot more trouble than we are. Neither of us could defend ourselves if that had happened. How could we both have gotten to the doctor?'

Lyssa waved a hand apologetically. 'I know, I know. I don't wish you had been hurt as well, or even instead. I just wish I hadn't been. Talking about it isn't going to change what happened, so why don't we talk about this?'

They studied the maps and Jeremy showed Lyssa what he had discovered while recopying them. 'It's not just the shapes that almost match. Look at the different neighborhoods in town, and the different levels in the House.' He pointed to a couple that corresponded.

'The town is the House,' said Lyssa slowly, pointing to more. 'The House is the town. Is this what Aunt Burchie wanted us to find?'

'I'd be willing to bet,' Jeremy said. 'But it leaves us with even more questions than it answers.'

Lyssa groaned. 'Oh, look!' she exclaimed, leaning forward slightly. 'Those strange living rooms around the jungle!'

Jeremy nodded. 'The shops downtown and the park on the side.'

'Jeremy, why is there heat radiating from the chest at the foot of the bed?' she asked suddenly.

He looked up and frowned. 'I don't feel anything.'

'Open it, please?' she asked. 'Show me what's in there.'

'Just what we put in it when we cleaned up,' he protested. 'Have the painkillers taken effect?'

'This has nothing to do with drugs,' Lyssa said sharply. 'There's something going on in there, and we'd better check it out quickly.'

With a poorly muffled sigh, Jeremy stood up and went to the foot of the bed. He lifted the lid and began removing the contents, stacking them on the bed for Lyssa to examine.

She kept shaking her head until he pulled up the false bottom. 'There it is!' she cried excitedly. 'It's in there.'

'Just the cloth and the sock full of jewelry,' he said, picking them up and putting them with the other things on the bed.

'Give me the sock, please.' Lyssa held out her hand. Jeremy obliged. She dumped the items onto the quilt in her lap and examined them.

'What's going on?' he asked finally.

'I'm not sure,' Lyssa said. 'But I think there is some connection between these pieces. There's a definite energy between them that wasn't there before.'

'Before what?'

Lyssa thought about it for a long time, picking up one piece after another and turning them over and over in her hands. 'Before I put this necklace in with the other items.' She held up the necklace she had found in the pocket of the tattered velvet robe in the cupboard. The carved stone was now clearly neither jade, nor marble. It glowed so that even Jeremy could see it when he looked closely.

'What is it?' he asked.

Lyssa shrugged. 'Magic? Something we probably should-n'tbe messing with if we don't know what it is. Were you able to get in touch with Millie?'

232

Jeremy shook his head. 'I checked back with David, but he hadn't seen her.'

'Maybe he would know,' Lyssa mused. 'Could you take these to show him?'

'No,' he said immediately. 'I'm not taking those things out of here. Why don't I ask if he could come here instead?'

Lyssa tugged her lower lip as she thought about it. 'I guess it can't hurt to ask,' she said at last. Then she looked around. 'But we need to clean the place up first.'

'Who's *we*?' Jeremy grinned.

'Okay,' Lyssa laughed a little. 'Clean this place up! And let me get a little more sleep.' She put the brooches, ring and pearl necklace back in the sock and handed it to Jeremy, then slipped the silk cord of the other necklace over her head. She fell asleep holding the stone in her hand.

Jeremy cleared the contents of the trunk from the foot of the bed, putting the cloth and sock full of jewelry back into the bottom, then stacking the books on top of the false bottom. Then he straightened Lyssa's covers and made sure she was comfortable. He watched her sleep for a long while before turning back to the cleaning.

'Incredible,' said the Speaker as he stepped across the threshold into the Room. 'It hasn't changed a bit.'

'You should have seen it before I cleaned,' Lyssa grinned. She sat, swathed in the quilt from the bed, in a rocking chair beside the window. 'How long has it been since you were last here?'

David shrugged. 'This place was abandoned fairly quickly, actually,' he said, looking around. 'The Family was very successful in establishing this particular industry, and was able to move to more luxurious quarters in only a few years time.' He indicated the weaving alcove with a nod of his head. He moved to take a chair opposite Lyssa, and stopped halfway to his seat. 'What has happened?' he asked in alarm, staring at the raw wound on her face.

'The aunts caught us by surprise,' she said drily. 'The

rest of me is worse, but we got the maps completed.'

'Maps?' David took his seat and looked at Jeremy as if studying him for marks of the conflict.

'We've mapped the town and the warrens,' said Lyssa, drawing the Speaker's attention back to her. 'Aunt Burchie wanted me to know them both, so now we do. We just have no idea what to do with the information and were hoping you might be able to help. Also, we've been hoping you might see Millie and tell her we'd like to speak with her. We have no way of knowing what's going on up at the House since we fled down here. Uncle Haskell told me Aunt Burchie had a stroke, but beyond that, and the fact that Uncle Haskell is now dead, we don't know anything.'

'Haskell is dead?' David leaned forward.

Lyssa nodded. 'Evidently, I killed him.'

'How did that happen?'

'I'm not sure,' said Lyssa. 'He was blocking our way and threatening us. I held up my hand and pow, lightning shot him down the hallway. I guess the aunts didn't like that, because they showed up next, using a projection spell, and nailed us.' She looked at Jeremy and then back at the Speaker. 'Well, me, anyway.'

'How badly are you hurt?' David asked solicitously.

'Bad enough,' Lyssa said briefly. 'Would you like to see the maps? Maybe you have some ideas about where we go from here.'

David nodded, and Jeremy brought the papers over. They studied them for some time, but came up with no additional answers.

'My head is starting to hurt,' Lyssa said after a while. 'Maybe there isn't anything here. Aunt Burchie might just have been wanting me out of the House for a while.'

The Speaker shook his head. 'There is a pattern here, but I don't have the connection with the magic to see it.'

'I don't see it either,' Lyssa complained. 'And I *do* have a connection to the magic.'

'Well, as long as you are recovering from these wounds,

you probably won't have the energy or focus to see what must be in front of our faces. Burchie may be ruthless in her methods, but she always has a reason for what she does.' David stood up. 'I'm sorry I can't be more help.'

'Can you stay for dinner?' Lyssa asked, trying to hide her tiredness.

David shook his head. 'You'll think more clearly if you rest, and you won't rest while I'm here.' He shook Jeremy's hand and walked to the door. 'I'll be sure to tell Millie to stop by when I see her.'

'Thank you,' said Jeremy. He shut the door behind David and turned to Lyssa. 'Back to bed?' he asked.

'Yes, please,' she said gratefully.

Jeremy picked her up gently and carried her to the bed where he settled her against the pillows. 'Would you like some soup?'

'Yes, please,' she repeated.

She was asleep by the time he returned with the steaming mug. With a small smile, Jeremy took the soup over to the table with the maps on it and sat down to do some more studying on his own. He might not have any connection to the magic either, but he had walked the pattern with Lyssa for a considerable part of the way. Maybe he could remember where some of their steps had led them, and discover the pattern himself.

He could hear Lyssa sleeping restlessly on the bed behind him, but she was in considerable pain, so he wasn't surprised.

They were playing hide and seek in the attic.

Lyssa couldn't remember who was 'it', but she needed a good place to hide because she'd been found too easily before and didn't want to be 'it' again. She opened a door she hadn't noticed earlier and stepped through, shutting it behind her as quietly as she could, trying not to give away her location by any sound.

As she turned, she realized where she was. Many of the

floorboards were missing, and she could see darkness and dissolving mist beneath her. If she stepped on a weak board, she would fall forever, never finding the bottom of the pit beneath her. There was a hallway stretching into darkness before her, but she never went down it. She always went up the stairs.

The stairs weren't much better, but they were well lit, and that made her feel safer in this place of no safety. There were boards missing in the stairs as well. Most of them, in fact, but she had to climb the stairs in order to get out of the attic and back to the rest of the world. She didn't know how she knew this, but it was a given, so she started to climb.

The railing was rickety, and provided nothing more than a false sense of security, but she held onto it, placing one foot in front of the other on the narrow boards of the stairs. Gradually, she moved up the treacherous flight and finally found solid footing at the top.

Another hallway stretched before her, no more lit than the one downstairs had been, but considerably more intact. Carpet covered the floor, and she knew the boards beneath were whole without being able to see them. There were doors at intervals on either side of the hallway and all of them were closed but one.

Lyssa knew that one was where she had to go, so she set off down the hall, certain of what she would find. There was no breeze in the hallway, but as she moved to stand in the open door, the wind suddenly picked up, through the broken glass of the window. The organ was playing silently, its bloodied keys moving on their own, making music Lyssa couldn't hear.

She turned toward the closet and began walking across the windy room. The door was ajar, so she pulled it open wider to let in more light. The upper hinge broke and the door fell toward her. It was heavy, but Lyssa pushed it back and out of the way, stepping closer to examine the interior of the closet.

*It was empty. Just as she had thought. She began to turn
away when something caught her eye. Hanging on a hook
beside the door frame was the necklace she had found in
the bathrobe pocket. Her hand went immediately to her
throat, where she had been certain she put the necklace
before Jeremy started cleaning. It wasn't there.*

*She reached for the necklace, and put it on again, hoping
it would stay put this time. She searched the closet again,
more carefully, but this time, it was truly empty, so she
turned to go.*

The eye was staring at her from the window.

*Even expecting it, Lyssa jumped. Unblinking, it stared
at her, golden and baleful and huge in the open window.
White feathers surrounded it, and she knew the wind came
from the beating of the bird's immense wings. The eagle
said nothing, but Lyssa knew it was time to leave the room.
She walked purposefully toward the door, knowing if she
ran, the bird would pursue her. She pulled the door shut
behind her and stared up the hallway. She knew what came
next and sighed, walking straight for the next door.*

*The room beyond was blinding in its whiteness. Circles
were cut into the floor at four-foot intervals, and into each
circle descended a metal railing and ladder. The floor
seemed unending, stretching out in front of her until she
couldn't see anything else, and every four feet in all directions were the circular holes. Only one ladder reached all
the way down to the next level, and she had to try each
one until she found the right path. The others vanished
after a few rungs, and she had to pay special attention in
order not to fall off the end and into oblivion.*

*There were floors and floors like this, and she would
have to repeat the process on each one, searching for the
path down. With another sigh, she began the search,
moving from one hole to the next, climbing a few rungs
down each ladder, checking and climbing back out when
it proved not to be the one.*

When she finally came to the last floor and found her

way into the rest of the House, she ran to find the other kids she'd been playing with, hoping they'd finished their game by now and were wondering where she'd got to. She ran all over the House, but there was no one home. She decided to go over to the house of one of the children she had been playing with, so she went out the front door and down the steps to the street.

Everything was eerily still as she walked down the road. There wasn't a sound; no dogs barking, no kids yelling, no cars driving by, no insects making their background noises.

She was utterly alone.

She ran down the streets into the center of town and found everything there as deserted. All the buildings were intact, trees still grew beside the sidewalks and cars were parked along the streets, but there wasn't a living thing except for her.

She sat up screaming and found herself in Jeremy's arms. 'It's okay,' he said, stroking her hair gently, trying not to hold her too tightly and risk injuring her again. 'It was just a dream. It's okay.'

'I went back to the room in the attic,' Lyssa gasped, trying to regain her sense of reality. The dream always seemed so real when she first woke up it was hard to reorient. 'I saw what was in the closet.' She pulled the necklace into his view and gasped again. It was glowing brightly now and the color had changed from a milky green to a deep, pulsing crimson.

'I hope Millie can answer this one,' said Jeremy grimly. 'Should you take it off?'

Lyssa shook her head. 'I don't think so. I think this may be the safest place for now.'

'I hope you're right,' he said. 'Can you get back to sleep?'

Lyssa shuddered. 'I don't think I want to,' she said.

'Then why don't I show you something I've been working on,' he suggested, going to get the maps he'd been studying. 'I think I may have something.'

Lyssa lay back and rubbed her eyes. 'I think you may be right,' she said. 'But what can we do to correct it?'

'Well, the book I read suggested something, but I couldn't make any sense of it,' Jeremy admitted. 'I was hoping if you read it, you might be able to figure it out.'

'Right now, I can't read anything,' Lyssa said. 'I can hardly keep my eyes open.'

'Do you want some soup?' Jeremy picked up the maps and moved them back to the table.

'That would be nice.' Lyssa grinned shyly. It was amazing to her that she had seen nothing of Jeremy's anger since being injured. He had been solicitous and surprisingly gentle and she wasn't sure what to make of it. He dressed her wounds and rewrapped her bandages daily without complaint, cooked and cleaned voluntarily and was working hard to find the answers they both sought, on his own. He didn't seem much like the boy she had grown up with, and little like the temperamental man she had been fighting with since she got back.

Jeremy brought her a steaming mug and helped her sit to drink it. 'How are you feeling?' he asked.

'The burns are hurting less,' she said. 'But I feel stiff and sore in my muscles and my head still aches.'

He nodded. 'The backlash, shock and adrenaline. I've got some of those symptoms, too, but moving around helps. When you feel up to it, you should get out of bed and start walking around a little.'

'You see them more often than I do,' Lyssa said, referring to her burns. 'Are they starting to heal?'

'The edges are starting to look pink, and the swelling has subsided quite a bit,' he said.

'Then maybe now would be a good time,' she suggested.

'Maybe after you take a nap,' said Jeremy. 'You look like you can barely keep your eyes open.'

'I don't want to go back to that dream,' Lyssa said warily.

'Have you ever had it twice in one night?' he asked curiously. 'I never did.'

Lyssa shook her head. 'I could never get back to sleep afterwards.'

Jeremy laughed. 'There's always a first time. You need sleep, now lie down.'

'How much longer will she be asleep?' asked a small voice in a stage whisper.

Lyssa smiled to herself, luxuriating in the space between sleep and waking.

'I don't know,' Jeremy whispered back. 'But we have to let her rest as long as she can. Remember, she got pretty badly hurt.'

Lyssa lay still a few moments longer before making a show of waking up. She wasn't sure she wanted Jeremy to know she'd heard that. Moving carefully, she turned to see Molly standing beside the bed, staring solemnly at her. 'Well, hi, sweetheart,' she said, reaching out to stroke Molly's soft, black curls. 'I'm sorry I haven't been able to come see you recently. I've felt bad about that.' She smiled, hoping to ease Molly's shock. There was something else in the little girl's expression she couldn't make out. 'I don't look too good, do I?' she asked.

'You look beautiful,' Molly whispered, reaching out to touch the burn on Lyssa's cheek in disbelief. 'You look just like –' She caught herself by biting her lip and said nothing more.

Lyssa laughed uncomfortably, looking at Jeremy for help, but he shook his head. 'I thought it might be nice to have some company.'

'Well, in honor of company, I think I'll get up,' said Lyssa, sitting up carefully and pushing back the covers. Molly helped her swing her legs out of bed and stood so Lyssa could use her shoulder to stand up. 'Thank you,

Molly,' said Lyssa as they walked to the rocking chairs. Lyssa sat down and smiled at the little girl. Molly sat in the chair beside Lyssa and smiled back.

Jeremy brought a plate of cookies he'd bought on the way back from town and put them on the table. 'I helped pick them out,' said Molly eagerly, picking up the plate and offering it to Lyssa.

Lyssa grinned. 'Good choices,' she said, picking one. 'These are my favorite.'

'I know,' said Molly, taking one herself and putting the plate back on the table. 'They're my favorite, too.'

Lyssa felt a chill, but shrugged it off and bit into the cookie. 'When I feel better, we'll have to bake some of our own.' She turned to Jeremy. 'Still no word from Millie?'

He shook his head. 'I checked with David Baker on the way over to get Molly, but he said he hadn't seen her in quite a while. They must be keeping her hopping up there.'

'Maybe we should be speaking to the owner of the grocery store instead,' Lyssa mused. 'They have to eat something and Millie usually does all of the shopping for the Household.'

'Can't hurt,' said Jeremy. 'I'll stop in on my way back here later.'

Molly's face fell at that. 'Do I have to go back to Marnie's?' she asked. 'I hoped I could stay here with you.'

'I don't know if that's safe,' Lyssa said, turning back to the little girl. 'I would love for you to stay here with us, but I think for now you're still safer with Marnie at her house.' She studied Molly's face for a long moment. 'Are you okay there? Are you happy?'

Molly nodded reluctantly. 'Marnie is nice,' she said. 'But she's not you. I want to be with you.'

Lyssa frowned slightly and glanced at Jeremy. He was frowning also, and mouthed the word 'later'. She nodded and looked back at Molly. 'Why don't you tell me about what you've been doing since I've been gone? Have you found any friends your age in the neighborhood?'

Molly immediately launched into a story about some children she'd met at the park, and the games they played, and how she had been to some of their houses, and had some of them to Marnie's house for lunch and to play. Lyssa listened with half her attention on the story, and half focused on the way Molly was telling it, trying to find meaning behind the words; trying to find out if there was more going on in Marnie's house than the little girl was telling.

Lyssa was ashamed of herself for thinking Marnie could be capable of any wrong-doing where Molly was concerned, but it struck her as odd that Molly was still so attached to Lyssa even after spending so much more time with Marnie. She'd have to remember to talk to Jeremy about this when he got back from taking Molly home.

In the meantime, Molly seemed determined to make up for all the lost time in one afternoon, and talked non-stop until Jeremy said maybe Lyssa needed some more rest and they'd better get going before it got dark and Marnie started to worry.

Molly went to stand in front of Lyssa. 'Would it hurt you if I hugged you?' she asked shyly.

Lyssa smiled. 'Maybe we can do it very gently,' she said, putting her arms around the little girl.

Molly kissed her uninjured cheek, and hugged her gently. 'I'm glad you're getting better,' she whispered.

'Thanks,' Lyssa whispered back. 'Me too. And thank you for coming to see me. That made me feel really good.'

'Then maybe I can come again?' Molly asked eagerly.

'Definitely,' said Lyssa. 'Soon.' When the door shut behind Jeremy and Molly, Lyssa stood slowly and hobbled back to the bed. Even that little bit of exertion wiped her out, and she was sound asleep when Jeremy came home.

'Were you able to find anything out?' Lyssa asked.

Jeremy started and turned to see Lyssa sitting up in bed. 'How are you feeling?'

'I'm still pretty stiff,' said Lyssa. Her burns hurt unbelievably and she still couldn't get over the fact that it was her own family turning against her had caused it. In the end, that hurt even more than the wounds. They weren't much of a family, but they were all she had and they were trying to kill her.

Jeremy nodded, seeing the dilemma play on her face. 'I stopped at the grocery and left word for Millie. They said they hadn't seen her in a while. The chauffeur has been doing the shopping.'

'Will they tell her to pass the message along to Millie?' asked Lyssa.

'Yeah,' said Jeremy. 'I figured that way we've just about got our bases covered. It's that or go up the hill ourselves.'

Lyssa shuddered. 'I just hope she's okay.'

'I'm sure she is. They can't really do anything to her except restrain her,' Jeremy said. He had meant to be comforting, but it came out sounding wrong. 'You know what I mean,' he finished lamely.

'We'll hope for the best,' said Lyssa. 'What were you working on?'

'Just seeing if I could put together more of the pattern,' Jeremy gestured behind him to the maps on the table.

'Is it working?'

'Uh, actually, yes, it is,' said Jeremy.

'Why don't you bring me the book you thought I should go through and I'll give it a crack while you keep puzzling that,' she suggested.

Jeremy brought her the book. As she took it, he reached out and gently touched the burn on her cheek. 'It's starting to look better,' he said. 'The edges are turning pink.'

'It itches ferociously,' she complained. 'I wish the salve the doctor gave me could do something about that.'

'At least that's a good sign,' said Jeremy. 'But most of the burns are still pretty bad. It could take months for them to heal completely.'

'We don't have months,' Lyssa protested, brandishing the book.

'Then why don't you see what you can do with that magic of yours,' he said facetiously. 'It ought to be good for something.'

The thought had never occurred to Lyssa. 'I could try,' she said, surprised.

Jeremy laughed. 'You do that while I go back to this,' he gestured at the maps.

'Each of us with a job to do,' Lyssa grinned. She watched Jeremy settle back down at the table before turning her vision inward, searching for the strange magic that had taken up residence in the center of her being. The small, hard kernel had grown larger since she last accessed it. The knot was loosening and the throb of power increased. Warmth radiated outward from it, causing a faint tingle in her arms and legs that she only now noticed.

Not knowing what to do, Lyssa tried to envision the energy going directly to the burns on her body, but she didn't seem to be able to control the flow. The power diffused itself before she could hone or direct it. After a long while, Lyssa noticed that the itch of her wounds had intensified a bit, but when she lifted the dressing on her left arm, there was no noticeable difference.

With a sigh, Lyssa abandoned the approach and thought for a while instead. There had been little in any of the books about directing the old magic. The only oblique references to directed energy had nothing to do with the actual working of spells, and there was no mention of rogue magic connected with any of the rooms in the House. She racked her brain trying to think of anything she might have overlooked, but in the end, she could come up with nothing.

Well, if at first – she thought to herself, and returned to the central core of the magic to find another way. Since directing the flow didn't work, and the magic seemed to want to diffuse, Lyssa tried increasing the output, allowing the diffusion and trying to send it to the outer layers of skin in the hope that an all-over barrage might do the trick. She peeked under the dressing again, and there seemed to be a small improvement, but not enough to remark on.

She was getting a headache again. She lay back down and closed her eyes. Quietly, she monitored the energy flowing inside her, feeling where it went, and observing the patterns it created in her system.

There were blocks in some of the streams, causing short-circuits in the currents, so Lyssa focused on one of the bigger ones, and removed it. The energy immediately started flowing in the direction it was supposed to and she watched where it went, feeling life being breathed back into tissues that now seemed to have been dead. Fascinated by the effect, Lyssa began searching for and removing the other obstacles in the energy streams.

When the last one was gone, she stepped back mentally and observed the pattern of the flow, marvelling at the beauty of the power. Everything was now where it was supposed to be, and everything seemed to be working more smoothly than it ever had. It felt good to lie in bed, but she knew it would feel even better to wake up.

When had she fallen asleep? Lyssa opened her eyes and stared at the ceiling. There seemed to be a new awareness in her, but she didn't know what it was. Then she remembered her burns. Lying still, she did a mental inventory on the aches and pains that had been constant company since the aunts attacked her in the warrens.

They were gone.

She sat up and pulled the dressings off her arms. The scars were vivid pink, but the wounds themselves had healed completely. She stripped off her shirt and removed the bandages from her body as well. All the burns were gone, and in their place was smooth, shiny scar tissue. 'I did it,' she whispered.

'Hmm?' Jeremy turned, distracted by the sound of her words. His mouth dropped open when he saw her. 'H-how do you feel?' he asked.

Lyssa burst out laughing. 'Like going for a walk,' she said, pulling her shirt back on. 'Want to go clear our heads?'

Jeremy shrugged. 'Can't hurt. I've hit an impasse. Maybe we can come back to it with fresh minds.' He stood up and stretched.

Lyssa pulled on her pants and rummaged for her shoes and socks. 'I may be able to help you, finally,' she said, pulling them on. 'I think I can sit up for a little while without getting a headache now.'

Jeremy grinned. 'I'm glad you're feeling better.'

'Me too,' said Lyssa. She opened the door and stepped out into the late afternoon sun. Taking a deep breath, she looked around as if seeing the place for the first time. 'It really is very pretty here.'

'Still a gilded cage,' said Jeremy, stepping outside and pulling the door shut behind him.

'So maybe we'll find the way out,' said Lyssa. She felt too good to let his pessimism affect her. 'Come on.'

They walked down the hill and into town, headed nowhere in particular. It felt good just to be walking, and Lyssa enjoyed the outing, but soon it was dusk, and they turned back toward the hill, heading home for another evening of studying.

'Shall I fix some dinner while you look at the maps?' Lyssa suggested as they closed the door to the Room.

Jeremy shook his head. 'Why don't I cook and you look at them for a while? I've about had it with patterns and sitting.'

Lyssa moved the maps to the kitchen table and adjusted the wick on the lamp. She sat down and immediately lost herself in the task. The sounds of Jeremy moving around the kitchen faded into the background as she tried to decipher the marks he had been making, both on the maps and in the margins.

Jeremy dropped a plate and jolted her into awareness.

'Sorry,' he murmured, returning to his preparations.

Lyssa looked back down at the maps and gasped. 'There it is!' she cried, pointing. The flow of energy was as clear to her in the House as it had been in her own body.

Jeremy came and looked at where she was pointing. 'Where?'

Lyssa sketched the pattern on the House. Then she did it on the town. 'Here,' she said. 'It's the same in both of them. It was the same in me.'

'What?' Jeremy looked puzzled. 'Isn't this the way we walked it?' He used his index finger to draw a different pattern on the map of the House.

'Yes,' said Lyssa excitedly. 'That's the way we walked it. That's the pattern Aunt Burchie set in motion. That was the pattern I was looking at before I cleared the blocks in my own energy flow. After I removed them, the burns were healed.'

Jeremy sat down. 'Lyssa, what are you talking about?' he asked with exaggerated patience.

'Aunt Burchie is playing fast and loose with the rules! She changed the pattern that the Family has been walking for generations,' she said, becoming agitated. 'The book that talked about the spell for transition detailed a pattern very different from the one we've been walking. That's why nothing made sense! Every time the House moves things around, a barrier is formed in the spell, changing the pattern we walked, and the spell we wove. I don't know what we were supposed to be doing, and I don't know what the House was making us do, but I do know that with this information, we can choose the pattern we do walk, and control the spell we cast. Why didn't we run into the Others when we were mapping the House?'

Jeremy was unprepared for the subject change. 'Huh?'

'We didn't see anyone but Family when we were mapping the House,' Lyssa said. 'Where were they? No room looked any more lived in than any of the others. Where was your room?'

Jeremy's mouth dropped open. 'How could we miss an entire section and not even notice?'

'Not noticing a room I can understand,' said Lyssa. 'We weren't exactly compos mentis by the time we'd been doing this a while, but I don't even recall seeing that whole area. It just wasn't there.'

Jeremy leaned forward and looked again at the maps. 'There isn't anything corresponding to it on the town map, either,' he said with a slight frown. 'Dinner is going to burn.' He stood up. 'Maybe we'll have more answers after we eat.'

Lyssa sniffed in appreciation and got up to move the maps back to the other table. 'If the Others' quarters aren't in the warrens proper, then why is their entrance right there by the side of the road, and where is the door we always went through that connected them?'

Jeremy set plates and silverware on the table and sat down. 'None of this is making sense anymore,' he complained.

Lyssa laughed a little, but it wasn't from amusement. 'It never did,' she said, also sitting. 'We definitely need to talk to Millie. I think we're going to have to go find her because she should have been into town by now if everything was okay.'

Jeremy looked grim, but he nodded in agreement. 'Do you have any better handle on the magic? Can you use it to protect us?'

Lyssa nodded slowly. 'I think so.'

'You'd better be more certain than that,' he said with feeling. 'That trick with the burns was neat, but you came way too close to dying. I don't want to take that kind of risk anymore.'

'Risk is part of it,' Lyssa shrugged. 'I don't want to die, because then we probably wouldn't get to finish the spell the way we want it to go, but without talking to Millie, I don't even know how we'd go about getting started. It's a chance we've got to take.'

'How many aunts and uncles are there?' Jeremy asked, hardly reassured by Lyssa's attitude.

'Even Millie didn't know for sure when I asked her,' grinned Lyssa. 'She said she couldn't even remember any of their names. I think that's why I think of them as the aunts and uncles. That's how she thinks of them, too.'

'So there's lots?' asked Jeremy in growing frustration.

'That or they all look alike,' said Lyssa, feeling a little devilish. 'My guess is we're going to find out.'

First they went to talk to David Baker.

'You're planning to do what?' he asked in disbelief. He sat down in the pew and stared up at them. 'You can't be serious.'

'She hasn't come to town,' said Lyssa defensively. 'We need to talk to her.'

'You can't just walk up to the front door and ring the bell,' David protested. 'They'll kill you before you get that close.'

'Why are they trying to?' Lyssa asked. 'I thought I was supposed to finish walking the pattern. If they kill me, I can't do that.'

'I think they've pretty well figured out you've decided not to finish the spell,' the Speaker said. 'They didn't want you to succeed Burchie in any case. Each wants to be the one to inherit, and if you're out of the way, one of them will.'

'Swell,' said Lyssa, sitting in a pew near David. 'So Aunt Burchie is the only one who wants me to inherit, and since I'm not playing by her rules, she's mad at me too?'

David shrugged. 'She may be out of the picture already. You may already have inherited. That doesn't mean they won't try to remove or replace you. If you die, there has to be someone else who's next in line.'

Lyssa sighed. 'I have to see Millie,' she said. She felt a thump against her solar plexus and remembered the strange, glowing necklace. She reached into her shirt and pulled it out, looking at it. Staring at the pulsing, crimson stone, she missed the expression on the Speaker's face. She took it off and held it out to him. 'Will you keep this for me?' she asked. 'I don't think I ought to take this up to the House.'

'Are you sure?' asked David and Jeremy simultaneously. They looked at each other and back at her.

She nodded. 'It doesn't want to go.'

David reached for the necklace like one who couldn't believe his good fortune, restrained, but barely. His fingers closed on the silk cord below where she held it and excitement trembled his hand. 'I'll keep it safe,' he said in a voice of contained excitement.

Lyssa studied him with a frown, but she felt she could trust him, so she decided not to worry about his reaction to her request. 'I'll come back for it,' she said softly, reminding him that he was only holding the necklace for her, and letting him know that she would be careful while in the House.

He smiled. 'Good.'

Lyssa stood up and motioned Jeremy to follow her out of the church. Once they were out on the street again, she said, 'You were awfully quiet in there.'

'There wasn't anything for me to say,' he smiled.

Lyssa grinned. 'I don't think we should just walk up to the front door, though.'

'Where's your sense of adventure?' Jeremy objected.

'It was cauterized,' Lyssa snorted, smiling grimly. 'I think we should try using an alternate mode of transportation.'

'Can you take us to wherever Millie might be?' asked Jeremy more seriously. 'It's not like we know where to find her.'

'I have a little better handle on this stuff now,' said Lyssa. 'But I don't know if I have any better control. When I cleared the pattern inside myself, it felt like I got more in touch with the magic, but I still don't know how to use it, so I suggest we hope for the best and go someplace where our disappearing won't raise any eyebrows.'

'Home it is, then,' Jeremy said, turning in that direction.

'Home,' Lyssa repeated softly. 'Home.' Jeremy didn't seem to hear, or pretended not to, so Lyssa followed him back out of town and up the hill to the Room. The House was no longer home to her, and the warrens were evidently no longer home for him. She thought about Marnie and her heart ached. He might think of the Room as home, but his heart didn't belong to her, and that would always hurt.

Once they were on the path around the hill, away from prying eyes, Lyssa said, 'Here is as good a place as any.'

Jeremy stopped and turned to face her. 'Are you ready?'

Lyssa smiled weakly. 'No, but we have to do this eventually. We might as well get it over with.' She reached out and took his hand, feeling the strength in his grip and the dry touch of his skin against hers, and caught her breath.

'What?' he asked, leaning toward her slightly.

Lyssa shook her head. 'Huh?'

'You were going to say something?' Jeremy searched her face.

'No,' Lyssa denied. 'Just trying to get up the nerve to do this.'

'Either it'll be okay, or it won't,' he answered, giving her hand a reassuring squeeze.

Lyssa laughed. 'Okay.' She touched the magic flowing in her veins, and thought about Millie, picturing her as clearly as she could, and thought about going to her.

'Miss!' Millie gasped a second later. 'You shouldn't be here!'

Lyssa opened her eyes. 'We had to come.'

'Who's we?' asked Millie, looking around.

Lyssa gasped. Jeremy hadn't come with her.

Chapter Nine

'There is a price to be paid for using the magic, and if you choose to do so, you should be prepared to pay in full.'

The Magic Book, Chapter Six

'We were holding hands!' Lyssa gasped, sagging onto the bed. She looked around Millie's small room again, as if he might be there this time. 'That always worked before.'

Millie glanced nervously over her shoulder at the door and came to sit beside Lyssa. 'You shouldn't be here,' she repeated.

'We've been leaving word all over town, trying to get a hold of you, but you haven't been coming down from the hill,' Lyssa explained. She put up wards finally, remembering she was inside the lion's den. 'Are you being held here?'

'Yes and no,' said Millie slowly. 'I've been trying to monitor what the aunts and uncles are doing, and I can't do it if I'm not around. Also, I just don't feel like I'd be able to leave if I tried.'

'You haven't tried?' Lyssa demanded.

Millie made a small gesture. 'There's been so much to do.' She reached out and touched the scar on Lyssa's cheek. 'I'd heard about this. They were bragging that they'd probably killed you. They certainly tried to.'

'You should see the rest of the marks,' Lyssa said wryly. 'They came very close.'

'Was Jeremy with you then?'

Lyssa laughed. 'Behind me. He wasn't touched. We were mapping the warrens.'

'That's what they thought you were trying to do. They were trying to stop you from seeing the pattern,' Millie sighed.

'Well, they didn't succeed,' said Lyssa. 'Not only do we have the layout for the warrens, but the town and the old magic as well. I fixed the kinks in my own system and everything is flowing much more smoothly now.'

Millie nodded. 'You're certainly doing better than the last time I saw you. Did you finish the books?'

'Yeah, but Aunt Burchie has messed with everything so that most of the information is no longer accurate.' Lyssa sighed. 'The House is frozen until I start walking the pattern again, but I had to talk to you about changing it first. I don't know any spells and the books didn't help with that at all. Who is the old man in the jungle?'

Millie looked startled. 'Who?' she asked.

'There is an old man in the jungle, who calls himself the Keeper, and a weird little boy he refers to as his companion. I've talked to them mostly in dreams. Jeremy and I went looking for them physically one day, and couldn't find them, but when the aunts burned me, we woke up there, and he gave us a salve to keep me going until we were done with the mapping. Who are they?'

'The balance of power,' said Millie slowly, ignoring Lyssa's question. 'Everything is a balance: the House and the town, Burchie and Cornelius, you and Jeremy.'

Lyssa nodded. 'Jeremy was brought here for me.'

'He is supposed to replace Cornelius when you replace Burchie,' said Millie.

'That's what the Keeper said, but that isn't going to happen now, is it?' asked Lyssa.

Millie shrugged. 'I have no idea what's going to happen now. All I know is that none of us are safe here, and the Family is in a frenzy of activity that largely makes no sense to me. I've never seen this behavior at a transition before.'

'Burchie walked the pattern,' said Lyssa.

'Only in part.'

'What really happened with my father?' asked Lyssa.

'Burchie was just beginning to tinker with the rules. The House hadn't caught on to her manipulations and Jordan fell through a hole. When it became evident he knew more than he should, she sucked him dry and then turned him inside out. He never recovered and finally she couldn't bear the reminder anymore, so she threw him out.'

'But kept me,' Lyssa said with a bitter twist of her mouth.

'Who knows her reasons, but I guess it didn't seem likely there would be any more Family members except from you, so she wanted to keep you close.'

'Until she sent me away, too. Odd way of handling things. I found a necklace.' Lyssa said abruptly changing the subject again. 'I put it with some other old jewelry in a sock in the trunk, but a strange energy started vibrating between them, so I separated them again. I gave the necklace to David Baker before I came here.'

'Had you been wearing it then?' asked Millie casually.

'Yes,' said Lyssa.

'What color is the stone?' asked Millie, a little less casually.

'It was green. Now it's red.'

'The balance is shifting,' Millie murmured. 'The contrast has changed.'

Lyssa frowned. 'What are you talking about?'

There was a sound in the hallway outside the door. Millie put her hand on Lyssa's arm. 'You have to leave now!' she whispered urgently.

Lyssa nodded and stood up. She closed her eyes and focused on the Room.

'Where the hell have you been?' Jeremy demanded, grabbing her by the shoulders, shaking her gently. 'Why didn't you take me with you?'

Lyssa opened her eyes and focused on him. Jeremy looked worried, not angry. 'We were holding hands. I thought that was enough.'

'Did you see Millie?' he asked, relaxing his grip on her.

Lyssa nodded. 'She's okay. We were able to cover a good amount of ground before the old folks caught on to the fact that I was there.'

'You saw them?'

'No,' Lyssa replied hastily. 'We only heard a noise in the hall. I'm not even certain it wasn't the cat.'

'You don't have a cat,' said Jeremy frowning.

'Then maybe we should get one,' Lyssa said with a smile.

Molly ran down the lawn to meet them. She caught Lyssa around the waist, hugging her tightly. 'I'm so glad to see you,' she cried, pushing away to inspect Lyssa's wounds. 'Are you okay?'

Lyssa smiled and nodded. 'See?' she pointed to her cheek. 'Much better. Jeremy and I thought you might like to take a walk with us.'

'I'll go tell Marnie!' Molly yelled, racing back up to the house.

'You're not going with her?' Lyssa asked.

Jeremy shook his head. 'I guess she can get permission without my help.'

Lyssa raised an eyebrow, but said nothing more. Shortly, Molly returned, grinning ear to ear.

'I can go,' she said, grabbing Jeremy and Lyssa each by the hand. 'Where are we going?'

'Why don't you choose,' Jeremy suggested. 'We've done a lot of the picking before. I think it's your turn.'

'Can we go into town for ice cream?' Molly asked slyly.

Lyssa laughed. 'That sounds really good.' She turned to Jeremy. 'Can we, huh?'

'Since when am I in charge?' Jeremy laughed also. 'Ice cream it is.'

'Goodie!' yelled Molly, pulling them in the direction of town. 'Hurry,' she begged.

'What have you been doing since I saw you last?' Lyssa asked as they trotted down the street.

'Playing,' said Molly briefly.

'Do you play with Marnie or the other kids?' asked Lyssa, wondering what she was digging for.

'Mostly by myself,' said Molly. 'With the doll houses and stuff. Marnie is very busy right now, and I can't go to the park by myself.'

Lyssa looked at Jeremy. 'What does Marnie do?' she asked.

Jeremy gestured that he had no idea. Molly said, 'She spends a lot of time in her room with the door shut. Sometimes I hear voices, but I think mostly she's alone too.'

'Do people come to the house pretty often?' Lyssa pressed. 'Do you get to see them?'

'No one comes to the house but you and Jeremy,' said Molly a little impatiently.

'But you hear voices in Marnie's room?' asked Jeremy.

Lyssa shot him a glance, but he seemed as surprised by the news as she had been.

'Not very often.' Molly pulled them faster. 'I want chocolate marble on a sugar cone. What are you going to get?'

'I hadn't thought about it,' said Lyssa. 'I guess that sounds pretty good.'

Jeremy agreed. Shortly, they arrived at the ice cream parlor, having traveled most of the distance at a jog. They purchased their cones and went back out on the street to continue walking while they ate.

'Molly, have you been alone at Marnie's a lot?' Jeremy asked.

'Yeah,' said the little girl. She was engrossed in her cone and walking slowly now. 'Especially since the House at the top of the hill started glowing.'

'You noticed that?' Lyssa asked, surprised.

Molly looked up at her somewhat disdainfully. '*Everyone* has noticed it. That's all they talk about. Can we go to the park?'

'Sure,' said Lyssa. While Molly played with the other kids, it would give Lyssa a chance to talk to Jeremy. They watched her run to join a group playing on the slides before sitting on a bench to watch. 'I'm worried about her.' She looked at Jeremy, studying him for his reaction.

He nodded. 'I don't think she should be spending so much time alone, unsupervised,' he said.

'Should we talk to Marnie?' Lyssa asked uncertainly.

'I should probably,' Jeremy admitted. 'Maybe when we take Molly back we can go in for a while.'

The house was quiet in the early evening when they returned. The only light on was in Marnie's room. Molly opened the door, and Jeremy and Lyssa followed her in.

'Marnie? We're back,' called Jeremy. He went to the living room, even though she wasn't there.

To Lyssa it looked like long habit, but she didn't comment, following him instead. Molly brought up the rear. All three sat on the couch.

Soon, they heard footsteps on the stairs, and Marnie came around the corner into the room.

Lyssa was shocked by the changes in her. She glanced at Jeremy, who was likewise struck dumb. Marnie appeared to have aged considerably. The youth and beauty Lyssa envied had faded, and Marnie looked tired and ill. Lyssa was about to get to her feet and offer Marnie assistance when the look in Marnie's eyes stopped her. 'Are you okay?' she asked instead. 'Is there anything we can do? Do you need a doctor?'

Marnie smiled bitterly. 'I'll be just fine,' she said in a hard, brittle voice. She continued to stand in the doorway, looking at the three sitting on her couch. 'What a sweet little family,' she said, raising a hand.

Lyssa felt the hair stand up on the back of her neck, and raised a shield around them even as she grabbed Jeremy and Molly by the hands and pulled them to their feet. 'We've come to take Molly home with us,' she said, rather too loudly. She started purposefully forward, hoping fervently that Marnie would give way. Lyssa wasn't prepared to risk Molly's life on whether or not the magic was working.

Marnie lowered her hand. 'Run away,' she hissed as they walked past. 'I'll deal with you in time.'

Lyssa could feel Marnie's eyes burning into her back as they went through the front door and down the steps. She was squeezing Molly's hand so tightly she could hear the little girl whimpering, but she didn't loosen her grip until they were out of the neighborhood. 'What was that?' she asked Jeremy finally.

Jeremy shook his head, still too dumbfounded to speak.

'Lyssa, where are we going?' Molly asked plaintively. She was trotting alongside, trying to keep up, but it was evident she was tired.

Lyssa slowed her pace immediately and turned her attention to Molly. 'We're going back to the place Jeremy brought you to visit when I was hurt and in bed. You're going to be staying with us until I can find a way to get you back to your parents.'

'What's the matter with Marnie?' Molly asked.

'I don't know,' Lyssa answered truthfully. 'But she can't take care of you right now, so Jeremy and I are going to, okay?'

'Okay, but where am I going to sleep?' Molly wanted to know.

'We'll find somewhere,' Jeremy laughed. 'How about we make up a special pallet on the floor of the weaving room? It won't be as nice as the room you had at Marnie's, but maybe you could pretend you're camping. It might be fun.'

'Okay,' said Molly again. Once her fate was settled, she seemed to regain her happiness, apparently unruffled by the scene she had just witnessed.

Lyssa and Jeremy, however, were both still shaking from the incident, and wondering now just what they were really up against.

*　　*　　*

258

After dinner, they tucked Molly into her bed and kissed her good night. 'Sweet dreams,' said Lyssa, smoothing the black curls from the little girl's forehead. 'Sleep well.'

Molly smiled, snuggling down into the blankets. 'It feels good here,' she said.

Lyssa smiled. 'I'm glad. If you need anything, we're right over there, okay?' She pointed at the living area. Then she kissed Molly again, stood up and moved aside for Jeremy who had come in with them.

He knelt and kissed Molly on the forehead, stroking her cheek gently with his index finger. 'Everything's alright now,' he said. 'Do you have everything you need?'

'Yes,' Molly said earnestly. 'Good night.'

'Good night,' said Jeremy and Lyssa together. They stepped out into the living room and Lyssa trimmed the wick on the lamp, turning the light low. They sat in two of the rocking chairs in silence for a long while, rocking gently and savoring the relative calm.

'I have to go back in,' said Lyssa finally, keeping her voice low so as not to disturb Molly. 'Do you have any idea what's going on with Marnie?'

Jeremy shook his head. 'She's connected to what's going on up there,' he said, nodding toward the top of the hill. 'I had thought she might be, but I wasn't certain until this evening.'

Lyssa sat up. 'You suggested we send Molly there and you thought she had a tie to the Family?'

Jeremy held up his hands. 'No, no!' he said hastily. 'I only began to discover things after Molly went to stay there, but she seemed safe, and I knew we weren't in a position to take care of her, so I thought she'd be best where she was. Up until tonight, I think everything was okay.'

'She's unharmed,' said Lyssa. 'What made you think Marnie might not be what she represented?'

Jeremy shook his head. 'It wasn't anything specific. Things she said sounded like your aunt sometimes, or like something you would say. It just wasn't necessarily what she would have said when we were kids.'

'You've known her for a long time,' Lyssa said slowly. 'Did you know her well?'

Jeremy smiled wryly. 'Yes and no. We were friends. I don't have a whole lot of those. People in town don't much trust the people from the hill, and the people from the hill don't usually last too long,' he shuddered, remembering what he'd read in the books Lyssa had found. 'Anyway, even though I stuck around longer than most, I didn't do much to make myself popular, and I defended the girl with the funny accent, so the other kids left me alone. I guess I thought Marnie was enough and she seemed willing to be. We spent a lot of time together.'

'You're in love with her?' Lyssa couldn't believe she'd actually spoken the words.

Jeremy's head jerked up and he looked her in the eyes, astonished. 'Love?'

'You've been . . .' Lyssa couldn't stop herself from asking. 'Intimate?'

Jeremy's jaw dropped. 'We've scratched an itch from time to time,' he said bluntly. 'Am I in love with Marnie? Maybe there was a time I thought I was, but no, I do not love her.' They rocked again in silence for a time. 'You have to go back in?' Jeremy came back to the start of the conversation. 'What for?'

'To change the pattern,' said Lyssa. 'I was looking at the pattern you traced, and the pattern I saw in the maps when I looked at them. Then I saw the pattern in my body when I healed the burns. I know what I have to do, and I have to go back into the warrens to do it.'

'What about the aunts and uncles?' he asked. 'What about Millie and David? What about Molly and me?'

'Millie and David can't help any more than they already have, and if I try to contact Millie again –' she shrugged. 'I'm not sure, but I think it would be a big mistake to go back into Aunt Burchie's part of the House. In the warrens, I have more control over what happens. In the House, even if Aunt Burchie is ill or dead, she still has control over what happens there. As for you and Molly, it's probably safest if you stay here. I can't defend you both and still protect myself. The aunts and uncles are going to find out what I'm doing and they'll try to stop me; I think we can treat that as a given. I just know I have to walk this other pattern.'

'I just don't want to see you get hurt again,' said Jeremy.

Lyssa grinned. 'I'll either succeed or die trying. How's that? Nothing in between.'

'That's not funny,' Jeremy said.

Lyssa held up a placating hand. 'I was trying to take the edge off. I'm tired. I think maybe I'll go to bed and get an early start in the morning.'

'You're going back in tomorrow?'

Lyssa frowned. 'Do you have a reason I should wait?'

'Well, no,' he admitted. 'But don't you have to prepare or something?'

'How? For what?' she wanted to know.

He shrugged. 'I guess I just wasn't ready for everything to happen so fast.'

Lyssa grinned and stood up. 'You and me both,' she said. She went to the bed and sat on the edge to take off her shoes and socks. 'Leave the lamp on in case Molly wakes up and gets disoriented.'

'Shall I turn it down some more?' Jeremy leaned forward to adjust the wick.

'Sure,' said Lyssa, pulling off her pants and crawling under the covers. She moved over against the wall, leaving Jeremy room, and was asleep immediately.

Molly cried out in her sleep in the middle of the night, but didn't waken. Lyssa came awake immediately, listening for another cry, and realized she and Jeremy had been sleeping back to back, comfortable with the contact. When Molly settled back down, Lyssa snuggled back against Jeremy and fell asleep again, smiling to herself.

*   *   *

The pattern started at the jungle; the green heart of everything.

Just as the town had started with the church, and life began and ended with the heartbeat, so the House had started with the jungle.

It had been a garden at first. The Room was far from it in relation to the hill, but closely tied by the magic used to create them. As the House had expanded and taken on a life of its own, the jungle became the heartbeat that kept the organism living and growing. Eventually, the House made the organ internal, swallowing the jungle as the hill swallowed the House.

Then Burchie had started changing the rules and the pattern became twisted, bent to her purposes. By the time Lyssa began walking the pattern, the jungle had been cut out of the loop and the pattern no longer had a heart. The soul was gone from the magic, which could no longer purify itself in the lush growth protected by Cornelius and his companion. Removed from the process, the Keeper was unable to balance the power he was supposed to help control. The best he could do was defend himself if Burchie came looking for him.

So this was where Lyssa took herself first thing the next morning. She stood outside the doorway she and Jeremy were becoming familiar with, and warded herself as best she could, hoping this time it would be enough. Then she looked inward, tracing the pattern and overlaying it on what she remembered of the map Jeremy had drawn.

Opening her eyes, she marked her first steps. She would have to hurry. Almost at a jog, she set out, threading her way through the maze of living rooms. There was no way of knowing how long it would take her to complete the pattern, but Lyssa was hoping to be able to set the magic in motion before being forced to quit for the day.

Completing her first circuit, she headed for the hallways beyond, and the ballrooms and bedrooms that made up the next part of the spell. She could feel the magic starting to pulse within her in response to what she was doing, and wondered how long it would take for the elders upstairs to get wind of her actions. Darting from one room to the next, waking long dormant magic, Lyssa checked again and again on her wards, sensing nothing and hoping it was a reliable read.

She ran across balconies, up and down stairs, drawing on the power inside her for the energy to keep moving, and gradually she felt the House begin to respond. Slowly, like long-rusted machinery stirring to life, the spell began to work. The House was rearranging itself to correspond to the pattern Lyssa had created in herself when she moved the blocks from the energy flow.

She was able to move faster now, and that meant the danger was greater. There was no way the aunts and uncles were unaware of her actions. Lyssa sped across a large, dark foyer and started up a flight of stairs.

They were waiting for her at the top, and she ran right into them. They were old but, en masse, they were strong. They closed around her like a net, but her momentum took her through it, tearing the webbing apart, still it slowed her down.

When they regrouped, they were stronger, and she was slower. The energy she was using began to dwindle as she drew from it with such speed and so little reserve. When the net closed around her the second time, she had to fight to break free.

She was forced to a walk now, struggling to continue the pattern. Her wards were useless. Lyssa was fairly certain they had never been much good. She had no idea how the magic worked, only that it didn't serve her.

Feeling defeated, she didn't even see the net the third time. It caught her tightly and held her so that she couldn't move, then took her upstairs to Aunt Burchie's room. The net released her so that she dropped into the chair beside the bed. She looked up and saw her aunt watching her with blazing eyes. Lyssa shrank away from her. She tried to stand, but her legs were too weak.

Looking again at Aunt Burchie, Lyssa finally understood. 'Marnie?' she asked carefully.

'You will pay for what you've done,' spat the creature in the bed. 'Where is the necklace?'

Lyssa shook her head. 'What are you talking about?'

'The heartstone,' said the old woman urgently. 'Where is the necklace? You have it. Give it to me.'

'I have no idea what you're talking about,' said Lyssa, spreading out her empty hands as if that might appease her aunt. 'I don't have a necklace.'

'You told Millie about it,' hissed Aunt Burchie. 'I was listening. You said you'd found it.'

Lyssa sighed. There was no point in lying, and no profit in telling the truth. There was no way of knowing just how much the old woman knew, and what lies might work, but she thought she'd better try. 'I found a necklace,' she admitted. 'I used it as a barter in town. I had no money for groceries.'

'That's a lie. You may not know how to use your magic, but you'd better believe I know how to use mine. I can see through you easily. Where is the heartstone?'

Lyssa studied her aunt for a long while. 'Who are you really?' she asked at length.

'Who I am is unimportant to you. I've asked you a question. I have other ways of obtaining the information if you choose not to give it voluntarily.' The old woman's eyes snapped and sparkled.

Lyssa thought she'd probably enjoy using other methods rather than just questioning, so Aunt Burchie was probably bluffing or she'd have used them by now. 'We're trading information. Are Family members actually related?'

'We are cut from the same cloth,' said Aunt Burchie. 'That's close enough to related.'

'Do you mean literally?' Lyssa shuddered, remembering the cloth in the trunk downstairs.

The old woman threw back her head and roared with laughter. 'What a silly notion. Where did you get an idea like that? No, I simply mean we reproduce differently than the humans that surround us. We are not stitched, stuffed and animated.'

Lyssa blushed. Her thoughts were that easily read. Then why couldn't her aunt see the whereabouts of the necklace in her mind as well? She searched her mind, trying to remember what she had told Millie about it. She thought for sure she'd mentioned leaving it with David Baker. Maybe Aunt Burchie wasn't tracking the name, only associating the person with the title. Had she said 'Speaker'? No, Aunt Burchie would have had time to think about it, and would have asked other people if she couldn't remember. She couldn't have heard the entire conversation. 'I've put the heartstone in a safe place. I'm the only one who can retrieve it.'

'That's not all,' her aunt prompted, leaning forward greedily.

'Why do you want it?' asked Lyssa. 'What is it for?'

The old woman chuckled. 'If you haven't even figured that much out –'

'None of this comes with directions,' Lyssa snapped. 'And when you play fast and loose with the rules, you make it difficult to follow what's happening on the field of play.'

'You're no dummy. It's all right there in front of you, and you can't even see it? Jeremy must have your head turned more than I thought.' Aunt Burchie waited for her reaction, but Lyssa remained passive. 'He is good in bed, though, I can see how that would happen.'

Lyssa froze. She wasn't prepared to hear this. When Jeremy referred to scratching an itch, it didn't conjure the images she was now faced with. Then, mentally, she transposed Aunt Burchie's face on to Marnie's and started to laugh. Well, everyone came out looking foolish on this one. 'If you want the necklace, I'll have to go get it,' she said.

Aunt Burchie shook her head. 'You don't think I'm stupid, do you girl? There are –'

'Better ways to get what you want, I know, I know,' Lyssa finished rudely. 'If there were, you'd have done it by now. Tell you what: If you won't let me go, let Millie go.'

'*NO!*' shouted Aunt Burchie.

Lyssa jumped. That was definitely not the reaction she'd been expecting. 'Fine,' she said sullenly. 'Don't send her. But you'll never get your hands on it if you don't send one of the two of us.'

'We could send your little girl,' said the old woman slyly. Her eyes glittered at the thought.

Lyssa felt a chill run down her spine. 'You leave her out of this,' she spat. 'Either I go, or you don't get your precious necklace.'

'You'll send for it with your magic,' Aunt Burchie said, shaking her head at Lyssa's statement. 'You aren't leaving this room until it is safely in my hands.'

'Why do you want it?' Lyssa asked, determined not to retrieve it.

'If that were any of your business, I might tell you,' said the old woman, settling back into the pillows. Evidently, she thought she'd won.

Lyssa leaned hard on the magic coursing through her veins and visualized the Room. She could hear her aunt howl in anger as she disappeared from her chair. 'The church!' she gasped as she appeared in the Room before Jeremy and Molly. 'You've got to go to the church!' They stood for a long moment gaping at her. 'Now!' she shouted. 'Run all the way, and don't take the most direct route. Tell David he has to hide you. Burchie and the aunts will come looking here if they can.'

'Lyssa –' Jeremy began, taking a step toward her.

She fell back and held her hands out in front of her to stop him. 'Go now, please,' she begged. 'The wards are useless, and I don't have much control over what does work. I can't protect you, but I think he can. Please! I have

266

to try to finish the pattern.' With that, she disappeared again, back into the warrens to where she had stopped working the spell.

Once again at a run, Lyssa moved through the House, trying to change the pattern she and her relatives had walked for lifetimes.

Jeremy looked at Molly, who was staring solemnly at him. 'I guess we'd better do as she says,' he said, holding out his hand.

Molly stood up and came over to him. She put her hand in his and looked up. 'I guess,' she said, nodding.

Jeremy picked her up and hugged her tightly. 'She'll be okay,' he whispered in the little girl's hair, not sure whether he was trying to reassure her, or convince himself. Still carrying Molly, he went out the door and started down the hill toward town, and the church.

A stitch was burning in her side. Her throat was dry and her new pink scars ached with her efforts. Still, Lyssa ran. She could feel the magic vibrating around her now; see the power twisting the House into a pattern never seen, even before Aunt Burchie began wreaking havoc with the spell. The old woman had done a tremendous amount of damage in one lifetime. As the pattern developed, Lyssa could feel the magic strengthen within her. She began to feel invincible in spite of the physical discomfort hindering her.

Then the counter-surge hit.

Like a tidal wave it roiled up out of nowhere and struck her flat, roaring past her and unraveling the work she had just done. With a scream of feral anger, Lyssa leaped to her feet and chased after it, trying to use the power she had garnered to stop it before it did more damage.

This was the power of the aunts and uncles combined, and they knew what they were doing. Aunt Burchie had spent her lifetime learning how to use her magic. The other relatives had probably done the same.

Lyssa felt feeble and inadequate, following in the wake of their spell, unable to stop it. She had been running for so long, she was having trouble even keeping up with its destructive pace.

She had the overview.

Lyssa almost mis-stepped when the realization hit her. She had stared at the maps long enough to have them memorized. The patterns were the same for the town, and her internal energy flow. Somewhere here there had to be a way she could bypass the rogue magic and stop it head on. As she ran, Lyssa frantically searched her memory and surroundings, and finally found the place. She stopped by grabbing the doorknob and using it as an anchor. Twisting it, she threw open the door and lunged through.

She wasn't where she thought she was. Or more specifically, she would have been where she meant to be, but the spell had changed things again. She was back to playing the Game by other rules.

Oh, god. She was back to playing the Game. Agitated, Lyssa turned, trying to find the way she had meant to take to get in front of the magic she had been chasing. If they could rewrite the rules as they went, she was going to have to learn to do the same. She hoped fervently that Jeremy had listened to her for once, and taken Molly to the church. She had a bad feeling she was going to be here a while. At least she would be able to practice with the magic she had been harboring for entirely too long, ignorant of its use.

Unable to return through the door she had entered, Lyssa found another way out of the room and started down a hallway she didn't remember seeing on the map, or from the Game before. Tapping into the flow of energy inside her, Lyssa began to experiment as she walked.

She started out by using the magic to see where the other power was working, and to try to see beyond it, to how things should be, in much the same way she had seen the various doors in and out of the Room after she had finished cleaning it for the first time. It took time to begin to see what she had been looking at all along, but eventually, she could fathom a little of what she was up against.

And she knew exactly where she was. They were trying to get her to resume the pattern where she had originally broken it. They could try to disguise the hallways and rooms, but Lyssa could see through their spell.

This meant they still needed her to complete the job. They needed her alive. So the aunts either had not been trying to kill her, or were trying to scare her into co-operating, or were so angry they had acted first and thought later.

Lyssa was too tired to decide, let alone care. She was worried about Jeremy and Molly, and she was frustrated that all her hard work was being undone while she was powerless to stop it. There was only one place to go.

The room outside the jungle was exactly as it always was; neat, sterile and frighteningly decorated. Lyssa found herself again marvelling at the tastes that had produced the maze of living rooms.

She helped herself to some fruit, and then lay down inside the doorway, on the ground inside the jungle, feeling it might be safer than lying on a couch, even if it was less comfortable.

She was being chased.

She ran across the long balcony overlooking the dark hall. There were no lights on, and only the gibbous moon to illuminate her flight.

There should be no light here at all, she thought in passing. The stairs were before her, and she sped down them, looking over her shoulder to see if she could catch a glimpse of who was behind her.

No one was there. It felt like a panic manufactured by the House, but she knew it wasn't. Someone was in the darkness behind her, and the chase was quite real. There was a door near the base of the stairs.

Glancing back again she could see a shadowy figure on

...cony above her. The door was too obvious. She ...ed it open and let it bang against the wall before ...arting under the stairs she had just come down.

Her breath came in gasps, and she desperately tried to quiet down so as not to give away her hiding place. Her heart pounded so loudly in her ears, she was certain the sound filled the room. There were doors at intervals along the wall stretching away from her, and any one of them would do once she was certain her ruse had worked, but her pursuer paused on the stairs for what seemed an eternity.

She didn't dare put her head out to see what was happening. The longer she stayed hidden, the calmer her breathing became and the more regular her heartbeat, but the terror that filled her didn't abate.

Then she heard the footsteps on the stairs above her. Unexpected, she started violently. They were right beside her ear, as if the person following her was right next to her under the stairs. Then she realized what had happened, and hoped she hadn't made a noise that would betray her location. By now she was holding her breath.

Her eyes were adjusting to the dim light. She could see the room before her clearly, and realized it was one of the ballrooms, but all the furniture was missing. The marble floor stretched before her unbroken, gleaming in the half-light of the moon that shouldn't be shining in here. There were no windows, and the ceiling was intact.

The shadowy figure finally walked through the door at the foot of the stairs.

She waited until the footsteps faded before going to another door and stepping through it. The long corridor beyond led to stairs that went back up, so she mounted them and began to climb.

At each landing, the stair narrowed until there was scarcely room to step, and still she climbed, coming at last to a door. There was nowhere else to go, so she opened it.

The garret was lit only slightly more than the ballroom she had come from, but after the darkness of the stairs, it felt like she had come out into broad daylight.

Her sense of panic hit full force as she stepped into the room. Looking wildly about, she could see no one. Nothing that would indicate danger. Still, she was driven by the panic inside her. She plunged across the room and through the only other door.

The maze of rooms looked familiar, but she couldn't place it. Somewhere here was her pursuer. She moved carefully, using the furniture as cover, crouched on hands and knees in order to move more surreptitiously through the rooms.

How had the person chasing her found her here? she wondered as she crept from behind a couch. She caught a flicker of movement out of the corner of her eye and froze, searching the area. Her heart was in her throat as she waited, crouched against the couch, hoping her own movement hadn't been detected.

At last, she decided it was safe to move again, and she headed toward a chair. She saw the movement again, and knew she'd been spotted.

She stood up and sprinted for the door, getting through it only moments before the person she was trying to evade. She still had no idea who was chasing her, only that if caught, she was as good as dead.

She slammed the door and ran as fast as she had ever run before, passing doors in the hallway that she probably should have taken, but stopping was more than she could manage right now. Her only goal was to put as much distance between her and her follower as possible.

Finally, a door loomed in front of her at the end of the hall. She found a large kitchen beyond. The tile floor was slick and she felt like a poodle scrambling for traction as she rounded the corner of the long counter and headed toward the pantry. There had to be a way out.

The dumbwaiter beckoned as she looked wildly around

the room. Shelves lined the dead-end, but promised a way her pursuer might not think of.

Glancing over her shoulder, she climbed into the dumb-waiter and shut the door. The platform on which she sat moved smoothly down into the depths of the warrens and she wondered where she would finally emerge.

Her sense of panic decreased slightly as she descended, but she was in no less trouble for having temporarily evaded capture.

The small platform came to a halt with a gentle bump and she threw open the door, tumbling out onto the floor, searching the darkness to discover where she should go next. The rooms were smaller here. It felt like places where her friends had grown up. One room connected to the next rather closely, and she could go around in circles before realizing what she was doing.

The platform began to rise. She slammed the door shut on the dumbwaiter and ran, hoping to find her way without any idea where she was going. The rooms began to look alike in the half-light of a moon which shouldn't be able to shine through the hill and into the House. Still she ran, knowing that somewhere behind her in the dark was the danger she had to destroy.

Where was her weaponry? How had she been taken by surprise?

The old magic.

She tried to focus on it as she ran, fighting down the panic. She could hear footsteps behind her now, certain they were no longer echoes of her own. Reaching into herself, she held onto the core of the curious power within, willing herself to safety.

She awoke in a panic, unable to pinpoint the cause. The dream was only half-remembered, as was the day before, and she was so tired she was disoriented. She lay on the ground for long minutes trying to steady her breathing and recall what was frightening her. Eventually, as her breathing calmed and her mind began to function, she remembered.

Lyssa found her scars ached from the previous day's exertions, and were pulled in places so the skin around them had bruised, or was torn and scabbed from bleeding. She was sore all over from the hard ground and still fatigued, so she lay still, and concentrated on the energy flow to which she was only just becoming accustomed.

It was a relief to discover that despite what had happened in the House yesterday, it hadn't affected her internal functioning. With her eyes still closed, Lyssa began to turn her attention outward, seeing what she could do with the magic that way.

An image of a spider in the middle of its web flashed into her mind, but Lyssa brushed it away, deciding that was more apropos of Aunt Burchie than of herself. She would never take root in this House the way her aunt had, and there was certainly no time now to establish the network her aunt had constructed over the course of her lifetime.

Lyssa wished she'd had more time to ask questions, now there was no possible opportunity to have them answered. With a sigh, she stirred and sat up. She felt a little better, but that wasn't saying much. She breakfasted on more fruit and thought about her options.

She might as well start walking the pattern she had tried to finish the day before. It needed to be done, but also Lyssa hoped if she angered the old folks enough they might either tip their hand, or do something foolish. If they did, she would be there to take advantage of it.

In the meantime, she would use the walk to continue probing the magic to find out what she could do with it. Wearily, she set off, back at the beginning, hoping to reweave the spell. Hoping, as well, that she would manage this time to finish.

Molly sat up and rubbed her eyes, looking around, disoriented. 'Mommy?' she quavered in the darkness of early morning.

Jeremy reached out and touched her shoulder. 'Will I do?' he asked, voice roughened with sleep. He shifted position to accommodate her beside him on the floor, trying to make the blankets more comfortable for them both. Molly snuggled up beside him and he put his arm around her, feeling her shake with fear and fatigue.

'Where is mommy?' she whispered. 'Is she okay?'

'I don't know, sweetheart,' he whispered back. 'I hope so.' He thought about Lyssa, wondering where she was. He felt so helpless, hiding in the church, unable to help her. But Molly needed him, and this wasn't his battle, so he hoped for the best and slept badly.

The House at the top of the hill was taking on a life of its own, scaring the people in the town below as they watched the nightly fireworks, and saw it glow with misused power. There was talk, but only Jeremy knew some of what was going on, and even he wasn't certain of that. He just hung on to the hope that if Lyssa was dead, somehow he would know it. Since he didn't, she must still be alive. If she was alive, there was hope.

Lyssa moved slowly and cautiously through the hallway and out onto the balcony. The ballroom stretched into the darkness before her so that she could make out only sketchy details. The opulence of this room never failed to amaze her. The entertaining the Family must have done in a place like this would have been something to see. The marble floor was highly polished and the frescoed walls and ceiling showed dancers ghostly pale as they waltzed in the dimness, lost in flight across the ceiling.

Movement caught her attention and drew it to the far end of the balcony. A waxen figure in a floating white gown stood looking at her. She was much too young to be one of the aunts, and from what Lyssa could see, she was beautiful, with flowing white-blonde hair and a faint smile on her full lips.

Given the circumstances, Lyssa thought she ought to be

terrified, but she stood, looking back at the silent woman, wondering instead who she was.

'You don't recognize me?'

It took Lyssa a moment to realize the apparition had spoken. Her voice was familiar, but Lyssa couldn't place it. Finally she shook her head. 'I'm sorry. I feel like I ought to know you, but I don't.'

The woman laughed, a low gentle laugh that made Lyssa feel good all over. Then she knew. *This woman held three-year-old Lyssa in her lap, tickling her under the chin and laughing as Lyssa giggled.* 'Mother?' she gasped in disbelief. 'Mother?' She took a step forward and stopped. 'Is it really you?'

The woman nodded, but remained where she was. 'I thought you might like to talk.'

Lyssa felt her knees grow weak. *They were taking a walk in the garden; Lyssa was chasing butterflies while her mother clapped her hands in delight.* 'They said you left. Where did you go? How have you come back?'

The woman shook her head. 'I didn't leave. They couldn't make me go. I would never have left you behind and they couldn't let me take you. They tried to do to me what they do to the Others.' She shuddered delicately as she said that. 'It didn't work, but they did succeed in killing me. I've been here ever since.'

'How is that possible?' Lyssa asked in a very small voice. *They were cuddled in bed with the lights low, and mother was telling her a story.* She felt her legs buckling under the chore of supporting her weight and she leaned against the balcony, trying to stay upright.

'Nothing in this House ever really dies,' the woman laughed, a little less pleasantly this time. 'The magic and the lies keep everything going, and Burchie rules it all with an iron hand, pulling the strings.'

'Where are the Others?' Lyssa asked, afraid of the answer, but needing to know for sure. *Mother had introduced her to Magrite. Mother had told her that Jeremy's mother would always love Lyssa just like she did.* Lyssa shuddered. Mother had known she wouldn't be able to raise Lyssa herself.

Her mother shook her head. 'All converted to the energy that runs this place,' she said sadly. 'I tried to help them, but the magic is too strong for us to fight, and their anger and fear are a perfect power source.'

Lyssa crumpled to the floor. *They were splashing together in the bathtub.* 'Is that the power I've been using?'

'No!' said her mother emphatically. 'The old magic may be confused and in the wrong hands, but it isn't evil.'

'Confused,' Lyssa whispered. *Mother was hugging her and kissing the scraped knee Lyssa was sobbing about.* 'Is that why it doesn't really work?'

Her mother laughed. 'It works just fine. You just haven't learned how to use it.'

'Can you teach me?'

'Darling, I wouldn't even begin to know.'

'You're not here to teach me?' Lyssa was dismayed and overwhelmed by the resurfacing memories. Aunt Burchie had blocked everything away, but now they came bubbling to the surface. 'Why are you here?'

'I told you, to talk,' said her mother firmly. 'I know you weren't able to ask Millie everything you wanted to, and you won't have the opportunity until this is all over, and I thought there might be some questions I could answer.' She stopped for a moment and looked at Lyssa longingly. 'Besides, I had to see you again, talk to you again. I've missed you so much. I've missed loving you for too many years and this will be the last chance I get.'

'How can you know that?' Lyssa wondered. *She was being carried down the stairs, and her mother stood at the bottom, smiling up at Lyssa with shining eyes.*

'Because of the pattern you are walking. You may not know what it's for, but I do.'

'What?' Lyssa prompted when her mother stopped. *What, mommy? she asked. What?*

'You're going to have to see for yourself.'

'Is it the right pattern?' Lyssa asked in frustration. *Mommy, am I pretty? she had asked. Mother held her close, and kissed her hair. What you look like is unimportant, mother had said. It's who you are that counts.* No one answered her questions the way she wanted them answered.

'Yes, you're doing the right thing, but the aunts and uncles are going to do everything in their power to stop you. What they want, and what needs to be done are two very different things.'

'The Family is a matriarchy. I thought the uncles had no real power. What can they do to prevent me from reweaving the spell?' Lyssa asked. *What, mommy? She asked. What?*

'The aunts will assist them to maintain the illusion under which the uncles prefer to labor. You're right that they are weak, but together, they still pose a threat and should be taken seriously.' Her mother swayed slightly, as if a breeze passed through her.

'How do the rooms stay so clean?' Lyssa blurted, thinking about the state of the Room when she found it, in comparison to the rest of the House. She wondered also how she was managing a conversation when her mind was in such chaos.

Her mother laughed in delight. 'The questions you come up with! Each matriarch is allowed to stay in her portion of the House, tending it until the end.'

'The end?' Lyssa echoed.

'The end of the cycle. I think you and Millie have talked about this a little. Transition. It will soon be time to return to the center.' She nodded, as if trying to encourage Lyssa to understand.

Lyssa figured eventually she would, and by then it would all be over and a moot point. Slowly she stood, testing her legs and finding them adequate. She began walking toward her mother. A series of images of herself as a toddler, walking toward her mother, almost overwhelmed her. 'What is the cloth for?'

The woman shook her head. 'I don't know for certain, so I'd better not speculate.'

'Why didn't you ever contact me before?' Lyssa asked in a voice barely above a whisper.

Her mother shook her head. 'I couldn't let Burchie know I was here. I watched you. I wanted to let you know I was here, but I couldn't take the chance.' She held out her hands and Lyssa tried to grasp them, but went right through them. With an inarticulate cry, the woman held up her hands. 'All I ever wanted was to love you,' she whispered. Then she disappeared.

With a hoarse sob, Lyssa sat once again and cried for a long time in silence, missing her mother all over again and knowing what she had said was true. She would never have left voluntarily. But it didn't ease the pain of losing her mother a second time.

Eventually, Lyssa dried her eyes and stood up. She would find a way to set her free from this House, and everyone else who was trapped here. There had to be a way to undo what was being done, and in the meantime, she had a pattern to walk. Still shaky, and drained by emotion, Lyssa left the balcony and re-entered the spell.

The pace was working to her advantage. Since the spell was being woven so slowly, the old folks seemed not to have taken notice of her activities. Still, it was hard to put one foot in front of the other, and Lyssa was longing for sleep.

She had experimented with the magic, but found there just wasn't much she could do voluntarily. Getting from one place to another, healing wounds and seeing where the other magic was working, seemed to be the extent of her control over the strange energy that had taken up residence inside her. Beyond that it just didn't serve her and finally she gave up trying, too tired to fight it any longer. It was using up energy she needed to concentrate on the route she had to take through the House in order to reweave the spell.

The good news was that, having studied the maps and moved through the House again and again, it was becoming smaller. Not literally shrinking in size, but familiarity was making it seem less huge; more manageable. Lyssa had a better idea of what would be on the other side of the door when she opened it, and the knowledge helped her keep track of where she was. This was important especially since she was so fatigued by the process.

It occurred to her that it could be the House inducing the lethargy, since it had demonstrated itself capable of goading her with anxiety to complete the old pattern more quickly, but Lyssa was more inclined to believe it had to do with emotional overload, lack of sleep and still recovering from her wounds. There was also the disappointment of having to redo the work she'd thought already completed and the worry over Molly's and Jeremy's safety. A lot was riding on her success.

So she moved through rooms and down hallways, trying to visualize the pattern being anchored so that no spell the aunts and uncles tried could undo her work, blind to the beauty around her, no longer seeing the incredible and conspicuous wealth that had created the place.

The Others were all gone now. Her mother had verified that. So, by extension, the wing the Others had occupied was gone also. That explained why she and Jeremy hadn't come across it in the mapping they had done. There was Family, and they were all here, with the exception of Uncle Haskell, who had the misfortune of being the sacrificial lamb sent by the aunts to determine the extent of Lyssa's power. There were Millie and David Baker, long-lived and part of the situation without being part of the problem. There were House and church, essentially unknown quantities in Lyssa's experience. House was flexible. Was church?

Then there was the Bell family. Family, but not Family.

They lived in town and had little contact with the Family in the House except at building time. Did they actually create the entity that was the House, or did the House use them to create itself?

Lyssa's head spun with the questions raised by the few facts she seemed to possess. She had to sleep and the only safe place was in the jungle. Hoping she would be able to pick up the pattern where she left off, Lyssa went back to the room outside the greenheart, and walked inside the door. She found the nest she had created for herself the last time she'd slept here, and curled up in it again. She was asleep immediately, too tired even to dream.

Since day and night had no meaning here, Lyssa slept until she woke up. She ate more fruit, wishing there was something else, *anything* else, then straightened herself up as much as possible. She could also wish for a change of clothing and a hot bath, but it would have to wait until she was done and safely out of the House.

She went back to where she had left off, and was relieved to find the spell still intact and waiting for her to resume. As she set off, reality hit and Lyssa began to wonder if she would spend the rest of her life walking the pattern.

'Ah, there you are,' said the voices of the uncles. They were taking no chances, not even materializing in the hallway. The voices were projected from wherever they were in Aunt Burchie's quarters.

'Are the aunts going to sacrifice all of you at once?' Lyssa asked, feeling like it was time to unmask the deceit about the balance of power.

The uncles laughed. 'Do you think we don't know?'

'I'd be willing to bet you don't know as much as you think you do,' she said. 'Is my father with you?'

'I'm here,' said Jordan. 'Lyssa, you have to stop this foolishness and come home.'

'Mother says hello,' she said, ignoring his command. Her mother had, of course, said no such thing. Lyssa was hoping to throw him off balance.

'Your mother was sent away years ago,' her father said with assurance. 'She would never contact you without permission.'

'That's what Aunt Burchie told you?' Lyssa scoffed. 'And you believed her?'

'Why would my sister lie to me?' Jordan sounded now as if he wasn't quite so sure.

'Your *sister*?' Lyssa gaped, caught off guard. She'd always thought the title 'aunt' was courtesy, not actual. She couldn't remember who had told her that the Family wasn't necessarily genetically related, but it had seemed the only thing that made sense.

'Yes, my sister. Your aunt. What did you think?' Her father sounded irritated now. 'How could your mother say hello?'

'She's been trapped here since Burchie killed her,' said Lyssa, not pulling the punch even a little.

'Burchie would never do that!'

Lyssa didn't recognize the voice. 'Would and did,' she snapped. 'I think you don't realize to just what lengths Aunt Burchie would go to protect what she's doing here. She sent Uncle Haskell to find out just what I could do, and then she tried to kill me. Now she's sent you to slow me down, fully expecting to lose you in the process, I'd bet. She's probably monitoring this right now. Aren't you?' she called, hoping to draw her aunt into the fray by angering her. If she could get them to lower their guard, she might have a chance.

'You're finally getting some smarts.'

Aunt Burchie's voice startled everyone. The uncles muttered among themselves and Lyssa found herself pressed against a wall hoping not to be seen. 'You are that much older than my father?' she asked, trying to goad the old woman. 'I mean, Dad's middle-aged, but you're ancient. Was there a second marriage or something?'

'And a pretty smart mouth you're developing with it,' said Aunt Burchie. 'You're on shaky ground. Perhaps you'd like to reconsider some of what you're saying?'

'Look, either you kill me or you don't,' said Lyssa. 'If you were going to do it, you would have by now, so you must have a reason for keeping me alive. Given that, I imagine there's no limit to what I can say, just on how much you're going to hurt me for saying it. How old are you, Burchie? That magic you're playing with comes at a high price, 'cause you look like you're going to die any day now. What did it cost you to maintain Marnie?'

The bolt sang past her ear and scorched a good portion of the wall beside her, but Lyssa didn't move. 'You're going to have to give everything over to me eventually. What difference does it make if I give you the necklace now? It'll just come back to me in a little bit and it won't have done you any good at all.'

'You have no idea what that necklace can do,' Aunt Burchie hissed. 'You don't actually have it, or you'd have discovered by now.'

Energy coursed around Lyssa, pinning her to the wall, crackling against her skin. 'I've hidden it where you'd never think to look,' Lyssa taunted, wishing she could brush away the crawly-bug feeling, but unable to move. She could feel the energy in her body responding to the flow surrounding her; not a clash of magic, but like one was igniting the other. Desperately she tried to damp the pulse inside, terrified of what might happen, and unable to stop it.

'Burchie, we need her. Stop it,' said her father from somewhere in the distance. He sounded completely unconcerned for her well-being, only her ability to do whatever it was they needed done.

'Gee, thanks, Daddy,' she said sarcastically. It shouldn't have surprised her, but it hurt anyway. Still, the build-up of energy abated and she found she could move again.

'Any time, my sweet,' he answered, just as sarcastically. 'Now why don't you tell Auntie what she wants to know?'

'Why don't you all just go take a hike?' She stood straight and squared her shoulders. Raising her hands above her head, she could feel the energy gathering and flowing toward her palms. Burchie was probably in her room, Lyssa thought vaguely as she felt the discharge. She had no idea how this was happening, or even what was happening. All she was sure of was that when she lowered her arms and came back into herself again, the voices were gone, and she was able to resume walking the pattern. She had bought herself some time, so she moved down the hall, hoping to make progress.

Sometime later, Lyssa became aware of what she was doing. She had been walking for hours, knowing she was following the path she should, but doing so only by rote. The encounter with Family had taken her farther out of herself than she'd thought.

Now she stopped and looked around, seeing where she was for the first time. The pattern was nearly complete. She was almost back to the maze of furniture.

Glancing around to make sure she was alone, Lyssa started to run. She wasn't going to take the chance of being stopped again. The feeling of fear grew behind her, but she didn't turn around, afraid that if anything was in fact back there, turning would slow her down enough to be caught. The fear gave her speed, and she burst into the maze so fast she almost fell over the overstuffed furniture. Recovering, she ran the pattern through the room and down the stairs into the atrium.

She came to a halt in front of the door leading up to Aunt Burchie's quarters. The pattern was complete, but her job had only just begun. She had to go up there and face the Family. She had to find Millie. She had to wait for the magic to work, and wondered how long it would take. The spell Aunt Burchie had been weaving was centuries in the making. Lyssa didn't think the new one would take anywhere near that long, but it wasn't going to be instantaneous either.

Reaching out she put her hand on the knob. She took a

deep breath and held it, but didn't open the door. Standing in the atrium, she exhaled slowly and tried to screw up the courage to walk up the stairs. Knowing what she had to do, and doing it, were two very different things.

Also, she realized, it had been ingrained in her from childhood that you never went back the way you came when playing the Game; she had never walked up those stairs. As a result, it felt wrong to do so now, as if the House would punish her by sending her somewhere else in the warrens for violating the rules.

'This is silly,' she said out loud, shaking herself and twisting the knob. She pulled the door open and stood looking up the flight of stairs. They were no different than any of the stairs between any of the other sections of the House. She had been walking up flights just like this for days, but she had known those sections were empty. This time, she knew Family was there, and she had no idea what she had done to them with the last blast of energy. Taking a deep breath, Lyssa held it as she walked up the stairs and through the door at the top. She walked down the narrow hallway and stepped out of the cupboard in her childhood room.

Millie was waiting for her.

Chapter Ten

'One of the portals will be the Door, as well. Until the
spell is completed, you will not know which one it is.
Do not destroy, or allow to be destroyed, any portion
of the House.'

The Symbiosis of Builder and Family, Chapter Eight

There was nothing he could do, and Jeremy had never been
so frustrated in his life. Living at the church didn't have
any up-side that he could think of besides being safer than
the Room, and of that he couldn't even be certain.

He and Molly had spent their first night on the floor of
the sanctuary, huddled on the few blankets David Baker
had scrounged together. They were neither warm enough,
nor well enough padded against the hard floor, but Molly
slept snuggled up against him, and that made Jeremy feel
pretty good in spite of their situation. He could comfort a
small child and make her feel safe, and that felt pretty good
indeed.

The next day, they resolved to find a more comfortable
spot, and more blankets. After clearing out a spot in the
basement storage room and stacking boxes in such a way
as to give each other a little privacy, they had declared
their home suitable for now. In the middle of the night,
Molly crawled out of her bed and snuggled up against
Jeremy again, saying she'd had a bad dream.

Jeremy was having bad dreams also, but he didn't tell
her that. He just put his arm around her and lay silent in
the darkness, listening to her breathe and wondering what
was happening in the House; wondering if Lyssa was okay.

On the third day, they ventured out into town. People

looked at them strangely, knowing they were from up the hill, but were otherwise polite and Molly didn't notice anything unusual in their behavior. Jeremy tried not to let it bother him, but it did. Finally, he suggested they take a walk around the neighborhoods to stretch their legs a bit.

Molly readily agreed, and they set off. They went from one area to the next, up one block and down another until Molly asked to be carried.

With a pang, Jeremy looked down at her. 'Am I walking your legs off?' he asked.

'No,' said Molly with a small grin. 'I still have them on. I'm just tired.'

'How about a piggy-back ride?' he suggested.

'Yeah!' she said with enthusiasm.

They had been walking this way for quite a while before Jeremy realized what he was doing. He had studied the maps for so long he'd internalized the patterns he and Lyssa traced over the one they had walked for so many years. He was walking the pattern in town.

It felt right, and no one was stopping him, so he picked up the pace, determined to finish. 'Are you okay, back there?' he asked. When he got no response, he realized Molly had fallen asleep with her arms around his neck and her head on his shoulder. Since she was comfortable, and he could walk for hours more like this, Jeremy kept going, weaving the pattern with determination, hoping in some small way it would help Lyssa with whatever she was doing in the warrens.

She should have finished by now. At least, he thought she ought to have, but he had no way of knowing what was happening. If they had injured her again, or were holding her in some way, preventing her from weaving the spell, he didn't know if he could to finish it for her. If he went back into the warrens, they would surely kill him. There was also no way he was going to leave Molly, even in the Speaker's care.

By the time he finished the pattern, he was bone tired and Molly was stirring.

'Are we still walking?' she asked sleepily, picking her head up off his shoulder and looking around.

'No,' Jeremy chuckled. '*I* am still walking. But I think it's time to head back to the church. Can I put you down?'

'Yes, thank you,' said Molly. 'I'm hungry.'

'Okay, how about we get some supper and then go back to the church?' he amended, helping her slide down off his back. He did a few arm circles to restore circulation.

'Can I have ice cream?' she wanted to know.

Jeremy laughed. 'After supper.' It was then he realized the pattern had not taken them past Marnie's house. He wondered about that, but only for a moment. He was much too tired to think seriously about anything more than feeding Molly and getting them back to the church.

'How did you get back here?' Millie asked. She stood aside and pulled Lyssa into the room, shutting the door quickly and silently behind her. 'Where is Jeremy?'

'He's at the church if he followed my instructions,' said Lyssa, keeping her voice low, as if that might help. 'He and Molly needed a safe place to stay. I wasn't sure the Room would be protection enough once the aunts and uncles figured out what I was doing.'

'I thought Molly was staying in town,' said Millie. 'Couldn't Jeremy have stayed with her?'

Lyssa shook her head. 'Marnie turned out to be a cover for Aunt Burchie, or an extension of her, or something.' The image of Marnie's distorted face made Lyssa tremble. 'Anyway, we got Molly out of there just in time. No, I still think the church is the safest place for them.' She paused a moment. 'How is Aunt Burchie?'

'She's in a bad way,' Millie said.

'How old is she?' Lyssa asked.

Millie shrugged. 'I don't think she's really that much older than your father.'

'It's not the years, it's the mileage,' said Lyssa drily. 'The years of playing with the rules have cost her dearly?'

Millie nodded. 'Cost us all.'

They sat in silence for a long time.

'It might be another stroke,' she said slowly. 'She's unconscious. The aunts and uncles are taking turns sitting with her and trying to make plans around what she had told them before all this happened.'

'All this,' said Lyssa. 'You mean me?'

Millie grinned. 'You do mix things up a bit.'

Lyssa grinned back. 'Well, when you're good at something –'

Millie laughed. 'You stick with it.' Then she sobered. 'You're not safe here, you know. They'll find out soon and come for you. They're pretty angry.'

Lyssa sighed. 'Millie, I walked a new pattern. Do you know how long it will take for the spell to start working?'

Millie frowned. 'It should have started immediately after you finished. When was that?'

'Not too long ago.' Lyssa thought for a moment. 'Was there more to it than that?'

'How did you know what pattern to trace?' asked Millie.

'I kept seeing it,' said Lyssa slowly. 'On the maps Jeremy and I drew of the House and the town, and inside me when I healed the burns.' Her hand stole up to her cheek to touch the vivid pink scar.

Millie nodded, inspecting the marks on Lyssa's face and neck. 'You did a good job healing yourself. The pattern was inside you?'

'That was how I recognized it on the maps,' said Lyssa. 'Then, I walked it in the warrens.' She grimaced. 'It took a couple of tries, but I just finished it, and now it's not working.'

'Maybe it was only a part of the spell you're trying to weave,' Millie suggested. 'Maybe you have other places to walk.'

'But I'm tired and I need to sleep!' Lyssa protested, flop-ping down on the bed. 'Why can't what I do ever be enough?'

Millie laughed softly. 'No rest for the wicked,' she said. 'I think you'd better get back down to the church.'

'But what about the questions I still have?' Lyssa wailed.

'When you've figured it out, I'll meet you at the green-heart,' said Millie, gently but firmly. 'Until then, I'll keep an eye on things up here, and you have to take care of yourself down there.' She nodded down the hill in the general direction of town.

Lyssa pulled a face, but she got up. 'I guess I'll see you eventually.' She drew on the energy inside her and visu-alized the church.

'You came back!' cried Molly, running to hug her.

Lyssa opened her eyes and smiled, opening her arms to catch the little girl. She gave Molly a big hug and buried her face in her hair. 'Oh, I've missed you so much,' she said.

'I missed you too,' said Molly, hugging Lyssa enthusiasti-cally. 'Are you going to be staying?'

'For a while, at least,' Lyssa said. 'I still have a lot of work to do, though, so I can't promise for how long.'

'Oh,' said Molly, disappointed. 'I thought you were done.'

'I wish I was,' said Lyssa fervently. 'But I'm not, and I don't know how much more I have to do, but I want to be able to send you home to your parents, so I have to do whatever it takes.'

'I know,' said Molly. 'I was just hoping.'

Lyssa smiled and put the little girl down. 'I was hoping for more, too. It just didn't work out that way, so now I have to figure out what to do next. Is Jeremy around?'

'Downstairs,' said Molly. 'He needed more sleep.'

'More sleep?' Lyssa raised an eyebrow. 'What have you two been up to?'

'We took a walk,' said Molly. 'We went all over town. Jeremy gave me a piggy-back ride and I fell asleep.'

'How long did you walk for?' asked Lyssa.

'All day, I think,' said Molly. 'Most of it, anyway. A really long time. I don't know.'

'Should I let him sleep, then?' Lyssa grinned at Molly. The little girl nodded. 'Okay, what shall we do while we wait for him to wake up?' Lyssa was dying for sleep herself, but she wanted to spend time with Molly more.

It was mid-morning before Jeremy came upstairs. By then, Lyssa was just about out on her feet, so he sent her downstairs, shutting off her protests and saying they would talk when she was coherent. Lyssa gave up arguing and went downstairs to find the makeshift beds in the storage room. She was asleep before she managed to get under the covers.

'Is she still alive?' Molly asked in a stage whisper.

'Sh-h. Yes,' Jeremy whispered back, only somewhat more quietly. 'See? The way her chest rises and falls? That means she's still breathing.'

'Oh-h,' said Molly, leaning in close. Lyssa grabbed her in a hug, startling and delighting the little girl. Molly shrieked, then giggled, hugging her back. 'You're awake!'

'Well a herd of elephants stampeding is quieter than you two!' laughed Lyssa, struggling to sit the two of them up.

'I kept her away as long as I could, but she was certain you were dead,' Jeremy apologized. 'I couldn't think of any other way to reassure her.'

Lyssa gave Molly another big hug. 'It'll take a lot more than over-tired to kill me, sweetie,' she said. 'I just needed to sleep. How long was I out?' She looked questioningly at Jeremy.

'Just since yesterday morning, but it's almost three in the afternoon. You had a good rest?'

'I feel like I could sleep another week and still not catch

up,' Lyssa grinned. 'But yeah, I had a good rest. What have you two been doing?'

Jeremy looked sheepish. 'We walked the pattern in town a couple of days ago. Other than that, we haven't really done much besides worry about you.'

Lyssa looked at him sharply, hearing something in his tone she wasn't sure of, but she saw nothing in his face to back it up, so she dismissed it as wishful thinking. 'You walked the pattern?' she repeated, finally realizing what he'd said.

'I know, it's silly, but it was the closest I could get to actually helping, and I've felt so helpless recently –' He shrugged, spreading his hands, palm up. 'It just felt like a more constructive thing to do than sitting here in the church hoping you were walking the pattern in the warrens. How did it go?'

Lyssa made a face and told him. She held Molly in her lap, rocking gently from side to side as she described the journey and its setbacks. 'I think I blasted Aunt Burchie,' she finished. 'The aunts and uncles are sitting vigil, and no one is sure what's wrong, but I know it was the energy I let loose. Just like with Uncle Haskell.'

Jeremy shuddered. 'She had me coming and going. I don't know when she took Marnie over completely. I didn't even know Marnie was in danger.' He looked long and hard at Molly with an expression Lyssa couldn't interpret. 'Otherwise I would never have suggested –' he reached out and touched Molly's silky dark curls with gentle fingers. 'I certainly wouldn't have –' he shuddered again, violently, and this time Lyssa had no problem reading his face.

'You had no way of knowing,' Lyssa offered him defence. 'She played me for a fool, too. I was actually jealous of Marnie.'

'Why?' asked Jeremy, surprised.

Lyssa shook her head. 'I just was,' she dissembled. She was certainly not going to admit it to Jeremy; she could only just barely admit it to herself. The idea of him with her – she shuddered even thinking about it, and hugged Molly tighter to quell the feeling rising inside her. Mercifully, Jeremy let it go.

'So were you able to find out what they're doing up there?' he asked, changing the subject.

'No,' Lyssa sighed. 'No one really seems to know. The aunts aren't talking, and Millie said only that she'd meet me in the jungle when it was time.'

'I don't suppose we have any idea when that will be?' he asked, pulling a face.

Lyssa laughed wryly. 'When the spell is complete?'

'Yeah, but how do we know when that is?' Jeremy asked in exasperation.

'When it starts to work, I guess,' said Lyssa. 'You've walked the pattern in town, and I walked the pattern in the warrens, but the spell isn't working yet. Millie said the spell should start working as soon as it's complete, so there's something we're missing.'

'Are you supposed to do all the walking?' asked Jeremy with a frown.

'You've walked almost every step of the old pattern with me, so maybe we need to do this together,' Lyssa said.

'The town?' Jeremy asked. 'The warrens?'

Lyssa shook her head. 'I don't know,' she said in frustration. 'What I did felt right!'

'Is there someplace else we're supposed to walk the pattern?' Jeremy asked, obviously casting about blindly.

Still, it made Lyssa think. 'I first saw the pattern inside myself,' she admitted. 'Maybe the only pattern left to walk is the one inside me.'

'The pattern has to be walked three times? Why?'

'I didn't make up the rules,' said Lyssa impatiently. 'I'm just trying to figure out what they are so I don't do the same number on them that Aunt Burchie did.'

'Okay,' Jeremy placated. 'You're right. It just seems excessive is all.'

Lyssa shrugged. 'I agree, but we have to do what needs to be done.'

'How are you going to do it?' Jeremy asked.

'Probably the same way I did before when I healed the burns,' she said in a voice that sounded like a question. 'I'm not really sure, but that seems the logical place to start.'

'When are you going to do this?' he asked.

Lyssa laughed. 'After I get something to eat!' She gave Molly a squeeze. 'What do you think, are you hungry?'

'No,' the little girl laughed. 'We just ate lunch. But I'd love some ice cream.'

Jeremy laughed outright. 'You always want ice cream.'

After lunch, they went for a walk and did some shopping. 'Have you gone back to the Room?' Lyssa asked.

Jeremy shook his head. 'You were so emphatic that we get out of there immediately, it didn't seem like a wise thing to do. I bought us each a change of clothing and David scrounged up enough bedding for us to be comfortable. We eat every meal out and spend a lot of time walking around or doing nothing. That's why I finally walked the pattern. I couldn't handle doing nothing while we waited to see if you were okay.'

'You've been taking good care of Molly,' said Lyssa in a low voice. 'That's a lot right there.'

He nodded. 'I didn't realize what hard work it can be. She's a good kid, though,' he ruffled Molly's hair affectionately. 'But don't tell her I said that.'

Molly giggled. 'I heard you!'

'Darn,' he said.

'I wonder if your walking the pattern here is sufficient, or if I have to do it as well,' Lyssa said.

Jeremy shrugged. 'We'll find out, won't we?'

Lyssa sighed. 'Another question. Well, why don't we head back to the church, and I'll give the internal thing a go. Once that's done, I'll have a better idea.'

'What do you want me to do while you're doing that?' asked Jeremy.

Lyssa grinned. 'Buy me a change of clothing?'

'Why didn't you do that earlier?' he demanded.

'I didn't think of it until you mentioned it,' she protested. 'Molly, help him find something nice, okay?'

Molly shook her head. 'He picks nicer things than me,' she said. 'He showed me lots prettier things than I was looking at.'

Lyssa looked at Jeremy with one raised eyebrow.

'My mother taught me what to look for,' he admitted grudgingly.

'Magrite had good taste,' said Lyssa with understanding. 'I'm sure whatever you choose will be fine.' She left them at the square and returned to the church on her own.

She lay on the pallet and closed her eyes self-consciously. She lay still for a time before realizing she was stiff as a board and completely unable to concentrate. Deliberately, she began with her toes and made herself relax, working her way up from her feet to her head, and by the time she reached her scalp, she was in a much better frame of mind for the task at hand.

Reaching into the energy stream, she went straight to her heart, knowing the pattern had to begin there. Painstakingly, she traced every inch of the web, feeling the changes in the power in a way she hadn't when she was walking the pattern in the warrens. She cleared the few blocks that had occurred since the healing, and closed the spell.

Stepping back to observe, she saw the completed pattern and was satisfied with her work, so she opened her eyes and sat up. Since there were no windows and the basement was dark, she had no idea how long she'd been working, but she was stiff when she stood, so she guessed it had been a while.

Lyssa went to find Jeremy and Molly, and to see if anything had changed as a result of her work. David Baker was waiting for her on the stairs.

'How are you doing?' he asked. 'Is everything alright up at the House?'

'I'm fine,' said Lyssa, sitting down a few steps below him. 'Millie is alright. I don't think Aunt Burchie will last too much longer. I have no idea about the aunts and uncles, except for Uncle Haskell. I killed him.'

'Jeremy told me,' said David gently. 'It sounded to me like you did what you had to do.'

Lyssa shook her head. 'I don't know. All I did was raise my hand and that was it for Uncle Haskell. I don't feel like I had any say in the matter. I certainly didn't know him well enough to know if he posed any kind of threat, and I don't recall waiting to find out. It just sort of happened.'

'The old magic is like that,' he answered thoughtfully. 'It just does what needs to be done, and doesn't worry too much about what the vessel thinks.'

'Vessel.' Lyssa seized on the word. 'Yes, that's exactly what it feels like. How did you know?'

'The old magic is what the long-lived used to wield before the Family tipped the balance of power,' he said. 'I remember what it was like, even though it was a very long time ago.'

'How old are you?' Lyssa asked in wonder.

David shook his head. 'I've lost track.'

Lyssa knew it was a lie, but she let it pass. 'If it treated you the same way, did you ever control it, or was it just in you and popped out at strange moments to do what it pleased?'

'We had a degree of control, but only in the way that you can sometimes get a two-year-old to obey. It's sort of like herding cats. You have to hope you give a command they feel like obeying.'

Lyssa chuckled. 'Pretty much.' They sat in silence for a time. 'The spell doesn't seem to be changing anything yet. Have I done something wrong?'

David shook his head. 'I don't know what you've done.

You'll have to evaluate this for yourself and decide if you need to be doing something else.'

'I was afraid of that,' said Lyssa. 'Do you know where Jeremy is?'

'I believe he's upstairs.'

Lyssa stood up. 'Thank you,' she said.

'Certainly.' The Speaker moved aside and Lyssa walked past him, up the stairs to go and find Jeremy.

He was sitting in one of the pews with Molly. She was nestled into the crook of his arm and he was reading a book to her. His deep voice resonated in the sanctuary, quiet but clear, and Lyssa stopped a moment to listen, enjoying the sound even though she couldn't quite make out the words. She hated to interrupt, so she waited until he reached the end of the page before gently clearing her throat.

'That was lovely,' she said when he looked up.

'Are you done?' he asked, giving Molly the book and gently disengaging from her. 'We'll finish this in a while, sweetheart, okay?' Molly nodded and Jeremy stood up. 'Do you want to go somewhere?'

Lyssa shook her head. 'I haven't felt any change in the web, have you?'

Jeremy paused a moment. 'No.'

'I think I may have to walk the pattern in town,' said Lyssa reluctantly. She hated having to tell him, even in a roundabout way, that the thing he had done to help had been useless.

He nodded but said nothing.

'I guess that's what I'll do tomorrow. Do you want to come?'

Jeremy lifted his shoulders once and let them drop heavily. 'There's nothing else to do,' he said in a defeated voice.

'What about Molly?' asked Lyssa gently.

'She'd love to come along. There's nothing to do here that's any more interesting. When she gets tired, I'll just do what I did last time and piggy-back her.'

'Okay,' said Lyssa, feeling only slightly relieved. 'Why don't you finish the story and let's get some sleep.'

They started right after breakfast and walked all day.

The pattern wasn't difficult to trace, just long, and by now, tedious. At least Lyssa had Jeremy and Molly to make this walk different from the House. She had company, scenery and a lack of Familial intervention.

From almost everywhere, the House could be seen, glowering down at the town from the hilltop. Lyssa could feel the power emanating from it like a tangible force, but she doubted the rest of the people in town were as aware of it as she was. The building glowed and quivered with magic and Lyssa shuddered when she thought about what might be going on up there.

She would have to confront it eventually and she was utterly unprepared. If what David had to say about the old magic was correct, she would never get a handle on it. That would make dealing with the aunts and uncles even more dicey and she was beginning to think the best she could hope for was to come out of it alive.

When Molly grew tired, Jeremy piggy-backed her and she slept. On they walked through neighborhoods that had become entirely too familiar.

'Where is Marnie's house?' Lyssa asked when she noticed they had not walked past it.

Jeremy stirred from his reverie. 'What?'

'The pattern didn't take us past Marnie's house,' Lyssa said.

'I noticed that,' said Jeremy with a frown. 'I don't know.'

'And the Others are missing from the House,' said Lyssa softly, hoping Molly wasn't paying any attention to what they were saying.

Jeremy nodded. 'They must correspond to each other,' he said bleakly.

Lyssa nodded. There was nothing else to say.

The town seemed much smaller than it ever had before,

but the walk was endless. It was dusk by the time they had completed the pattern and returned to the center of town.

'We should get some supper,' said Jeremy softly, trying not to disturb Molly, who was once again up on his back with her head down on his shoulder.

'I'm too tired to eat,' said Lyssa, stifling a yawn. 'Do you feel anything different? Is the magic starting to work?'

Jeremy shook his head. 'I can't feel anything, including my arms.' He jerked his head in the direction of the cafe. 'Come on, let's at least get something to drink and sit for a little while.'

Lyssa followed him down the street and into the restaurant. They slid into a booth, placing Molly so that her head rested in the corner between the cushion and the wall. She barely stirred during the transition.

'She's really out,' said Lyssa, looking at the sleeping child. 'She's so beautiful.'

Jeremy smiled. 'She's a really neat kid. She's very special.'

There was no mistaking his tone this time and Lyssa looked at him in surprise. 'I thought you didn't like children much.'

Jeremy looked equally surprised. 'Where would you get an idea like that?'

'I–I don't know,' Lyssa stammered, embarrassed. 'I guess – I don't know.'

'There weren't any kids around besides the ones our age at school,' he suggested. 'I never thought about it when we were kids. We've never talked about it since you came back. Yeah, I like children, and Molly is special.'

Lyssa nodded, floored by Jeremy's revelation. In truth, she had assumed that since she loved children, Jeremy would dislike them. As if he felt entirely the opposite of what she did. Sort of stupid, but she guessed she hadn't been thinking all that clearly since she came home. The strangeness of her situation was opening her eyes to the possibilities in others she had never seen before. Suddenly, seeing Jeremy as a father wasn't so improbable.

Looking from his face to Molly's, Lyssa was struck for the first time by the resemblance.

Then the waiter came over and the thought went straight out of her head. They ordered their meals, and something for Molly if she woke up, and by the time the waiter left, the conversation turned to the spell they were trying to weave.

'Millie seemed to think the magic should start working right away,' said Lyssa, frustrated. 'If we're doing it right, shouldn't it have begun?'

'Are we doing it right?' asked Jeremy.

Lyssa shrugged. 'I'm making this up as I go along,' she admitted. 'But there have only been three places I saw the pattern, and I've walked it in all three places. The same pattern, the same steps in the House, the town, and inside myself. I don't know what else to do.'

'Has it felt right all the way along?' asked Jeremy, watching for her reaction.

'What do you mean?' asked Lyssa, confused.

'I mean, when I was walking the pattern in town, it felt like the right thing to be doing. Is that how you felt in the House?'

Lyssa thought for a long time about exactly what she had felt beneath the fear and exhaustion that pervaded her journey in the warrens. Finally she looked at him and nodded. 'Yeah, it felt right. I was scared all the time, and tired, but I knew I was doing the right thing, so I kept going.'

'Now, what about when you did it again internally last night?'

She thought about it for only a moment. 'No,' she said decisively. 'It wasn't like I was doing the wrong thing, but it felt redundant, like today walking through town. I'd already done the internal pattern. It didn't need to be done again.'

'Then why isn't the magic working?' he pressed.

Lyssa reddened slightly. 'You,' she whispered. 'You and

me together. You were right. The House was mine to do, the town was yours to do. This is all a matter of balance. The last pattern we should have to do is yours.'

'Mine?' Jeremy's voice jumped. 'I don't think so.'

Lyssa smiled gently. 'I'm not sure, but you're as connected to this place as I am. If we are supposed to be yin and yang, it would make sense. Think about it. To me, it feels right.'

He nodded, looking unhappy and embarrassed. 'If it has to be done,' he said, leaving the sentence unfinished.

'I guess the question is when,' said Lyssa.

Jeremy glanced at Molly, who still slept in her corner of the booth. 'My guess is not tonight.'

Lyssa chuckled. 'I could use a good night's sleep. But we should do it as soon as possible.'

'Do we have any idea what's going to happen once the spell starts to work?' asked Jeremy suddenly.

Lyssa shook her head. 'None whatsoever. It'll be a surprise for everyone I'll bet.'

Supper came and they ate in silence. Molly slept on in her corner, so they carried her out of the cafe and back to the church.

That night, all three slept soundly, but Jeremy and Lyssa had strange dreams about the jungle and the church which neither could explain to the other the next morning.

Feeling more than a little self-conscious, they set Molly up with some books and toys, and asked her please to play quietly so they could do some meditating. She nodded and took herself off to a corner of the sanctuary, leaving Jeremy and Lyssa facing each other with no excuse.

Finally he gestured toward the pallet. 'Soonest begun,' he said.

'Soonest done,' she sighed, following him and lying down.

They lay side by side and held hands, both for the magic and the reassurance. Then Lyssa reached into the energy stream and took them both down into it.

He gave her hand a reassuring squeeze.

Jeremy's internal energy was a mess. It was tangled, clotted, swollen and broken. The flow was misdirected in unbelievably circuitous fashion and blocks of immense proportion absorbed energy, unable to let go and ready to burst.

'Oh, Jeremy!' cried Lyssa, dismayed.

'I'm sorry,' he said, humiliated. 'I had no idea.'

Lyssa squeezed his hand hard. 'We just have a lot of work to do, is all. We might as well do it as we weave the spell.' She took them to his heart, skimming over the surface because there was no other way to get there through the mess. Jeremy stumbled along behind her as if afraid to open his eyes and look around.

Once at his heart, Lyssa stopped and took a deep breath. 'Okay, you have to go first. I want you to draw on my energy and use it to clear up your flow. Remember the pattern we're tracing and work through the blockages so we can complete the spell.'

Jeremy nodded, taking a look around and shuddering. Then he leaned into Lyssa's energy and began to move. It was an extremely slow and painful process, wading through the havoc wreaked by years of anger and bitterness, fear and loneliness.

Jeremy had no overview. After a time, it felt like they had never done anything else. Everything depended on the blocks and where the energy had been diverted to. If the diversion wasn't too convoluted, he could clear it up fairly quickly and move on. If the block was small, it posed little problem.

Often, though, the diversion was complex, or the block an absorption that, like a boil, had to be lanced. The energy coming from those was putrid and required cleansing before it could be allowed to rejoin the stream, so care had to be taken in releasing it.

Lyssa could do no more than follow him, supporting his efforts and staying out of the way. She was beginning to understand how he felt when she was in the warrens by herself. At least here, there was something constructive she could do to help. She provided him with the energy to deal with years of damage. Still, she said nothing, following him on the painful journey through himself.

There was no way of knowing how much more was to be done. Even though he was familiar with the pattern, and knew where they were within it, some portions had gone very quickly, others had dragged interminably.

Lyssa grew tired, got a second wind, and grew tired again. Still they plodded on, doggedly working a pattern they could barely see anymore. 'How are you doing?' she asked finally, unable to remain silent any longer.

'Okay,' Jeremy mumbled without stopping.

'Do you want to take a rest?' she asked, half-hoping he would say yes, knowing he'd better stick with the task.

He shook his head. 'We're almost done,' he said. 'I can see the end. I have to make it through.'

Lyssa looked back behind her and was astonished by what she saw. The energy flowed clear and true, pulsing with the same power as her own. She could see clearly the path they had followed and knew this was the last portion of the spell. He was right. They were almost done and it had been worth it.

There were a few areas not included in the pattern where energy was still blocked, but the clots and diversions weren't bad. Checking to see that he could handle the remainder on his own, Lyssa left him to go straighten out the last messy areas.

By the time she was done, so was he. When she rejoined him, he was standing back and admiring his handiwork.

'Not too shabby!' he exclaimed jubilantly as she approached.

Lyssa grinned. 'You did a great job. How do you feel?'

He did a brief jig, grinning ear to ear. 'Famished. Let's go get Molly and find some lunch.'

302

'Oh, god!' said Lyssa, with a sudden pang. 'What time is it? Is she okay?'

'I have no idea,' said Jeremy, pulling them back to the surface. 'But she's a pretty strong kid. She knows where we are if there's a problem, and she can take care of herself just fine. Besides, David is around. He looks out after her.'

Once they were back to consciousness, they sat up and self-consciously disengaged hands. Molly was still in the sanctuary, but the light coming in through the windows was dim with approaching night.

'Hi!' she said cheerfully as they approached. 'Look!' She held up a new book so they could see the cover. 'David is lending it to me,' she said, relishing the word 'lending'.

'That's nice of him,' said Jeremy. 'What's it about? Did you two get some lunch?'

'Yeah,' said Molly. 'It's about a little girl who gets lost, and the things that happen to her while she's trying to find her way home.'

'So it's kind of about you?' asked Lyssa.

'No,' said Molly impatiently. 'It's about another little girl. The one in the book, not me.'

'Oh,' said Lyssa, properly chastened.

Molly jumped up from where she sat and grabbed each of them by the hand, dragging them down the aisle. 'I've missed you all day,' she announced.

'We missed you too,' said Lyssa, giving her hand a squeeze. 'But thank you for letting us get our work done. I think now we have a little time to play.'

'You mean it?' asked Molly, with a little skip-step.

Jeremy nodded. 'For a little while.'

'And we can read any books?' Molly demanded eagerly. 'Please?'

'All of them,' Lyssa promised.

By the time they fell into bed that night, sleep was a welcome respite. Lyssa slept deeply, seeing brilliant pulsing energy flow and swirl around her, pulling her toward the center of the vortex. Instead of fear, she felt a euphoric curiosity. She knew she was caught up in the pattern, and that now the magic was working. She flowed with the energy, knowing where it led, but wondering where it was going.

As she grew closer to the end of the pattern, the rush of energy was loud in her ears, rumbling deep bass as it pushed her inexorably forward. She could feel the power shake and toss her and she began to be afraid. In the distance, someone was crying, and vaguely Lyssa knew she should be responding, but she couldn't place the sound or its location.

Gradually the cry pulled her from her dream and Lyssa realized it hadn't been a dream at all. Reality was impinging on her dream-state, and while the energy pattern wasn't manifest, the rumbling and shaking were.

Boxes were being jolted from their stacks, falling to the floor all around them. Molly was crying.

Lyssa sat bolt upright. 'Molly?' she shouted over the noise of the earthquake. 'Molly?'

A box glanced painfully off Lyssa's back, knocking her forward into her knees. She swore and pulled herself from the blankets, crawling in the pitch dark toward the little girl's pallet.

'Are you okay?' Lyssa shouted to her above the noise. She couldn't see anything and there was no hope of finding a light in the chaos. 'Molly?'

'Mommy!' cried the little girl pitifully. 'I'm stuck. Help!'

Lyssa followed her voice and found her trapped under a heavy box. 'Jeremy! I don't know if I can lift this by myself,' Lyssa called to him. Then she realized she hadn't heard from him since she woke. She lifted a corner, but Molly gasped in pain as the weight shifted onto her shoulder and hip.

'Ow,' she moaned softly.

Guiltily, Lyssa lowered the box again. 'Jeremy!' she shouted.

'Huh?' came his groggy response.

'Come help me now!' she demanded, hoping he was okay. She had to get the box off of Molly.

'Jeremy!' she shouted again. 'Jeremy, are you awake? Are you okay? Come here now!'

'Umm,' was his response.

Over the noise of the earthquake, she couldn't tell if he was moving. '*Jeremy!*'

'Coming,' he called back. It seemed an eternity before she could feel him near her, and all the while, the shaking and rumbling continued.

'What's happening?' he asked as he moved around to get to the other side of the box. 'Okay, I've got it.'

'This has to be the longest damned quake I've ever heard of.' Lyssa grabbed her side and together they lifted the box off of Molly and put it aside. Lyssa felt for the little girl in the dark. 'Lie still, sweetheart,' she instructed. 'Can you feel if everything is alright? Can you breathe?'

'I hurt,' Molly whimpered. 'I'm scared.'

Lyssa smoothed the hair from Molly's forehead, and wiped the tears from her cheeks. 'Can I pick you up without hurting you more?' she asked gently.

'I think so,' said Molly, trying to sit up. 'Ow!' she cried again.

'Let me do it,' said Lyssa, helping the little girl up into her lap. She hugged her gently, rocking back and forth while Molly buried her head in Lyssa's shoulder. 'I don't know what's happening,' she said over Molly's head to Jeremy. 'Are you okay?' She asked the last a little guiltily. She hadn't even thought to check him when the shaking first started. She just assumed if she was alright, so was he.

'Uh, yeah,' Jeremy responded slowly. 'I guess all that internal work earlier just wiped me out. I wasn't even awakened by the noise. It was you shouting at me that finally got through. Do you know what's going on?'

Lyssa shook her head, but in the dark, he didn't see it.

'I have no idea. I guess we'll have to wait until morning to find out.'

Footsteps sounded on the stairs. 'Are you all okay?' asked the Speaker as he opened the door to the storeroom. He held a lantern aloft and they could finally see the damage done by the quake. They sat amid a heap of boxes. Everything they had so carefully stacked and arranged was tossed about and the contents spilled where boxes had broken.

'Molly was crushed by a box,' said Lyssa quickly. 'Please bring the light here so we can see if she needs medical attention.'

David obliged, stepping over the mess gingerly, trying not to slip on any of the loose papers, or break any of the more ornate religious artefacts now in his path. Lyssa gently disengaged the little girl and lay her back down on her pallet to examine her better.

'I won't hurt you,' she said, pulling up Molly's shirt to look at her chest. The bruising was nasty already, but careful palpation showed nothing was broken, and there were no cuts. Since Molly could breathe easily enough, and there were no sharp pains, they decided she could wait until morning to see the doctor. 'Is there anything the old magic can do?' Lyssa asked David.

'I have no idea,' he answered. 'You can try, but I think you should come outside first, and see this.'

'What's "this"?' asked Jeremy. He was still having trouble getting his mind around being awake, and what was going on.

'You've got to see it to believe it,' said David cryptically. 'I've never seen anything like it before.'

Lyssa looked at Molly. 'Do you want to stay here, or come with us?' she offered. The rumbling had finally stopped, and Molly would undoubtedly be more comfortable not moving, but Lyssa figured she probably wouldn't want to be left alone right now.

'Could Jeremy carry me?' asked Molly shyly.

Lyssa looked at Jeremy. She wondered if he could carry himself, but she asked him anyway. 'What do you think?'

Jeremy nodded and moved to pick Molly up, even more gently than Lyssa had managed. He cradled her against his chest and stood.

Lyssa stood up as well and gestured for the Speaker to lead the way. As David left the room, Lyssa stepped aside for Jeremy to follow him, then she brought up the rear.

Outside was ablaze with light in spite of the dark night. Everyone, it seemed, had come out to see the spectacle. Lamps, flashlights, candles, every means of illumination had been employed, and everyone stood in their bedclothes staring at the brightest blaze of all.

The hill no longer covered the warrens. The House had somehow risen from its grave and stood, tier upon tier, in plain sight. Most of the light was coming from the windows, now free of dirt and debris. The effect was spectacular, and the crowd was dumbstruck. No one said a word, they just stood and stared, rubbing their eyes in disbelief and shaking their heads.

The splendor was undeniable, with no evidence of what should have been the inevitable damage of centuries of interment. Rare woods, highly polished, survived with the help of the magic that made the place possible to begin with, and the glass was unbroken in spite of the upheaval. The carvings and external adornment were just as richly detailed as the day they had been installed.

'My god,' said Lyssa softly.

Heads near her turned, and a murmur swept the crowd, drawing everyone's attention to her. She came from up there, and they stared at her now, wondering what she knew about this.

Lyssa was unaware of this until David nudged her in the ribs. Turning, she noticed she was the center of attention. 'Uh,' she said to him under her breath. 'What do I do about this?'

He shrugged and said nothing.

'Thanks,' she muttered. Then she took a deep breath and raised her voice. 'I have been estranged from the Family,' she said. 'Living in the cellar of the church. I don't know any more than you do.'

'Why should we believe that?' asked a man nearby.

'Because it's the truth,' she said simply. She stood, shivering in the cold night air, waiting for their verdict. More voices rippled through the crowd, and heads began to turn back to the incredible sight on the hill, drawn in spite of themselves.

'Is this what the aunts and uncles were up to?' Jeremy whispered.

Lyssa shrugged. 'I guess, but what for?'

'I'm cold,' whimpered Molly. Then she threw up. 'Ow,' she cried. 'Oh, my – ow!' She began sobbing, clearly in pain from her injuries and the shock they had caused.

'Why don't you come home with me and clean up. You can spend the rest of the night there,' David suggested.

Silently, they followed him out of the square and down a street toward his house.

'I'm sorry,' Molly whispered. 'I'm sorry.'

Lyssa took Molly's cold little feet into her hands and rubbed them, cradling them against her. 'Sweetheart, you've done nothing to apologize for,' she reassured. 'We'll have you warm and snug in bed in no time, and everything will be okay.'

By the time they'd gotten Molly cleaned up it became apparent a doctor would be necessary that night, so David went to fetch him while Lyssa and Jeremy stayed to comfort the little girl.

Wrapped in a soft towel, Molly snuggled miserably into Lyssa, who rocked her and sang every song she could think of in a quiet voice. Jeremy sat nearby holding a bowl just in case Molly vomited again. He looked sweet and silly to

308

Lyssa; dressed in a tee-shirt and rather over-sized pants of David's in the aftermath of cleaning up his concern for Molly clear on his face. She smiled at him over Molly's head as she sang and hoped nothing was seriously wrong with the little girl.

Tapping into the old magic, Lyssa tried to use it to envelope and heal Molly, but she had little hope it was actually working. In spite of the physical contact, she was unable to get inside Molly in order to do the sort of cleansing she and Jeremy had done.

The doctor finally came and checked Molly over. Lyssa was appalled all over again by the extent of the bruising on Molly's chest and arms, but the doctor said there was no damage to her internal organs. 'She'll be very sore for a while, and her body is in shock still from the damage and the fright, but she'll be fine,' the doctor said. 'I'll give her a shot to ease the pain and help her sleep, and then I'd suggest you all do the same. If you have any other problems, come see me in the morning.'

'Thank you,' said Lyssa as she gently eased Molly into another of David's tee-shirts. On the little girl, it was the perfect size for a nightshirt. She looked up to see the doctor staring at her strangely.

'The burns healed . . . quickly,' he commented.

She nodded, unsure of what to say.

'You're very fortunate,' he said. 'Perhaps Molly has inherited your ability to heal.'

Lyssa opened her mouth to deny genetic involvement when Jeremy intervened. 'We can hope,' he said. 'Thank you so much for coming to the house. I know tonight is a busy one for you and we appreciate your time.'

'Was anyone else injured?' the doctor asked.

'A box landed on me, but I think all I got was a bruise,' said Lyssa.

He took a brief look at her back and agreed. 'Well, then, if I'm not needed here any longer, I'll leave you to get some rest. I'll check back tomorrow to see how Molly is doing.'

The doctor followed Jeremy and David out of the room and Lyssa turned back to Molly, looking at her closely and frowning.

'Did I do something wrong?' Molly whispered sleepily.

'No, sweetheart,' answered Lyssa quickly. 'Let me tuck you in and you can get some rest, okay?' She eased Molly under the covers and smoothed them up under her chin. 'Jeremy and I will be right here if you need anything,' she said, kissing the little girl good night. She turned off the brighter lamp and climbed into the pallet Jeremy and David had made up on the floor. She was asleep before Jeremy came back in.

'I have to go back into the House,' said Lyssa reluctantly over breakfast the next morning. Molly was still asleep, and they were content to let her remain so until the drugs wore off and she awoke on her own. Lyssa, David and Jeremy had gotten up only slightly later than usual, and were drinking strong coffee in an attempt to jolt themselves awake. The spectacle of the night before prevented any of them from going back to sleep once they realized it was daylight.

When they went outside to check, the House was still there, rising up out of the hill in solitary magnificence, level by level, connected by covered stairs. They stared at it for some time before going back inside.

'It's too dangerous,' Jeremy protested. 'You still don't know what they're doing, besides trying to kill you.'

'I think it's pretty evident they aren't going to wait for you to continue the pattern,' said David wryly. They had told him about the four patterns they had used to reweave the spells. 'How can you be sure this isn't the result of the spell you wove?'

Lyssa shook her head. 'It doesn't feel right. I don't know what we were trying to achieve, but this wasn't it. This is what the aunts and uncles were doing. I'm certain of that much. I think what Jeremy and I were doing had to do with closing doors.'

David frowned. 'That makes sense,' he said to himself. When he looked up, both Lyssa and Jeremy were looking questioningly at him.

'What do you mean?' they asked in unison.

'Sorry, I'm not sure, but I think you were closing the Door to the meeting place; where we're returning to at the end of the millennium. If the Door is shut, the aunts and uncles can't leave here.'

'Then neither can anyone else,' said Jeremy pointedly. 'What about you and Millie? What about Lyssa? And how do I get home?'

'Is that a place you want to go?' asked David, giving Jeremy a strange look.

Jeremy thought for a moment before shrugging. 'I've never given it much thought. It was always the goal my mother had. I just took it over when she died. I don't have a life wherever I came from, regardless of whether or not my father is still alive. I guess my life is here now. I just don't want to be tied to this town any longer. I want to be able to go other places, have a job and a family.' He stopped abruptly, embarrassed.

'These are normal things to want,' said David.

'I've never allowed myself to want anything other than going home. It seemed the only safe dream,' Jeremy said.

'You said you had no dreams,' whispered Lyssa. Tears stood in her eyes, a sure sign she'd gotten too little sleep on top of the stress of the last few days.

'I lied,' said Jeremy.

'What if it turns out all I can do is make sure all the doors are shut?' she asked. 'Will you be happy here?'

'I've never known anything else,' he said, not answering the question.

'Well, I still have to go back into the House,' said Lyssa, shaking off the melancholy as best she could. She turned to David. 'Is there *any* help you can give me with the old magic? I could use any edge. If the old folks want me dead, there doesn't seem to be much I can do to stop them.'

David shook his head. 'I can give you this, though,' he said, reaching into his pocket and pulling out something. He reached across the table and handed Lyssa the object.

It was the necklace she had given him for safekeeping. The stone was green again, no longer pulsing like a living entity. Lyssa slipped it around her neck and tucked it into her shirt. 'Thank you for taking care of it for me,' she said. 'How will it help?'

David shrugged. 'I just know you have to take it with you back into the House. When are you going?'

'After Molly wakes up,' said Lyssa. 'There are some things I need to talk to her about first and I want to be sure she's okay. I can't leave without knowing she's okay.'

David smiled. 'I understand.'

Jeremy gave her a measured look. 'What about me?' he asked.

'You're okay,' said Lyssa. 'I know you'll be fine whether I am or not. Molly seems really attached to me. I have to explain things to her.'

Jeremy shook his head. 'I mean I think I should be going back in there with you.'

'No!' said Lyssa too quickly. She paused for a moment. 'I don't have any control over the magic. I can't protect myself, let alone both of us. Remember what happened last time I tried?'

'Yeah,' said Jeremy. 'I don't seem too much the worse for wear. What I mean is, if I am the balance of your power, like Cornelius is the balance for Burchie, then I should be going back in with you. I can't tell you why, but I feel I should be part of this.'

His argument made sense.

Lyssa hated that, but there was nothing she could say against it. He was right. It made sense on a gut level she couldn't deny. He should be there. Finally, she nodded. 'Then we go together.' She turned to David. 'Please take care of Molly?'

He nodded.

312

'We might be gone a really long time,' she said.

David nodded again. 'For as long as you're gone,' he said.

'What if we don't come back?' Lyssa whispered, afraid even to voice the thought.

'We'll cross that bridge if we come to it,' David said reassuringly. 'As long as you are gone, she'll be safe with me.'

'Thanks,' said Lyssa, trying to surreptitiously brush a tear from her cheek. As important as she was to Molly, the little girl was equally important to Lyssa. She had really grown attached to her since finding her in the warrens. It seemed like forever ago by now and Lyssa was hard put to remember a time when Molly wasn't a concern for her and a joy to her. She sighed. 'Thanks.'

Molly awoke finally, and tearful good-byes were said. The little girl was still too woozy from the drugs to be fully coherent, and in too much pain despite them to be concerned with much beyond herself, but she cried and hugged Lyssa and Jeremy tightly. 'I love you,' she whispered, kissing Lyssa on the cheek.

'I love you, too, sweetheart,' Lyssa whispered back, blinking away the tears she didn't want Molly to see. 'David will take care of you, okay?' She laid Molly back down on the bed and stroked her cheek. Molly nodded and Jeremy and Lyssa rose to leave.

During the night, the crowd attracted by the emergence of the House had dispersed, but there were still quite a number of onlookers as Jeremy and Lyssa made their way through the square and down the road toward the hill. As they passed, murmurs rippled away from them, speculation, conjecture and some ridicule, but they were allowed through unmolested.

As they approached the House, their pace slowed a bit and Lyssa reached for Jeremy's hand without even realizing it until he gave her a gentle squeeze. 'I don't feel so sure of myself,' he said softly. 'This whole thing is giving me the creeps.'

Lyssa chuckled. 'The creeps?' she asked. 'How about a complete fit of the horrors? What are the old folks trying to accomplish by digging up the warrens? You wouldn't think they'd be so eager to draw attention to what's going on here.'

Jeremy shrugged. 'I guess we'll find out soon enough.'

They passed the trail to the Room and Lyssa was surprised to find it was the only portion of the House that was still underground. 'Maybe we would have been safe in there after all. Maybe Molly wouldn't have gotten hurt if we'd stayed.'

'Stop,' said Jeremy softly. 'You can second guess yourself forever. It won't change what happened. We'll check on it later and see if the loom is still standing, okay?'

Lyssa sighed. 'You're right. I'm just trying to put off dealing with the inevitable here.' She nodded up the hill toward Aunt Burchie's quarters. 'Bearding the lion in her den isn't my idea of fun.'

'We don't even know if she's still alive,' Jeremy pointed out. 'Let's just wait until we know what we're dealing with before we panic.'

Lyssa smiled grimly and they continued up the hill toward the House.

Chapter Eleven

'In case of emergency, wait.'
The Book of Rules, Chapter Thirteen

The front door was open, as if they'd been expected.

Jeremy and Lyssa stood outside on the road for a long time, looking into the foyer and wondering; holding hands and trying to screw up enough courage to walk up the steps and into the House.

'It's so difficult,' she said in a low voice. 'I used to go through it all the time.'

Jeremy gave her hand a squeeze and started forward, pulling Lyssa with him. Reluctantly, she followed. They walked through the door and stopped as if waiting to be challenged.

Nothing happened.

'Should we go find Millie?' asked Jeremy in a whisper.

'Yeah,' Lyssa whispered back. 'Maybe she's been able to find something out.' She pressed her hand against the necklace tucked inside her shirt. They went down the hallway to Millie's quarters and knocked on the door.

'Come in?' Millie sounded surprised.

Jeremy opened the door and stepped quickly inside, tugging Lyssa inside after him and shutting the door behind them.

'You made it!' Millie exclaimed, rushing to them and hugging them tightly together. Then she pushed them back and inspected them. 'You weren't hurt by the quake last night?'

Lyssa shook her head. 'Molly was.'

Millie nodded. 'She'll be fine,' she said confidently. Lyssa wondered how she could possibly know, but before she could open her mouth, 'I'll bet it's quite a sight out there,' Millie continued. 'You should have heard the aunts and uncles cackling over it.'

'What are they doing?' asked Jeremy.

Millie shrugged. 'They keep their own counsel,' she said. 'I have some ideas, but I wouldn't even begin to know for certain. They don't let me see much, and I don't have eyes all over the House.'

'Are these ideas you'd like to share?' asked Lyssa.

Millie chuckled. 'They're pretty far-fetched. Is the entire House above ground now?'

'Everything except the Room,' said Lyssa. 'And you're right, it's pretty amazing to see. The people in town are completely in awe and extremely suspicious of what's going on. They seem to think I have an idea of what's happened.'

'That would be a logical assumption,' said Millie.

'What happened?' asked Lyssa, somewhat more pointedly this time.

'We have to go to the greenheart,' said Millie. 'Do they know you're here?' she nodded her head in the direction of Aunt Burchie's room.

'Probably,' said Lyssa. 'They haven't done anything to prevent me from coming this far. Is Aunt Burchie still alive?'

Millie laughed. 'It'll take a lot more than a few strokes to kill that old bat. Shall we go?'

Lyssa felt a sudden pang. 'What about Bertie?' she asked, remembering Millie's husband.

Millie looked regretful, but not particularly sad. 'He was Other,' she said.

'I'm sorry,' said Lyssa.

'Don't be,' said Millie with a smile. 'We had a good time together while it lasted, but I can't tell you how many husbands I've outlived over the centuries. I've never been happy to see one go, but it's the price one pays for becoming involved with the short-lived. His health was poor and he wouldn't have lasted much longer anyway.'

'Then I guess it's time for us to leave here,' said Jeremy, opening the door.

The aunts and uncles all stood outside in the hallway, smiling. 'We're delighted you came,' they said with one voice. They all had the same look in their eyes and moved at the same time, in complete unison. The spell they cast was a powerful one.

Lyssa found she was unable to move. Jeremy appeared to be equally frozen, still holding the knob to the bedroom door. Lyssa couldn't see Millie, but assumed she, too, was immobile. Gently, they were lifted off the floor and moved out the door.

The old folks gave way and the paralyzed trio were pulled down the hallway by the unseen force which held them. Lyssa knew where they were heading, and she was positive the aunts and uncles were following along behind, no longer in control of themselves either. Aunt Burchie was surely not incapacitated by her strokes. She was still in charge and making the rules up as she went along.

She had gone from using the energy of the Others, to using the energy of Family, and Lyssa had no doubt that she, Millie and Jeremy were the next victims. She tried to speak, but that was also beyond her control. In desperation, she reached into the old magic.

It wouldn't free her. Try as she might, the spell held fast, resistant to her efforts. She couldn't even use it to free her vocal cords. Desperation made her struggle harder, but the more effort she put into it, the more hopeless the situation became. They were being pulled inexorably toward Aunt Burchie's room. The rooms they passed, which had once seemed so comfortable and familiar to her, now seemed alien and foreboding as they were drawn down the hallways, followed by their silent entourage.

Lyssa reached with the magic toward Jeremy, hoping that, even though they weren't touching, they might have a connection from their earlier work.

Lyssa?

His voice sounded loud in her head, but it was unmistakably Jeremy. *Yeah, got any ideas?*

Not a one, he said. *But maybe we can get the old lady to talk. She used to love to talk to me about things. She might tip her hand and tell us more than she had intended.*

It's better than anything I've thought of, but it still doesn't help us get out of here, said Lyssa. *You want me to see if I can get Millie in on this conversation?*

Jeremy gave her a mental shrug. *Can't hurt, and it might give us an edge the old lady wouldn't anticipate.*

Okay, then, hang on, said Lyssa, reaching out for Millie. This would be a lot tougher; they'd never had the kind of connection she and Jeremy did.

It was worse than tough. It was futile. Nothing Lyssa did established even a flicker of communication between her and Millie. With a sigh, Lyssa gave up and returned her attention to Jeremy. *Sorry, I guess we're on our own.*

Well, two heads are better than one, he said, obviously disappointed. *As long as we can keep it a secret from your aunt, we've got a little advantage.*

I guess that's better than nothing, said Lyssa.

They were pulled through the open door and deposited on the floor at the foot of Aunt Burchie's bed.

'Ah, there you are, my dears!'

The hospital bed was gone. The old lady was gone. In her place was a beautiful young woman who looked a little like Marnie, and a little like Lyssa. She stood in front of what looked like an altar or shrine, holding a cup with which she gestured. 'Quite a change from the last time we saw each other?'

What is she up to? Jeremy asked Lyssa.

Like I'd know? Lyssa demanded, trying to keep her eyes as deadpan as her face had become. It was to their advantage that whatever magic Aunt Burchie was using on them held them rigid. *The only consolation is that this is costing her dearly, and she won't be able to keep it up indefinitely. Eventually the magic exacts a price, and I'd be willing to bet this one will be stiff. She looks like she's our age or younger. What could she possibly gain?*

'And how do you like the House?' Aunt Burchie continued. 'I decided to turn back time in order to finish the pattern you so stubbornly refused to complete. Unfortunately, while I was ill and working the new spell, you seem to have worked one of your own. This is what happens when magics clash.' She smiled and put down the cup, coming out from behind the odd structure she had built and bending to put her face very close to Lyssa's. 'You have caused me problems since the moment you arrived, and now even the House is rebelling. What did you do to cause the House to unbury itself?'

Lyssa remained paralyzed, unable to answer, but her mind was working furiously, trying to sort out what her aunt was implying. How could she possibly have known what would happen? She hadn't even known what pattern she was walking, only that she had seen it so often it was the only thing that made sense.

Then she remembered what her mother had said about each matriarch remaining with her section of the House, keeping it and tending it until the transition when they all returned to the meeting place. Could they have been involved? Obviously magic was keeping them there and able to affect the material things around them. Did they wield any magic of their own? If Aunt Burchie had in fact gone back in time, how would that affect the different sections of the House, and why didn't the rest of them go back in time with her? Why then was she still here?

Why did Lyssa keep finding herself with more questions? Every time she thought she was finding out what was happening, something else pulled the rug out from under her.

'You want to answer me, don't you?' asked Aunt Burchie sweetly.

No! shouted Lyssa inside her head.

Ow! Jeremy objected. *I'm having enough trouble keeping up with your panic. Try to keep the noise down a little.*

Gee, sorry, said Lyssa sarcastically. *Is she trying to delay transition, or hasten it?*

Aunt Burchie waved her hand and Lyssa felt her throat and facial muscles relax. She worked her jaw a little to cover her reaction and then asked the question. 'Are you trying to make transition or stop it?'

Aunt Burchie chuckled. 'My dear, transition is the only thing worth living for. Why would I want to stop it? I'm struggling vainly to understand why you tried to stop it.'

'Why does the House want transition to occur?' asked Lyssa.

'It's not the House, darling,' said Aunt Burchie. 'You really should have been paying more attention during the Game. The spirits want transition to happen. They are the ones who guide your footsteps and weave the spell.'

'The spirits?' Lyssa asked, trying to keep the disdain out of her voice.

'The energies of those who have gone before,' said Aunt Burchie with exaggerated patience. 'The women who take care of the House.'

'Why are men powerless in the Family?'

'Not powerless, exactly,' said Aunt Burchie. 'They have their uses, but they don't connect as deeply to the magic. It limits them severely.'

'Then what about my father?' Lyssa pressed, knowing the answer, but trying to find out how much knowledge Aunt Burchie actually had.

'I have no idea.' Aunt Burchie was visibly disturbed by the question. 'I've never found that out.' She looked past Lyssa and Jeremy at the aunts and uncles in the doorway. 'Still, it's a moot point now.'

Lyssa felt her insides grow cold. She had never really known her father, but he *was* her father.

'Why would the spirits allow me to walk a new pattern, then?' asked Lyssa, fighting down her anger and disappointment. 'Why wouldn't they try to stop me like you did?'

'That's something I still don't understand,' said Aunt Burchie with a frown. 'Any more than I understand why the House suddenly uprooted itself. Quite a shaking it was; you should have felt it.'

'I did,' said Lyssa curtly. 'So did the entire town. I wouldn't be surprised if by now half the region is crawling around down there, wondering what's going on.'

Aunt Burchie shook her head. 'Our reach doesn't extend that far. Did you ever contact the Bell family?'

It was Lyssa's turn to frown. 'Yes,' she said. 'Why?'

'Their magic built this place. I was wondering what they might have told you about it.'

'Nothing,' said Lyssa. 'They told me to contact them only when it was time to build.' She stopped and thought for a long moment. 'Transition isn't supposed to occur for another few decades, is it? You aren't supposed to make transition, are you?'

'Not in corporeal form,' said Aunt Burchie, looking uneasy for the first time.

'What advantage is there to being alive when we go to the meeting place?' asked Lyssa.

She doesn't want to die, whispered Jeremy in the back of her mind. *She has a complete horror of it.*

'You'll never know,' Aunt Burchie said, smiling maliciously.

'Of course I will. The Family members are all still here, including my mother. I'll translate with the rest of you, I'll just do it as energy instead of skin,' said Lyssa, trying to call her aunt's bluff. 'Isn't that how it works?'

Aunt Burchie shrugged. 'It doesn't matter. You'll still be out of my way.'

Lyssa grinned. 'How can you be sure of that?'

Aunt Burchie leaned in close again. 'Because I have control over my magic,' she whispered. She smiled slowly as she stood up again. She went back to the altar and picked up the cup. 'Would you care for a drink?' She came back and held the cup to Millie's lips.

'No!' Lyssa growled, her voice coming from deep inside. Connected to Jeremy, she had twice the energy to draw on and the bolt came from both of them. Burchie flew backward and hit the wall. The cup spun away from her and crashed to the floor, spilling its contents onto the carpet. Suddenly free from her aunt's paralyzing magic, Lyssa turned to Jeremy and Millie. 'Can you move?' she asked urgently. They nodded. 'Then let's go!' she cried.

The old folks gave way as the trio darted past them and down the hall. Lyssa headed straight for the cupboard she knew led to her Room. Still underground, it might be safe for now. Once there, they could decide what to do next.

Everything was as Jeremy and Molly had left it.

'Oh, god,' moaned Lyssa, looking around. 'She'd have been okay if we'd stayed. The loom is still standing.'

Jeremy came to stand behind her and put his arms around her shoulders. Giving her a gentle squeeze he said, 'You had no way of knowing this. You were thinking of our safety. Second guessing yourself won't change the way things are. Molly will be fine and that's what's important in the long run.'

Lyssa sighed and slumped against him. 'Intellectually, I understand this. Emotionally, I feel like I could have gotten her killed.' She could hear rummaging behind her and disengaged from Jeremy to see what Millie was doing. 'What do you think?' she asked.

Millie was bent over the maps, which Jeremy had left on the table between the rocking chairs. 'I hadn't realized how much everything had grown since the last time I looked. You did a good job putting the Room to rights. The magic feels well balanced.' She straightened up and continued her inspection. 'I haven't seen this place in quite a while.'

'Did you live here?' asked Jeremy bluntly.

Millie laughed. 'No, no. We couldn't afford the appearance of affluence until much later. I lived in town for quite a number of years after I came here, and walked up the hill to work every day.'

'How long did you wait before coming?' asked Lyssa.

'I started working for the Family when they lived in the third House, helping out with the industry as well as doing the housekeeping. I moved in when the fifth House was built. By then, it was becoming a problem explaining away my longevity to the people in town who saw me every day.' Millie chuckled wryly. 'It's always nice for the first couple of decades in a new place. No need to deceive anyone.'

'Why are the Houses deserted fully furnished and with all the clothes and knick-knacks?' asked Lyssa, finally unable to stand not knowing.

Millie laughed. 'The Family has always been very possessive. Each matriarch holds on fiercely to her things. It's up to the new builder to fill her own House with things. I think also, having her own possessions anchors the matriarch to her House once she stops existing as a physical being. And there's probably a degree to which affluence is demonstrated by purchasing all new things to fill the new House.'

'Then why is there such a strange assortment left behind in this cupboard?' Lyssa gestured.

'Because they weren't so very affluent at the time,' said Millie. 'They left behind only those things which were no longer useful or necessary.'

'Then why did they leave behind the loom?' asked Jeremy.

'At first they didn't,' said Millie. 'They returned this only after they could afford the second one in the new House.'

He shook his head. 'You people are just too strange.'

Lyssa pulled a face. 'But why all the rigmarole? Why all the new Houses and why do the old ones get covered up by the hill?'

'Because of the portals, and the patterns, and to avoid suspicion,' said Millie. 'You read this in one of the books, didn't you? The Bell family builds the portals at whim, and you never know when they'll build the one that takes everyone back to the meeting place at transition – and because there has to be room to weave the spell that transports everyone to the meeting place, and because the Others need to have a place to live while they're here.'

'Don't the town people remember the other Houses?' asked Lyssa, dubiously. 'Just because they vanish from sight doesn't mean they vanish from memory.'

'You'd be surprised,' said Millie. 'Memory is a funny thing. Especially when magic is involved.'

'Where is the portal for transition?' asked Jeremy.

'No one knows,' said Millie. 'It gets opened once the pattern is complete. This time, the pattern wasn't completed, so we may never know.'

'The pattern wasn't due to be completed for decades,' said Lyssa. 'What was Aunt Burchie doing trying to change that?'

'I told you,' said Jeremy impatiently. 'She has an incredible fear of dying.'

'It's not just that,' said Millie. 'The matriarch who takes the House into transition gets to lay the foundation for the next cycle. Burchie couldn't stand that she was so *close* to being the one, without *being* the one. She was used to getting her way and just assumed she could bend the rules to her whim.'

'So far she's been pretty successful,' Jeremy noted.

'But she still doesn't know where the portal is, and she isn't sure how to find it,' said Millie. 'Her magic has its limits, and up against Lyssa's, time is one of them.'

'So where do we go from here?' asked Lyssa. 'And how can I expect to stop Aunt Burchie when I have no control over my magic? It was a fluke that I got us out of her room like that.'

Millie shook her head. 'The magic won't let itself be destroyed. While you harbor it, it will take care of you.'

'Swell,' said Lyssa. 'But where do we go from here?'

'We have some work to do here first,' said Millie. 'And evidently, we have some time in which to do it.'

'Work?' asked Jeremy.

'The power symbols,' said Millie. 'Where are they?'

Jeremy and Lyssa looked blankly at one another and then at Millie. 'We read every book. There were no symbols anywhere.'

Millie shook her head. 'These would be some items of jewelry and some lengths of cloth.'

Lyssa nodded toward the trunk at the foot of the bed. 'Everything is in there,' she said. 'Except this.' She pulled the necklace from under her shirt. Once again, the stone glowed crimson.

There was an unmistakable gleam in Millie's eyes when she saw it, but she turned to open the trunk. She unloaded the books quickly and pulled out the false bottom. 'Ah,' she said, pulling the cloth and the sock containing the jewelry from their hiding place. 'Help me with this please,' she gestured for Jeremy to restore the contents to the trunk.

While he obliged, Lyssa watched with interest what Millie was doing. She handled the cloth without any trace of the difficulty Lyssa had experienced, unfolding it quickly and wrapping it around her like a sari, over the clothing she already wore. Each piece went on in a specific fashion.

'Are those wrapped in a certain order?' asked Lyssa, leaning forward to watch what Millie was doing.

Millie smiled. 'Each its own order, each its own path.'

Lyssa groaned. 'Not more patterns!'

Millie laughed outright. 'Always another pattern. Our lives are based on them. You can't live without the patterns.'

Shortly, Millie was covered in cloth, shapeless with the bulk.

'What pattern are you weaving?' Lyssa asked.

'When the magic was stolen,' said Millie, 'the Family wove the spells of the old magic into these lengths of cloth, each thread imbedded with a spell, and fashioned some of

325

them into several pieces of jewelry, which were kept out of reach, along with the books.'

'So if I'd completed the spell and started transition, the books would have made sense?' Lyssa asked. 'I would have put the old magic back together and started a new – *colony*?' Lyssa shuddered violently at the thought.

'No,' Millie shook her head. 'The books would have been more useful, but you would have continued to keep the cloth hidden.' She looked at Lyssa fondly, but her smile was sad. 'Yes, you would have started another colony. And sent the Others to establish hundreds more.'

As they spoke, Lyssa began to notice the fabrics were fading and melting into Millie until finally they completely disappeared.

'Wow,' Jeremy whistled appreciatively, still kneeling beside the trunk. 'What was that?'

'Step one,' said Millie with grim satisfaction.

'What's going to happen now?' Lyssa asked apprehensively.

'First the jewelry, then we go to the jungle.' She reached into the sock and pulled out the brooches, the pearls and the tiny ring. Her hands shook, so she gave the necklace to Jeremy. 'Help me with this, will you dear?' She turned so he could fasten the clasp at the nape of her neck. 'Thank you.' She turned back around and began pinning the brooches down the left side of her dress from the shoulder toward the center of its rounded neckline. Lyssa could see she had already slipped the gold ring onto her little finger as far as the second joint. 'What do you think?' she grinned, displaying her finery.

'You look like a Christmas tree,' Jeremy laughed. 'All you need are lights.'

'In good time, dear. All in good time.' Millie made a gesture and all three of them were standing in the jungle.

'I thought you said you had no magic,' said Lyssa.

'When I said that, it was true,' said Millie. The pins and necklace had vanished just like the cloth. 'But you have returned almost all of the objects of power that were taken so many millennia ago, and now the balance is returning. There is only one more thing that will make the return complete.'

'You can't possibly think I'll let that happen,' said Aunt Burchie.

They swung around at the sound of her voice and shuddered to see her. She had become hideous to look at. The hate and anger inside her had twisted her features, deforming them. Her eyes were wild and staring, red-rimmed and blood-shot against the pallor of her skin. Her lips were cracked and swollen. She had been reduced to skin and bones as the power she misused ate at her from the inside. Her limbs were gnarled, huge joints appearing stiff and arthritic, and her hands were like claws.

The aunts and uncles were no longer in attendance. Lyssa could only assume they had been sacrificed to keep Aunt Burchie alive. 'Can you actually force transition to occur earlier than it should?' Lyssa asked, hoping to catch her off guard. 'What about the other Families in other places. How will they know and why should they come earlier?'

Aunt Burchie grinned and her lips began to bleed. 'Once the spell is woven, the message is in the web. Of course they would know and respond. We're the branch that's in charge. Why do you think we have the talismans and baubles?'

Millie shook her head. 'You don't have them anymore.'

'You still don't have them all,' Aunt Burchie cackled. 'And until you do, you can't hope to match my strength.' Her claw-like hands rose above her head, and raw energy, pent-up rage shot at them from across the clearing.

Millie stood her ground, but Jeremy and Lyssa dodged, each going a separate direction. Lyssa wasn't going to stick around and be burned a second time. She paid no attention to where Jeremy went, running for her life and praying to whatever deity might be listening. Periodically, energy shot past her, fueling her flight, but the going was tough, through undergrowth so thick she really needed a machete to cut through it. Still, she ran on until she found herself facing the door out into the maze of living rooms. She flung herself through it even as another bolt of raw blue rage singed her hip and destroyed the couch she had slept on.

Careful not to follow any specific pattern, Lyssa ran from room to room, feeling her heart pounding in her throat and the necklace thumping against her chest.

The heartstone.

This was the final object of power. The last talisman. She was supposed to give it to Millie in the jungle.

Millie had stood her ground and her power was incomplete.

Lyssa had no control over her own power, and the key to Millie's. With this realization, she turned and started back to the jungle, but Aunt Burchie shot her again. This time the bolt took her in the shoulder.

Screaming in pain, Lyssa headed off in a new direction. She knew her aunt was driving her away from the jungle, but she could do nothing to prevent it. In the back of her mind, she wondered where Jeremy was, but her primary concern was with her own safety, and finding a way to get back to the jungle.

She could feel the energy inside her working to heal the new injuries as she searched her internalized maps of the place to find a way to return to the jungle without Aunt Burchie suspecting.

There had been holes in the web. That was how Jeremy had described it. Places where Aunt Burchie was unaware of the new structure of the House. It had changed itself in response to her manipulations, but she had been unable to keep up with the differences since she wasn't able to get around and into the warrens herself.

Where were those holes?

Lyssa found herself wishing she had paid more attention to the conversations she'd had with her aunt about the places she went when she played the Game. Where had Aunt Burchie asked for the most detail? And where would those places lie on the map?

Lyssa ran. Her flight was driven more by fear now than physical evidence of being chased. She was afraid Aunt Burchie might manage to kill Millie or Jeremy, and afraid that she would still prevent Lyssa from returning to them.

She was afraid she would never see Molly again.

The sob caught in her throat, and Lyssa felt a burst of impatience with herself for being so maudlin, but it didn't slow her pace. She began to think more clearly, seeing the conversations and managing to overlay the missing areas on the map she carried in her head of the warrens she was sprinting through. There had to be a pattern, if she could only see it.

Then she got shot again. It knocked her off her feet and slammed her into the floor. She lay stunned, wondering what had happened, but even as the thought occurred to her that she was in trouble, she felt the darkness close in and she passed out.

Jeremy dodged the old lady's strikes and found himself separated from Lyssa once again. She was evidently the target, because once Jeremy was out of sight in the tropical growth, Burchie paid little attention to him.

He tried to follow Lyssa's flight while staying out of the way of the energy being blasted about, but gradually found himself being driven away and left behind. The old lady might not want to kill him, but she surely didn't want him helping her niece either.

Then he realized he was lost. Of course it wouldn't have taken much, he rationalized, everything looked the same in here, but he had absolutely no idea even of the direction he'd come from. Looking back, there was no discernible path cleared by broken or crushed foliage, and no noise coming from the attack. He couldn't get to Lyssa, but maybe he could return to Millie.

It was a vague hope, but the best he had to go on, so Jeremy reversed course and tried to find his way back to the clearing. He struggled for hours through the dense vegetation, wishing he had a knife and aching with the exertion, but he didn't find the clearing. Millie was on her own with the old lady, and Lyssa was who-only-knew-where. Come to think of it, Jeremy had no idea where he was, either. The jungle was huge, or he had been going in circles, but it was clear he was getting nowhere. Finally, exhausted, he sat down with his back against a tree to rest.

When he woke up, Cornelius was sitting in front of him, watching him. The young apprentice was nowhere to be seen. Jeremy sat looking back at the old man, saying nothing.

'It's begun?' asked Cornelius finally.

Jeremy nodded. 'I guess so. Do you know what's going on?'

Cornelius nodded slowly. 'I knew as soon as Lyssa came home that no good would come of this. Marnie and Apato are gone and the hill is receding. The forces that eddy through this House are too much for any one individual to control, but Burchie is going to try, and I'll have to try and balance her.'

'Apato?' asked Jeremy blankly.

'My young friend; Marnie's balance,' said Cornelius sadly. 'He wasn't much, but he was company.'

'Marnie's balance?' Jeremy echoed, beginning to understand.

Cornelius smiled a little. 'As the magic twisted Burchie, she needed a way to stay in touch with the village. I don't think the poor girl even suspected until it was too late. As a result of that transference, Apato was created to maintain the balance. Since Marnie required only the energy of maintenance and not creation, Apato was a tiny balance.'

Jeremy frowned in acknowledgement. 'What did Lyssa

coming home have to do with this? Burchie sent for her.'

'She controls the next stage of power. Burchie needed Lyssa in the House in order to take it from her.'

'Needed?' Jeremy sat up urgently. 'Is Lyssa alright?'

The old man shrugged. 'For now, alright, but she isn't safe. None of us are.'

'What can we do?' asked Jeremy.

'Balance the power,' said Cornelius vaguely.

'How?' Jeremy demanded.

'The only way is to be here. This is where the power comes from. If we leave, the balance is upset.'

'We just sit here?' Jeremy was incredulous. 'There has to be something more we can do.'

Cornelius shook his head.

'I thought the power came from the spells they've been weaving,' said Jeremy.

'No. That gathers and directs the energy, but it all comes from here to begin with. That's why everything is so wild and impenetrable. That's the way this magic has become since the theft took place. Before that, it was a beautiful and exotic garden, tended by both yin and yang. Now it is tended by no one. Since it is uncontrolled, so is the power it creates. This is dangerous for everyone, but especially those of us who live here.' Cornelius sighed, vision turned inward.

'Where did you come from?' asked Jeremy.

The Keeper shook his head. 'I have no more idea where I came from than you do,' he said. 'We all come from somewhere else. Those of us who are here to balance come at a much earlier age so that we have no memory of another time and place. I guess the theory is that we can't miss what we've never known.' He looked pointedly at Jeremy. 'We both know that's not true.'

Jeremy nodded. 'Can we go help Millie in any way?'

Cornelius shook his head again. 'We balance the old lady and the young one. They are Family. We leave the long-lived to themselves. Besides, Millie has managed to reclaim much of the power that was taken in the theft. She can probably take care of herself.'

'It's the "probably" that worries me,' said Jeremy, standing up and stretching his cramped muscles. 'She and I go way back. I can't just leave her to the mercy of a crazy old woman.'

'There is nothing you can do to help her, and if you try, you risk getting us all killed. You are here for Lyssa only. Stay out of the rest of it.' Cornelius rose also, holding out a hand to stop Jeremy.

'Sorry,' said Jeremy brusquely. 'I can't just sit around and do nothing.' He strode off into the jungle with no idea where he was going, and no idea what he would do if he got there.

Cornelius watched him go and shook his head. 'Son, you're going to get us all killed.'

Lyssa had definitely been the object of Burchie's attack. Shortly after she and Jeremy had disappeared into the jungle, Burchie disappeared also.

Evidently, Burchie had no idea of the significance of the power restored to Millie, or she would never have let Millie remain alone in the jungle. Grateful for the small boon, Millie hoped Lyssa would find her way back so they could complete the task they had come here for. She wished there was something she could do to help the girl, but there wasn't. Hoping Jeremy was still in the jungle, Millie, left alone and unharmed, sat down to wait.

When Lyssa finally came to, she was back in Aunt Burchie's room. Her heart sank as she realized she was alone, and in a great deal of trouble. Her aunt was nowhere in sight and Lyssa was confined by the same paralysis used earlier. Aunt Burchie was taking no chances that her niece might manage to free herself by attacking.

Well, this gave her time to think, Lyssa decided, and that was something she needed very much to do. She had been on the verge of putting together the holes in Aunt Burchie's memory of the warrens. Now she had the opportunity to do so.

But first, she searched her mind for the traces of Jeremy she had used to contact him earlier.

Are you there? she called to him, hoping for, but not expecting, any answer. *Jeremy, please?*

Lyssa? His thoughts sounded excited and relieved. *Are you okay?*

Yes and no, she thought to him wryly, picturing her situation for him. *Tell Millie I'm doing my best to get back there.*

Assuming I find her again, said Jeremy. *Take care of yourself.*

You, too, said Lyssa softly. Then she turned her attention to the problem at hand.

She must have fallen asleep. When she awoke, Aunt Burchie was in the room with her, rummaging through the drawers of her bureau, looking for something she wasn't finding. Clothing spilled out and landed on the floor, unheeded as she went from drawer to drawer. Lyssa, unable to move, watched with interest.

The search continued, from bureau to armoire to bedside tables without success and Aunt Burchie grew more and more agitated. She began muttering to herself, but Lyssa couldn't make out the words. She was still paralyzed, so she couldn't speak, or she might finally have asked what Aunt Burchie was looking for.

'You have it, don't you,' Aunt Burchie turned on her suddenly, making the question a statement. 'You took it before you left. Where is it? Give it to me!' She lunged at Lyssa, ripping her blouse to get at whatever it was she was looking for.

Lyssa tried to move, but it was no use. The heartstone lay against her chest, and there was nothing she could do to prevent Aunt Burchie from taking it. Instead of grabbing

333

the necklace, her aunt reached into Lyssa's jeans pockets, still searching for the mysterious missing object.

'What have you done with it?' she hissed, putting her face right up to Lyssa's.

Lyssa wished desperately to be able to move back, but wishing wasn't enough to break the spell her aunt held her under. She settled for closing her eyes. Then she felt her mouth and tongue freed from the spell.

'Answer me!' Aunt Burchie demanded.

'I don't know what you're looking for,' said Lyssa, opening her eyes again. The abuse of magic was taking a hideous toll on her aunt. She barely looked human anymore.

'Liar!' the old woman screamed. Spittle foamed at the corners of her mouth and her skin stretched tight across her bones, translucent and shiny, like an old scar. 'There was a bracelet. A gold bracelet with a pattern carved on it. It was in my dresser and you stole it. Where did you put it?'

'I don't have it,' Lyssa said. 'When I left the House, you were still confined to your bed and not sleeping. When would I have come in here and stolen from you that you wouldn't have noticed?'

'And where did you get that?' Aunt Burchie asked, reaching for the heartstone, avarice sparkling in her eyes.

'It was a gift,' said Lyssa. This was it. She closed her eyes and held her breath, not knowing what would happen when her aunt controlled that bit of magic too.

As Aunt Burchie's hand closed over the stone, Lyssa heard the crackling and her eyes flew open, but her head was still immobilized and she couldn't look down. Her aunt's eyes widened and her mouth gaped open. Then Lyssa smelled burning flesh and felt the jerk of the cord around her neck as her aunt tried to let go of the stone.

The smell intensified until Lyssa's stomach rebelled and still Aunt Burchie was unable to let go of the necklace. The old woman was screaming in pain and frantically pulling on the cord around Lyssa's neck. She couldn't get the necklace off Lyssa, nor could she free her burning hand. Lyssa vomited.

'You beastly child,' raged Aunt Burchie, slapping Lyssa with her free hand.

Lyssa began to cry. 'Leave me alone!' she sobbed. 'You selfish, greedy old witch. You can't have the necklace and you're going to have to die eventually. These things aren't my fault.'

'I will never die!' shrieked Aunt Burchie, yanking harder and harder on the cord. 'I will manage the transition and become immortal.'

'W-who told you that?' gasped Lyssa, trying to breathe over the stench of burning flesh and vomit.

'The matriarchs.' With one more vicious jerk, Aunt Burchie was suddenly freed from the stone. She held up her arm and both she and Lyssa gasped in disbelief. Her hand had been burned away and they were staring at her bloody, charred wrist.

'Well, the matriarchs lied,' said Lyssa bluntly. 'And it looks like the bracelet won't do you any good now.'

'What do you mean they lied?' her aunt asked weakly, staring at her stump.

'Well, do you see a matriarch still hanging around here from the last transition?' Lyssa demanded. 'Who were you talking to? Was she alive? Are any of them?' She could feel the spell relaxing, and she was starting to regain movement, but she had to keep her aunt distracted until it was too late for her to do anything about it. 'Are you that gullible, or that fearful?'

'You can't talk to me that way, young lady,' Aunt Burchie snapped. It was a pro forma reprimand. She was in shock over the loss of her hand.

Lyssa took that moment. Grabbing whatever came to hand, she clubbed her aunt's wounded wrist as hard as she could and then ran for the door. She knew she would never get another chance. If she was caught again, Aunt Burchie would kill her.

It hadn't been just a nightmare.

It hadn't been about her mother.

It was a premonition, dreamed over and over again during her childhood. A warning she hadn't heeded, not knowing what it was about.

Once again Lyssa ran through the warrens, carrying a map in her mind, but following a route she was uncertain of, pursued and fearful.

This time she knew who was chasing her. The nameless fear of her dreams was the aunt who had raised her from early childhood, but the aunt had been transformed, made grotesque by rage and misuse of power.

Lyssa hoped she had put together the correct route back to the jungle based on areas of the House her aunt was no longer familiar with. She dashed down hallways and through rooms, barely taking time to shut doors and hoping the slamming sounds weren't enough of a trail for her aunt to follow.

Her heart pounded in her chest and her throat constricted, making it difficult to breathe. There was no sound behind her to let her know she was being followed, but she knew Aunt Burchie was there somewhere.

With a scream, Lyssa threw herself back out the door she had just opened, dodging a bolt that barely missed her. Miscalculating Aunt Burchie had been a problem for her all along, and she was still slow to see it. The old woman didn't need to move through the warrens on her feet, she had control over the magic she wielded.

And Lyssa had been able to use hers to transport herself. Was her brain that addled? Tapping into the magic she possessed, she visualized the jungle and willed herself there. Something happened, but when Lyssa opened her eyes, she was not among the undergrowth. She was in another part of the House.

Tearing wildly through her brain, she finally figured out where she was and readjusted her course. She was closer to the jungle than she had been, but that was small comfort. She was supposed to have gotten herself there. How had she failed?

She heard her aunt laughing behind her, but a quick glance revealed no one there. *I can do anything to you I want,* Aunt Burchie's voice mocked her in the back of her mind. There was nowhere she was safe. She was a lab rat running in a giant maze with no control over her destiny.

With a shudder, Lyssa shook off that image. She was *not* helpless. Aunt Burchie could play games with her, but the necklace was Lyssa's, and there was only one place she was going with it. No one could stop her from reaching her goal. Temporarily deter, yes, but not stop. She burst through a door and onto the dance floor of the grand ballroom where she had seen the ghostly dancers.

The church. She needed to go to the church.

'Lyssa?' David Baker was surprised, and shocked by her appearance, she could tell from his voice.

'I can't stay,' she gasped, looking around for any sign that Aunt Burchie had followed her there. She grabbed the necklace and held it out to look at it for the first time. The stone and cord were pristine. There was no trace of the earlier horror. Holding it tightly, she closed her eyes and tried again to picture the jungle.

This time when she opened her eyes, she was in the room outside the door. With a quick look around, she darted inside, running as best she could through the impossible tangle of plants and vines. 'Jeremy?' she screamed. 'Millie?'

They can't help you, hissed Aunt Burchie.

Lyssa slewed around, arms up, prepared to defend herself from a physical attack. She could see Aunt Burchie, but between them stood Cornelius.

How could you have betrayed the Family? Aunt Burchie demanded, advancing a step.

Lyssa gaped for a moment. *You didn't kill my mother soon enough,* she said slowly.

Cornelius looked at Lyssa for a long moment, then nodded in the direction she should go. 'I'm here to balance the power,' he said.

Lyssa turned and ran. In no time at all, she had no idea if she was still on the course the old man had indicated, but she kept moving. 'Millie?'

'Lyssa?'

She veered toward Millie's voice without slowing her pace. 'Is Jeremy with you?' she panted, hoping her voice would carry.

'I'm here!' he called.

Lyssa tried to run faster, but the branches caught at her legs and she struggled to remain upright.

'Hurry!' they called together.

She burst into the clearing and fell flat on her face. Jeremy and Millie rushed to help her to her feet. 'Burchie is in the jungle,' said Millie urgently. 'We've got to get out of here now.'

'I have no control over the magic,' Lyssa protested. 'I can't guarantee I'll get us all out safely.'

'You have to give me the necklace,' said Millie. 'Then I can do it.'

Lyssa backed up a pace, putting her hand to the stone. 'The necklace is mine.'

Millie shook her head. 'If you think about it, you know that's not true,' she said gently.

Lyssa looked at Jeremy. He shrugged. 'I don't know, but I trust her,' he said.

Looking back in the direction she had come, a sickly yellow light was beginning to glow through the foliage. She hesitated a moment longer before pulling the cord over her head and handing Millie the necklace.

Millie slipped it over her own head and settled the stone proprietorially between her breasts. As she did so, a change seemed to come over her. 'You've done the right thing.'

There was an elaborately carved gold bracelet on her left wrist that Lyssa hadn't seen before, but she could guess where it had come from.

In a heartbeat they stood outside on the road in front of the House. 'I thought we needed to find the portal to take us to the meeting place,' Lyssa protested. 'What are we doing here?'

'The portal is in the jungle and Burchie found that out. We have to close the door before she can get through,' said Millie.

She seemed physically larger than before, even though she was no taller or heavier. Lyssa looked at her, but couldn't put her finger on the change. Then she looked at the House. The unhealthy yellow glow was spreading, pulsing above and around the area in which the jungle must be located. The House seemed to be shaking with the effort to withstand Burchie and Cornelius at war inside.

Millie stood muttering quietly to herself in the peculiar language the books had been written in. Lyssa had never heard it spoken, so, even straining to catch the words, she couldn't understand what Millie was saying. She glanced at Jeremy, who was riveted by the scene before them. Then she looked down the hill toward town.

People had begun to gather again, drawn by the repulsiveness of the activities on the hill, unable to look away. Millie stopped speaking and held up her hands. Then the rumbling began, as if the House was going to levitate from its foundation. The people below ran to take cover and Lyssa wondered if she, Jeremy and Millie shouldn't do the same, but neither of them moved, so she stayed put.

The entire structure imploded.

It caught fire as well. Dust and sparks billowed up into the sky as green flames engulfed the wreckage. There ought to have been tremendous heat, but Lyssa felt cold. Jeremy fell back a step, shaking his head as if coming out of a trance. He looked at Lyssa with a bewildered expression and reached for her hand. 'Are you okay?' he asked.

Lyssa gaped at him. 'I was just going to ask you the same question.'

With his free hand, he rubbed his eyes and looked back at the conflagration. 'I guess so,' he said. 'That's the only home I've ever known. All of my things are in there.'

'Millie, is the Room burning as well?' Lyssa asked.

Millie shook her head. 'We still need that.'

Lyssa turned back to Jeremy. 'Some of your things are still there.' It wasn't much, but it was all the reassurance she had. 'We won't be able to walk the rest of the pattern in order to get to transition now, will we?' she asked Millie.

Millie chuckled. 'No, we won't,' she said. She turned and started walking down the hill.

Jeremy and Lyssa followed, no longer questioning her right to lead them. They walked through the crowd at the outskirts of town and headed straight to the church. David and Molly were waiting for them on the front steps.

'You did it,' said David as they approached. He was studying Millie as intently as Lyssa had done. 'It finally happened.'

Millie smiled. 'Lyssa did it.'

'What?' Lyssa demanded, shocked out of her daze. 'All I did was hand you the necklace. *You* blew the place to bits.'

Millie and David laughed. 'The necklace was the final object of power,' said Millie gently. 'You have returned to us all the stolen items. You restored the balance.'

'What do you mean?' asked Lyssa, touching the livid scar on her cheek. Jeremy squeezed her hand and she turned her face from him, blushing.

'I mean the magic is back where it belongs, and now you will have the chance to grow up,' said Millie. 'We can never rectify the damage done by millennia of misuse, but suffice it to say the inmates are no longer running the asylum. The adults are once again in charge.'

'It was children who stole the magic?' Lyssa asked, struggling to comprehend.

'Adolescents,' corrected Millie, 'but basically, yes.' She sat down on one of the steps, looking thoughtful for a long moment. 'You've been asking me about transition,' she said, finally, gesturing for Lyssa and Jeremy to sit as well. When they had complied, she smiled. 'Before transition was passage. You see, only one child matures every few generations, and that maturation process is called passage.'

'What happens to the ones who don't mature?' Jeremy asked reluctantly. He thought he knew the answer already, but he needed Millie to say it.

She nodded understanding. 'As with the Others,' she said gently. 'They become energy.'

Lyssa shuddered. 'That's cannibalism,' she whispered in horror.

'Cannibalism is a human taboo. If the young don't achieve maturation, and indeed most of them don't, it makes sense to reap their energy and make use of it rather than waste it,' said Millie sharply, in defence.

'Is that why the young ones stole the magic and created the symbols of power?' Lyssa asked, equally sharply. 'So that you couldn't suck the life out of them?'

Millie laughed. 'Nothing so dramatic as that,' she said. 'They just wanted passage, and thought that way they might get it.'

'Didn't they?' asked Jeremy. 'They lived out their lives, grew up and had children –'

Millie laughed again. 'Passage is instead of dying,' she explained. 'You translate to the next level, still corporeal, but, well, mature in the species.' She turned to Lyssa. 'You are that one in generations that is ready for passage. You returned the magic to us just as we knew you would.'

'How could you have known that?' Lyssa objected. 'You had no magic, and I wasn't born until thousands of years later.'

Millie shook her head. 'Not you, specifically,' she back-pedalled. 'The one we were hoping would be bred, given time and patience. There have been others in other Families

341

over the millennia, but those were not Families having access to the talismans. We just had to be patient. And now that we have the talismans back, we can take the proper steps to make sure this never happens again. We have a lot of damage to try to repair to a lot of worlds and peoples, and the truth is we can never fix the lives destroyed by this childish rampage, but we will do our best to make right what we can.'

'In the meantime,' said David, looking down at Molly, 'I think it's time to say good-bye.'

Jeremy and Lyssa looked at Molly, seeing her as if for the first time. Then they looked at each other. 'Oh, my,' breathed Lyssa. She went and knelt beside the tiny girl, taking her in her arms and hugging her gently. 'Did you know?'

Molly nodded solemnly, touching the scar on Lyssa's cheek. 'But Millie told me not to tell. I always wondered what you looked like before this happened.'

Lyssa looked sharply at Millie. 'How could you?' she mouthed over Molly's head.

Millie held out her hands and shook her head. 'I haven't yet!' she said softly. 'But you were going to leave. I can't let that happen.'

'Your tenses are mixed up,' said Lyssa.

'Time is a difficult thing to keep track of,' said Millie.

'How could you have known I was going to go home? I never said anything out loud, and you claim to have had no magic at the time,' said Lyssa sharply.

Millie shrugged.

Lyssa frowned and turned back to Molly.

Jeremy sat on the steps beside Molly and Lyssa and put his arms around both of them. He kissed Molly on the temple. 'When will we see you again?'

Molly smiled. 'Soon.' She turned back to Lyssa. 'Thank you for helping me find my parents. Maybe we can make the doll house again?'

She sounded so unchildlike Lyssa barely knew how to

respond. She nodded through the tears pooling in her eyes, not trusting herself to speak.

'I love you, mommy,' Molly whispered, kissing Lyssa on the cheek. 'I love you, daddy.' She kissed Jeremy as well. Then she disappeared, leaving Jeremy and Lyssa alone on the steps of the church, hugging each other and sobbing for their loss, trying unsuccessfully to comprehend that they would see her again.

Millie and David stood by quietly, allowing them to grieve, and watching to make sure the House was consumed utterly by the odd green flames.

Finally the ashes were dead.

David and Millie walked up the hill to make sure everything had been burned. Jeremy and Lyssa took the path to the Room, not really wanting to see the devastation above them. It was strange to them that everything was as they had left it not too many days before. They looked at Molly's pallet on the floor by the loom, and walked past it to the kitchen.

Silently, they prepared a meal and sat to wait for David and Millie to return. The wounds from the previous days would heal, but Lyssa was feeling banged up and tired, so she used the down time to aid her healing with the magic still permeating her system. She knew Jeremy was feeling Molly's loss as keenly as she was right now and left him to his own thoughts.

When Millie and David came through the door, it woke both Lyssa and Jeremy. 'I'm sorry,' Millie said softly. 'Should we go?'

'No,' Lyssa protested sleepily, rising awkwardly from the rocking chair, every joint in her body objecting. 'We made supper.'

'Then we should eat,' said David, a trifle too heartily.

'How is it up there?' asked Jeremy.

'It's gone,' said Millie. 'Everything burned. The Door is shut.'

'So now we can't get back,' said Lyssa. 'What happens when we don't make the next transition?'

Millie shook her head. 'The message went into the web when the House burned down. The magic was released and a new spell was woven.'

They sat and ate in silence. When their plates were empty they found they all felt much better.

'What will you do now?' David asked Jeremy.

'I guess I can do anything I want, now, can't I?' Jeremy grinned, looking at Millie. 'I can leave town if I want to?'

Millie nodded. 'You can go anywhere you want,' she smiled.

Lyssa felt a sinking in the pit of her stomach, but she remained quiet. Jeremy looked at her and grinned even wider.

'I thought I might like to get out of here. I've never seen anything beyond this town, and I'm well and truly sick of it. Maybe I could find a job, settle down; get married and have some kids.' He looked across the table at Lyssa. 'What do you think?'

She smiled weakly at him. 'I think you should do what's going to make you happy,' she said. 'I can't blame you for wanting to be someplace else, see some different faces.'

'What about you?' David asked Lyssa.

She shook her head. 'I hadn't thought about it. I don't know. I suppose I've got some things about passage to learn from Millie.'

Millie looked from Lyssa to Jeremy and started laughing. 'You've got years for that,' she said. 'What do you want to do in the meantime?'

Lyssa looked timidly at Jeremy. 'I wouldn't mind leaving town for a while,' she admitted. 'It wasn't the most pleasant homecoming I could have had.'

They all chuckled.

'Maybe you could show me some of the places you've been,' Jeremy suggested. 'I wouldn't even know where to begin my explorations beyond here. I'm not positive I can find the highway by myself. And I've never learned to drive.'

'The car burned in the fire,' said Lyssa. 'I suppose I ought to go home and get back to work and school. She sat up straight. 'My god, Millie, what *am* I going to do?'

David and Millie laughed outright. 'You have no idea how wealthy you are, do you?' asked David. 'You never have to work again.'

Lyssa looked blankly at him.

'The aunts and uncles are all dead. You are the sole beneficiary of the estate. There may be no goods and possessions, and millions of dollars of antiques just went up in smoke, but the estate is wealthy beyond imagining,' he explained.

'But what about the trust?' she asked. 'The allowance was fairly small.'

Millie shook her head. 'The size of the allowance depends on the number of individuals drawing from a finite amount. If there is only one controlling individual, they have the legal right to rewrite the trust. You're it, kiddo. If I were you, I'd talk to my lawyer.'

'Soon,' Lyssa agreed. She looked at Jeremy. 'That could be our first stop?'

He laughed. 'You'd better have something more adventurous planned after that.'

Lyssa smiled. 'I can probably come up with a thing or two.'

'Should we get married before we go, or find someplace along the way?'

The smile froze on Lyssa's face and her heart stopped beating. She couldn't breathe. She had seen the proof of Molly, and known that there was a possibility she and Jeremy could be together, but the future isn't something that can be counted on, and she had been afraid to hope things would really turn out that way.

'Lyssa?' he asked, watching her face carefully.

345

She forced herself to breathe again and then turned to David. 'Could you perform the ceremony?' she whispered.

'Yes,' he smiled.

She reached up and touched the scar on her cheek, lightly tracing the path it took across her face, and thought about the damage done to her body. Jeremy had seen all that while he was treating her wounds. He knew what she looked like, and he didn't care. She drew another shuddering breath and turned back to Jeremy. 'I'd like to get married here. Then let's leave.' She looked at Millie. 'What about you?'

Millie smiled. She stood up and went to the alcove where the loom was and ran her hand lovingly along the frame. Then she picked a basket of deep blue yarn and started to string the warp threads. 'I'll stay here,' she said at last. 'I have always loved this town, and David and I have a life here. Besides, you have to have a place to come home to, and this is where the other Families and long-lived will come to find us. Someone should be here when they do.'

'When will they come?' asked Lyssa.

'Eventually,' said Millie with a smile.